THE OLD
RAZZLE DAZZLE

To the theatre kid in all of us

And though we are divided
Our hearts beat in parallel
No more could I desire
Than to ride the longest rail
And share the journey
With you to the end

"The Longest Rail"
from "Stations of the Heart"
Music by T. Whitley
Lyrics by E. Pound

believe it," he groaned. "This has been the worst day of my life."

"What are you on about?"

"The audition. The entire day's been a disaster. I tried…tried so hard to get here on time." The lad was gasping, weeping, wiping his face in vain against his tears. "Is there any chance you might—"

"What, give you a private audition on account of you can't manage to show up on time? Un-bloody-likely, my son. Come back tomorrow like the rest of 'em."

"But I can't! Please, you don't know what this is costing me. And I'm so close, and please, sir, it's only just gone five o'clock."

"Which means the theatre's locked up for the night. It'll have to be tomorrow."

"I can't! He won't let—" The man caught himself, took a deep breath and exhaled, before going on in a shaking voice that rose with his anguish. "Please, Mr Pound, I'll do anything. I'll audition right here. Please!"

"Hey now, no need to be making a scene. And I'm sorry but I can't be making exceptions."

"You can't imagine what I've sacrificed for this."

"Welcome to theatre, laddie. It don't get any easier from here."

Izzy hadn't gone five steps when the lad began to sing. Some jumped-up modern tune, but damn if the fellow didn't have a voice, a ringing tenor without that nasal warbling too many young men adopted these days. Izzy let him get through the first verse and the chorus before turning around.

"Very nice. You ought to do well down Brighton

Pier."

"But I want to be on the stage. A proper stage. Yours, if you'll let me."

"If you want to be on a proper stage, then you better learn how to properly audition. You're not the only one who's made sacrifices to get where he is. Better luck next time." Izzy turned away before he broke out in a case of sympathy. He'd gone another dozen paces when the singing started again.

He very nearly told the lad to shove off permanently. Every fool thought he could *Figaro*, except this was for real. Vigorous, swiftly sung, not missing a syllable, of which there were loads, many of which Izzy himself couldn't have sung for love or money. The lad knew it by rote, and was giving it all he had, pink in the face, puffing out his chest, going up on his toes as he brought the short aria to its triumphant end. A courting couple had paused on the path behind him and offered a smattering of applause as he stood shaking.

You're the one who's the fool if you turn him away. But having such a voice didn't mean one could survive a life on the stage. Izzy sighed, weighing his armchair, his teapot, his privacy against the finest raw talent he'd heard in ages. Whitley had a teapot. Besides which, he ought to hear this as well.

Muttering unspeakable curses, he started back the way he'd come. The man yelped and stumbled out of his path, treading on the lawn. "Come along then, if we're going to bother," Izzy said over his shoulder.

"What? Where?"

"Back to the blooming theatre, you twit. I want to know how that sounds indoors. Odds are, we'll have to train you up from the ground all over again. Bloody *Figaro*…" Shaking his head, he kept on, not looking behind. Footsteps followed.

THE THEATRE

PICTURES TOLD MUCH, but a reprinted photograph in the back of a theatre program was no substitute for meeting a man in person. Mr Pound was both shorter and more vivid than Telford expected, with a quick step that kept easy pace with Telford's longer stride. He was dressed sharply if rather out of date in maroon velveteen, a gold chain crossing his brocade waistcoat, an emerald in his tiepin, and he carried a cane with a pewter raven's skull as the head. Carried being the word, for despite his age he didn't once lean on it, holding it by the middle like a marching band leader's baton.

"You married?" Mr Pound asked him as they passed onto Tavistock Street.

"Married? Certainly not."

"Stepping out with anyone?"

"May I ask why—"

"So as I know who you're going to be disappointing on the regular. I'd rather have a half-arsed singer with no family to speak of than a virtuoso with a fussy wife."

This was not the time for Telford to mention his household's unyielding expectations. Better to get the role and sort out the rest of it afterwards. "I've no one.”

“You get much work?” Mr Pound asked. “I mean on stage.”

“Oh. Yes, I’ve been in a number of productions, but never professionally.”

“You don’t say. I’d have never known.”

“I must apologize again. I really did do all I could to be on time today.”

“You don’t think that wasn’t fate trying to spare you?”

“Spare me? From what?”

“A lifetime of misery,” Mr Pound cried, gesturing with the raven’s beak at the theatres lining the roadway. “Being skint, and tired, and missing meals, and missing your family, and making an absolute hash of things in front of a packed house, and then having to do it all again the next night whether you like it or not.”

“I understand there are sacrifices one makes for this career. But I can’t imagine wanting anything else.”

The old man chuckled, a low growl that set Telford’s teeth on edge. “That’ll come with time.”

As they neared the theatre Telford’s hands began tingling, as they tended to before a performance. Though due for a refurbishment the Palmetto was a lovely old building, the façade decorated on a Moorish theme with soot-dusted plaster arches framing trompe l’oeil frescoes of walled gardens under starlit skies. He followed Mr Pound down the alleyway beside the building. Very little light fell between the high walls, and the bricks were black and slimy-looking even on a sunny day. Ahead the alley bent to the left. Just before the corner was a plain wooden door with a badly dented kick plate and a slot at eye level.

The stage door. He was about to go through it, the stage door of one of the West End's most loved little theatres, in company with its legendary director, for a private audition he didn't deserve and which he was certain to foul up—

Telford's toe caught on the rough paving and for a terrifying second he was falling forward, but Mr Pound grabbed his arm with surprising strength and jerked him back, allowing him to get a foot out.

"When we say break a leg you know that ain't for real, hey?" he said. Telford nearly answered, but Mr Pound was smirking, or trying not to, his eyes sparkling.

"Just working on my pratfalls," he said lightly, his heart unclenching as the old man rasped another laugh and began patting his pockets for keys.

And then they were inside, and Telford couldn't keep from staring about him. The stage was to their left and stood shoulder high, supported on open scaffolding which allowed crew members to move about beneath. To the right, the coarse brick of the rear wall disappeared behind a partition wall beyond which must be the dressing rooms and stores. Far above and all but invisible hung the rails and gantries to support the backdrops and lighting. St Barnabas had no auditorium, and their major works had been staged under a canvas tent in the school's quadrangle. This…was everything he'd imagined, everything he'd ever wanted and immeasurably more. Pictures couldn't convey the sense of space, of huge volumes barely contained, the air laden with the scent of floor polish and greasepaint and phosphor from flash-pans, old canvas and some subtle other thing that he later decided was the smell of his own fear.

Mr Pound pulled off a glove, put two fingers in his mouth and whistled sharply. He then led Telford up the short flight of steps and onto the stage. The curtain was raised and they faced the empty theatre, but before the enormity rendered Telford helpless, they were joined by two others: a pale man with a close-cut moustache and a permanent crease between his dark eyebrows whom Mr Pound introduced as his assistant director Mr Whitley, and the stage manager Mr Unger, as solid and brown as Telford was slim and rosy.

"And your name?" Mr Whitley said, a clipboard and pencil at the ready.

"My name is Telford. Telford Vandurenburg."

Mr Pound swore again and started to laugh with his wheezing cackle, Mr Unger snorting in his effort not to join him. As for Mr Whitley, the crease between his brows merely deepened. "That'll never fit on the marquee, love. What else do you go by?"

"How about we talk of stage names once he's earned the right to be on stage," Mr Pound said dryly before turning to Telford. "As for you, you get your arse out there and sing something."

"Yes, Mr Pound. Thank you so much for this opportunity."

Mr Unger snorted again. "Take it from an old hand, it's too soon to be kissing his arse. Save it for when you've pissed him off."

"About which you know loads, am I right?" Mr Pound said. Laughing together, the two followed Mr Whitley down the few steps at the side of the stage, as Telford rubbed his numb cheeks, tried to even his breathing, any of Father Gilchrist's tricks to prepare. This was all in that dear man's honour, and there had to be a touch of the divine in the fact that Telford had made it this far, when all the world had stood in his way. He pressed his hand to his chest one more time for the hard comfort of the crucifix beneath his shirt, then walked to centre stage.

The men were seated in the middle several rows back, the dark theatre stretching away beneath the balcony. He'd be singing to hundreds and hundreds of—

"Get on with it, son," Mr Pound called. "I did you a service coming back for this."

"Sorry! Yes. Ah. Accompany. An accompanist. A pianist. Is there one?"

"Gone home."

"Right."

"Besides which, you didn't have no accompanist in the park."

"True."

"So get on with it."

Not the Bizet again. He'd never top his attempt of twenty minutes ago, which had come from somewhere outside himself. Nothing too popular either, or he'd seem frivolous. Instead a song tender to his heart, a song he knew like his own soul. The theatre was a sort of cathedral, filled with that same air, that expectation of the miraculous. *Dear Lord, let their ears and hearts be not hardened…*

> *O Holy Night! The stars are brightly shining, it is the night of the dear Saviour's birth…*

He had to sing louder. The rising melody demanded ever greater devotion, and so he gave, sang as though he stood witness to that holiest of holies, as though this was his sole purpose in life, his calling. The men sat and watched without speaking, letting him finish the verse. When he stopped, they leaned together and began to whisper. Telford stayed where he was, his legs trembling, stomach flopping. They were taking too long. They were debating how to break the news, Mr Unger stabbing his finger against his other palm to make his point. If Telford had found time to eat lunch, he would have vomited it up on the stage. He'd done everything he could, given his all, given everything, and it had still lead to—

"How does the name Terry Fords strike you?" Mr Pound called to him. "As your stage name," he added as Telford stood mute.

His stage name. "Yes! Yes, Mr Pound."

"Very good, Mr Fords. Mr Unger will take you up to my office. You and me'll have words."

THE MEETING

THE DELAY HAD nothing to do with strategy and everything to do with Izzy's knees, which were lately quite belligerent about climbing stairs in a hurry. Still, it put the lad on his back foot, to be taken to what they all called the headmaster's office to get stared at by Unger across the scratched desk. Every bloody thing in the place was decrepit. Starting with himself, but he was used to getting by on next to naught. Just another day on the job.

The headmaster's office meant he could get away with a bit of the old routine, the one that used to drive them lords mad. Shameful what one could achieve in this rat-bastard nation with no more than a twist of the tongue. One way or another.

Chuckling at his own enduringly perverse sense of humour, Izzy reached the top of the stairs and paused to check the time. As if he could see his watch in the half dark of the upper walk, but it masked his genuine need to catch his breath. And to think, he could have been at home, rugged up in his chair with a bit of toast and tomorrow's racing form…

And piss away your last hurrah, your swansong? You berk…

"Shush. I know, I know, I'm going. Angel of my

bloody conscience." His muttering came back to him in whispering echoes, and for a superstitious second he nearly looked behind him, but he'd done that enough to be tired of seeing no one there.

He entered the office without knocking. The boy half leapt out of his skin, falling back with his hand pressed to his heart as Izzy swapped places with Unger behind the desk. The big man stopped beside the boy—Telford, his name was—and clapped his broad hand on the tweedy shoulder.

"Remember what I told you. Don't take none of his shit. If he didn't like you at least a little, we'd have tossed you out by now." He gave Telford a friendly shake that flopped him about like wet laundry, then went out, thudding down the shoddy wooden steps. Izzy waited for quiet, then sat forward, his hands folded on the desk.

"Well. Not a fluke, then, the singing."

"No, Mr Pound," the lad gasped, sitting upright. "I've worked very, very hard at it."

"I can tell you've had training. Church choir?"

"School, mainly. Father Gilchrist was a marvellous teacher. And a good friend." The lad smiled crookedly, a telling brightness to his eyes. "He passed not long ago."

"I'm sorry to hear that." Izzy cleared his throat and went on. "If only as I think you've done him proud. He's made you a hell of a singer. If you'll pardon the language."

"Thank you."

"Have you auditioned elsewhere I should know about?"

The kid goggled at him, but before he could answer,

Whitley came in with the tea. The sly chap had been a butler for a grand family and had that high-class domestic's way of moving without sound, even up that blasted staircase with a tray of chinaware. As Telford clutched his chest again, Whitley set down the tray and handed Izzy the papers held under his arm. Notes from the audition, Whitley's swirling hand illegible to Izzy's poor eyes and scant talents, as it ever was.

"Can't this wait?" he asked as Whitley served the tea.

"Of course."

"Grand." He shoved the papers in the top drawer. "Now bugger off. And close the door on your way out, there's a dear."

"Yes, love," Whitley drawled. Hardly a joke, for they spent more time together than most marrieds. A fact of life in this cursed business and one which Noel had struggled to accept at times, wanting every bit of Izzy for himself. A testament of his devotion, even if it had caused some wicked fights.

Telford had gone very still, his eyes flicking between them. Shit, not him as well, but the lad said nothing as Whitley poured and then departed. Izzy took a good drink of the tea, brewed to tarry perfection, then set down his chipped old enamel mug and resumed his pose.

"So, young man, it comes to this. I want you. And mark my words, I'm going to have you. But I'm going to put you through hell. How you feel about starting on the bottom?" *Don't cringe. If ever you've acted before, pretend you just said none of that.* Telford only stared, trembling a little. "Of the pecking order. Christ, why do I bother?" His heart thumping, Izzy snatched up his tea, glaring at the lad over the rim as he drank.

"Sorry, I understand completely," Telford stammered. "I'm sure it entails cleaning the latrines and fetching things and such."

"That'd be the measure of it. I can't be handing out favours to newcomers, not and keep control of this pack of mongrels. So mind your manners, do what you're told, and I'll see if I can't get you in the chorus for this one."

That lit a fire under the lad, who frowned and sat forward again. "Chorus? But you said—"

"I said you could sing, not that it earned you anything. Don't ever make the mistake of thinking this is a democracy. There's no voting. No recourse, except by pleading a very strong case to yours truly." He tapped his chest. "But it's the only way we work. And as regards you, vis a vis we? You ain't nobody yet. If you want a seat at the table," and he knocked on the desk to punctuate, "you gotta earn it."

"Quite a way to run a business," Telford murmured.

"La, if it were a business it'd want to be a shade more profitable. Why in blazes do you even want to ruin your life this way?"

"It's all I've ever wanted."

"I see. In that case, you're completely fucked. Welcome aboard." He reached across the desk. After a moment, Telford took his hand and they shook. He went to sit back and Izzy tightened his grip, wanting the man's full attention. "And there's one last thing you'd do well to remember. No matter what it is you think I'm saying, it won't be an approach. I'm as good as married, me. And the husband ain't the sharing sort. Now go fetch me a sandwich."

He let go of Telford's hand and the young man sat back abruptly, rubbing his knuckles. "A sandwich?"

"It's where they take a piece of bread, and another piece of bread, and stick something between 'em and…" He slapped his hands together in mime and Telford jumped to his feet.

"Sorry! I understand, I'm going. Any preference?"

"I'll have whatever you put in front of me. Not an approach," he said sternly as Telford gulped and blushed again. "Thank Christ this eejit can sing. Go, go!"

THE SANDWICH

HE WENT CLATTERING down the listing stairs and came to a halt. He'd been following Mr Unger on his way up, passing through a warren of partition walls and badly hung doors, and he hadn't a clue how to even get out of the building. Nothing for it but to knock on and then try each of the three doors he faced. The first two were locked, but the last let him into a vaguely familiar corridor, with an open doorway at the end through which Mr Whitley now came. He didn't quite smile when he saw Telford though his stance eased.

"The old man hasn't rattled you too badly, I hope."

"He wants me to fetch him a sandwich," Telford stammered, his face prickling with foolish heat, but Whitley nodded at once and fished out a handful of silver.

"Ham for him and Unger, and I'll have cheese and pickle. From the pub across the street."

"Right. And to get back in?"

"Knock on the door," Mr Whitley said with a hint of impatience.

"Right. And the door is…where?"

Mr Whitley blinked. Slowly, deliberately, a tiny gesture that expressed incalculable contempt. "Follow me."

It was coming on dusk as Telford scurried down the alleyway. He was due at home by seven. He'd never make it, and five minutes late might as well be five hours, five days, for the trouble he'd wear for it. Praying for Auntie and Uncle to find the grace to not despise him, he went to buy the sandwiches.

Unlike the stinking gin holes of his most wretched childhood memories, the public house was well-kept, with polished wooden booths and stained glass transoms over the doors. The barman had the meal ready in a flash and very soon Telford was back at the stage door, rapping as loud as he dared.

Unger let him in. He took the paper sack, retrieved his sandwich and had half of it eaten in two bites. Flashing his cohort an inscrutable look, Whitley took his own sandwich, then gave the sack to Telford.

"Run it up to him, there's a dear."

"Yes, Mr Whitley."

Following his directions, Telford returned to the staircase, wincing at every creaking step. Mr Pound's door was ajar. He was speaking with someone. Telford ought not to listen, but he had the sandwich, and he dithered on the landing, afraid of the sound of the stairs, of letting Mr Pound know he'd been there and run away. Afraid of meeting Whitley and Unger, who would laugh at him and—

He approached the open door, but paused again at the ache in Mr Pound's voice: "I just don't know. I don't know why I bother anymore. It's like to kill me, and then where are we? And don't say pearly gates, that's as unlikely as it ever was." Some piece of furniture scraped over the floorboards, and Telford was about to knock when Mr Pound went on.

"Oh la, you should have heard it though. Well, perhaps you did. Right there in the park. Got the old chills, I did. When's the last time that happened, hey?"

They were talking about him, and he knocked on the doorframe before the thought overwhelmed him. The furniture scraped again and Mr Pound's quick steps came to the door. He opened it farther, looked Telford up and down with red-rimmed eyes.

"Is that my sandwich?"

"Oh. Yes it is." He offered the sack and Mr Pound snatched it from him.

"Go see Whitley for your papers," he rasped, then shut the door in Telford's face.

Mr Whitley took him to his own office, a tiny slot of a room tucked beneath the stairs. Bookcases lined the walls stretching clear to the ceiling and laden with books, folios, reams of documents, all neatly arranged with a little brass ticket on the front of each shelf showing the year. Whitley took a printed form from a folder, asked Telford to fill in his details, then added his signature and above this scrawled a disorderly hash of letters that might have read *E. Pound, director* to an imaginative eye. He blotted then folded the page, tucked it in an envelope and gave the lot to Telford.

"Thank you, Mr Whitley. You can't know how this helps me, to have it in writing. I was afraid my family wouldn't believe me."

"Should we expect a problem, Mr Fords?" Whitley's face was impassive, the nuance all in his buttery voice drawing out the words.

"A problem? No. None at all. Thank you. What time tomorrow?"

"Half nine."

"Very good," Telford replied, as his stomach filled with stones. He'd never gotten away from the bakery before eleven. He would manage it, go directly home and do as much as he could now, chop the wood, measure the coal, set out the crockery, anything to speed up the morning's work. This was his future at stake. He would find a way.

It was now after eight, and he fairly ran the whole way home, dodging other pedestrians, barely apologizing when he knocked someone's elbow or stepped in their way. His own impending unpleasantness was nothing compared to the grief he had heard in Mr Pound's voice. He had said he had a *husband*, a word so improbable that at the time Telford's mind had skipped over it, too busy being shocked by the reason Mr Pound was saying it.

Head spinning, heart pounding, he checked his stride as he came around onto his street. His best choice was to come in the back and get stuck into a task straight away. He might even lie, say he'd been there the whole time, working through supper in his desire to improve himself. Anything to curry favour with his uncle. Who would demand to know why he was in his best clothes. *Dear Lord, soften his heart…*

He eased closed the latch on the back gate. One gauntlet run, and a familiar voice hissed from the high slatted fence that divided the yard from its neighbour. The back of the house was dark, so he slipped across to the fence and pushed his fingers through the gap, felt his friend Cian's fingertips.

"Did you get the part, Telly?" he whispered.

"I did."

"Gosh! Oh Telly, that's grand! Are you not over the moon?"

He leaned against the fence, his forehead to the slats, Cian on the other side merely a gleam of eyes and teeth and the scent of pine-tar soap. "It was a very long day. I nearly didn't make it in time. And now I'm sure to catch an earful."

"Never mind," Cian murmured. "Tell me about this Mr Pound. Did you finally meet him? What's he like?"

"He…likes ham sandwiches."

"That's all?"

"Sorry, Cian. I'm absolutely shattered. I ought to go in."

"We'll talk tomorrow. I'm so happy for you, Tel. You're going to be famous."

"Don't count on it. But thank you anyway. I'd not have got this far without you." He closed his fanned hand, holding Cian's fingers between his for a moment as his friend returned the pressure.

"Anything you need," he murmured, "promise you'll ask."

Telford was about to demure, turn aside Cian's generosity, unwarranted when he had so little to give. The words died on his tongue as the back door of the bakery opened.

"God bless you," Cian whispered as he retreated, leaving Telford clinging to the fence, numb with fear as he awaited the fall of his uncle's scarred hand on the back of his neck, the violence that followed even his slightest transgression. He started breathing again as he smelled not Ned's bitter sweat but his Aunt Beryl's lavender water.

"Come along, Telford," she murmured, one eye on the gate. "It's time you were inside."

"I'm sorry to be so late, Auntie—"

"Never mind that," she said, backing towards the house. "He's still down the pub. Come in and settle and he'll never know what time you got in."

"Thank you, Auntie." And God bless you, Cian.

THE REHEARSAL

IT WENT THIS WAY every production, and there was nothing to be done but get through. Still, the first two weeks of rehearsal were a trial like no other. Besides which, Izzy's joints were paining him night and day, keeping him awake and making it hard to sit still, so that he spent most of the rehearsal on his feet, stomping up and down the aisles when he wasn't on the stage itself. The veterans associated this with his very worst moods, hence the whole cast was on tenterhooks, blundering through the libretto without confidence even though they were no worse than usual.

Telford's voice was making up for a great deal. Physically he was a danger to himself and others, too eager with gestures and fancy steps, and the cast were giving him wide berth to avoid being trod on. Time to cure him of that or he'd smash up the sets. Time as well to cure him of his squeamishness over the subject matter. Why a good little Catholic like him wanted to mix with this gang of Godless sybarites was a mystery worth solving. The sooner the better, for if the lad cracked up at show-time, Izzy would crack him into little Catholic bits.

There he went again, stepping right in Mignon's path. She dodged sideways, bumping into Alex, who stumbled back against the row of wooden chairs standing in for the train carriage set.

"Stop! Stop! God damn it, I said stop!" Izzy had to smack his cane against the back of the nearest seat to get Larson the pianist's attention. "By the stars!" he shouted into the ringing silence. "Once, just once in my four decades in this cursed business I would like to not regret having started a new production. Everyone go the hell home. Learn your bleeding lines. We'll start fresh tomorrow. And where the hell is Bowen?"

There was a shuffle of feet. Someone coughed. Then Alex cleared his throat. "I heard he got picked up. They've took him to Cannon Street."

Fifth on the bill. His character the linchpin of the second act. And the randy git had to pick this time go swanning about the bath houses… Izzy pinched the bridge of his nose where the headache was building. "Everyone go home. Learn your lines. God help you if you don't know them by tomorrow."

He didn't bother with his office. Whitley would come up and they'd bitch about what they couldn't fix, which at this point was everything, and then Unger would come in with his whiskey and there went dinner. It'd be pub sandwiches again, and he'd eaten so many of the buggers he could have built a pub from their crusts. Instead, he chose the far more cheering prospect of visiting the police station to tell his second tenor that there wasn't money for bail. He hadn't kept a legal fund for his people in twenty years, and there was no chance the theatre's liability covered getting caught with one's trousers down.

The next day was, against all odds, worse. Telford was frequently late for rehearsal, but he failed to show at all. Izzy left the principles with Larson to work through the first number and went to Whitley's office. The door was open which meant he was in, for he'd suffocate with it closed. The desk touched both walls and Whitley kept a shaving mirror standing on it to spy people coming up behind him.

"How was it today?" he said to Izzy's reflection.

"God help us all."

"That bad?" he chuckled as he returned to his green-lined ledger.

"They're dropping like flies. Bloody Fords wasn't in."

"Really? He seems so…obedient."

"He's as bad as the rest. At least with him away, no one got stepped on."

Whitley swivelled his chair to face Izzy. "He's hardly more than a child. Give him time."

"I don't bleeding have time. And don't you talk about me leaving things to the last minute."

"I wouldn't dare. What will you do about Bowen?"

"Nothing. We're in hock up to our eyeballs. He made his bed, didn't he?"

"And Fords?"

"Also nothing. Unless he skives off tomorrow. In which case I'll wring his bloody neck."

"He'd do well as Jeeves."

"Why do you think I'll be wringing his neck if he don't come in tomorrow? I'm not having some pissant papist ruining my show."

"*Pissant papist*, that's a good turn of phrase," Whitley smirked, getting out his pocket book where he kept such scraps for future song-writing.

"Tell us the lad's direction while you're at it."

"Why, what are you planning?"

Izzy raised his hands. "Nothing. Just a bit of the old razzle dazzle. Impress upon him the importance of meeting one's commitments."

"You don't know what sort of commitments preceded us," Whitley said as he tore a slip of paper from the back of the pocketbook to write down the name of Telford's street.

"That's exactly what I intend to discover."

"Please don't start any trouble. For him or yourself."

"What you mean, trouble? I'm golden."

"Then make sure there's no gilded cage in your future."

"Hush up, you old woman. Now tell me what this says." The slip was more to aid passers-by if Izzy got turned about, as there were very few parts of the old city with which his feet weren't familiar. Coming up the alley, he gauged the distance to his flat versus Telford's place. It did no good to wait until tomorrow. By then he'd have to be running the next round of auditions.

Like flies to a corpse they were already gathering, for stepping onto the street he spied a young man lurking round the Palmetto's ticket window, his pert face marred by a broad patch of pinkly puckered skin spreading from the corner of his mouth to his jawline on the left side.

"Are you Mr Pound?" he blurted as Izzy strode past.

"Auditions ain't till tomorrow."

"I'm not here to audition," he said in the flat brogue of a man trying not to sound Irish as he fell into step beside him, though the scar obliged him to speak from the right side of his mouth. "I need to speak with you."

"You're speaking with me right now."

"I would very much appreciate this conversation remaining private."

"And I'd appreciate it not happening at all. What is it you want?"

"It's to do with Telford Vandurenburg." The name rolled off his taut lips like he'd practiced it. Izzy stopped to give the fellow a better look. He had the thin frame of one who'd had a hungry childhood, topped with a shock of curling auburn hair and a finely-boned face that made him pretty rather than awkward. Even the scar hardly detracted from his charm, for his eyes were wide and full of light.

"What this about Telford?" Izzy asked.

"He's a friend of mind," the young man said, blushing so deeply his freckles all but disappeared. "A good friend. And, well, he's talked about you so much I thought I ought to make sure of you. That no one was…well, he's such a lamb, ye know? I worry about him."

"You were right," Izzy said as they stepped out of the way of a trio of quick-stepping women in enormous hats. "We ought to be having this conversation indoors."

Back to the Palmetto they went, Izzy fingering his keys in his pocket as he walked, feeling for the one that opened the hidden door behind the ticket booth so he didn't look like an old fool hunting for it. He brought the lad through the cramped booth to the lobby, which at mid-afternoon was a dusty, echoing cavern, wan sunlight falling through the glass of the doors and gleaming off the scarred tiles, the muffled sound of Larsen's piano filtering through from the auditorium.

"And who am I speaking with?" Izzy said as the young man stared about them.

"Gilbert, if you please," he said, whipping off his worn cap and clutching it to his chest. "Cian Gilbert."

"Pleasure to make your acquaintance, Mr Gilbert. And let me start by saying that any friend of Telford's is a friend of mine." Izzy put out his hand. The lad stared at it before shaking it gingerly. "So what is it that's troubling you, Mr Gilbert?"

Being addressed politely seemed another novelty as he gaped at Izzy, his eyes somehow bluer in the muffled gloom of the lobby than they were in broad day. "It's like I said in the street," he replied at last. "I wanted to be sure he wasn't mixed up in, well, bad business."

"Such as what?"

"You hear things. About people who work in theatres. Not you personally, sir, but people, and...faith, I've insulted you terribly, haven't I?" he finished in a small voice.

"Not as much as some, but let's not worry about that. Mr Gilbert, I've faced down plenty of bad business, but I don't have any of that in my shop. Theatre, that is. Strictly above board, we are, and you can ask whomever you like, anywhere on the Strand."

"It's just that Telly's so kind. I hate seeing him mistreated."

The lad would make no kind of actor, his thoughts betrayed by his hot cheeks, his trembling jaw.

Someone had been cruel to Telford. Cian had seen it happen. Wished it not to happen again.

"He missed rehearsal today, you know," Izzy said quietly.

"I know. That is, he's my neighbour. I can't help but know what goes on next door."

"May I assume what goes on ain't so good?" Cian merely nodded and Izzy went on. "Sorry to say but that's hardly in my power to amend. I do what I can for my people, however. He'll always be treated well here. In fact I was on my way to look him up at the bakery, find out why he's been skiving off."

"Oh no, Mr Pound," he said with a shake of his head that set his curls bouncing. "It'd never be that. Telly's very responsible. Too much so, at times."

"You might come with me, if you like."

Again his thoughts showed on his face as his eyes flew open in alarm. "I couldn't. I'm meant to be— well, not here, that's for certain."

"Fair enough. Shall I send your regards?"

This frightened him worse than anything as he gasped and took an urgent step towards Izzy. "Oh no, please don't let him know I was here. He trusts me."

"I can't see as how this meeting breaks that trust, but that's between the two of you. He shan't hear a word of this from me." He steered the lad back outside where he disappeared in the afternoon crush.

Izzy stood in the shadows a little longer, for he'd lost the dash-fire that had sent him hurtling out the door. Yes, Telford had a voice, and a key role in the play if he proved his worth, but woe to a director accused of coddling an actor, no matter how fine his voice.

He wasn't worried for his own reputation, which he had thoroughly ruined years ago. Yet he'd seen more than one company torn apart by jealousy. A director playing favourites was one of the surest methods of invoking it, for which reason Izzy kept actors and actresses alike at arm's length, not taking them as friends except for particular people admitted to his circle only under particular circumstances. There was no good becoming friends with someone whose livelihood depended on your opinion of his singing voice.

Telford's natural talent set him far above his peers, however, and Izzy would gladly challenge anyone who disputed it. Weighed against a round of last-minute auditions, a short walk to the bakery and a hard word to a biddable young man was a lark. All in a day's work, and pinching the bridge of his nose to blunt his worsening headache, he set off for the Vandurenburg's bakery.

THE STAND-OVER

"SOME LITTLE OLD man's out there asking after you," Uncle Ned said as Telford slid the last tray of pies into the oven. "I told you not to have them theatre people coming round the shop, they'll put off the customers."

"I didn't ask anyone to come round, Uncle." His hands grey with flour, Telford wiped his sweating brow on his shoulder.

"Well, get him to clear off. Go on, what are you waiting for?"

"Sorry, Uncle." He edged past the thickly built man and went out through the swinging doors. Mr Pound was on the other side of the counter, dressed in his old finery, a steely glint in his eyes though he was smiling.

"Mr Fords. It does me good to know you're not dead in a ditch. I am however led to wonder why you weren't at rehearsal today. Because being dead in a ditch is pretty much the only acceptable excuse for missing rehearsal, in my books."

"I'm so sorry. There was a problem with the ovens, and we had to remake so much stock, and—"

"Mr Fords," Pound repeated in a voice that was not so much louder as clearer. "I don't much care what the cause is. Only that you never allow it to happen again."

"It was entirely beyond me. Otherwise you know I'd have been there."

"That I do not, for I know exactly nothing about you, Mr Fords. Other than you've been putting in time making cake while you wait for an opportunity. I cannot imagine a better opportunity for a man in your position than the one I'm offering. So what's holding you back?"

"I can't speak right now. Mr Pound, please believe I want this more than anything."

"Then bloody well work for it, lad!"

The bell jingled against the door as a customer entered. Telford beckoned Mr Pound nearer and whispered across the counter. "Is there any way at all we might speak about this tomorrow?"

Pound stepped back. "No. Now or not at all."

"Then meet me around the back. The gate painted yellow. Please." Then Aunt Beryl came out to serve the woman, and he had to retreat. His uncle was luckily occupied in the storeroom so Telford darted through the kitchen and out to the yard, praying for Mr Pound to be guided to the correct alley, for his heart to be softened by Telford's plight and not hardened by disappointment.

A few agitated minutes passed before he appeared, swinging his cane, looking about with lively interest. Telford met him in the alley, swinging the gate nearly closed in case Uncle Ned glanced into the yard.

"Don't bother to apologize again," Mr Pound said before Telford spoke. "I'm here on other matters."

"Please don't sack me."

"Sack you? Boy, I need you. I've got to pull you up in the cast."

"Come again?"

"Bowen's gone and..." He grunted in disgust, rolling his eyes. "Let us say he's likely indisposed for the duration. Which puts me in the position of needing to find a new Jeeves, quick smart."

"Who were you thinking of?"

"I'm thinking of you, you twit."

"Are you really?"

"Of course it'll mean more lines, more rehearsals. And we'll have to do something about the flailing about, won't we?"

"Yes. In fact I've been thinking of—beg your pardon, did you say more rehearsals?"

"It's a speaking part, innit?"

"Oh. Yes. That may however pose a problem."

"Then bloody well unpose it," Mr Pound said with a forehead crease to rival Whitley's.

"I...can't. I couldn't possibly take any more time away from my work."

"Your work?"

"Yes."

"Your work?"

"I—I—"

"Fucking hell, Fords!" the older man cried, stamping his cane on the stone paving. "What in blazes do you think *I'm* giving you? A bleeding pastime? Theatre's the hardest work you'll ever do in your entire damned life."

"I know, I know! It's not me who needs convincing."

"Who then? That lumpy bugger?" Mr Pound

jerked his head towards the bakery.

"I can't just come and go as I please. They need me."

"The hell they do."

"If you could please keep your voice down. I'll wear this hard enough as it is."

"For what, five minutes in an alley? Forget I said that, but honestly, son, is this how you want to be spending your time? What is it you even do for them?"

"Nearly everything. Chop wood for the ovens, get them lit, start the yeast, sweep and clean the shop and the bakery and—"

"Stop. Do they let you touch the money?"

"Never. I'm not even meant to be seen in the shop."

"Do they let you make decisions?"

"About what? And no."

"I see. So is there anything they oblige you to do that couldn't be done by, say, a couple of trained monkeys?"

Telford stared, torn between insult and utter confusion. "What do you mean, monkeys?"

"I mean they're bleeding well exploiting you!" Pound cried, throwing up his hands. "They don't need you. They need a boy, some neighbour's son who will do it for tuppence and a currant bun. You're half a man. Probably a whole man if you stopped letting your parents shove you about."

"They're not my parents."

"Ah shit." He calmed on the instant, letting his breath out in a sigh. "More to this than meets the eye, hey?"

"My aunt and uncle. They took me in when my

parents…passed. I owe them everything.”

“Up to a point. And so tell me, what’s their snit with us theatre people? Ain’t that what I heard him call me? Odds are that’s what disturbs him, the company you’re keeping, rather than that you happen to like prancing about on a stage.”

“It’s all one in their minds. It’s a God-fearing household.”

“In that case, God help you.” He laughed his dusty old laugh and Telford smiled along as best he could. “So then tell me how much time you can give me. It’s not a huge role but it’s important, and you get a good song in the middle.”

Before Telford replied, the yard gate swung open. “I told you to get rid of him,” Uncle Ned barked, stomping towards them. “And here you are gassing—”

“Me and your nephew are negotiating his new role.” Mr Pound winked but Telford couldn’t respond, his dreams shattering around him at his uncle’s next words.

“There is no new role. In fact there’s no role at all. You’re done with this theatre rubbish, if it’s people like him you’ll be associating with. I didn’t waste ten years on bringing you up—”

“Excuse me, waste?” Mr Pound said in that low but inarguable tone.

“Get inside, boy.” The clench of Uncle Ned’s right hand was enough to send Telford scurrying for the gate. “And as for you,” he said to Mr Pound, “this is none of your business, you…criminal.”

Mr Pound inhaled sharply, fire sparking in his eyes. “Well, now you’ve insulted both me *and* him. I’m afraid I can’t let that pass.”

The son of a Frisian cheesemaker, Uncle Ned was a stony block of a man, with a baker's straining biceps and a longstanding membership at the local boxing club. Mr Pound was a good six inches shorter, half his width and nearly twice his age, yet as he approached, cane tucked under one arm while he adjusted his immaculate cuffs, something made Telford's uncle take a step back.

"I feel it best," Mr Pound said in a soothing tone as he continued to advance and Uncle Ned continued to retreat. "Given that we'll be *associating* on the regular, that I let you know a couple of things about me. See, I've had a lifetime of dealing with hard cunts." His uncle gasped at the foul word, but Mr Pound carried on, indifferent. "Men so hard a rat like you'd shit your pants they so much as looked your way. Powerful men, and I got them on their knees, and I made them weep. Turns out, I ain't afraid of nothing."

Ned glanced about as if his mates from the club were about to step forth and uneven the score. There was only Telford, lingering in the doorway. Ned's heel caught and he stumbled, fetching against the wall. "So you ain't afraid? What's your point?" he spat.

"My point?" said Mr Pound, not stopping his slow approach until he stood nearly on Uncle Ned's toes. "My point," he repeated as he stared up at the other man, "is that I've taken a real shine to that nephew of yours. I got a warm feeling for him. Like he's someone worthy of my protection. And the more I go on feeling this, the angrier I get when someone fucks with him."

From nowhere the cane appeared, pressed against Uncle Ned's chest. The bigger man gasped with a childish sound of instinctive fear before batting it away. "How dare you threaten me!"

"Threaten you?" Mr Pound repeated, cocking an eyebrow, the cane down by his side as if it had never moved. "I've done no such thing. I'm merely informing you of my sentiments for young Telford."

"It doesn't change anything. He's done with that sinful business."

"And I say it's none of your business at all what he does. He's age of majority, you've wrung a good many years labour out of him, and from what he tells me you treat him like dirt. Do you even pay him a wage?"

"He's family," Ned mumbled.

"Fuck family!"

"How dare you use language like—"

"I ain't done talking!" Mr Pound snarled. The cane reappeared, the raven's beak poised over the hollow of Ned's throat. "Family ain't license to exploit a man. From where I stand, it appears that you're treating my good friend and an essential member of my cast—my employee—very poorly, for no other reason than you feel your shared blood entitles you to his labour."

"That's not it at all," Ned stammered, eyes crossing as he strained to look down without moving any nearer to the raven's head.

"Is it not? What precisely am I misunderstanding? Please, enlighten me."

"Me and Beryl took him in," Ned said to the raven. "Fed him, clothed him. Gave him what no one else did."

"How charitable, that you didn't turn away your nephew when he came to you in his lowest hour, so that you might keep him in what amounts to indentured servitude. How deep is thy well, hey?" He stepped back and the cane disappeared again. Uncle Ned slumped a few inches down the wall, chest heaving, face several shades of red.

"Now," Mr Pound went on. "Before you go thinking I want to leave you high and dry, I've a proposal, which I suggest you accept. You release my young friend here, and I'll supply you a worker that will do his job for fair value."

"Who'll pay him?"

"I will. For two months. If you don't want to keep my boy on after that, so be it, you can make your own arrangements. But that gives you time to learn to manage without our lad Telford."

"I'm barely scraping by as it is," Ned moaned. "You'll ruin me."

"If the scant wage of a boy with a broom is enough to ruin you, I dare say your business has bigger problems than the cost of labour. Come along, Mr Fords. We've got to discuss your star turn. Might as well do it over dinner. My shout."

It took Telford no more than ninety-five seconds to bolt upstairs, leap out of his bakery whites and into the nearest clothes to hand, vault back downstairs and meet his saviour, waiting for him in the alley.

"What a charmer, your uncle is," Mr Pound said as they set off.

"That was terrifying. He could have snapped you in half."

"If he had, by tomorrow there'd have been a pile of rubble where the shop stood. People will notice, something happens to me."

"What do you mean?"

"I weren't making that up. I'm not much to look at, but trust me, I'm not to be trifled with. I been around, and I've made some friends who take notice of those who get on my bad side."

"I'll endeavour to remain on your good side, in that case."

"You? You're golden. And if you pull off a good Jeeves, you'll be my bloody saviour."

THE REASON

Izzy HADN'T LAID on the killing charm in years. Like as not he'd overdone it, but there was an unbeatable thrill in taking charge of a man. Anything he wanted, he could have got from that nasty piece of work Telford called an uncle. Not there'd been much to want from the bloviating bully. Just Telford. Or rather, Telford's freedom.

What a lamb, just like his friend Cian had said. The kid wouldn't last a season if he didn't toughen up. He could barely blush his way through the libretto of the play he was presently in, given the racy language, the outré subject matter. Stock in trade at the Palmetto, yet the kid had said it was the only place he'd auditioned.

After the rousing encounter, Izzy craved an equally rousing meal. Noel's blood had run with capsicum thanks to his Jamaican parentage, and he had inured Izzy to its effects over years of brutal exposure. Now Izzy's mouth fairly watered at the thought of a good curry. Besides which, it would put Telford on the spot, to have to manage such a different sort of food.

One could smell Brick Lane from two streets away. Settled in the corner of his favourite Bengali shop, he ordered a korma for the lad and a vindaloo for himself, little masochist that he was. *Also your fault…*

Telford was conspicuously out of place, his nostrils twitching at the wealth of aromas spilling from the kitchen as he stared about him at the brightly painted walls, the red-shaded lamps, the conspicuous fact that of all the diners they were the only two white people.

"So, Mr Fords," Izzy said without warning.

Telford flinched but didn't spring out of his seat. "Yes, Mr Pound?"

"Let's leave that be for the time being, all right? I'll call you Telford, Terry, whatever you wish. You can call me Izzy."

"I couldn't possibly disrespect—"

"Don't come the Rothschild, lad. We're not so far apart on the social scale that we've got to keep up appearances. I hear *Mr Pound, Mr Pound* all damned day. This is a meal between friends, ain't it?"

"Certainly, Mr—Izzy."

"Good. In which case, might I ask you a question?"

"Of course."

"Out of all the trades on earth, why have you chosen theatre?" An immensely useful question, and one he asked of nearly all his cast at one point or another, for he had patience for neither starry-eyed fame seekers nor swooning poets who couldn't see it as a job.

"It hardly felt like a choice, to be honest," Telford said with a sheepish smile. "I've wanted to become an actor for as long as I can remember. I was in every play at school, at church. We did a very compelling *Passion* one year that still gets comments."

"Please tell me you weren't our lord and saviour."

"No, I played Thomas. Fewer lines, and that way I

could help with props. And costumes. And getting the younger children to pay attention. And…well, you know what it's like. But I love it. It's tremendously difficult and exhausting and I can't imagine wanting anything else. That's all."

"But why'd you come to me? Out of all them theatres, why the Palmetto?"

"You had a notice up," Telford replied as if nothing could be clearer.

"Yeah, but I'm not the only rep in town. And beg my pardon for saying, but you seem well out of your depth. You don't drink, you don't gamble, you don't curse, you spend more time in church on a given week than I have in the past year, and I can't even imagine what you'll say when you find out the rest. So what is it?"

"*The Alabaster Angel.* Your play."

"I know it's mine, but I haven't put that one on in ten years."

"Twelve years, to be precise."

"And so what about it?"

"My parents brought me to see it."

"Your parents?" Izzy did some quick reckoning. Telford was, what, twenty-two or -three? Which meant the lad had been all of ten years old when he'd seen a play so infamous it had almost gotten Izzy arrested. Twice if one counted the punch-up at the print-shop when the printer's wife got a look at the libretto. "Your *parents*?"

"They were very broad-minded. Scandalously so at times."

"I'll say. What were they thinking?"

"We were always at the theatre, one way or another.

And I suppose they'd run out of other shows to bring me to, and it had been running for ages and was going to close soon."

"But golly…that one pulls no punches."

"I know. It's genius."

"Now you're having me on. Genius, it ain't."

Telford shook his head, almost frowning. "I'm not joking. It's a magnificent play. A work of art."

"It's sentimental bilge." What bits of it weren't irredeemable filth. "I'm sorry, your *parents*?"

"Sentimental it may be," Telford replied with a little laugh, "yet the story itself is so very beautiful. One longs for their happiness so much, even if they're meant to be terrible men."

"No honour amongst thieves, they always say."

"But they're not bad-hearted. Yes, they sin, but so do we all. Given a chance, they might have been happy." He had been speaking with passion and now sat back, his hands in his lap. "It's been years, but that's how I remember it. Perhaps I've misunderstood."

"Nah, you've got the general shape of it," Izzy said, his throat catching on the words, the moment itself too sentimental by half. "Though that's not usually the first thing people notice, if you know what I mean."

"That's why I say it's genius. You fooled the audience into having sympathy for men they'd been taught to despise. You took the most profane subject matter and made it into something…well, something sacred."

"Sacred? Are we talking about the same bleeding plays?"

Telford laughed again—the boy was laughing *at*

him. "Love is how we acknowledge the presence of God in others. *The Alabaster Angel* is a love story, isn't it?"

"Not all have said so."

"But what do *you* say? Why did you write it thus, with no female lead?"

Why did it feel like he was confessing? And to this man-child, whom he had just had to rescue from his evil stepfather like a fairy-tale princess; to whom he owed nothing. "You know why. And if you don't, I sure as hell ain't telling."

"But have you never felt God's presence in your love?"

"God don't generally get involved in my sort of love."

"I don't believe that. Not at all."

"What, your bible's missing that page?"

"Would you rather I condemn you?"

"It's hardly your place to do so. And in truth I would rather you leave well enough alone. The plays are what they are. I don't have to justify them, to you or anyone else."

THE SAUCE

Telford was fudging it completely. He had meant to comfort him, uplift him, show the man that he'd been doing God's work the whole time. Instead he was causing a fight, Mr Pound glaring at him across the table with a hint of that power he'd used on Uncle Ned.

"I'm sorry. It really is none of my business."

The older man sighed, resettled in his chair. "Nah, it's me. I've always got my feathers ruffled about something or other of late. Comes of getting so frequently shat on. You come to expect every cobber's out to get you. Speaking of," and he nodded towards the approaching waiter.

The man set the food between them: small metal dishes brimming with bright sauces and a larger bowl of rice. Mr Pound—Izzy—waved off the waiter and plated the food himself. "They ought to know by now not to stand on ceremony," he grumbled as he ladled rice onto Telford's plate. "I'm in here often enough."

"It smells extraordinary. Do you eat like this all the time?"

"My friend's parents were from Jamaica. It was him what gave me a taste for spice. Plain food is a bit like eating a boiled boot." He was patting over his pockets and with a gasp of delight pulled out a small brown vial. He gave it a shake, then with one eye towards the kitchen unscrewed the cap.

"What is that?"

"Shh."

"Is that opium?" he hissed. No matter Izzy's other sins, Telford didn't truck with addicts, but the old man laughed.

"Christ, no. Capsicum sauce. The cook goes spare if she sees me messing with her spices." Izzy's dish was mutton in an orange-brown stew, to which he now added several drops of bright red liquid from the vial. "You want a dash?" He waggled his eyebrows, his lip curled in a dangerous grin.

"I've eaten spicy food before. Why not?"

"I can think of a few reasons, but let's see what happens." He put a single droplet at the side of Telford's plate. "Take a bit of meat and dab it."

Dutifully, Telford cut a piece of chicken and touched it in the red sauce. He put the meat in his mouth and chewed, preparing to tell Izzy about the Szechuan restaurant he'd gone to once. Then the pain set in. Then accelerated, spreading across his tongue and down his throat like he was chewing fire. His gums were burning. His nose began to run. His legs wanted to, but there was no escape. He could barely see for the tears, but it sounded like Mr Pound was laughing again.

Someone passed him a glass of beer. "I don't…oh, forget it." It was drink this beer or cut out his tongue. Whatever stopped the pain, and he set his sizzling lips against the cool glass and gulped, flushing down the incendiary mouthful. "You…are a wicked little man."

Izzy swallowed the bite he was chewing and gave him a devilish smile. "Bet you're wishing that *was* opium, hey?"

Compared with the contents of the vial, the 'korma' was mother's milk, and Telford ate more than he expected, though he declined any more beer, the giddy effects as unpleasant as he'd been told. Mr Pound's face got red and shiny with sweat but he ate the entirety of his meal without flinching.

"Might I ask a question?" he said as Mr Pound was mopping his plate with the last scrap of flat bread.

"Seems only fair."

"Will you tell me how you started? What was it that made you choose this as a way to ruin your life, as you say?"

"Mainly a lack of options. Honour bright, if you'd told me when I started that I'd be doing this for the rest of my days, I'd have laughed in your face. In fact, I'd have laid odds on me being dead by now. Certainly not that I'd be so hale as I am," he added hastily as Telford crossed himself. "I mean that I thought I'd have gotten my head cove in, or just got plain old locked up. But I haven't. So there. Dunno that it means much other than our Maker having a peculiar sense of humour."

"What do you mean by that?"

"I mean that plenty of good, God-fearing men die young, while a shit like yours truly gets to ride the long rail. Ain't much sense in it."

A question Telford had asked himself too often, the answer the only one that had ever made sense. "I believe we can't always know the meaning of the life we're granted," he said carefully. "That's why we call it faith.   God is great not only because He encompasses all but because that *all* is more than we can possibly understand. The grace He grants comes from so far beyond us that at times it terrifies. The voice of God is not always still and small. Sometimes it comes ringing from the mountaintops and calls us to it, and we follow as if we hadn't a choice. And sometimes we hear it in the words of those we encounter in our lives." He indicated Izzy with an open hand, a knowing smile.

"Voice of God? You can't possibly mean me."

"But what if I do?"

"Just sounds a bit, I dunno, transcendentalist for the good little Catholic I thought you were."

Telford laughed, finally out of humour and not nerves. "I won't claim it's a popular doctrine. Father Gilchrist was an iconoclast. A rabid Pythagorean. Music of the Spheres and all that."

"Now you've lost me," Mr Pound said, frowning. "Is that some kind of church music?"

"In a sense. It's more an idea. The notion that there are heavenly sounds. That music resonates beyond the audible, and the reason we find certain songs, certain melodies more spiritually uplifting is due to these resonances."

"Is that another one of your Voice of God deals?"

"Simplified for human ears."

"Still don't reckon it has naught to do with me."

"That may be for the best, that you think thus. Pride goeth before the Fall, they say."

"Don't I know it."

The waiter had come to clear the table. Mr Pound finished his drink and waited for the man to leave, then sat forward, hands clasped on the table, as intent as at their first meeting in his office. "Look, I came on pretty strong with that uncle of yours. Be honest, have I made things worse for you at home?"

"I…don't know. I've never stood up to him before. I don't know how he'll take it." Poorly, as he took anything that Telford had done wrong, which was often everything.

"If he hurts you—" Mr Pound broke off, his jaw trembling. He exhaled and unclasped his hands and set them flat on the table, then went on, his voice ragged. "Well, I ain't never had a son. Not one I know about. But no young man in my care would have to endure that. If it comes to it, I want you to come to me. I'll put you up."

"What do you mean?"

"I mean, I don't want you going home if that home ain't a proper home. If he's going to hurt you, don't go near him again. You can stay at the theatre if you'd rather not bunk at mine. But you come to see me, and I'll get you out of that gaol he keeps you in. Day or night, doesn't matter. I'll not turn you away."

Dumbfounded, Telford only stared, unwilling to admit how badly he needed this. His uncle's violence was so unpredictable that he'd given up anticipating it. There were too many ways to earn it, and no way to avoid it. Naturally his first instinct was refusal. "You can't possibly make such an offer."

"Like fun I can't," Mr Pound retorted, but his eyes were merry. "I can, and I have, and you can't keep me from making it again. If I've learned nothing else from four decades in this cursed business, it's that no one gets by on their own. Take what help is offered you, when it's offered. Because a time will come when you'll wish you had it, and no one will have an ounce to spare."

Telford merely nodded for if he spoke he'd start to cry as Mr Pound found a scrap of paper and the stub of a pencil then told him his address on a street not far from the Palmetto.

It was late afternoon, and by rights he ought to go home. There'd be something in need of doing. But were his doing days done? Mr Pound was sending a boy in his place… Reeling from the whirlwind of a day, from the alcohol and the spice and the staggering possibility of freedom, Telford followed the older man out to the street.

THE CITY

"LA, IT'S BEEN an age since I had a slap-up like that." Strolling towards the high street, Izzy rubbed his belly, full to bursting.

"Thank you for the meal. And for everything else you've done," Telford added quickly. "No one's ever made me feel so welcome."

"What else could I do? I was the one who went and mixed it up with your uncle. Figured I owe you."

"You don't, and really he started it, years ago. I've learned by now I'll never please him."

"He don't deserve you."

"I hope they don't suffer without my help."

"They'll manage. And if they can't, you can be sure they'll be begging you to come back."

"Do you think so?"

"Maybe. Either way, the choice will be yours. Which brings us to the present moment. Feel like taking a walk?"

"To where?"

"Round and about. Stretch our legs, see what's what. Maybe I'll show you a couple sights. You seem unreasonably interested in my history. I reckon I ought to exploit that." Telford startled at the insinuative word and Izzy went on. "The rest of them have heard it all before, see? To them I'm just some old fart mumbling away."

"Not at all. You're not that old."

"Tell that to my rheumatism."

"And I'd love to take a walk, see some of your history."

"What of it's still standing. This way."

They crossed Whitechapel High Street and entered the narrow lanes beyond. Nothing like as coarse as when he was coming up, nearly all of the neighbourhood having been rebuilt in his lifetime. Most of his old landmarks had been removed but after a few wrong turnings they reached Horlick Close. The tilting, soot-stained tenements that had ringed the dead-end street, the ragged children warring in the oily gutters out front, the sound of the Goldmeiers' chickens bickering in their coop: all gone in favour of matched rows of red brick townhouses with green shutters on the windows and a brass flap for the post on every door.

"Here we are, where it all started going wrong."

"Why, what happened here?" Telford said, looking about with the sidelong glances of a man with something to hide.

"I got born." Telford laughed, then covered his mouth, as if Izzy had meant it as anything but a joke. "This ain't the place though," he went on. "I mean to say, it's the same street, but the building's long gone. Slum reform, they called it. Gave them three weeks' notice, I recall. Whatever you couldn't shift, you lost for good. And that was for ordinary folks. The city wanted you gone, they moved quick. That's how Ursula lost the first house, off Leicester."

A door opened and a tiny boy came outside, his left index finger up his left nostril as far as he could get it. Izzy nodded to the scamp, who made a rude gesture with his free hand. Izzy returned it, making Telford gasp and the boy dart back inside, howling.

"I see bugger all's changed about the residents. Let's shift before him and his little friends come out and start asking for money." They returned to the high street and started westward. It was some distance to the old House, but the weather was fine and he was more full of dash than he'd felt in an age.

"It must be difficult living in a time of such rapid change," Telford said as they passed yet another construction hoarding, the iron girders rising a good six stories above them.

"There is no other sort of time. You think this city's a fixed thing, but I tell you, it shifts like the tides. I can remember back before they put in the sewers. Cor, the smell of the Thames of a summer could knock a man flat. Trust me, by the time you're an old codger, they'll have knocked these buildings down all over again. Be putting up some Jules Verne affair with electric elevators zipping all over, and I dunno, wings or something."

"Wings?" Telford chuckled.

"Eh, why not? Consider that, no sooner had man swapped out the horse and buggy for engines like that," and he pointed at the motor conveniently rattling past, "then some mad bastard strapped wings on it and hurled himself off a cliff. And there you have it, the aeroplane. A whole new thing. As a boy I imagine I would have shit myself sideways if one of them came hurtling overhead. Now people take them across the ocean like it's nothing. Next you know, they'll be aiming them at the moon."

"More Jules Verne?"

"His guess is as good as anyone else's. Like the cu—cobbers round these parts," he said, as they came to Threadneedle. "Bankers and pollies and all the little men hiding behind their big doors, who want us to think they've got it all sussed. They're making it up as they go, just like we all are."

Some ways further they passed the solicitor's office he wanted, the old brass nameplate blackened round the edges. Three more streets brought them to the alleyway. "We'll not go in as there's nothing to see that you can't see from here," he said, pointing with the raven's beak. "But down there's where I met my first proper employer, Ursula. Right after I seen her smashing a man in the face with this here." He waggled the stick and Telford's eyes sprung open.

"In the face?"

"His fault for trying to pinch her purse. She had no patience for pricks like Joycey. I got there just as she was wiping off the blood. Not a woman you crossed, not without an army at your back. Whatever possessed her to offer me work..." He shook his head, no less surprised a lifetime later. "I weren't much more to look at back then than I am now. Bit faster on my feet, couple extra teeth, but still a milky shortarse. I reckon all she was looking for was compliant, and boy, I was that in spades." He led Telford onward, making for that odd corner of Mayfair.

THE RIVER

MR POUND'S TALES were so vivid Telford could easily imagine how the city used to be: smaller, darker, damper, stinking of the unwashed and washed alike, set to the music of stall-men singing their wares and the clatter of hooves over cobble. Easy as well to think of the spry old chap beside him as a gap-toothed scallywag, the runt of the litter, with five older brothers who had made him their proxy for all the worst mischief. Eight to a one-room flat. Two beds, and a mother cooking dinner over a fire in the lane, when there was a dinner to be cooked. Telford would be adding a thanks to his nightly prayers that God had let this precious man live.

Yet here they were in Mayfair, not known for its tolerance of Cockney scallywags. Spencer Street was a-bustle on this fine evening with suited gents on their way to homes gleaming with welcome and quick-stepping groups of women concluding their day of shopping.

They came around a corner and Mr Pound slowed then stopped, peering at the frontages across the street. "See that door?" He nodded towards an old haberdasher's.

"The shop?"

"Nah, beside it. That real old one what looks like a Tudor might have knocked on it once or twice." He pointed the cane at a heavy affair of silvered planks held together with weighty black hasps and huge, square-headed nails. "That's all that's left, that door. I heard it goes up to flats or something now. Main floor's a handbag shop. Frontage on the other side."

"What was it in your day?"

"My place of employ," he said in a strange voice. A stagey voice laden with implication, though the door gave nothing away. He led Telford across the street and further along to a laneway jogging between the buildings. A door was set into the left-hand wall similar to the Palmetto's stage door but without a pru-hole. The door opened and a lad in shirtsleeves and a canvas apron came out with a bicycle, the panniers laden with parcels wrapped in brown paper. He wheeled the bicycle past them with a glare, and Mr Pound guided Telford on, chuckling under his breath.

"Goes to show, don't it?" he said. "That door was once the best kept secret in town. That's where Ursula's staff came in. Custom had to use that street door I showed you. Then they had to get past Clyde, which they didn't if he didn't want them to. Welsh giants indeed. You never seen such a man." He raised his arms overhead to mime the size, nearly smacking Telford with the foot of the cane. "And then a bit of a chat with Ursula. Rare that she needed to use the stick. Our custom weren't the sort to argue. Not given what they were asking of us. And then, if one was paid-up, and deloused, one might be allowed in the parlour to mingle with the trade. Exit on the far side, after your service. Magnificent set-up. Ran like a greased wheel for years. Good old change, though. Ruins the best of plans."

Staff, trade, custom, the stick, and Mr Pound had yet to mention anything to do with the theatre. Unless this Ursula operated some form of private club. One that needed a giant as a doorman and a delousing before the show. "You'll have to forgive me," Telford began, "but you've painted a rather peculiar picture. Is this what you were doing before you took up directing, working for this Ursula?"

"It is."

"You were a performer for her *custom*, as you said?"

"I was."

"And so what was your act?"

Mr Pound coughed, or was he holding in a laugh? Lips pursed, he glanced around, but the foot traffic had dwindled as they neared Leicester Square. "Pretending to like them," he said in that same purring voice as before. "Though more often than not, it was pretending to hate them."

"Hate them…" Understanding eluded Telford once more, like trying to grasp a wisp of fog. "I feel like this should make more sense. Like you're telling me a secret that I'm meant to already know."

"I was rather hoping." When Telford didn't reply, Mr Pound sighed heavily. "All right then. Lemme put it this way. Your old mate *Alabaster*? Very little of that was made up. I just wrote it the way it happened."

"What…what do you mean?"

"Exactly what I said. Aside from it being set in Fairyland and the bit with them singing to the statue without knowing the other chap was there. But la, how else was I going to pull off a trick like that? How else was I going to fool 'em, like you said, into pulling for them lads in the story?"

The conversation with his parents while walking home after seeing *The Alabaster Angel* had been more astonishing for young Telford than viewing the show itself. Intent humanists, they had carefully led their son through an occult history of the West, its vestal virgins and gymnasia, and the now-forbidden love that had sustained some of the greatest men to have lived. To a boy of Telford's eager intellect and acute sensitivity, their words had been both a comfort and a challenge, opening to him a larger and stranger world than he had thought existed.

And yet…

Yet even the Lord had space in his heart for the so-called fallen, for had not Christ Himself blessed the Magdalene? He stopped walking. Mr Pound stopped as well, his lips tight, shoulders rigid, poised to defend himself.

"Do you mean…" *Please Lord, let this not be when he learns to despise me.* Telford took a breath and tried again. "Do you mean to tell me you used to be a prosti—"

Mr Pound threw up a hand to cut him off. "Never mind that dirty old word. Never did like it. Besides, the custom were the ones what were prostrate." He laughed, that dry chuckle that made Telford's hair stand on end.

"What does that mean?"

"What'd you call me before, a *wicked little man*? Son, you got no idea how wicked I can be." Still laughing, he turned and carried on walking. Head spinning, heart slightly breaking, Telford followed.

They crossed Leicester Square and went down a street on the far side, where Mr Pound pointed out another missing piece, the site of the other 'house' owned by his employer Ursula. Here young Ezekiel had worked as a runner and look-out. The bawdy had been demolished not long after he had gone up to Ursula's Mayfair house.

"*House of Lords*, she called it," Mr Pound explained. "Right cheeky, that. The clients got a good laugh, I tell you. *I'll pretend I didn't see you at the House of Lords*, said one MP to the other."

"And so that play, those men…that's your life? Just…with costumes?"

Mr Pound shrugged, swinging his cane as they walked. "More or less. But where else do writers get ideas except their lives? I tell the story, and Whitley figures out how to make people pay to hear it sung."

They carried on towards Covent Garden, Telford's feet growing heavier with every step. He wholly believed Mr Pound, who had nothing to gain by inventing such a tale when so many adherents to Telford's faith would have used it against him, denounced him not merely for his profession but for having conducted it with men. And Telford had spent half his life denying the truth behind this man's art, imagining the gods and angels and statues and impossible creatures that populated his plays were allegorical of something far more spiritual, and not this debased sensualism.

And yet…

Nothing had changed. Not in the plays or in Mr Pound or even in Telford, who ought to have known. Unspeaking, he followed the other man down past the rail station and so to the top of the Victoria Embankment, its verdant parkland extending along the riverbank to Waterloo Bridge.

"None of this were here before," Mr Pound said, nodding about as they started on the combed gravel path. "Cleared out a ton of buildings to put in the sewers, then slapped this bougie bit on it."

"Bougie?"

"Bourgeois, you know? Fancied up for the middle classes. Hey, like my plays. Take something revolting and make it beautiful." The park was certainly that, graced with trees and flourishing garden beds, and the fine evening had drawn many Londoners to walk its paths and sit about on the smooth lawns. In a few minutes they had crossed it, and went over the roadway to the footpath which ran along the riverbank. Here they stopped, Mr Pound leaning his elbows on the stone wall as they looked out over the sluggish water, green-gold from the lowering sun.

"Now there's something no one can change," Mr Pound said, pointing with his chin. "That stinking river is always going to be half made of mud."

"I…think I need a minute."

"I don't doubt."

Telford walked a few yards further, set his hand on his crucifix and recited the Hail Mary until his teeth stopped chattering. *Pray for us sinners now*, and he had never meant it more. Mr Pound was a sinner, right across the board, yet he had shown Telford more kindness than anyone had in years. Save for Cian, who was more his guardian angel than his friend. The thing for Telford to do was to let go of his need to understand. If God had a plan, then this was in it. If

God loved the world, He loved this man as well, as He loved Telford or any other part of Creation.

He returned to Mr Pound who was leaned on the stone wall, reading a chap-book. No, he was looking at a picture in an embossed card frame, though he tucked it away when he noticed Telford approach.

"Thank you for showing me your side of London," Telford said, resting his elbows on the wall.

Settling beside him again, Mr Pound hissed through his teeth. "My side of London don't hardly exist no more, except up here," and he tapped the side of his head. "All the rest of them are gone. Even Esme, I heard. Poor little moppet. Though if that were last year, she'd have been going on fifty years. Christ, I'm old."

And for the first time he looked it, his shoulders drawn, head drooping, eyes seeing not the murky surface of the River Thames but some far distant shore. Telford waited for the dry chuckle, but Mr Pound remained as he was, his face haggard.

"You'd better go now, lad," he muttered.

"Will you be all—"

"You're still here," he growled, his grip tensing on his cane.

Telford stepped back. "I'll see you at rehearsal."

Gazing into the green-gold roll of the river, Mr Pound didn't reply.

IT WAS NEARLY eight o'clock before Telford got home. Standing in the alley, he whistled to Cian, who appeared at the window in the rear of the house. He met Telford at the gate and they sat in the corner behind the trellis where Mrs Gilbert grew beans, to hear of Telford's long, strange day.

"So I left him, like he asked. And now I'm worried he'll have fallen or been mixed up with some troublemakers and—"

"Telly, give it over. Maybe he's an old fellow, but if he really did what you said to your uncle, he's like to be hale enough to protect himself from near about anything. Or do you think he's really in danger?"

"I don't know. I just don't think I ought to have left him like that."

"Like he asked you to?"

Telford didn't reply. Couldn't, his tongue pinned to the roof of his mouth, his breath stilled in his lungs, for Cian had put his hand on Telford's knee. A casual touch, a gesture of friendship: a disaster, as a betraying heat crept up Telford's thigh while Cian went on reassuring him in his soft lilt about…something Telford had wholly forgotten.

At the sound of an opening door Cian jerked his hand away. "It's getting on," he whispered. "I ought to get inside. As for you, might be best if you're not seen at home tonight."

Telford nearly asked why before recalling his act of defiance, the facts of the day. "Perhaps you're right. May I—"

"Of course," Cian said at once. "Whenever you need. I even managed to wash the blanket."

"Heavens. You'll spoil me."

"If I could offer you more—"

"Hush. You do more than enough for me. Now

go before you're missed."

"As long as you know you have only to ask."

Once Telford heard the scullery door scrape shut he slunk closer to the house and carefully let himself into the brick shed built against the wall. Inside, he waited for his eyes to adjust, then felt his way around the barrels and crates to the broken armchair he and Cian had secreted here. It was dusty and sagging and better than nothing, more comfortable than the ground, and immeasurably safer than facing his uncle's rage. The blanket was more patch than fabric but it was clean and smelled of the piny soap Cian's foster mother used. No, it smelled of Cian. Wrapped in the blanket, Telford settled into the musty cushions, and began again to pray for Mr Pound's immortal soul. And his own.

THE DIRECTOR

TELFORD WOKE WITH the birds and slunk to his own house, where he set about his chores before it was light. The boy Mr Pound had promised arrived not long after, a sturdy, quiet fellow of fourteen who took well to instruction and didn't flinch when Uncle Ned yelled, which had the peculiar effect of causing the man to yell a great deal less. Telford left at half-past eight, arriving at the theatre early for the very first time.

The rehearsal ran smooth as glass, as did the following two. Everyone knew their lines and was swiftly learning their stage directions. Costumes were fitted, sets were rising, the enterprise running like clockwork, and he hadn't seen Mr Pound once. No one spoke of it, and perhaps their director's absence was doing more good than his presence, as the cast lost some of their self-consciousness without a cross old man stomping about in the aisles, looking for a reason to blow his top.

By the end of the third day, Telford felt sick with worry. Cian had tried to soothe his fears, but he couldn't forget the state of melancholy in which he'd left poor Mr Pound. When rehearsal was finished, he went around to Mr Whitley's poky office to see if there was any news.

"No. Why would there be?"

"Is it usual for him not to be here?"

"Usual?" Whitley drew out the word like an insult.

"Only we were talking the other day and when I said good-bye he seemed awfully low, and I really am worried that something's happened to him."

"What would happen?"

"I don't know!"

"Well, I can't possibly get away. You might as well go round and check on him yourself."

"Me?" Telford yelped.

Whitley blinked in eloquent frustration. "It's not far." He took out his little book and began to tear another strip from the ragged rear page.

"I know where he lives." Whitley paused, the paper's edge between thumb and forefinger, and slowly raised his eyes to Telford's reflection in the mirror on his desk. "He told me. In case of an emergency. Why don't I just go?"

He all but ran from the tiny room, heading for the stage door via the twisting route past the dressing rooms and storerooms and standing bits of set. Ten or so minutes later, he was climbing the slightly sagging stairs of an older building off a run-down stretch of Shaftesbury Ave. Mr Pound's flat was on the third floor, the carpet in the corridor worn to threads, the various noises and smells of the other tenants creeping from under the peeling doors.

Mr Pound's was the last, and as Telford neared the door he heard him speak with the same cadence as in the office, as if he expected an answer. Telford's stomach unknotted a little. At least the old fellow was alive, and he was about to knock when there was a shout and an almighty crash. Then silence.

He began pounding on the door. He'd have to kick it in. Mr Pound had fallen, and Telford had to save his—

Cursing a blasphemous streak, Mr Pound yanked the door open. "For Chrissakes, quit it! Knocking like the bloody peelers."

"What happened? Are you hurt? What fell?"

"Bleeding cat, knocked over a flowerpot. What're you doing here?"

"Well, you weren't in, and it's been a few days, and I do recall you telling me that the only reason for missing rehearsal was that one was dead in a ditch, and I wanted to make sure that you…well, that you weren't. Dead in a ditch, that is."

Mr Pound snorted a laugh, leaning on the doorframe. "I just about feel it. Does that qualify?"

"Why, what happened?"

"My blasted knee happened. Gone and seized up again, what with carting you all over the city, and that gut-buster of a meal, and that stand-over job on your uncle, and having done a full morning's work before all that. I didn't reckon on getting back up the stairs once I went down them. So I stayed up. I'll have to go out soon, though. I'm out of liniment."

"I could go for you. In fact if there's anything you need, I'd be glad to help."

Mr Pound looked at him for a long moment, then sighed, shrugged, and rolled his eyes in one. "Well, as long as you're here. I've got a few things on high shelves that want reaching down."

Favouring his right leg and leaning heavily on the

cane, he shuffled away from the door. Telford followed him into the flat, which was nicer than the building had promised, with clean carpets and a charming old writing desk by the window. The broken pot lay on the floor there, a fern and its dirt spilled beside. The largest wall was covered with playbills from every theatre in the West End, some yellowed with time and overlapped by those from more recent shows.

"What a collection!"

"Wallpaper had a stain," Mr Pound said from the doorway to the kitchen. "Then we just kept going."

"How long have you lived here?"

"Six…no, seventeen years. But on and off. We spent a lot of winters away." He emerged with a dustpan and started for the desk and the fallen plant.

"Please, will you allow me to help?"

"All right. You can go put the kettle on."

"I meant—"

"And you'll find the broom behind the door. And bring a bowl or what have you, something to put this poor fellow in. He ain't quite dead. Just bashed about a little, like his owner."

Telford made tea. He put the plant and what dirt he could salvage into an empty coffee tin. Then Mr Pound had him retrieve a number of cups and dishes from the highest kitchen shelves and a cracked leather valise from atop the wardrobe in the rather squalid bedroom.

He left Mr Pound to inspect the contents of the valise in private and returned to the sitting room where he looked over the wall of posters in search of the names of actors he knew, shows he'd seen. Nearer the door hung several photographs, the largest of which showed a group of men and women gathered on a sandy shore. They were dressed in all manner of costumes: a pair of redcoats, a Roman goddess in a toga and laurel wreath, fortune tellers and harem girls and a top-hatted villain complete with monocle and twirlable moustache.

"Wager tuppence you can't find me," Mr Pound said as he came to stand beside him.

"This is your first troupe?"

"So to speak. Mad bastards, the lot of them."

Telford looked over the men again, whose faces ranged from paper-white to deeply coloured. None of them had Mr Pound's pointed chin, his sideways smile. On a whim Telford began to inspect the women, lingering over a strong-featured girl in the centre of the photo with short curling hair, dressed in a rather louche frilled gown that fit slackly on her boyish frame…

"There you are." He pointed at the young man in the dress.

Mr Pound snorted, shaking his head as he began patting his pocket for coins. "Eh, I might have to owe you—"

"Oh no, keep the money. I never took the bet."

"That you didn't."

"And what role were you playing that you were dressed like that?"

"Nah, that was us clowning. Bloody Alanson had us pose for press cards, and the photographer had a few plates left at the end. There's Ursula."

He indicated a severely dressed woman seated in the centre, her skin so fair it was hard to make out her features, her sole concession to the mood a large plumed hat, the raven's head cane resting against her knee. A young girl with the same flaxen hair but darker eyes stood beside her.

"Her daughter Esme. She's the one I told you passed away not so long ago."

"And the man you're with," Telford asked, pointing to a handsome black man in the centre of the group, his arms crossed over his bared chest, his gaze uncompromising. "Who is that?"

He hardly needed to ask, the way young Izzy had his arms wrapped around the man's waist. Mr Pound's expression told the rest as he gazed at the photograph with a soft smile, a look of purest love.

"That's Noel," he said simply.

"Your husband?"

"Yep."

"Is this when you met?"

"Nah. Knew him for years. Since we were small. Prick just about broke my arm."

"He did what?"

Mr Pound rasped his wicked little laugh. "We sure as hell didn't start out as friends."

"YOU KNOW THE plan, right?"

Izzy merely grunted at his elder brother John. He knew the plan. He hated the plan. He hated it because it meant he was going to get hurt again. Him getting hurt *was* the plan. Not going through with it meant getting hurt so much more, however, that he hadn't once thought of backing out. The plan meant getting hurt by only one boy rather than five.

"His ma's gone and he's turned away. Get on," his brother hissed. He slapped Izzy between the shoulderblades to propel him out from behind their cover of a stack of crates at the corner of the alleyway.

Stinging, grumbling, he dodged passers-by to get as close as he could to the stall. That Peters boy had a fine set of lungs, tailor made for drawing customers to his family's produce. One found him all over the city, and it was Izzy hanging about to hear him sing that had started the other Pound boys on their cursed plan. The thing was to not be too skilled. He'd lifted plenty from other carts, even shimmied the odd drainpipe (typically because his brothers had sent him up it) and never been so much as seen, which was exactly what he didn't want.

Scuffing his heels, he strolled past the Peters boy and gave him a look over. The taller boy frowned at him briefly, then took another big breath and went back to his song about *ca-bbages, cut fresh and green.*

Izzy circled the end of the cart, dodged a woman with a basket perusing the carrots, and with exactly no concealment plucked an apple from the top of the pile. Peters didn't notice. Cursing silently, Izzy went skipping past and waved the apple at him.

"Oi! You little shit!" Peters bellowed. Izzy took off, the bigger boy in pursuit, shouting blue murder. Close pursuit, his long legs a match for Izzy's general quickness.

He had just about reached his target, an alley with a scalable fence at the end, when he trod on a loose cobble and went sprawling. Peters was on him at once, wrenching his left arm painfully behind his back, while with his free hand he rained blows on Izzy's skull, cursing him roundly.

Suddenly Peters shrieked and let him go. Then he was on the ground, a thick-armed woman in a bright kerchief standing over him.

"You rass! We leave you be five minute and them boys rob us blind!" She resumed smacking her son about the head and shoulders with his own cap, as he howled and writhed and begged for mercy. Izzy meanwhile scrambled to his feet and took off at top speed, rubbing his smarting elbow, regretting more than anything that he'd dropped the apple.

"WHAT A STORY," Telford said when they'd stopped laughing. "Someone ought to be writing this down."

"You think so?"

"You've made plays out of other parts of your life."

"Yeah, but this is just kids messing about."

"It still has humour and friendship and family drama."

Mr Pound grinned, rubbing his neck. "It has me getting my narrow arse beat, so yeah, humour I'll give you."

"And it clearly has a happy ending. Eventually."

"It does. It does at that. Took a while. Almost ruined his life along the way. Probably broke his heart, or at least dinged it. Dunno how he put up with me."

"Perhaps because he loved you?"

"And God bless him for that. Theatre wasn't my life. Noel was. It was all for him. Ah, but you don't want to hear all this soft soap," he sniffed, pressing his eyes with the heel of his hand.

"I do, actually. Very much so. If you ever felt inclined. I could listen to your stories all day."

Izzy frowned, but before he answered, the bells on the nearby steeple began to chime. "Five o'clock. Tea room's closed. Bar's open, though. If you'll pour me a bit from that bottle in the kitchen, that is. Pour a glass for yourself if you like."

"Will you tell me something else?"

"What d'you want to know?"

"Anything. How you and Noel became friends. Or tell me more about that photograph. Who was Alanson?"

"A proper cu—I mean, he were Marisol's husband. Her there, in the flamenco dress." He pointed to a statuesque woman with penetrating eyes, her frilled dress cut to show a stunning amount of leg. "And there's old Bill." He indicated a corpulent fellow with oiled curls and a grandiose moustache and the incongruous costume of a paperboy's knickerbockers and flat cap.

"He's *her* husband?"

"No accounting for taste, am I right? Nah, I'm joking. It were strictly on paper. *Mariage blanche*, don't they call it? Cor, he were so bent he was nearly straight. As for her, she was wild. Massive family, hugely wealthy, but most of them mad as pants, and she whored for the hell of it, for something to do. This was her beach we're standing on. Her house what we lived in. So I suppose it's all thanks to her.

Her and Ursula. And hard work and luck and all that rubbish."

"And Noel?"

"Yeah. Him too. Otherwise, I dunno…I dunno what would have happened to me. I can guess, and it wouldn't have been half as pretty."

"Why, what happened?"

"You get us that bottle from the kitchen, I might be inclined to tell you."

I'm going to have to ask you to [*] off
Though it's not the sort of thing I like to ask
But it's come to my attention
That a few of your intentions
Are the very sort which I must take to task

*[*INSERT LOUD SOUND EFFECT]*

"Have to Ask (The Unsingable Song)"
from "Stations of the Heart"
Music by T Whitley
Lyrics by E Pound

L'arrivée

GOOD INTENTIONS ASIDE, Noel's mother's cooking was as relentless as ever, in both quantity and intensity. She had been feeding Izzy non-stop, every dish more violently spiced than the last, since he'd arrived an hour ago at the Peters' cottage on the northeast fringe of London. All his old favourites, like she'd known he was planning a visit: run-down, brown stew, callaloo, an avalanche of pasties with all manner of stuffings, and a murderous yellow curry made with coconut cream that she'd learned from Mrs Patel from down the way. Glutton that he was, he'd kept eating, until his lips burned and his sides ached and he'd had to hitch his trousers over his swollen belly to toddle to the sofa in the sitting room while Mrs Peters tidied the kitchen.

When he was once again able to move any part of his body, he retrieved the mysterious envelope he'd picked up from Auntie Owen's laundry. Postmaster, broadsheet, town crier and keeper of secrets for just about every household in the district, Auntie was among the few left England-side who knew how to reach Noel and Izzy since their hasty change of address after the disasters of last November.

Though made of fine paper, the envelope was

sealed with paste rather than a gentleman's seal, and bore no return address. The lightly perfumed card inside was from Lord Leslie, who had sent as well a pair of theatre tickets. Izzy was sounding out the name of the play when Noel's father came into the room.

"You not been wearing your hat in the garden?" Mr Peters grunted as he eased himself into the armchair opposite. "You gone all speckled across the nose."

Nervous as he always was around Noel's sternly caring father, Izzy was trying to stick the tickets back in the envelope, but they slipped from his twitching fingers onto the floor. Mr Peters bent to retrieve them.

"Who sent you those?" he asked as Izzy stuffed them loose into his inside pocket.

"An acquaintance."

"An acquaintance invited you to see a French play at the St James?" Mr Peters said, raising a grizzled eyebrow. If the man knew the truth of his son's relationship with Izzy, he had grace enough to never say an indictable word on the subject, even though his curiosity was as relentless as his wife's cooking and equally inescapable.

"He's a viscount," Izzy said, his face afire.

"A viscount, is he?"

"It's a long story, but I swear he's harmless."

"Hmm. I'd not be letting that boy of mine know that you're getting invitations from viscounts, harmless or no."

"Noel shouldn't mind. He knows his lordship as well as I do."

"And I know that boy of mine," Mr Peters replied as he looked Izzy over with a flick of his rheumy eyes.

"He gets stuck on a thing, he's like a dog in a fight. He don't like to let go."

"Are you going to tell him about it?"

Mr Peters hissed as he settled back in his chair. "Me, I can't tell that boy of mine nothing. You, though, you listen to what I say."

"Yes, sir." He slipped the envelope into his pocket as well then got groaning to his feet, his trousers pinching everywhere. "I best be getting on. I've got my own family to pay a visit to before I meet Ursula."

"You going so soon?" Mrs Peters said, popping her kerchiefed head around the door. "Wait and I'll make you up a plate."

"Oh no! I mean to say, I couldn't eat another bite."

"To take with, for on the train."

"Never mind him, where's my plate?" Mr Peters griped, scowling at his wife over his shoulder.

"Hush up, you," she retorted. "You ain't going to starve for waiting another minute."

"That's very kind of you," Izzy said as he began backing towards the front door. "But I may have to help Ursula. You know, with her things. It's best I have my hands free."

His cheeks smarting from Mrs Peters' pinches and his hand from Mr Peters sturdy grip, his guts threatening generalized rebellion, he staggered from the cottage and down the road towards the bridge. A long walk was just the thing he needed to settle his stomach before he reached his next destination.

Crossing the bridge he stopped to tear the theatre tickets into bits and let them drop into the Thames' oily murk. The card as well, for he had no intention of mentioning either to Noel, who would kick up some fuss or other, question Leslie's motives or worse, Izzy's. A conversation he preferred to avoid for it had never amounted to anything but Noel apologizing for his fits of jealousy.

Giving the tickets away was no better. Izzy had felt eyes upon him from the minute he'd stepped off the ferry at Dover. If he was expected somewhere, whoever went in his place might face a host of dangers, none of them deserved. Not that Izzy had himself done a thing to deserve them. Simply worked in a dangerous business, been pursued by dangerous men. Even the viscount was a danger in his way, for he had once been a client of Ursula's. Unlike men of similar privilege, dear old Leslie had never taken refusal as an insult.

For the fetid, freezing cesspool it became in late winter, London was quite pretty of an April midday, with the trees in dancing green, the flowers on the windowsills blooming with bees. The more London it became, the prettier it wasn't, the neat rows of new houses giving way first to shops then to windowless warehouses and stinking factories. The streets grew narrower as the buildings grew taller and dirtier, the facades stained by decades if not centuries of smoke.

Again he began to feel the creeping sense of being watched, like someone was breathing down his neck. A trick of the mind, for after spending the winter confined to the manor in France, seeing the same dozen faces and never another, he'd become accustomed to not being around strangers. London was full to the brim with them, clogging the streets and stepping on his heels, and as the nearest church began to chime the hour he surrendered to the press of time and hailed a hansom. This took him as far as Whitechapel Road, where he was forced to take to his feet again as the streets were too narrow for vehicles, if the jarvey had even been willing to drive his cab into a neighbourhood that could credibly pass for a ring of hell.

Shortly after Izzy had found his own lodgings, his parents had moved house. Had been obliged to move if one were being truthful, as part of the city's program of slum reform, a fancy way to sum up kicking out all the residents of a building, then tearing it down and replacing it with houses slum-dwellers could never afford, reforming the unfortunates straight into the last of the worst of the housing, when it wasn't directly onto the streets. Standard practice for English landlords in other words, and it had driven Izzy's parents from their dingy single room atop a creaking tenement on the wrong end of Horlick Close to an even smaller, darker, ranker room in a slumping wooden rooming house down a nameless back alley which served as the local commode to judge from the smell and the texture of the cobbles.

It took Izzy ten minutes and three shillings to get past the grunt who answered the door. Now he stood with increasing discomfort in his parents' meagre room, his hands in his pockets to keep from touching anything. Thankfully there was nowhere to sit, so that he needn't refuse. He didn't know what vermin were lurking in this squalid place, but he had a reliable number of guesses, none of which wanted confirming.

Thanks to a fallen load of bricks on the jobsite, his father had recently lost a toe. He sat in the only chair, his right foot propped on the bed, the bandages stained orange by the surgeon's iodine. Mrs Pound sat on the other end of the bed, slim shoulders drooping, her wispy hair gone stark white. Izzy did not ask if they were well.

"So is this where you'll be stopping for a while?" he said instead. "I'd like to know how to look you up when I come back."

"Are you coming back?" Ma asked, lurching forward, her clasped hands pressed to her chest.

"On visits, like. I've business abroad."

"Business," his father spat. Izzy ignored him. He'd kept the old dog alive for two years off the so-called wages of sin and not once heard a word of thanks.

"I've been out Bromley way," he said to his mother. "There's a lovely little room come free, up the road from the Peters' cottage. About the size of our old digs. But proper clean. None of this city stink. And it made wonder how you might feel if I were to help you—"

His father hissed, grabbing the arms of his chair as if to rise. Izzy's mother sprung up instead, but sat down as Mr Pound shot her a piercing glare. Misery: a one act play, repeated and repeated and repeated, and Izzy was sick to the teeth of it. As he drew a cautious breath to apologize for trying to be kind, for existing in general and in the wrong form, if only to draw his father's ire away from his mother, someone knocked on the hollow door. In swaggered Izzy's elder brother Peter.

"By my lights, the prodigal returns," he drawled around the frayed toothpick dangling from his lip. Fifth of the sixth Pound boys, Pete had long been a scrounger, refusing all work, living off his parents and brothers, until he'd got drawn into a dirty job for that capital shit Muldoon, central London's most merciless crim, with a finger in every pie. Muldoon, whose machinations were the cause of Izzy's exile, first to Liverpool, thence out of England entirely. Who had ruined Ursula's business, nearly her life.

So that prickling sensation traveling up and down Izzy's spine hadn't been mere revulsion but his intuition of imminent trouble. "Howzit, Pete?" he said, measuring the distance to the door, the gap between Pete and the wall.

"Top shelf, my brother. You look like you've made out well." Pete himself was flash as anything, from his crisply blocked hat to his silk cravat to his polished boots, though those were showing the muck he'd stepped through. "I was hoping to catch up with you. Got a proposal you might wish to hear."

The prickling intuition was now a scraping cat's claw of fear. "What a shame. I was just about to take my leave."

"In that case, let me walk you out," Pete said, gesturing grandly toward the door directly behind him.

"No, it's no bother. You ought to stay, have your visit. I've friends expecting me. If I'm late, they'll wonder what's happened."

He met his brother's gaze unflinching. Pete returned the stare, his lips working. Then he smiled, a staged grin, a baring of teeth. "In that case, carry on. We all know what your friends are like."

"Et tu, Brutus?"

"Wot?"

"Never mind. I've got to shift. God bless you," Izzy said to his mum as he bent to kiss her cheek.

Muttering under his breath, his father looked away. Izzy returned the favour. "And God keep you," he said to Pete, whose grin tightened to a snarl.

"What in blazes is that meant to mean?"

"Only that I wish you well, my brother."

Pete stood between him and the door, mostly as there wasn't anywhere else to stand. Still, a long and sickening moment passed before Pete turned his body enough for Izzy to step past. The cat's claw was now a scraping blade of terror as he unlatched the door and let himself out to the piss-reeking corridor.

Ready money had it that his brother hadn't aimed to catch up on old times but to rob him. At the very least. Given the link between them all, the link named Muldoon, kidnapping wasn't out of the question. Hence the odds of Pete coming alone were exactly none.

Rather than chance the front door, Izzy went through to the coal-box of a kitchen. A pair of old molls were chattering by the stove, and he paid them a crown apiece to let him out the back door then forget they'd ever done any such thing. The alley behind the house was no less wretched but seemed deserted. Fear gripping his spine, he stepped quietly as he could around the puddles and the lumps and gained the street.

At midday the city was running full tilt, the pavement busy with workmen and delivery boys and women with baskets and flocks of squalling children. Standing on the curb waiting for an omnibus to pull away, Izzy caught his own reflection in the glass of its windows. Amid the other people waiting behind him were two men he recognized, lingering at the corner of the wall. A pair of Pete's chums, the one peering about for his fellows.

The 'bus hadn't moved, blocked by the press of traffic ahead, and Izzy turned right and started along the pavement, hoping enough of his old maze-like routes through the streets had been spared from development. The last thing he needed was to lead the brutes directly to Ursula.

He wanted to run. He kept on at his usual sprightly pace, obliging himself to whistle now and then as if he wasn't walking a razor's edge, waiting to slip and fall as he led them round and round, up one street and down the next, avoiding dead ends as they were likely to be his end, until he began to worry he might miss the train to Dover. Another chap had joined the first two, the three more than a match for Izzy even if he were fighting for his life, and he doubled back towards Charring Cross where he was to meet Ursula and Sal.

Reaching the square in front of the station, he spotted Pete in his garish suit of green and navy check, loafing against a lamp-post. Izzy had his train ticket in his pocket, needed only to pass the gates to be sure of his safety. As Pete shoved off the lamp and started on a course to intercept, Izzy played his last card. Drawing on every bit of courage he possessed, and a great deal more that he was merely pretending, he walked calmly up to the police constable standing in the centre of the square.

"I beg your pardon, officer," Izzy began in his most meticulous accent, the one he'd learned from his high-tone clients in order to intimidate them better. "I fear my watch has stopped. Have you the time?"

"Of course, sir." The constable snapped open his

dented watchcase and displayed the face to Izzy. "A quarter-hour to ten, sir."

"Much obliged. I say, my good man, and not to tell you how to do your job, but there's a veritable plague of pickpockets working this square. I dare say there's a gang of them after my own self. Been following me for some time."

"And might you be able to provide any distinguishing details of this gang?" the constable asked as he pulled out his little book. As Izzy obliged, a luxe carriage pulled up at the curb. Itself not a remarkable event, except that the passengers being aided from its upholstered cab by the footman were Ursula and Sal.

Sal flagged a porter and began aiding the fellow with piling the luggage on a cart. Still Izzy ignored them, for he had no desire to make himself known to the occupants of any more posh carriages. At last the vehicle pulled away, and Izzy thanked the constable then caught up with his employer and her aide as they passed under the brick arch leading into the station. Ursula greeted him with a brief nod, Sal with an eager handshake and a twitchy smile.

"Whose trap was that?" Izzy asked Sal as they fell into step behind the cart.

Sal snorted, shaking their head. "You don't want to know, and I don't want to tell you. How're your folks?"

"Same answer. Now let's get the bloody hell out of England."

"Amen to that."

Between the picnic of sandwiches and ale and everyone's general relief to be safely away, they made merry on the train. Sal had a deck of playing cards and showed off their newest shuffling tricks. Once Ursula's barkeep, the wiry American had quicksilver fingers, and had made an art of pouring. The same skills could make cards dance, until even Ursula smiled when Sal extracted the Queen of Hearts from her coiled hair.

On the ferry they played whist, though as always Ursula refused to wager, a mercy given she was nearly unbeatable. It was all quite jolly until they disembarked in Calais. Officially, Izzy had nothing to hide. What he had in his case was wholly permissible. And yet his heart fair doubled its pace as he followed Ursula and Sal down the ramp from the ferry and across the concourse to the baggage inspectors.

Hat tipped back, chewing a toothpick, and generally playing the guileless errand boy, Sal bore an enormous basket from Fortnum & Mason. Beneath the biscuits and preserves and costly port lay an envelope stuffed with francs, destined for the head man's pocket, a bribe Ursula would have gone to great pains to arrange in advance. The cost of doing business, which in this case was buying disinterest in the contents of Ursula's other goods, not to mention the several hundred pounds sterling secreted about her person in various pockets and pouches sewn into her thick dress. Izzy made to join them, but an official in his little drum-shaped hat obliged him to halt, then sent him to a different counter.

"Ouvrez, s'il vous plait," barked the sallow faced guard, pointing at Izzy's bag. It pleased him not at all, but Ursula was paying no mind, leaning on her cane as she conversed with another guard, likely the chief to judge from the extra set of bars on his shoulder and the coloured band around his hat.

Perhaps this chappie wasn't getting a cut. He began to rifle through Izzy's open Gladstone, which contained not a stitch of his own things, given the amount of goods the others had pressed him to bring back. A dowry's worth of women's underclothes, everyone's favourite cosmetics, jam for Brigid and ribbon for Rosie and a life's supply of hairpins and hatpins. The guard looked up, lip curling with contempt as he weighed the odds between Izzy being a smuggler and merely being bent.

"J'ai des sœurs," he offered in his atrocious French. The guard's eyebrow curled to match his lip. Izzy held up four fingers. "Beaucoup des sœurs."

The guard snorted, but before he replied the head guard called to him. "Il est avec Madame ici."

The fellow snapped to attention. "Très bien. Fermez."

"Merci beaucoup." Izzy snapped the case shut and joined the others. Sal had been relieved of the basket and was carrying Ursula's valise, and they followed their madam away from the customs counter to the cargo office, for her to arrange the transport of their other goods. Izzy got out the packet of Noel's lemon drops from his case, which he left to be sent with the rest. For the indignity he'd just endured, the girls could damn well wait for their frilly bits.

Once they were well away from the customs buildings, Ursula straightened her shoulders and set a lively pace through the streets of Calais to the country road which led to the house. If the tide was out they might have taken the shorter route by the beach, but it was a fine day and the road was dry and easily walked and offered a wealth of beauty, carrying them past newly furrowed fields and orchards coming into blossom, the air cracking fresh and smelling of the sea beyond the dunes a quarter-mile to their right.

Though Izzy had been glad to see London, glad to be in a lively city, he couldn't help but be cheered by the scenery around them. The other two were discussing Ursula's plans to launch her new enterprise. None of his business until she made it his business, and he dawdled behind, thinking on whether to give the sweets to Noel directly or make him earn them. One by one, straight from Izzy's—

"Hang on, ma'am. Do you hear that?" he asked. They had reached the head of the gravelled drive leading to the house, from whence came the sound of shouting, unheard until now thanks to the endless shushing of the surf. Then a woman screamed.

"Is it a raid?" Sal said, stepping nearer to Ursula.

"Against a private home?"

They heard another shriek, and Izzy bolted. Against all odds, directly towards the house. Straight for Noel, who had to be in dire straits if it had come to a riot. As he pelted past their little cottage, someone whistled, the sharp rising tone they used for a warning. He pulled up short, just about going head over heels into the turf. He spun about, seeing no one, then Noel whistled again. He was lurking behind the cottage, and Izzy ran into his arms.

Alive and well, and you'd think they'd been a year apart. Alive and well and still his Noel, strong and beautiful and so very wonderful to kiss, even more so for that kiss being in plain air. Proper romantic, under the windblown sky amid the gnarled old trees waking from winter. London could hang, if it didn't have Noel in it. Noel, who was trembling, clinging to him with unusual desperation.

"Thank heaven you're here," he breathed, resting his forehead against Izzy's.

"What's happened? Is it the French cops or the English?"

Noel raised his head and cast a foul look towards the house. "I wouldn't mind a bloody copper to show up. Bloody Marisol and that fool husband of hers."

"Why, what'd they do?"

"Went and started trading, is what."

"Fucking hell! Ursula's going to go spare. Where even did they get custom?"

Still glaring at the house, Noel let go of Izzy. "Bloody Bill went up to Paris and came back with a cartload. All of them English, but what a poxy bunch."

"You haven't had to—"

"Christ, no," Noel said with a shudder. "I'd not touch 'em with Bill's, no matter what the offer. I pity the women."

"Pity poor Marisol. Ursula's going to fair murder her."

The others had gathered on the drive where Noel explained the events of the previous days. "This is very much not what I wanted to hear, Mr Peters," Ursula said at the end. "And rest assured I don't blame you in the slightest."

"So what should we do now, ma'am?" Sal asked, vibrating with intensity, cracking their knuckles.

"Let's assess the situation first," Ursula replied. "You said there are five clients, Mr Peters?"

"Assuming they didn't slip anyone past me."

"Are they known to us?"

"I recognize a few."

"Excellent. And lastly, where is Mr Bevan? I'd like to have my forces assembled before we act."

Noel whistled for Clyde as they started for the house. A sprawling two-storey Spanish-style villa with arches and courtyards all over and a terracotta roof, they'd found it nearly a ruin. Months of labour and an untold amount of Marisol's inheritance had brought it up to better than liveable. With a ballroom, a dining hall, three ovens in the kitchen and a dozen bedrooms in the upstairs, it was ideal for Ursula's intentions, but not if all their hard work was undone by a pack of unfettered aristos on a spree.

Clyde met them on the front steps with a grim expression and very large and knobbly stick, and conferred with Ursula in their private language of hand signs and mouthed words. He had lost the power of speech in an accident years ago, getting by on his enormous size and strength as most employers took him for a dullard. Of course Ursula had seen his worth.

"Thank you for the information, Mr Bevan," she said to him. "Gentlemen, let us greet our guests."

The Spanish theme continued indoors, with whitewashed walls and a floor of blood-red tile. Several sets of muddy boot-prints led up and down the staircase which curved around the walls of the entry hall, though all the noise was coming from the open archway that led to the dining room. And what a noise: men and women singing and shouting and all of them at least slightly drunk, and someone had a mandolin and was playing it terribly, a disjointed plucking that gave the mood of a lunatic carnival. There went Bill's laugh, a put-upon sound of benevolent mirth as though he were playing a panto king.

Yet their own gang was nothing to sneeze at. Four pairs of fists, plus Clyde's size, plus Ursula's stick, plus the women's help if it came to a rout. Odds were, if these were former clients of the old house in London, Izzy had already beaten the stuffing out of at least one of them. That tended to put any lord on his back foot, coming face to face with trade outside the tidy confines of bought time.

Ursula in the lead, they passed into the dining room, a grand hall with a beamed ceiling and tile floors and a platform at the far end for a high table. The walls had once been panelled, but the years of neglect meant that Izzy and Noel had spent a solid week ripping down sheets of rotting wood, revealing scabrous yellow stains and leaving an infinity of nail holes, none of which the plasterers had yet attended to.

In the centre of the room was a long table and around this sat the custom, along with Bill and Marisol and several of the other women. They'd been at it for hours, cups and decanters scattered up and down the table amid teetering piles of soiled plates. Cigar smoke lingered above in a blue haze. Bill lolled at the head of the table, so soused his eyes were barely open. One of the men was sleeping, slumped forward on the table, his head on his folded arms. The rest were fixed on wee Noreen, standing on the table in her petticoat, the front of which was spotted with oil. One of the toffs shouted to her, and when she turned he tossed an olive. She caught it in her mouth and a great cheer went up. Chewing, she turned about, bowing here and there.

Then she saw Ursula. She shrieked, then covered her mouth as the party turned as one to the substantial and very angry gang standing in the doorway.

It got very quiet. One of the men began cautiously to stand, but the stricken looks and unsubtle coughing of his fellows changed his mind. Marisol had removed her hand from the lap of the man beside her and was wiping it on the tablecloth. "You're home earlier than I expected," she said through a set smile.

"Actually I'm a day late," Ursula replied. "Might I speak with you in private?"

"Of course." Marisol sprung to her feet, nearly knocking over her chair. Hiccupped, pressing her fist to her lips.

"Cor, she's absolutely littered!"

"Mr Pound, please," Ursula said. Leaving Noel and Clyde as persuasion against any client's desire to flee, Ursula ushered Marisol out of the dining room and across the entry hall to the study. Another grandiose space, long and high-ceilinged though the bookcases were largely empty, most of the volumes having succumbed to rot, leaving behind the smell of mildewed paper. Ursula took the armchair by the hearth. Sal stood behind, a hand on the back of the chair. Marisol hesitated in the doorway, but with a glance at Izzy she went to stand before Ursula, who regarded her with perfect calm.

"Please tell me why you thought this was at all a good idea."

Several excruciating seconds crawled past as

Marisol seemed to shrink, her face paling, shoulders drawing in. "It is my house," she finally said in a small voice. "May I not entertain here as I wish?"

"Is that what this is?"

Marisol opened her mouth, paused, closed her mouth. "No," she muttered.

"We've discussed this."

"I know."

"We were going to open as soon as I returned from this trip."

"I know."

"Well then?"

Marisol stared at her unblinking. Then she sunk to her knees with a pitiful groan and laid her head on Ursula's lap. "But it's so insufferably booo-ring out here. And haven't you always admired my initiative?"

"It's not that which distresses me, darling" Ursula replied, petting Marisol's matted pompadour. "It's that you've put so many of us at risk. Consider why we're here. Why we left England."

"I'm sorry."

Another sudden silence, the room holding its collective breath as they came to grips with having heard Marisol apologize. Ursula resumed stroking her hair.

"Thank you. Now, how much have they paid for this?"

"Ah. Yes." Marisol sat back on her heels. "Paid. You see…"

Ursula took a deep breath. It was like seeing an enormous wave build, a great swelling that promised harm when it at last came crashing down on one's head. Her voice dropped to a stony whisper, infinitely cold. "Do you mean to say they're here on *credit?*"

Marisol ducked the word like a slap. "Not entirely. Merely that we didn't negotiate a rate in advance."

Ursula took another breath, exhaled with a long hum. "I see. Regardless, it's now time for our guests to settle their bill and take their leave. Who's top man?"

"Lord Haversham."

Ursula smiled, a sight even rarer than her anger, and not a bit comforting. "Very good. That makes this much easier. Sal, I'd like you to return to the dining room. Keep our guests entertained. Marisol, you and Mr Bevan will return in the company of Lord Haversham."

"And me?" Izzy asked her as the others departed.

"You, Mr Pound, are here for atmosphere."

Le départ

WITH MUCH HOOTING and lewd shouts, Marisol removed Haversham from the party. He came into the study grinning, perhaps with the presumption of getting a special service. Instead she delivered him to Clyde, who brought the man to Ursula then took up his post at the door.

A beef-fed blond with an artfully trimmed beard and a scooped-out waist line that implied a girdle's firm imposition beneath the tailoring, Haversham glanced around, his blue eyes growing wide as he took in the situation: the derelict room, the business woman, the beast at the door, and Izzy, perched on the front of the water-stained desk, paring his nails with his pocket knife. Waiting.

"Lord Haversham," Ursula purred. "I must say this is a very great surprise."

"Isn't it just?" he blurted, smiling fixedly as he attempted to flatten his creased shirt-front. "Jolly little place you've got, by the by. Smashing time and all that. As always under one of your rooves, ma'am. And may I say how wonderful to see you looking so well," he added with a flick of his eyes towards Izzy.

"Thank you. However Marisol has told me you failed to set a price for this smashing time, as you

102

called it."

"To be fair, she never did ask."

"Any lapses in good business practice are an entirely separate matter between myself and Marisol. What matters between your lordship and myself is the price."

"And what do you suggest might be the price?"

"Given that this is a new situation for both parties, I'm afraid we are quite outside our typical fee structure."

"We are?"

"We are."

"I see." Haversham's eyes flitted around the room again as the dire mathematics set in. He took a deep breath, swallowed with a tiny squeak deep in his throat. "Perhaps you might suggest an amount?" he went on in the same squeaky tone.

Ursula said a number. Izzy nearly lost a fingertip, while Clyde began rocking in his voiceless laugh, his massive shoulders quaking.

Haversham swallowed again, his voice reduced to a pained rasp. "I...I see. And how is it most convenient to pay?"

"Cash, if you have it," Ursula said serenely. "Bank drafts are also convenient. Promissory notes are not."

"Who carries that much—of course. I'll just have a whip round the lads, see what we've got on us."

"Please. Mr Pound, Mr Bevan, let's help his lordship remember where the ballroom is. We wouldn't want him going where he shouldn't."

"Not a worry, ma'am, we'll take care of him." Izzy snapped his knife closed, hopped off the desk, and ushered the man towards the door. "Right this way, sir."

Noel had been patrolling the hall and was there as they stepped out of the study. Frowning, he stopped Izzy with a hard finger in the centre of his chest. "If no one minds, I need a word with this one."

"As you like," Ursula said. "Mr Bevan and I ought to be able to assist his lordship." Grinning like a wolf, if wolves were six and a half feet tall and made of Welsh boulders, Clyde set his hand on Haversham's shoulder. His lordship made a pinched noise, his knees buckling under the weight.

As they steered him away, Noel backed Izzy into the study, then closed and locked the door. What was eating at him this time? Something Izzy had done? Or something he'd failed to do, some omission of care? Was it easier getting on with a woman? Or was every kind of love a tightrope walk, teetering over the abyss of heartbreak?

Izzy drew breath to apologize—for whatever, just in case—and was suddenly against the wall, pinned by Noel's hard body and desperate kiss. Beyond desperate and approaching hysterical, as he bit at Izzy's lips, one hand clutching his hair, the other seeking the buttons of his fly. Not like Noel at all.

"Steady," Izzy grunted, shifting away from Noel's clawing. With a shudder, Noel quit trying to undress him and pulled him close, simply to hold him.

"You can't imagine what it's been like," he rasped. "I've been going out of my mind."

"It's all right. I'm here now."

"I hate it when you leave."

"I'll always come back."

"I know. Still hurts." They stood like this for some

time, Izzy stroking Noel's back, their hearts beating together. At length, Noel took a deep breath, exhaled in a long sigh and loosened his tight embrace.

"All right, then. Are you hungry?"

Izzy raised his head from Noel's shoulder. "Am I what?"

"You been traveling, been on a boat. I dunno if you had lunch."

"I thought *this* was lunch." Izzy swivelled his hips, feeling Noel rise in immediate response.

"It's mid-afternoon."

"That didn't seem to matter a minute ago when you had your hand on my prick."

"So are you saying you'd nip off to ours?"

"You have to ask? I'm damn near dying for it."

He leaned up to kiss Noel, but his friend grinned and stepped back. "First we ought to make sure Ursula don't need us to put the frighteners on the custom."

"Fair enough. Plus, if Sal's going to sock a lord in the chin, I wouldn't mind being there to see it happen."

OF COURSE THEY hadn't the money. Luckily, at least for Ursula, Calais was equipped with any number of excellent pawn shops, to which the clients surrendered as much of their personal items as it took to make up the amount owing, along with the cost of hiring a cart to transport them from the manor.

Walking back along the beach after escorting the cart to town, Noel and Izzy let Sal and Clyde get ahead.

Izzy related the visit with his parents and Pete's intrusion, though it was hard to imagine harm of any kind coming to them here, what with the glorious sky and the calming hush of the waves and the strength of Noel's hand in his. Never did he ever think so simple thing could warm his heart so much.

"Can I show you something?" Noel asked.

"This is a public beach, you know."

Noel shoved him with his shoulder. "You tart. I mean my girls."

"Cor, they didn't arrive in the midst of all that, did they?"

"Too right they did. I was bloody terrified them louts would find 'em and have at 'em."

"Are they all right?"

"More or less. A few feathers ruffled, but I calmed 'em down."

"You do have a touch with the fairer sex."

This won a smile, and Noel tugging his hand. "Come meet 'em."

The little building was some distance from the house, set in a sandy yard surrounded by a stout fence high enough to rest one's chin on. "You lucky devil," Izzy said as Noel blushed with pride. "They're beautiful." Six in all, two big whites and four little black and white speckled hens, all busily pecking at scattered corn. "Seems almost a shame to eat them."

Noel elbowed him sharply. "Oi! They're working girls, they are. They're layers."

"You mean you make them into cake?"

"No, it means they lay eggs, you twit. Or at least they will once I get a rooster," he added, itching his left eyebrow as he did when losing a bet.

"So you're saying they only put out for a cock?"

"Just like you, in other words?"

"I make about as much noise too."

"Speaking of…" Setting his hand on Izzy's back, Noel looked around, and was about to lean in for a kiss when someone whistled sharply from the direction of the house.

"Ah hell, what's another half hour to wait?" Izzy said as Noel hung his head and groaned.

"If your balls felt like mine…"

"Who says they don't?"

"Yeah, but I *like* making you suffer."

All in good time, and with a peck on the cheek as scant consolation, Izzy followed his lover to the big house. In what he'd been repeatedly told was classical Moorish style, the manor had a grand courtyard in its centre. Other than Alanson who was sleeping off his shame, everyone was gathered here, sitting around the trestle tables Sal and Noel had banged together from old doors and bits of panelling. The yard itself was paved with a patchwork of the original slate filled in with field stones and hunks of brick and mortar, the oddest shaped holes packed with gravel and sand. A mixed-up muddle well matched to their odd-lot company, fourteen strong and not a respectable one in the bunch. Izzy was happy to be home. Less so when the cause for the gathering was made clear.

"We will operate much like a hotel," Ursula explained, calm and inevitable. "Overnight stays, breakfasts, holiday making and the like. This does however place a greater obligation on us to provide entertainment."

"What about our rates?" Brigid asked.

"Fees will of course be raised commensurate with our offering," Ursula replied. "That is to say, you will be making much more money per transaction than you ever have before."

"And I suppose we'd see each of them less often?" Rose said over the chatter of the other women.

"That is my expectation."

"No more popping in for a pop-off?" Noreen quipped to general laughter.

"Indeed," Ursula replied, nearly smiling.

"But what about this theatre business of Bill's?" Annie said.

The rest arced up at once, the matter of some importance Izzy had missed. He leaned near Noel, who wore a poisonous expression. "What are they on about?"

"I'll tell you later."

"But—"

"Hush." He nodded towards Ursula who had a hand up for quiet.

"Stage plays and parties aside," she went on, "at the end of the day it is of course business as usual."

"So let's say it's Saturday afternoon," Annie pressed. "We're out on the croquet lawn, he says, skirts up, and…" She waggled her hand and her eyebrows.

"And one conducts business as usual," Ursula replied. "Though I suggest greater discretion. You might retire to his room, for example, rather than occupy the facilities when others might wish to play."

"But what if that's all he wants to do?" Rose asked over the others' laughter. "That'd be proper dull."

Marisol snorted a laugh. "That presumes any one of them can outlast any one of us."

When the next wave of laughter subsided, Ursula continued. "It will be discussed at the time of booking precisely how much business a client expects to conduct during his stay. And remember they will be paying substantially more for said business."

"Like how much more?" said Annie with a calculating eye.

Ursula said a number, of a piece with the fee she'd charged the interlopers. The gang fell absolutely silent, each member weighing their labour against their opportunities.

"Is that every time?" Brigid murmured as they began to stir.

"Every time. And our expenses have been greatly reduced, given that our overhead costs are merely provisions, property upkeep, and whatever labour we wish to transfer to hired hands."

"Bloody well all of it," Annie groaned, winning a chorus of ayes.

Noel sat upright sharply. "Not the garden though, ma'am."

"No, Mr Peters. Not the garden. As we've agreed."

He slumped back, his arms crossed, chin jutting. Izzy plucked at his sleeve. "Come for a walk."

"Eh?"

"In the orchard. We'll go check for coddling moth or something."

Noel glared at him, brows knitted. "Since when do you give a rat's arse for that? And it's going to be night soon."

"Just come with, you berk. I want to talk without an audience." He jerked his head at the gaggle of excited women and Noel's expression softened.

Without excusing themselves they slipped away, through the house and out the kitchen door towards the ghostly forms of the blooming trees at twilight.

The sea breeze had sharpened and they walked with heads down, hands in pockets, saying nothing. When they were deep among the gnarled trees, he stopped Noel with a touch on his arm. Kissed him, for the strength it gave them both. Noel was trembling, his lips stiff, unyielding, until he broke, relented, returned Izzy's affection with full force.

Only a kiss, though they stood in each other's arms a little longer, until Izzy found the courage to speak his thoughts, thankful for the darkness that covered his face, the shushing waves that hid the tremor in his voice. "You don't want to, do you? Start up again, I mean."

Noel opened his mouth, closed it without a word. He shook his head, tried again. "I don't know that I can."

"So I'm not the only one thinking that."

"Serious?"

"Well…it's been months, ain't it, since either of us took a job. Shit, my last paying customer was the bleeding RPA." The Royal Pain in the Arse, their cant for the exceedingly powerful man who had fixed obsessively on Izzy last autumn. Fate had intervened, but Izzy had yet to shake the fear. Every posh carriage was potentially a trap, every shiny hat could be hiding that groomed mug, even though by all accounts the mug was on the other side of the globe, on a goodwill tour of the Commonwealth.

"You still having dreams?" Noel murmured.

"Not so often. A bad one while I were away." Of

a carriage door which wouldn't open, and a smooth hand closing around his throat, and his arm in a carpenter's vise, and... He had woken in a hotel bed, his arm numb from being laid on, his nightshirt tangled about his neck. He'd lain awake for a good hour before finding the courage to get out of bed and assure himself he was still in Ursula's suite. Seeing her cloak by the door, he'd nearly wept. To entertain such men again, no matter their wants, no matter the fee, was to put his neck in the noose.

"What do we do?" Noel whispered. "There's nothing else I'm any good at."

"The garden. That's something."

"True."

"Unlike me, who's only good at doing what I'm told, if I like who's telling me and the money's good."

"Proper useless, in other words."

Izzy laughed, but it came out wrong, too high, too much like a sob. Noel pulled him close and began stroking Izzy's hair, which was humiliating, and then so perfectly soothing that he laid his head on Noel's shoulder so that he'd keep doing it.

"I'm only gassing," Noel said. "Ignore me."

"Impossible," Izzy murmured, nuzzling into the curve of his neck.

"What are we going to do, Iz?"

"We're going to quit."

"Just like that?"

He lifted his head to look Noel in the eye. "All or nothing. Either you and me are in it together and all the way, or we ain't in it at all. Besides which, I reckon she'll need us as strong-arm men more than trade."

Noel tsked, shaking his head like a horse. "Bloody

right, the way them gits were carrying on."

"And there's only one of Clyde. He can't be everywhere."

"But do you reckon she'll go for it?"

"She might not like it, but if there's anyone in the world I trust to do right by me, it's our Ursula."

Le jardin

URSULA TOOK THE news with her usual aplomb, assuring them both that their service to the enterprise was welcome in whatever form it took. They had no choice but to believe her. But Izzy had never doubted his employer's honesty, nor her courage to say what needing saying, no matter how unpleasant.

In the time they'd been outside a party had erupted, the women in a mood and a half. The ballroom's doors opened to the courtyard, and for hours they caromed back and forth. Bullied out of bed, Bill remained inside where he hammered away at a repertoire of popular piano. One could barely turn around without getting a kiss on the cheek or the lips, or another drink, or an entreaty to dance, which Izzy indulged and Noel refused, citing an incurable case of left feet. Somewhat after midnight they escaped, their longed-for reunion a hasty game of mutual touch, swiftly resolved and leading almost instantly to sleep. Unimportant, when they had nights and nights to make up for it.

Or this morning, which was well on its way to noon by the time they emerged from their little cottage. Built away from the main house, it was meant for the property's caretaker. It was deigned the boys' by collective agreement, granting them the privacy their union was due, and a respite for the rest of the company from the noises they generated in the celebration of said union. Still, it was a rare treat to have Noel stay in bed of a morning. Most days he was up at the crack of, to inspect the vegetable patch for any damage done in the night by rabbits or moles. He ran off now to do so while Izzy made his way to the big house.

A covered cart stood on the gravel drive, from which Clyde and Sal were unloading Ursula's trunks. Izzy stuck into the chore alongside, and the cart was soon emptied and on its way back to Calais. They carried the trunks into the study along with Izzy's bag, which he set on the desk and opened at Ursula's request.

"Is there something of yours in here, ma'am? I thought I'd just shopped for the girls."

"I didn't know if I should mention it," she replied, feeling around inside the soft-sided case. "Pass me those scissors, if you don't mind."

He handed her the tiny pair of scissors, tooled to resemble a bird. "Is something wrong with my bag?"

"By no means, Mr Pound," she said, snipping through a row of stitches where the lining met the base. She gave him the scissors, then tugged the hole wider and extracted a thin manila envelope.

"Sending secret missives, are we? I thought we'd nothing to do with that espionage scheme—sweet mercy! Was I walking around with that on my person?" For Ursula had opened the envelope and was counting the banknotes it contained. "How much flipping money did I have on me? No, wait. Don't tell me. I don't expect I'll feel better knowing."

"As I said, I was unsure how this would affect your disposition."

"Poorly, ma'am. Very poorly indeed."

"I apologize, Ezekiel. It was careless of me to put you at risk. I must admit to not being entirely myself yesterday."

"Rough business in the Big Smoke?"

"Hmm. As well I missed a chance to…" Her sibilant voice died to a whisper. Then she looked up, her face blank as stone. "To see my daughter. I arrived late, and she'd already gone."

"That's a shame," Izzy murmured after a strained minute. "Better luck next time?"

She mouthed some word, then cleared her throat and tried again. "Yes. Next time."

"Well, if you don't need me, I'll take them seeds I brought for Noel."

Gazing at the items spread on the desk, seeing none of them, Ursula nodded. He dug the packet out from amid the lace and jam jars in his case then went outside. Noel hadn't left the garden plot, a spade in hand as he surveyed the rows.

"Just having a look, he says," Izzy called to him over the stone wall. "My milky arse. You'd have been here all day if I didn't come by for you."

"Nah. I'd have wanted dinner at some point." Noel wiped his forehead with his forearm, coming away with mud on his face. "Is that my seeds you've got?"

"Dunno where you're going to cram anything else. The allotment's bursting as is."

"Plenty of room," he said, weaving his way round

the beds to where Izzy stood. "We'll have eaten a good bit of this before most of that comes up."

"What all have you got going?"

"Not much," he replied with a shrug. He jammed the tip of the spade into the soil and leaned on the handle, nodding to the various beds as he named them. "Just some swedes, some turnip, cabbage, spinach greens, collards, carrots, potato. Radishes, of course. A couple patches of parsnips. That there'll be strawberries," he said, pointing to a long hummock of actual straw. "Them shrubs round the edges is currants, that there's going to be a bed of them little aubergine they grow here, and I reckon I can talk Monsieur Levesque across the way into some apple grafts and a pear tree or two, maybe some filberts… Why you looking at me like that?"

"Saints above, Peters," Izzy gaped. "Feed many armies?"

"What d'you mean?"

"Do you not think you're being a bit, I dunno, ambitious?"

He frowned, perplexed. "There's more than a dozen of us. And it's hard to only grow a little. We'll trade or sell what we don't eat."

"Who's gonna tend it all though?"

Noel looked from himself to Izzy and back. "Who d'you think, strong-arm man?"

He yanked the spade from the soil and proffered the mud-smeared handle to Izzy, who took a step back. "Like hell."

"You need to do something to earn a crust."

"What, my loving husband can't keep a wife?"

"You're the one made yourself wife to a man who

digs for his living."

Noel was smirking, and covered in dirt, and he was bloody well right. Biting back a number of uselessly unpleasant comments, Izzy took the spade from him, shuddering at the feel of wet dirt smearing over his palm. "Ah shit."

"Nah, just soil," Noel said with that irresistible grin. "Levesque don't deliver the shit until tomorrow."

Izzy was wearing his better trousers, so he left the spade and legged off to the cottage for the other pair. His worse shirt as well, for he knew how grubby Noel ended after a morning in the muck. And how pleasant it was to aid him in getting clean. He returned to the garden in better spirits. Noel was busy, crouched over a bed, so Izzy cleaned the muck off the handle of the spade and waited for instruction.

"Well?" Noel said over his shoulder. "Get to it, then."

"Get to what?"

He sat back on his heels, gesturing about the garden as if any bit of it looked any different from any other. "Are you joking?"

"You know I don't know bugger all about this business. Without you telling me what's what, I'm as like to pull up the swedes as the weeds."

"Fair enough," he said with a laugh. "I suppose I take it for granted."

"We've all got our particular talents. Ask me anything you'd like to know about sucking cock."

Laughing still, Noel set him to preparing a new bed at the bottom of the garden. There really was nothing to it. Izzy had done enough digging in the odd-job years before Ursula, constructing sewer trenches or mucking out stables, beside which this was child's play, a matter of moving bucket-loads rather than barrowfuls. He supposed the barrowfuls came tomorrow when Levesque brought the manure, and thank fun they hadn't been required to muck out the cow-yard themselves.

When Noel was satisfied with the beds, he opened the parcel of seeds and set Izzy to planting the beans, which turned out to grow from beans. Peas grew from peas, potatoes from pieces of themselves. Carrots and lettuce grew from what looked like sand, and all the rest fell somewhere in between. After the seeding, they set up a frame of crossed sticks overtop the bean patch for the plants to climb. Izzy was about to comment on the ease of the task when Noel handed him a pair of empty pails and sent him off to the water pump, to replenish the big barrel that served as a cistern. A dozen (or was it a hundred) loads later, Izzy's arms burned from the effort, but he kept mum, thinking of all the years Noel had endured performing the same dreary chores for his family.

At last Noel joined him at the pump, where they washed off the first layer of grime. Closer to the house, several of the women were sitting on the lawn, doing their mending to judge from the linens heaped about them, their work song audible between the creak and splash of the pump.

"I keep meaning to ask what they were on about last night," Izzy said as Noel rinsed his hands in the brimming bucket. "About Alanson and some play he's writing."

"Forget it. Marisol said he's always dreaming up plays and writing songs and such. I don't pay him any mind."

"Who would?" Izzy murmured, for Noel had stripped off his shirt and was sluicing water over his bare torso in a most distracting manner. A burst of laughter from the women recalled him to his senses. Time enough to indulge their appetites after they'd had a proper feed.

Noel's shirt clinging marvellously to his damp chest, they carried on towards the house in a line to pass by the women. Ursula was there as well in her wheeled chair, its seat densely padded with cushions and therefore the most comfortable in the house. Marisol lay on the chaise longue beside, a vision in pleated muslin peppered with bright blue bows, one bare arm draped across her brow to shade her eyes.

To her other side sat Bill, half leaning out of his lawn chair as he spoke breathlessly at her. Not *with* her, as she was so still she might have been a painting, a sensible attitude to adopt given the rubbish that tended to come out of her husband's mouth. When he spied Izzy and Noel, he gasped and struggled to his feet.

"How very fortuitous," he said, rubbing his meaty hands. "You're just who I wished to see, given your importance to my next and most likely greatest production to date."

"What are you on about?" Izzy said. Noel hissed him to hush, but it was too late as Bill turned to him, beaming.

"My next stage-play. Dare I say my master work, in which you, my dear boy, shall be performing as one of my leads."

No matter how often Izzy told him not to, the shit

persisted with his little endearments. "Look, you, I ain't your dear and I ain't your boy, and as for performing—"

"I know, I know," Bill went on loudly. "It's a startling opportunity indeed, but one for which I feel you're more than ready. As are you all," he said, gesturing to the women, none of whom were paying much attention. "In fact, it was your native talents, my dears, that have inspired me to write what I feel is my strongest work to date. If this doesn't pack them in, then theatre's all for naught. I could sense it as soon as I set pen to page, that this was to be—"

"Bill," groaned Marisol from behind her arm. "Get to the shitting point."

"Right you are, my dear. That point of course being the play. I call it *Very Missionary*. Though do bear in mind it's a working title," he added as the assembly broke out in groans and guffaws. "If I could beg your indulgence, ladies, gentlemen, I might explain why it's so very apropos."

"We may as well hear him out," Annie said over the rest of them. "He's a dab hand on the old ivories. Perhaps he's not all talk. Come on, Bill, tell us about your little play."

"It would be my pleasure. And hopefully yours as well, my dear." His grin stiffened as Annie laughed.

"Today, if you don't mind," she said. "As for the rest of you, hush up." They settled into various states of amused or derisive interest as Bill shook out his hands, bent his neck from side to side. In his faded linen trousers and billowing blouse, he looked like a sportsman gone to seed on good living, which was true enough if the sport was chasing young men and writing bad plays. Marisol conspicuously cleared her throat.

"Yes, dear," Bill replied through his teeth without looking her way. "Our dear Mr Pound shall of course be playing the titular role of missionary."

"God help us all," Izzy blurted. As the rest roared with laughter, he rubbed at his face, trying to shove his features into a semblance of a genial smile. "Never mind them, old bean. Do go on."

"Yes. Well. Our hero has been sent to the South Pacific, but his ship is wrecked at sea, and he washes up ashore on an uninhabited island." Bill bowed towards Rose, standing to Izzy's right. "You, my dear, shall be playing the part of the island."

Her cheery expression turned murderous. "So *you* say."

Bill took a small step backwards. "Ah. Yes, well, what happens is that you fall in love with him. But seeing as you're, er…"

"A mound of dirt?" she said through gritted teeth.

"No! By no means are you mere dirt, Miss Owen. You're an active volcano. A gigantic, er, that is to say great force of nature. That's why you're uninhabited."

"Because I'm likely to blow my top?"

Alanson's smile looked painful to wear. "Ye-es. In a sense. But before that happens, you fall in love with the pale-faced stranger you discover on your shores. Of course being a volcano you can't act on your feelings. Not without, er, damaging the object of your affection."

"So what's the play about, if one of the main characters can't do anything?" Noreen asked as Rose sizzled.

"Ah yes, that's the clever bit."

"Thank Christ, there's a clever bit," Izzy retorted. This was sounding madder by the minute, and Alanson had barely got going. The big man clapped his hands together with a resonant smack.

"And here it is. For our dear Miss Owen is of course no mere mound of dirt but Pele the implacable, the merciless, the Juno of the South Pacific. And so being a goddess, you craft a companion for your love object. Both to help him survive on the island, and to speak on your behalf. Knowing what you do of men, you decide to make another man and not a woman, to prevent your beloved from falling in love with your golem, whose part shall be played by you," he said to Noel, whose glare could have bent iron bars.

"What's a golem?" Brigid said, her nose wrinkling.

"A sort of Jewish homunculus, not that said denomination comes to bear on our story," Alanson replied, explaining nothing at all. "And so our dear goddess sends her beautiful golem out to persuade our man of the cloth to return her affections. But that would make for a very short story, wouldn't it? Hence the missionary and the golem fall madly in love. And then of course Pele becomes jealous, and attempts to smite them, and they must craft a vessel and flee her shores before she, er...blows her top, as you said, my dear Miss Owen."

"Call me *dear* again, I swear—"

"This of course is our opportunity for a grand set piece at the end," Bill said with a note of panic. "For you see, Pele's eruption causes a tremendous wave that capsizes our heroes' craft. Then her grief at having killed both her beloved and her creation drives her to madness. But some other god, Neptune I suppose, though I haven't quite worked out that bit, takes pity on them all, and transforms our heroes into dolphins, and embodies Pele's divine essence in the albatross, who soars above the sea seeking them forever more." Panting, he set his hand on his heart and gazed into the misty distance.

"And you mean for all this to happen in song and dance?" Izzy asked as the others began to mutter.

"Never fear, I've got that part in hand, my dear boy."

"I've told you not to call me that."

"That you have, Mr Pound. And yes, I admit the staging may prove a challenge, and it is of course a touch blasphemous, not to mention the tricksy business of not violating any statutory laws, which is why this venue is ideal. Couldn't play on the Strand, could it?" He laughed weakly, looking about for any sign of support. "Well? Don't be shy. I've heard it all. What do you think? Ready to get stuck in?"

"No," Rose said flatly, shaking her head.

"No," echoed Noel, crossing his arms.

"No, and are you out of your bleeding mind?" Izzy demanded. Damn Alanson, to whom he owed nothing. "She's a ruddy hill, and he's some dirt you scraped off the side, and I'm the shiny penny? Do you not know what missionaries are famous for doing to the natives?" Bill opened his mouth to say something useless but Izzy barrelled on. "And then we all get blown up or drowned or some nonsense, then turned into fish and a scrotty bird? Bugger that for a game of tin soldiers. This is the most degrading, insulting thing I've ever been asked to do, and I've done some low-down nasty things, so you best believe I mean it."

"But my dear boy——" Bill got no further as Izzy shoved past the girls to grab him by the shirt front, to be sure he was paying attention.

"Call me *boy* again, you sack of shit, I damn well dare you."

"Mr Pound, please." Ursula was the only one he might have obeyed. Aside from Noel, who he'd hoped would tell him to throttle the eejit. Izzy pushed away from Alanson, who staggered back gawping like a frog.

"Even were the subject matter acceptable," Ursula continued, "I can't see how Mr Alanson's *set piece*, as he called it, is at all possible, given the facilities and budget available."

"Facilities may be amended, my d—er, Ursula," Bill wheezed. "As to the budget, my dear wife and I have an understanding—"

"I'm not putting one centime into this farce," Marisol cut in, her voice dripping with contempt.

Bill looked about for supporters, finding only scorn. "Well. One must expect the occasional bad review, I suppose. As you were." Muttering to himself, patting his peculiar curls, he started towards the house.

As the others began chattering away, Izzy caught Noel's eye, tipped his head. Noel nodded and begged leave of Rose, who went at once to Ursula, dropping to a crouch by her chair to speak to her directly. He caught up to Izzy halfway across the lawn and they carried on towards the beach.

"Ready money says he's got a new play written by suppertime," Noel said once the sound of the waves was louder than the women's voices.

"Whatever keeps him busy."

Noel grunted, his jaw stiff. "About bloody time. The git's been hanging about the garden since you've been gone, trying to draw me while I work."

Izzy shuddered, too familiar with Alanson's presumptions. "Draw you into what?"

"Not entice. I meant sketch, like with pencils."

"He's done drawings of you?"

Noel's frown deepened, his shoulders shifting. "Course not. I told him to leg it."

"That's almost a shame. I wouldn't mind to have a drawing of you."

Noel's lips twitched. "What do you want with a drawing when you can see me in the flesh?"

"Ooh, may I? Right now?"

Noel hissed through his teeth. "You little flirt," he murmured, looking around as if they could be heard over the ceaselessly whispering surf.

"I missed you, is all," Izzy said, linking his arm around Noel's. "I can't help but feel I've got to make up for lost time."

"You were only gone a fortnight."

"I know. Half killed me, it did."

"Your fault for leaving."

"So how about we go back to ours so I can apologize?"

"You can say you're sorry right here, can't you?"

Izzy stopped in his tracks, letting go of Noel's arm. "For heaven's sake, Peters, take the hint…oh, you shit." For Noel had given up hiding his grin and his arousal. With a last glance around, more of habit than need, he took both Izzy's hands in his, pulled him close. Kissed him once on the forehead, once on each cheek, then spoke softly in his ear.

"Here's what we're going to do. We're going to forget all about Alanson and his plays. We're going to go back to the big house and have some dinner, so that you get your strength back, because you are going to bloody well need it." He tightened his grip on Izzy's hands, making known his intention. "I'm going to wring you dry, my little man."

THE DAYS SOON took on a rhythm. Izzy grew accustomed to rising early in the morning, the pain tempered by the fact that he often woke with Noel's hands on him, coaxing him to alertness. As the plants sprouted, then flourished, so flourished Izzy's confidence in raising them, though he could only follow so much of Noel's talk about ash versus lime, chicken manure versus cow. Mainly he dug and watered and weeded, often aided by Sal whose bright mood and sharp tongue made the work go swiftly. Afternoons were generally spent on repairs to the manor, which was fit to live in but not yet up to Ursula's standards for a place of business.

Business Izzy was happy to ignore. He was busy enough as it was, and aimed to remain so. The 'hotel' would need staff, of the kind who never disappeared behind closed doors. The bawdy in Mayfair had been easy to secure, having only one entrance with Clyde as its keeper. Here anyone might walk right up to them from any of a dozen directions, and with Marisol's purse-strings tightening by the day Noel set about sprouting a thick hedgerow of scrub willows along the road frontage in lieu of paying for a fence to be built. Bill kept to himself for the most part, hammering away on the piano in the ballroom at all hours as crumpled sheets of paper piled around him. Other times one saw him wandering up and down the beach, the gusty wind bringing snatches of his bellowed songs.

Yet another thing with which Izzy hadn't time to be concerned. What mattered more was Ursula. Whatever bad thing had happened on their visit to London had stuck with her. She seemed to age by the day, her back stooping, her cheeks hollowed, her eyes clouded. Hardly their Ursula, who had once been able to make dukes weep with a mere glance. Izzy himself had seen the woman do permanent harm to one of the hardest men alive, the day he'd met her, only three years ago. Not that it was in his power to amend whatever hurts she bore. She despised sympathy, doubly so if it had to do with her physical frailties. He knew the bent and scarred body she hid with her padded corsets and military posture. Knew and could do nothing to help, except to do his best to fulfil his duties and give her no cause for further distress.

In truth he had never worked so hard in his life. Odd jobs had come and gone, demanding only time, not heart. Being a runner for Ursula's house by Leicester Square had meant a lot of standing around with occasional bursts of activity. Trading for her had meant the same, except the standing had been indoors while dressed superbly, and the bursts of activity far more lucrative. Now he simply worked, at whatever task he was given, which was anything from good old digging to plastering the holes in the dining room walls to crawling about on the ballroom's parquet seeking loose planks in need of replacement, though he managed to get himself barred from the kitchen after mistaking salt for sugar and turning out a batch of biscuits so stiff they left a bruise when Mrs Owen threw one at him.

Barely a night came that he didn't fall into bed like a stone, his and Noel's intimacies reduced to a brief clinch, a stroke, then sleep. It was enough. Better than enough, because of Noel, because Izzy wasn't going it alone.

Except he was, but only for a week or so. A letter for Noel had come with the post, forwarded by Auntie Owen at the laundry—Mrs Owen's sister—who knew only that she might reach them under Marisol's family name in Calais. A wedding: Noel's sister, and hence unavoidable. Ursula had been forming plans for another visit, and agreed to make a party of it with Clyde as their chaperone.

The day before departure, Noel was in a proper sulk, replying in grunts when he paid any heed. Izzy soon gave up trying to raise his spirits, his every joke falling flat. Neither did he ask the cause of Noel's melancholy, his lover's feelings expressed by the vigour with which he attacked the hole they were digging for a gatepost.

Sitting on the stoop of their cottage after, Noel was rubbing salve into Izzy's chapped hands, an act of care that had been embarrassing the first time and was now a sort of sacrament. "I wish I weren't going," he said without warning, his voice catching in his throat.

"Then don't go."

Noel sighed again, shaking his head. "I've got to.

My folks will go spare.”

“They would, too.”

He was on the step above Izzy and planted a kiss on the top of his head. “I won’t be gone long. And you’ll be flat out, keeping up with the garden.”

“I’ll have Sal. We’ll be golden. Ow…” A blister had risen where his ring finger met his palm, paining him when Noel’s fingers brushed it.

“And wear your gloves, you rascal,” Noel chided, letting go of his hands. “And your hat. This sun will cook a milky bastard like you alive.”

“Yes, dear,” Izzy simpered.

Hissing, Noel prodded Izzy’s leg with his toe. “You’re already gone all freckled.”

“I have?”

“Not that it isn’t…”

“What?”

“Well…it is a bit adorable. Like you got dusted with drinking chocolate.”

“Go on with you. What a thing to say.”

Noel slipped down a step and put his arm around Izzy’s waist. “Not that you weren’t already delicious.”

“Oh stop. People will think you’re sweet on me.”

“How could I not be?”

“Let me count the ways, how about?”

“No. Let’s not talk at all.” He set his finger under Izzy’s chin, his thumb tracing the edge of his lower lip. “I’ve got better uses for this mouth.”

“Hoping for one to remember me by?”

“We’ll have time for two if we start right now.”

Le cirque

THE NEXT DAY, Izzy was back in the garden, and if he'd been asked could have said he was turning the compost, which in his sleepless state amounted to morosely prodding a garden fork into the rank heap of cuttings and straw and chicken droppings. Noel was convinced the heap would soon be soil, but for now it merely stank. The smell of loneliness… Izzy shook off the thought. Noel was gone for only a fortnight. No time at all once you'd quit marking time properly, when the hours and the names of the days were of less significance than the temperature of the breeze, the likelihood of rain.

Pointless poetry, and he shook himself again, shoved the fork in the heap and wiped his brow with his arm, leaving both dirtier. Gritting his teeth, themselves gritty with blown soil, he went to the cistern to wash. As he stood up from the barrel, chin dripping, arms wet to the elbow, he spied a whitish blur moving among the trees beyond the house.

Blinking away the water, he now made out two forms. Strangers—men by their silhouettes—wandering about the property as free as they liked. Grabbing up the fork, Izzy whistled for Sal, then went to intercept them.

They were dressed in sailors' garb of coarse linen slops and blue-and-white striped jerseys, their boots hung by their laces round their necks, their bare feet and ankles dusted with sand, the one carrying a guitar on his back. They were strolling arm in arm, casual as you like, conversing rapidly and more or less simultaneously in what Izzy guessed to be Spanish, for they sounded like Marisol in a snit. Both of them had him by inches, but neither of them had a pitchfork, which he brandished as they neared him, the taller one with the moustache looking him over boldly.

"Hey now," Izzy cried, taking a step back, wishing badly for Sal to arrive. "What's your business here?"

"You are a friend of Williams, si?" the one with the guitar said, beaming expectantly.

"Williams? Never met the man."

"Bill, he means Bill," the moustached one supplied, sparing a glance for the mucky tines of the pitchfork levelled at their middles. "We are seeking Señor Alanson." Of course they were. Only Alanson would consort with such rabble.

"Is Señor not at home?" asked the guitarist.

"I said this to you," the moustache said, wagging his finger in his friend's face, "that when one visits *un ingles* one has to first write a letter and only then might you arrive."

Throwing up his hands, the guitarist replied in rapid Spanish, both of them suddenly chattering so loud Izzy had to shout to make them shut up. "Oi! Given it ain't bloody Alanson's home but his wife's, I'm entitled to ask your business. So state it or shove off."

"Señor Alanson, he met us in Paris and said there was to be work here," the guitarist said.

"What sort of work?"

Grinning madly, the fellow slung his instrument around to his front and began to tune it, while his friend began to rummage through his rucksack.

"Never mind, you don't need to prove…ah shit." For here came Alanson from the house, puffing along behind Sal and Annie who were marching toward them with angry intent. Something Alanson shouted made the pair turn back to answer. By the time they reached Izzy, the musicians were well away on a merry jig, the moustached fellow keeping rhythm with a pair of castanets.

"Well at least Old Bill wasn't telling porkies," Annie said in Izzy's ear under the hollered chorus. "They ain't half bad, hey? You know, for Spaniards."

"I suppose it saves any of us being obliged to learn how to play."

"That's the spirit!" she said, jabbing him with her elbow. Even Sal was nodding to the beat, while Bill seemed to know the words and was clapping along. Rubbing his sore ribs, Izzy left them to make their own introductions.

By suppertime the musicians had pitched camp in the fallow meadow, helpfully downwind of the house so as to not pester the household with smoke from their fire. More peculiar people arrived the next day, then again the day after that. All friends of the Spaniards, naturally. Friends of Bill's, and it seemed he had made them wherever he went, until the meadow began to resemble a fairground, the parti-coloured tents dotting the grass occupied by men and women of all nations, their songs and chatter lasting long into the night, the joyful noise mocking Izzy, making the cottage and the bed seem even emptier, as if Noel had only ever been a dream.

On WHAT HAD to be the fifth day without Noel but which felt more like the fiftieth, Izzy was repairing a loose bit of the garden fence when a cart came rattling down the drive. With a mouthful of nails and wire in both hands he paid it no mind, trusting to Bill and the others to settle the new arrivals. The cart went and returned twice more through the morning, and when he was at last free Izzy followed its rutted tracks along the disused section of drive to the patch of sandy ground between the meadow and the beach, where the camp people had erected some kind of scaffold.

Four poles about the height of a man had been driven into the soil in a large square, though the canvas stretched between them hung too low to be much good as a tent. Two much taller poles stood halfway along facing sides of the square, a stiff hawser suspended between them as if awaiting another canvas to be laid over it to form a peaked roof. Rope ladders led from the ground to the little bits of board where the hawser was mounted, and Izzy had just about swallowed his pride and decided to ask what it all was for when the answer presented itself

A man was climbing up one of the ladders. He reached the board then stopped, leaning back against the pole as he looked towards the other. All around him on the ground, the other people were paying no heed, not even the gaggle of children engaged in raking the sand. Only Izzy was watching as the man in the air took a step forward, then another and another. Small, swift steps, his arms extended stiffly, his chin held high, as he walked from one platform to the other across a rope no wider than Izzy's wrist.

It was only when the man gained safety that Izzy realized he had been holding his breath. His palms stung, bitten by his own fingernails. He knew how it felt to fall from a height. What he wouldn't have given that long-ago day for a nice bit of canvas to fall onto, rather than that costerman's rag heap.

"It's not as hard as it looks, you know," said a velvety voice from the gloom of the trees.

Izzy spun about. "For shit's sake, Miguel. You ought not to sneak up on a man like that."

Miguel laughed, a soft *ha, ha* that would have felt forced from another but which was of a piece with his languid nature, his doe eyes and tautly waxed moustache. He'd been one of the first pair to arrive, the friend of the guitarist, and took pains to speak to Izzy whenever they crossed paths.

"Will you try?" He nodded towards the scaffold, where men were fussing with the staked lines holding up one of the high poles.

"Walking that rope? Doubtful. I've had my fill of high places."

"A shame. You look as if it would suit you."

"Beg your pardon?"

He smiled slowly, running his eyes up and down Izzy's form. "Strong but not too tall. Very good legs as well."

"Excuse me but my legs are none of your business."

"Still, I say you should try. Impress me." He clapped Izzy on the shoulder then carried on towards the tightrope, where his cohort greeted him with a hearty cheer. The lines had been properly tightened, and he at once went up the ladder. At the top he leaned out over the void to wave to Izzy who lingered at the edge of the clearing. Then he returned his attention to the rope.

Unlike the first man, Miguel strode resolutely to the centre then paused, his arms barely lifted. Then he hopped, landing on one foot, the other leg carefully bent. Another hop and he had switched feet. Bloody show-off, but Izzy couldn't look away, in case the man fell, or made it across, or, *sweet mercy*, did a blessed somersault in the middle of a rope hanging thirty feet in the air. Izzy was holding his breath again, but he didn't dare move until Miguel had regained his feet and crossed to the far side. He came down the ladder in haste to receive his friends' cheers and embraces. As the next person—a woman, her skirts knotted between her knees, her feet pinkly bare—began to mount the ladder, Miguel came loping across the grass, his eyes and cheeks aglow.

"You see? Nothing to it, my friend." Any reply Izzy might have made died in his mouth as Miguel slapped him on the arse as he passed back the way he'd come.

Izzy watched for a little longer, never losing that sick feeling in his guts. A thousand tasks awaited in the garden, which was feeling the strain of the extra residents, the food gone before it was barely ripe. How Noel kept on day after day…and Izzy had thought him overly ambitious, planting as much as he had.

Sick or no, bored or no, there was no one else to do the work, and so he trudged back to the plot. Mrs Owen was there ahead of him, uprooting new potatoes, meaning there'd be that many fewer big potatoes later.

"Spare a few of them spuds, will you?" he said to her as he hopped over the garden fence where an old post served as a stile.

"You want supper or no?" she replied over her shoulder.

"Yes, but have we really got to go on feeding…you-know-who?"

"Who you mean? Mr Bill?"

"He's at least in the family. It's them circus folks what are bleeding us dry." Speaking of the devils, here came a pair of them across the grass with empty hands and slanted grins. A boy and a girl, though she was in men's clothing, the overlarge trousers rolled to her tanned knees.

"Greetings, sir," the lad said, bowing his white-capped head.

"What is it you want?"

"Ezekiel, boy, where your manners?" Mrs Owen retorted on cue. "Costs you naught to nice." Biting his cheeks, Izzy gestured for the boy to continue.

He bowed again, his hands clasped. "Bien. We are to be of help. Yes?"

"You what?"

He glanced at his companion, who looked back with wide-eyed alarm. "The garden, yes?" the boy said slowly, hunching forward and moving his hands back and forth in some kind of mime.

"Is he off his head?"

"If anyone be mad it's you, boy," Owen said, holding her potato-laden apron by the corners as she shuffled up the path. "Put a spade in them hands and set them to work."

The boy sprang upright, beaming with delight. "Yes, madam! We are here to help with the work."

"Don't you madam me. And you'll be getting your orders from this one. Go on, then, boy," she said to Izzy. "Give 'em an order."

"I suppose they can turn over the muck heap."

"Yes, sir! We very much would like to do this for you."

"Yeah, well, let's see if you're still saying that when you're through."

"Sir?"

"I said grab yourselves each a spade and get cracking."

He left them to it, busying himself with weeding the beans, their long stems already grown well up their three-legged supports. With his head among the green, time melted away, and it seemed only minutes before the bare feet of the children came slapping along the beaten earth of the path.

"You again?"

"Yes, sir. Us again."

Grunting like an old man, Izzy got to his feet. The girl had lost that feral tension and now returned his gaze sedately, while the lad was bouncing on his toes, grinning as if he hadn't just dug through several hundred pounds of stink, remarkably little of it ending up on his long white shirt.

"Either of you know a thing about this business?"

Izzy asked them, gesturing around the garden.

"No, sir," the lad chirped.

"Of course not." He looked about with more purpose, seeking a task even he understood. "Well, you see them frondy things?" He pointed at the feathery green sprouts coming up from the bed behind the children. "Those are carrots. The orange bit is underground," he added as the children swapped glances again. "You're to pluck out everything that *isn't* a carrot. Just in that bit of dirt there," he said as the boy took an eager step towards the neighbouring bed of collards.

He stood over them for a minute until convinced they knew which was which, then returned to his own tasks. Again it seemed no time at all and the pair was back, this time with a companion, an unfamiliar boy of a similar age and richness of skintone. A vision rose in Izzy's mind of the lad's family: just now settling in at camp, greeting old friends, asking them what was to be had for dinner.

His own stomach rumbled. Broth and beans it was like to be, and soon neither of those if they didn't get more food growing. "Right," he said, clapping his hands together and startling the children into attentive silence. "Sure as sugar he'll tell me I've done it all wrong, but the head gardener ain't here and he ain't due back for days. So we're going to give it our best, and I'll wear the consequences."

"Sir?"

"You don't mind a bit more digging, do you?"

By mid-afternoon he had amassed a crew six strong, though all were of a piece with the first pair, with stick-thin limbs and unstoppable smiles and not a one over twelve years of age. They were biddable and untiring and he couldn't begrudge the help, by which the garden nearly doubled in size, the newly turned earth arrayed in somewhat neat beds stretching away from the narrow end of the garden. He knew enough to not plant until he'd got a fence around them, or else the blasted rabbits would take every leaf that dared poke aboveground.

Feeling very much the master, he left his charges and went to wash. He was still bent over the brimming barrel when Miguel's plummy voice addressed him once more. "How are my little helpers faring?"

Izzy stood up, water streaming down his neck. "Your helpers? You're who sent them kids to work for me?"

Leaning his elbows on the fence, Miguel grinned as he regarded Izzy with exceeding familiarity. "I said to myself, this is far too much for one man to see to alone."

"Yeah, well, the regular man ain't here this week."

"The regular man?" Miguel said as Izzy began hunting about for a cloth to dry himself. "Does that make you the irregular?"

"What is it you even want?"

"To be of service," he replied smoothly. "We are a large company. We ask much of your hospitality. It can only be fair to give something in return."

Not apparently his own labour, but Izzy said nothing, having resorted to his shirt tails to dry his face, thereby sacrificing any pretence of dignity. Being the subject of someone's covetous gaze had once made him swell with pride. Now it was a sour imposition, a reminder of how lonesome a man could get when he had given his heart to an absent other.

He turned his attention to cleaning his garden tools and after a few more minutes of being ignored Miguel wandered away. When he'd gone, Izzy dismissed the youths, then stole to the manor and availed himself of bread and a plateful from Mrs Owen's stew-pot. He was in no mood for the others' jollity, for Rose and Annie and Noreen's questions about his day and about Noel's visit home, never mind the bare fact of being among so many people who all knew his business and felt entitled to pass comment thereon.

In the quiet of the cottage, he lit a candle and spent some time on his reading practice, going over the first bits of Genesis for what was likely the hundredth time. It was Noel's mum what had first tried to teach him his letters, and the memory of her gruff voice sounding out the words along with him was soon too much to bear. Mere days, yet Noel's absence felt like a mortal wound, all the pains of life unbearable without that steady reassurance that today's failures were of no consequence, that tomorrow would be better.

Izzy woke in his chair, his nose wedged in the fold of the book. The stew had gone cold and he pushed it away in disgust. Wracked with exhaustion, he staggered the few steps to the bed and fell upon it. As he fumbled with his boot laces, the sound of revelry reached his ears. Every night had been like this, the circus folk carrying on long past sundown, though their encampment was far enough from the road that the sound failed to carry to other properties.

Izzy and Noel's cottage bore the brunt, the singing and strumming and shouts of delight seeming to draw nearer and nearer until they became one with his feverish dreams: of a magic seed and the plant that sprang from it, as tall as the sky, and Izzy's task to climb to the top; a wire between two walls, and now the task was to run across it. His task was to fall…

He woke in a sweat. Felt about in the murky blackness until he found Noel's pillow. Clutched it to his face to breathe in the last traces of Noel's musk. Prayed for morning.

Le surprise

HE WOKE IN the grey before dawn, Noel's pillow wedged beneath his chin. Alone, he had no cause to stay in bed. God knew there was work enough before him that day. The cottage had only two small windows, old and many-paned, the glass bleary, and one never knew from the light they permitted what sort of day awaited. So it was with great surprise that Izzy left the stale grey air of the cottage to find the greater world a paradise.

Really he ought not to have been so taken aback after this many months in the countryside. But if ever God's hand was visible in Creation it was here and now, with the rising sun gilding the tops of the trees, the sky a field of purest periwinkle, the birdsong like a holy choir rejoicing. How had he never seen those tiny white flowers sprinkled across the turf like stars? Enchanted, he found himself strolling not towards the garden but the shore, where he stopped at the crest of a dune. Mist swathed the beach, rising from the damp sand and stirred by the crashing waves. A fairyland, too beautiful for man's eyes, filled with untold danger. And twenty miles across the waves, his prince.

He left the beach, cutting through the loose copse of cypress and sand cherry shielding the grounds from the wind off the sea. He came out into the sandy lot where the circus scaffold stood, the blueing sky marked by the ink-line of the suspended rope. His stomach tightened as childhood memories imposed themselves, of being dragged by his brothers to Newgate to witness a hanging. His sense of ill omen dispersed as a flock of little birds alighted on the wire.

"You see? Heights are nothing to fear." Miguel, again appearing from thin air as he stepped out from behind a sprawling cypress at the clearing's edge.

"That's a terrible habit you've got, popping up out of nowhere."

"Are you thinking I am too secretive?"

Not by half. "I suppose I ought to thank you properly for finding help for me," Izzy said instead. "I was out of sorts yesterday. I may have seemed ungrateful."

"You seemed weary. I commend you. Myself, I cannot work nearly so hard as you do."

"Well, you must have to put in a bit of practice to do what you do." He nodded towards the high wire.

"My father likes to make the joke that I was born in mid-air. They both were acrobats. My mother performed into her sixth month of pregnancy."

"Saints alive!"

"And you?

"Me what?"

"Do you dare?"

"Go up there? Why would I even want to?"

"Because so many people don't believe they ever could. Yet it must be possible."

"For a man born to it, maybe."

"No. For any man who dares."

"I ain't doing none of that tumbling business."

"Yes, but to simply cross is no difficult thing. Come, you will start as a child would."

Swallowing a surge of indignation, Izzy followed him beyond the scaffold to a much humbler construction, no more than a pair of crossed stakes lashed together then driven into the ground about ten feet apart to support a pole. Without a word, Miguel stepped onto the pole and walked across it as if it were flat ground. At the end he dismounted with a clever little hop, landing facing Izzy.

"You see? Nothing to fear."

"Fine talk when you're all of six inches off the ground."

"There is no difference between six inches and six hundred."

"I beg to differ."

"No. In your mind, there must be no difference whatsoever. To fall from this height is as shameful as to fall from the greater."

"It's not shame that worries me so much as broken bones." Why was he still speaking to this weasel? More to the point, why was he kneeling to take off his boots, ready to take the weasel's dare? Too late to avoid it as Miguel offered his hand to help him step up onto the end of the pole.

"You may find it easier if I assist you to mount."

"I'll try it on my own, if you don't mind."

With a dip of his saucy eyes, Miguel demurred and stepped back. The pole was firmly lashed to its supports and remained steady under Izzy's foot. For once glad of Noel's absence, in case he made a right fool of himself, he took one last deep breath then shifted his weight and stepped up.

"That's right. Now—"

"Hush up. It's been a donkey's age, but I don't reckon much about this has changed." Only himself. But the game was the same: get across. At least if he fell it was only inches. Only Miguel who'd see, and not someone who mattered, or worse, Izzy's brothers, who'd punished him brutally for any failures.

The pole was a bit narrower than his foot. Eight or nine paces across. If he stood on the arches of his feet… The thing was not to stop, even when the pole bowed. Keep the knees bent and not stop until one reached the end.

Miguel began to applaud and Izzy hushed him at once. "Yes, yes, tremendous, I can walk in a straight line."

"Then you will have no difficulty doing so at a slightly higher elevation, yes?"

A WEEK IN, he'd just about got it: the feel of the rope, the dip and sway, though the thought of performing this trick even higher in the air, at the top of a circus tent was, well, something not to be thought about while doing the trick. That much he understood. Thanks to Ursula, he'd had plenty of practice in splitting his attention, separating his thoughts from his physical acts, for heaven knew there were nights enough when he'd have rather been anywhere other than where he was.

This was far easier, not least of all because everyone

kept their trousers on. Not always their shirts given the heat, though today he was glad of the linen of his sleeves. It was a trade-off between discomforts, as he'd yet to break the habit of trying to catch himself when falling. As a consequence the wire had bruised hell out of his ribs and the backs of his arms. What Noel was going to say about that was one more thing for Izzy not to think about, as he mounted the swaying rope ladder to the little platform once again.

Here he stopped, as one was wont, feeling every groove and knot in the planks through the thin soles of the leather slippers. Holding onto the nearest post of the scaffold, he looked towards the other platform. Twenty paces. He'd never made it farther than twelve. Granted it was years since he'd had to run walls, and a row of bricks was a far more substantial foot-path than a two-inch hawser. Beneath which was the canvas to break his fall, which would be nearly painless if he remembered to not try catching the wire on the way down.

He let go of the pole and stepped to the very edge, fixing his eyes on the flag affixed to the top of the other tower. One more attempt, then he'd make his daily pilgrimage to Calais, for the ferry most likely to be bringing Noel was due any time.

"*Vamos!*" Miguel shouted from the bottom. Izzy stuck out his tongue. He'd go when he was good and ready. Which was going to be in three…two…

"Oi! What in blazes you doing up there?"

Noel: he'd bet his life on it, and as he turned the man himself came stumbling into the clearing, bits of leaf stuck to his sleeves. He checked, staring up in horror. "Fucking hell, Pound…"

Later Izzy admitted to having chosen wrong, for rather than waste time on the wobbly rope ladder, he tossed himself off the platform onto the canvas, just as he'd been taught to do, landing easily on his rump, his limbs neatly splayed, his head forward to keep from knocking it about.

At the very least he might have warned Noel, who cried out in terror and fell to his knees. By the time Izzy had slithered off the canvas Noel had got up again and was fruitlessly brushing at the dirt staining his best trousers.

"Is this why you've let everything go to shit?" he said by way of greeting.

Izzy stopped short. "What about, *nice to see you?*"

"Is it? I'm surprised you even noticed I'm here."

"You bloody well shouted at—forget that. What's gone wrong?"

"What's gone wrong?" Noel snarled. "How about what's damn well gone right? I come back from a godawful trip away to find you mucking about on a circus wire while the house rots and the garden gets torn up by maniacs. How could you do this to me?"

"To you? You're the one went on holiday."

"It weren't no holiday. I had to go. And who the hell is he?" He pointed towards Miguel, or rather where he'd been, as the fellow had sensibly left them to their spat.

"That's Miguel. He's all right."

"What was he doing here?"

"Nothing. Yelling for me to hurry my arse up."

"And that's another thing—"

"Christ, there's another thing?" Taken aback, Noel lowered his accusing finger as Izzy went on. "It's been days and days. I was hoping you'd be at least a bit glad to see me."

"I might be more so if you weren't carrying on like this rather than doing what needs to get done."

"You think I've not been trying? God help a man, but you were right. It's awful here alone. It's awful without you. So I couldn't do it, couldn't spend all day every day in the garden, thinking how you ought to have been there, telling me what to do because I haven't a clue what's what. For all I know, I yanked out all the food and left the weeds. But it weren't for lack of trying."

Not knowing how else to persuade him, Izzy held up his hands to show the blackened, broken nails, the blisters, the nicks and scratches. "I know I could have done better, at least by your lights, but you gotta believe I did my best."

With a soft noise of sorrow, Noel took Izzy's hands, turning them over and back. He looked up, all anger spent. "I'm sorry. I don't mean to come the heavy, but fucking hell…" He glanced up at the scaffold, blew out a weighty breath. "You scared the daylights out of me."

"I ought to have come down by the ladder. Sorry I frightened you. And I'm sorry I've let you down."

"Nah, it's not you that's put me out of sorts." Yet as Izzy leaned near to kiss him he turned his head aside.

"What is it? Cobber, tell me."

"Not out here." He took Izzy's hand and led him to the cottage, where Izzy sat on the bed, expecting Noel to join him, not to begin pacing the narrow strip of floor between the bed and table.

"Come on, Peters, spill your guts. What's happened?"

He stopped pacing, tugging at his ear like he had something to hide. "There was this fellow at the wedding giving me a real funny feeling, see? Wouldn't let me alone. Not that I did anything to encourage him, mind. But he knew me from before. A friend of my sister's."

"So what'd he do?"

"Nothing, nothing. Look, don't worry about him. Thing is, I went outside to take the air, have a piss, you know, get away from him. From everyone really."

"What the hell kind of wedding was this?"

"Forget that, what matters is who was out there waiting for me." He settled on the edge of the table. "You know Vik Patel's kid? Him what started trading for Crabtree's?"

Izzy pictured the lad, who had hopefully grown from the rail-thin scrapper he remembered. Unless that's how Crabtree's touted him in their catalogue of diversely talented young men. "What about him?"

"He was hanging about. Came to tell me to mind myself, that people were looking for me. People I maybe didn't want to have finding me."

"How'd he know that?"

"He'd come round earlier in the week, left a letter for me at Auntie's. They picked him up on the other side of the bridge, put the frighteners on him bad. He looked it, too."

"Who was the letter from?"

"Forget the letter. It's not important."

"Fucking hell, Peters, what exactly are you telling me?"

"That they knew I was there. Muldoon's people. Now I reckon they'd followed me all over town. I just thought it was the usual sort of stares, that being over here I'd gotten used to not being in a city and just noticed it more. But no. I'm sure I was followed."

"What did you do?"

"Fair ran back to my folks' place. The next day I went to Ursula at the hotel and she put me up in the room next to hers. I didn't leave again."

"You were gone for a fortnight. You could have come home."

"Alone? Not a chance. I'd not have reached Dover in one piece."

"You don't know that."

"I bloody well wasn't in the mood to find out." He stood abruptly, the table legs scraping the stone floor. "Fucking hell, Iz. I should never have left."

"Forget about it," Izzy said, rising from the bed to intercept him as he began once more to pace. "You're here now. So let's get on with it."

"With what?"

"With being happy to see each other, you twit."

At last Noel laughed though bitterly, then pulled him close. At last they kissed, and such a kiss, made of want and waiting, so much waiting, for it hadn't seemed right to do anything in their shared bed besides sleep while Noel wasn't there to share it.

"Let's go to bed," Izzy murmured once they'd caught their breath.

Noel groaned, even as his hands tightened on Izzy's arse. "With all there is to do?"

"It's not likely to all get done today, is it?"

"No, but—"

"And it's not so bad it won't keep for an hour?"

"Suppose not," Noel replied hoarsely as Izzy hooked a leg round his.

"Please? We don't have to get up to much. Just kiss." He shifted his leg up Noel's thigh, curving his body against him.

"Kiss, he says."

"I didn't say which bit of you I intended to kiss, now did I?"

"You dirty little flirt."

"Am not. I had a bath last night. It's no joke," he said when Noel chuckled. "I had to after I fell in the manure heap."

"So that's what I can smell."

"Seriously?" Izzy yelped, dropping his leg. "Damn it, you won't believe how hard I scrubbed." His scalp still burned from the harsh yellow soap, but Noel chuckled again.

"Not you. I mean the cottage. You smell…" and he leaned in and sniffed at Izzy's hair, then his neck, his breath making Izzy shiver. "You smell like you want to be fucked. By me. A lot and right now."

"Please."

THE BOX

"**P**OOR BUGGER JUST about died all over again once he got my shirt off," Izzy said to the young man perching on the honest edge of his seat. "Thought I'd been flogged, the way the bruises cut across. Took some convincing to get him…well. That bit's not important." He was spared any further embarrassment as the bells of St Anne's began striking the hour.

"Is it really nine o'clock?" Telford gasped, staring about at the dim sitting room. "I'd best be getting on. Will you be…never mind."

"You wanted to ask if I'll be all right, didn't you?"

"Well, will you?"

"Not to worry. But if you happen to pass a chemists' tomorrow, you might do me the favour of bringing me a fresh jar of that business on the sink.

"The liniment?"

"Otherwise I ain't likely to make it to rehearsal ever again."

Making it to bed was effort enough. Though he expected to be kept awake by a host of memories, he fell asleep quickly. He woke at the same wretched hour as he ever did, the result of having lived so long with a man who kept farmer's hours.

By the grey dawn he shuffled to the kitchen and back to the bedroom with a brimming mug of tea. The cat had got in again and was curled up in the warm spot in the bed. If Izzy tried to join it, the thing would hiss, perhaps scratch him, almost certainly cause him to spill the tea.

"Fine, you toothless old bugger, you can have it. Time I were up anyway." The cat ignored him. It wouldn't want a feeding for at least an hour, so Izzy settled himself on the windowsill and watched the day begin, the sun rising rosy through the sooty mist, the pigeons on the roofline hopping and cooing while from below came the jingle of harness and rattle of hooves from a heavy wagon making its way up Shaftesbury.

The sill was wide, the boards strongly fixed down, and their window looked over the roof of the next house, but Noel had hated him sitting here, ever afraid of him falling. A soft touch on his ankle made him startle, just about slopping the tea down his front. The cat had left the bed and was rubbing against his leg. "All right, all right, let's see if we can't scrape up something for you."

Once he'd opened the sardines, it seemed foolish to waste them, so he grilled a bit of bread to go with. The cat scarfed its share in two bites and after a moment's preening it wandered into the sitting room. From the kitchen doorway Izzy watched as it paused, the tip of its tail twitching. Then it made up its mind and started for the bedroom again.

"At least let me make the bed first, you little stinker. Last time you left a mess of hair." Leaving his toast, Izzy hobbled after the beast, which hadn't climbed onto the bed but was disappearing under it. "Now you're going to mess yourself, you twit. No one's dusted under there in God knows."

Grumbling along with his knees, he got down on the rug and looked under the bed. There was its rounded silhouette beside a larger, squarer shadow. "For the love of… I swear, Peters, if this is another bleeding stack of seed catalogues…"

His cane was propped between the bed and the night stand and he used it to shove the cardboard box out the other side of the bed. Then used the bed to haul himself to his feet. Then used the cane to get around the bed. Was there an audience for geriatric acrobatics? If so, he had half a routine ready to go. Thankfully the box wasn't tied shut so he used the tip of the cane to push off the lid.

"Oh la…Peters, you cheeky bugger…"

There they were, breaking the law. Willingly and enthusiastically, to the amusement of the photographer, if Izzy recalled correctly. A private sitting, with explicit instructions that all plates remained their property, the prints not to be sold, not even for the inflated rates one got for mixed-race couplings.

Noel in his youth had been unbearably beautiful, with a labourer's hard musculature beneath his musky skin. Noel in his maturity had been handsomer still, if less sculptural. Noel in any form…

Seated on the edge of the bed, Izzy went through the blistered old photographs more slowly, lingering on the shapes and shadows, the power of Noel's gaze when turned to the camera. To himself he paid less heed. He'd been adequate to the task, man enough to please Noel and not an ounce more. Yet there was a charm in the way his body curved, in the contrast of Noel's skin against his. In the end, they were only pictures, and nothing like so good as his memories: the feel of that skin, the curve of their bodies together.

Amid the ordinary aches of a morning rose another, sharper and more urgent and focused on his groin. Yes, that was in fact his prick, rising to the bait like it ever did when Noel and nakedness were involved. For all the good it did him. Like as not the sorry old thing would break off in his hand.

He was startled from his maudlin self-pity by a vigorous knocking at the door. There was not a soul alive but him who deserved to see these photographs, and he shoved them under his pillow then pushed the paper-filled box under the bed with his cane.

"Leave off, will you?" he shouted as the caller knocked again. "I'm bloody well coming."

MR POUND SAID he'd be along as soon as he found clean trousers. Resisting the urge to help him look, Telford went on to the theatre. He'd never gotten there so early, and had to stand in the alley for several minutes before Whitley let him in.

"Can we expect to see himself today?" Whitley asked as Telford followed him into the bowels of backstage.

"I hope. He seemed quite lively this morning. And gosh, what a collection he has. Have you seen it, all those posters hung on the wall? And the photographs? What a curious life he's led."

"Curious is certainly a word for it." They had reached the door of Whitley's office, which really was the whole of the office, only enough floor-space inside the closet of a room for Whitley's swivelling chair. "Is there something else you wish me to know, Mr Fords?" he asked as Telford stood there pointlessly.

"Oh. No. It's nothing." Or perhaps it was everything. A question that had dug at him all night, an answer he didn't want to hear.

Whitley had been a butler to a wealthy family, and whatever he thought of Telford, his professionally placid expression persisted. "You know, Mr Fords, I believe you will make something of yourself.

"Will I? I mean…what do you mean?"

"You have a very charming way about you. Very natural. It's refreshing to find an actor who doesn't think he needs to always be acting."

Telford knew the sort. "Were you ever on stage, Mr Whitley?" he asked as the other man sat down and turned to face his desk.

"Never had the taste for it," Whitley replied in the mirror he kept for the purpose. "Nor the face."

"I'd have thought you're handsome enough."

He smiled with a brief press of his lips. "I'm much obliged, Mr Fords. But I have never doubted that my talents are best employed behind the scenes. To each their own, of course. I'd never expect you to take on my role any more than I'd be able to play yours."

The rehearsal ran smoothly, even with Telford keeping half an eye on the auditorium. It wasn't until the end that he spotted Mr Pound in the very back row of seats. As the other actors filed backstage,

Telford descended the little ladder to the orchestra pit then made his way to the rear of the auditorium. Mr Pound was three seats from the aisle, and Telford sat beside him, sinking low in copy of the other man's slumped pose.

"Cor, that was embarrassing," Mr Pound muttered. Before Telford came to the cast's defence, the director went on. "I half hoped you'd be lost without me. Arrogant little shit, I am."

"You thought we did well?"

"I ought to wreck my knees every show, if you lot are going to get on so well in my absence."

"To be honest, we're all terrified you're going to pop up at any moment and shout blue murder that we'd not got anything done."

"Is that so?"

"Does Whitley know you're here?"

"Figs to Whitley. He don't need to know." Something large and flat fell onto the stage with a resonant smack and he groaned. "I didn't hear that. Neither did you, right?" he added, looking sidelong at Telford, who shrugged.

"Not a thing."

"That's my boy. Whatever it was, it'll keep. Now, let's you and me scarper before Whitley does find me and doubles my misery."

They didn't speak again until they were outside, walking with purpose but without haste. Stepping lightly, carrying his cane as usual, Mr Pound cleared his throat.

"La, you'll have to forgive me, but I can't fix your blessed last name in my soggy old head. What's it again? Vandurberger?"

"Vandurenburg."

"Is that name yours or your uncle's?"

"His."

"And what's yours?"

"I suppose it's still Cline. Uncle Ned didn't adopt me formally."

"Telford Cline, that's not half bad. Good stage name. Specially if Terry Fords gets a bad reputation."

"Can one do that, start over with a new name?"

"With your voice, lad, you can likely get away with just about anything."

THE PHOTOGRAPH

IT WAS THURSDAY, when Maury's little bistro did onion soup and beefsteak with peppercorns. Telford asked many a question of the waiter regarding the soup, the bread atop it, the flour and yeast in the bread, until Izzy promised to acquaint him with the cook after their meal. The rest of the first course passed in silence, aside from the young man's helpless little murmurs of pleasure with every mouthful. As he scraped the bowl clean Izzy decided not to ask whether they were feeding him at home, for fear of hearing the answer. Ah well, he'd done all he could, made his offer of safe harbour. It was for Telford to ask, should he need it.

"While we wait for the main, you might like to have a peek at this." He offered Telford the manila folder he'd been carrying.

"I was wondering what you had in there," the young man said as he took it.

"Just a few bits and pieces I dug up."

"My word…"

Aside from the photographs, the box had held a wealth of memory. Programs and posters from shows he'd done thirty years prior. Handbills from even earlier, like the one Telford was now poring over, the central image an engraving of a youth with cherub curls and very tight clothes poised on one leg, his other leg bent sharply upwards and held arrow straight.

Telford's eyes grew wide as he read the text. With a child's glee, he turned to the next. "Are all these of you?"

"So far as I've had nerve to look," Izzy replied, with a regretful glance at his wineglass which he rather wished would fill itself. "I'd no idea he'd kept those, the bugger."

"You mean Noel kept all this without you knowing?"

"Good thing too or I might have tossed them in the rubbish by now."

"Whyever would you do that?" Telford asked, turning the pages over one by one. "These are marvellous. They're your history."

"Yeah, well, there's such a thing as having more history than one wishes to remember."

"Gosh. You were so handsome." Telford looked up again, face colouring. "Not that you aren't now. I mean, given your age. I mean—"

"I know what you mean, lad. I'm as well preserved as I could expect, given what I had to work with."

Grinning, Telford turned over the next page. "There's some photographs."

"There's what?" Surely he'd found them all, or at least all the compromising ones, his heart easing as Telford passed him a photo of a fair-haired young woman in a high-necked dress.

"Is that Ursula?"

"Nah, this is her daughter Esme. You gotta look for the beauty mark just above her lip. La, I didn't know that were in there."

"Here's another," Telford said in a tight voice as he passed the photo across the table.

"Shit…" Like a reflex, Izzy's hand went to his breast pocket, the square of card beside his heart, the mate of this photo, which he'd not laid eyes on in close on twenty years. It showed two men in their mid-twenties, both dressed superbly. The black man was reclined against the arm of his chair, his chin resting on his upraised fist, his legs kicked out before him. His head was in three-quarter profile, his eyes directed at the white man beside him. At Izzy.

How young they were, how long ago. It had been hot in the room where they'd sat for these portraits, and Izzy's carefully combed hair had succumbed to sweaty curls, his cheeks so bright they were shadowed in the photograph. He was staring at the camera, his gaze not defiant but assured, almost inviting: *don't you wish you were me?*

And who could disagree, given Noel's expression, the love in his eyes, plain as day. Telford sipped at his glass of water while Izzy tucked away the photo with its fellow, had a drink himself to refresh his parched throat. He wasn't much for surprises these days, even good ones.

Telford had begun to fidget, moving the dishes and cutlery about in quarter inch increments. Hoping the sommelier might pass by, Izzy let him stew for another minute before speaking. "What's on your mind son?"

He stilled his hands, glancing around in that nervy way he had. "Oh. It's not anything important."

"So you say."

Telford looked away again, blushing harder, as Izzy

steeled himself for the revelation. Something in his manner had made many a younger man spill his guts to him over the years. Rarely was it an overture, more often pure confessional, him the priest of perfidy, a turn of phrase worthy of Whitley's little book. Hopefully he'd remember it, for this was not the moment to ask the lad to write it down for him, as Telford sat forward and cleared his throat.

"I wanted to say thank you. Not just for the meal, but for trusting me."

"What, with my dirty secrets?"

"With your history. Your friendship. You understand how you've shaped my life, don't you? Not only by casting me, but through your plays, the stories you've been telling all these years. You gave me dreams to seek, and now you've made those dreams come true."

"No. Not me. You did it. I walked away, if you recall."

"But you came back."

"That I did."

"And you let me audition. And you cast me, and you didn't have to do any of those things. You might have said no at any turn."

"I might have."

"Instead you've given me so much. A chance. Your trust."

"A home if you need it."

Telford bowed his head, touching his chest in that way he had when moved. "Let's pray it doesn't come to that" he replied softly. "Not that I don't appreciate your offer, but—"

"Hush. And stop with this soft soap or you'll have

us both weeping. Cook will think it's over the meal, he'll be after us with a cleaver."

The meal kept them occupied, and it wasn't until they were waiting for coffee that Telford began to fidget again. Izzy was inclined to let it pass, but with his belly warmly full and time on his hands, he was feeling indulgent. "Is that chair of yours on fire, lad?"

"What?"

"The way you're shifting about, as if something's burning you up."

"Oh. It's nothing."

"Liar."

Grinning, Telford sat back. "The trouble is, you've got me hooked."

"Come again?"

"Clearly something took place between that Mr Alanson attempting to cast you in that play about the island and, well, the entire rest of your career. And I was wondering if he ever managed to complete another libretto. Not that you're obliged to tell me anything, and it's really none of my business, and—"

"Ah, what does it matter? You've heard this much. Who am I to leave my audience hanging?"

Like the first dawn on the newly minted earth
Like roses grown in paradise given mortal birth
Thy beauty is a blessing though it pierce me through and through
Mine eyes art open and all they see is you

"Mine Eyes Art Open"
from "Exasperating Times"
Music & Lyrics by W. Alanson

La pièce

"THIS WAS THE '70s, mind. Theatre's nothing like it is today. Even Messrs. Gilbert and Sullivan had barely got going. Whether he knew it or not, poor old Alanson was a bit of a vanguard. If only he'd been as honest as he was imaginative, he might have made a proper go of it.

He called the new play *Exasperating Times*. Much as theatre folk avoid saying the name of the Scottish Play, the cast and crew discarded the name almost at once, referring to it behind his back as *Bill Dies Suddenly*. One began to hope the new title was just as prophetic, given that exasperation was the prevailing mood.

Having little to do until Ursula resumed trade, most of her staff had thrown in with the inexplicable circus of itinerant musicians and other performers drawn to the manor by Alanson's summons. Alanson himself had come to terms with the paucity of money available to stage his masterpiece and had restrained his ambitions to setting the play backstage at a vaudeville theatre rather than atop a sentient landmass in the middle of the South Pacific. He had however kept to the supernatural themes, cobbling together three Shakespeare plays, some hoary old nursery tales, and a wildly interpretive reading of Old Testament verses, then patching the lot onto melodies cribbed from music hall to tell the story of an angel who falls in love with a man.

Izzy played the part of the man, which made sense enough. Rose and Noel together were to play the part of the fallen host, the character undergoing a titillating transformation from a woman to a man partway through the play after seeing the object of her, or was it his, desire dressed for the stage in women's clothing.

"I still can't believe an angel could be that stupid," Noel grumbled to Izzy as they sprawled in a pair of garden chairs set on the ballroom floor where the audience would eventually sit, while Bill attempted to explain once more to Noreen and Brigid the difference between upstage and downstage.

"Only an angel as writ by bloody Alanson," Izzy muttered in reply.

"If he thinks I'm kissing you for an audience, he's out of his mind."

"Hang on, how's that going to work in a love story?"

Noel snorted, his jaw trembling. "You saying it don't bother you? The thought of showing off like that?"

"Suppose. A bit. But it's different here, innit? The law's not like it is back home."

"Are you prepared to test that?"

"You're forgetting one thing," Izzy said as onstage the women once more walked into one another. "For us to get seen, there'd need to be an audience to see us."

"True. And there ain't a man alive who'd shell out for this farce." They broke up in a spasm of helpless laughter, covering their mouths as Bill glared down at them.

"If you don't mind, gentlemen——" he drawled, but they were already on their feet, scampering for the doors.

"If I'd know it were that easy, I'd have gotten us booted from every rehearsal," Izzy said, pausing to stretch his shoulders. Noel was headed for the front door and Izzy ran a few steps to catch up. He hooked his arm round Noel's but Noel shook him off then shoved his hands in his pockets.

"What's gnawing on you?" Izzy asked as he opened the weighty door.

"I don't need people knowing our business."

"What's there to know that ain't already known?" Noel replied with a sharp look but Izzy pressed on. "And what good does knowing do anyone? Not as if the two of us are worth the blackmailing."

"We might not be, but what about her?"

On the drive in front of the house, Ursula was advising Clyde, Sal, and a crew of helpers in loading a number of large crates onto a waiting cart. Half hidden behind a column, the tiny, fair haired girl watching from the porch ignored the boys as they passed.

No one knew why the girl Esme was here. A man claiming to be her father had approached Clyde while he'd waited for Ursula and Noel in St Pancras station and obliged him on the spot to take her, fleeing without further explanation. Stranger still, the child seemed not to know that Ursula was her mother. Yet she was unmistakeably Ursula's child, possessing the same porcelain skin, same unyielding expression, though her eyes were darker and her spine blessedly straight.

Hearing their steps on the gravel, Ursula turned, and the breath caught in Izzy's throat. The presence of her unacknowledged daughter had further sapped her vitality, her cheeks hollow, deep lines bracketing her mouth. "Mr Peters, Mr Pound," she said with her typical formality and an unusual hoarseness. "I had hoped for a chance to see you before I depart."

"Will you be away long?" Noel asked.

"I cannot say. Much depends on the speed with which I am able to conduct my business." She indicated the flat dray which was stacked with similar crates. "Through a former investor I have acquired a number of items of fungible value which require precipitous liquidation."

"I'm sure they do," Izzy said, nodding to show an understanding he lacked. "Best of luck, in any case."

"Thank you Mr Pound, Mr Peters, Mr Hastings," she said with a little bow of her head to each. She glanced one last time towards the house, then allowed Clyde to hand her up to the cart's bench. She took up the reins and cracked them smartly and they were away, Clyde walking alongside.

"So mum's still the word on, er, all that?" Izzy murmured to Sal under the sound of the cart's wheels, nodding towards the tiny witness lurking on the porch.

"Frankly, I don't have the guts to ask," Sal replied. "It's none of our business anyway." As they neared the house, Esme's head poked from behind the pillar. The resemblance was uncanny, as if she were a doll of Ursula found sitting on a shelf.

"Hey kiddo," called Sal. "Let's find you something to eat. You want?" Sal said to them.

"I could eat," Noel said, patting his firm stomach.

"Yeah, you're simply wasting away," Izzy said, laughing.

"He's a growing boy," Sal said with a grin.

"I'll say he is." Izzy pinched Noel's hip, receiving a filthy look in return.

"Don't talk like that in front of child, you—well, just don't, all right?"

Izzy stuck out his tongue and Noel turned away, shaking his head. If there were such things as paternal instincts, they were wholly lacking in Izzy, who felt not merely judged but condemned and executed by the girl Esme's unblinking stare. He followed the party inside and through the hall to the main kitchen. Here Sal cut up some fruitcake and gave a slice to Esme, then sat her on a stool by a door that opened onto the lawn and gave a view of a sliver of sea.

"Hey Ducky, what do ya say we go visit Mr Peters' hens after?" Chewing quickly, the girl nodded.

"You've got a touch with children," Noel said as Sal joined them. "Have you never wanted any of your own?"

"Oh, I wanted them. I just wasn't about to give any to that—" With a glance at the child, Sal went on more quietly. "That SOB I married."

"Whatever made you marry at all?" Izzy asked. "If you'll pardon me saying, you hardly seem the type."

"Trust me, it made sense at the time. He was such a sweetheart when we were courting. A little too sweet, but I was just a kid. Just turned seventeen. I didn't know bumpkus about the world." Hands splayed on the wood of the kitchen table, Sal paused, exhaled slowly. "Not an hour after we left the church, he hit me for the first time. I was his, see? He could do what he wanted with me. And me, I was too young to know how to get away. Didn't have anywhere to go if I did."

"Saints above! What about your family?"

"He had them stitched up from the start. He's got money, and they don't anymore, so…" Sal shrugged, made a ghastly face. "Anyway, he's got them in his pocket. As far as they know, he's a saint. I was just *being difficult*, like always. Just like they expected. That's half why they fell for his cock-and-bull, they were so desperate to straighten me out, make me over in their image of the perfect little debutante. Ursula, though, she takes you as you are. That's why I love her so much. Not like a romantic thing but like a sister. Or a mother. The kind of mother you always hoped for. You know?"

They did, and so they said nothing. After a little, Sal roused and returned to the child. "Come on, Ducky. Maybe the chickens want some cake too." They helped Esme from the stool, then hand in hand the pair went out by the scullery door.

"What about you?" Izzy asked, plucking a raisin from Noel's untouched slice of cake. "Do you suppose you'll regret it if you never father a child?"

"I can't know that. How can I know how I'll feel years from now?"

"You might spare a thought for it, though. While you can still do something about it."

"What are you trying to say?"

"Nothing."

"Come on, Iz. Don't hold out on me."

A fair cop, for all the times he'd wheedled the truth

out of Noel. "It's just that I'd never want to take anything from you. Never want to be the reason you weren't happy with how your life has gone."

Truth, but maybe too much of it, his voice ragged with it, Noel's eyes suddenly wet.

"Don't think of it so," he said, cupping Izzy's face between his hands. "You give me so much more than you realize." Gone was Noel's typical reluctance as he kissed him, first softly, then completely, bending him over the table before breaking off for them to catch their breath.

"Besides which," Noel panted, "I haven't time for another child."

"What you mean, *another*?"

"I'm already minding your milky arse, ain't I?"

"You shit!" He shoved at Noel's chest in mock outrage. Laughing, Noel grabbed Izzy's wrists, stretching his arms to the side and looming in to claim another kiss.

"We eat food from that table, you know." With a stifled groan Noel stepped away, leaving Izzy to struggle upright. Annie stood at the doorway, arms crossed. "You're wanted in the dressing room," she said to Izzy.

"Since when do we have a dressing room?"

"Since we got a costume department."

"I'm off to do some proper work," Noel said. He ducked out of the kitchen, leaving Izzy at Annie's mercy.

She brought him to the ballroom where Noreen and a pair of the circus women had drawn up chairs to the left of the stage. All were bent over various bits of sewing, bright gowns draped over their laps or lying in pieces on the floor around them. Even Marisol had humbled herself and was fitting Rose into her gauzy angel costume as Rose stood on a crate.

"What are you waiting for?" Marisol said to Izzy around a mouthful of pins.

"To know what I'm meant to be doing."

"Seeing if your costume fits," Annie said. "Hurry and undress."

"Out in the open like this?"

"There's not an inch of you we haven't seen already, love. We'll have Noelly bang us together some walls for the show. Now get cracking."

Cheeks ablaze, he looked about, but every direction he might face faced someone. Praying Noel kept busy for just a little longer, he stripped out of trousers and shirt, the summer air not warm enough to keep him from shivering.

"You can't wear that grotty thing in the show," Annie said, sneering at Izzy's admittedly worn underwear.

"This ain't the show. Gimme the damned dress and let's get this over with."

"Don't you know anything about women?" Marisol gritted past the pins between her lips. "Foundation garment first or it won't fit at all."

"You don't mean…oh, come on!" For Annie now held out a corset, stiffly boned, ribbon-trimmed.

"That angel ain't gonna know what hit him," she said with a leer. "Or her, I suppose."

It took a bleeding age. They'd stitched a lady's muslin combination for him, which was admittedly nice against his skin. The corset was less comfortable, being much too large in the top and so rubbing against his sides.

"I'll make you an improver for the show" Annie said as she yanked on the laces

"A what?" he grunted against the sudden increase of pressure round his middle.

"A bust improver."

"Oh hell…Noel's going to have a fit."

"I think you look very nice."

"Let's get the damned dress on and see if you still think that."

Looks were only half his worry, the tight clasp of the corset stirring his blood, putting him too much in mind of a certain gift of Noel's, an item he only wore on rare occasions. Now he was to prance about on stage in a similar state of confined breathiness. So much for his thought that no man would be foolish enough to pay to see it happen.

"Arms up, love," Annie said, a bulging bundle of white cloth in hand.

"What that?"

"Your bustle."

"Saints above, Annie…" Protesting would only prolong his humiliation so he raised his arms and let Annie drop the boned petticoat over his head. Marisol had done with Rose and came to help her position it. "You're out of your mind," he said to them over his shoulder

"It's only a costume, love," Annie said as she did up the tiny buttons at the back of the waist.

"It's not. You women go around in this gear on the daily. I wouldn't stand for it."

Then came a petticoat over the lot, and then the skirt of crimson silk and its matched bodice, both bedecked in swags of fabric and bits of ribbon and all of it very peculiar to see wrapped around his pointy frame.

"We'll have to make a few amendments, make it easier to put on and off," Marisol said as Annie fussed with the hooks that closed the bodice at the front.

"We can't just cut those scenes entire?" he pleaded. "Or write it different?"

"What's your worry, love?" Annie said, patting down the pleat that hid the hooks. "It's just clothes."

"I look ridiculous."

"You can't say that without having a proper look." She spun him about by the shoulders to face the tall mirror leaned against the wall. "See? You look just fine."

Fine wasn't the word. Ridiculous, maybe. Strange as could be, and that was inarguable, the scandalous cut of the dress leaving his shoulders entirely bare, though the neckline sagged at the front without a bosom to fill it.

"No one is going to put up with this." He gestured to his reflection.

"By no one do you mean Noel?" Annie asked, fussing with the bow on his shoulder.

"I mean the punters! Soon as I step on stage they'll be asking for their money back."

"They won't. Trust me, you look very pretty. Don't you think so, Marisol?"

She gazed down at him, as expressionless as ever. "Red's not your colour, but you look…very well." Given he'd never heard the woman deliver a compliment to anyone, this amounted to a love poem. His goose was officially cooked.

"See?" Annie gloated as she straightened the overskirt. "You're a vision of loveliness."

La danse

WORK CONTINUED APACE, on the garden, the house, the play, and the wire. Night after night, it seemed Izzy's head had barely hit the pillow before Noel was shaking him awake, some mornings more kindly than others.

Today at rehearsal he'd been short on words, long on silences, except in expressing his feelings about the wispy angel costume he was expected to wear. Marisol had joined her husband on the ballroom floor, and was viewing his notes over his shoulder as he explained the dancers' path back and forth across the stage. While most of the household had adopted a state of casual undress, going about in petticoats and shawls, Marisol persisted in full uptown regalia, from her follow-me ringlets to her silk taffeta gown to her buttoned boots.

"I know what the problem is," she said. She took a long draught from her cigarette holder, then exhaled luxuriantly while Bill fidgeted, his moustache wriggling like it wished to crawl off his lip and hide under a rock.

"Well?" he grated. "Are you ever going to enlighten us?"

"It's the same as it ever is." She had another pull on her cigarette, the smoke clinging round them in a haze. "You know nothing about dance."

With a strangled cry, Bill cast the papers on the floor. "For the love of all that's holy, woman—"

"Do you want my help or not?"

"Unfortunately for you the show has no need of a prima donna," he grated, his lips smiling, his eyes throwing daggers.

"No, but you're in desperate need of a choreographer."

The couple had faced off like fighters, Marisol indifferent as ever, Alanson vibrating with unspendable rage. Then his better sense or whatever passed for same in his fame-starved mind must have intervened, as he screwed a smile onto his red face and straightened his necktie. "Yes. Well, perhaps I can find some use for you."

Marisol's left eyebrow raised fractionally. She sniffed, and a hush came over the room, of the sort when the assembly had just collectively gasped in alarm.

"Holy waltzing Christ, Alanson," Izzy said into the quiet. "We're meant to charge money for this shambles of yours. So if you're begging for someone's help, you might want to do better than *perhaps I can find some use for you.*"

"Marisol, love," called Noreen from the stage, "can't you see we're drowning here? Throw us a blessed rope, will you?"

"For you, Nono, I will."

Clenching her cigarette holder in her teeth, Marisol reached under the waist of her bodice and undid her skirt, letting it slither to the ballroom floor in a magenta- and cream-striped puddle. At her most fearless when shocking, she hoisted her petticoat over her knees and clambered up onto the low stage. With nothing but glares and a fearsomely pointing finger, she ordered the dancers onto their marks.

"Alors, let me see your little dance so I can show you where you're wrong."

Soon enough Izzy and Noel were added to the ensemble. With Marisol's new steps there were fewer collisions and everyone ended up where they were meant to and not on the wrong side of the stage. Bill's accompaniment on the clanking piano became less forced and more authentic, and by the time he announced a rest Izzy felt the first stirrings of hope that the show might not be an absolute disaster.

Noel disappeared the instant he was allowed off the stage, to redo some chore already done by the circus folk but never to his standards. The rest remained, talking of the play and the dance and then of other things: the weather, the future, the readiness of dinner. Marisol had dropped a beaded hairpin and Izzy brought it to her as she was rebuttoning her skirt.

"How is it you learned to dance?" he asked.

"Prima ballerina in the national children's corps," she replied, not looking up as she fussed with the frilled hem of her bodice.

"You knew her?"

"I was her."

"Of course you were." Secretly an heiress to a thousand-year lineage, once among the highest paid courtesans in all of England, if Marisol had said she knew how to fly, Izzy wouldn't have blinked. "Don't suppose you know anything about singing?" he asked.

She laughed in her smoke-scarred voice. "If I could,

I'd not have bothered with whoring."

"Why didn't you keep at dancing?"

"Some idiot boy dropped me. Then trod on me. Shattered my ankle. I gave up ballet for opium."

IZZY JOINED NOEL at the plot, where there was always work wanting to be done and never hands enough to do it all. The new recruits were willing, but as not a one had ever lived in a home that wasn't on wheels, their collective knowledge about growing a garden was even sparser than Izzy's. Still, it was good to be able to send them up to the house with their arms full, to not begrudge every potato dug too early, knowing that the newly planted bed had already begun to sprout.

With their little helpers busy under the watchful eye of Khalid, the lad in white who'd been the first to volunteer, they found themselves with no pressing tasks to hand. Much to Izzy's quiet joy, Noel suggested a walk round the orchard.

The blossoms had mainly passed, the apples still only pebble-sized lumps on the ends of their stalks. After a quick peer around for signs of overzealous rabbits nibbling the tree-bark they simply wandered, hand in hand, Noel deep in thought. He gently led them beyond the orchard and across the fallow grass to the remotest corner of the property, where a loose stand of beech trees formed a sort of alcove, a room out of doors. Here Noel stopped to kiss him, which was exceedingly pleasant but did not at all answer why they had strayed so far.

"I didn't want to say this around Alanson," Noel murmured, brushing Izzy's curls from his forehead. "He'd only take it as an excuse to rub his eyes all over you, but you're a nifty little mover, you know?"

"I'm a what?"

He laughed kindly. "I mean you dance really well. I only wish I could get about on that stage like you do."

"You're not so bad,"

"I'm a joke. But I thought, maybe if I practiced a bit without bloody Alanson leering at us, smashing away on that rusty old piano, it might stick better."

"Is that why we're all the way out here?"

"Is it all right?"

"Of course. I'd love a dance, Mr Peters."

"Don't start that."

"You prefer I call you 'Jophiel'? Though perhaps we'll just worry about the dancing part," he added as Noel cringed at hearing his character's name.

In lieu of the balcony on the set, Izzy stood on a cypress stump. Noel knelt below, his hand on his heart. "How is this gonna work without the music?" Izzy asked after a few seconds of them staring at each other.

"Oh no, I ain't singing too," Noel said with force.

"Then count it with me."

"Eh?"

"It's a waltz, innit? Tra-la-la, tra-la-la, that three over four thing, right?"

"It's called a *time signature*."

"See? You already know more than me. So start with pretending you just sang that last line of the chorus, then stand up and take my hand. We'll go from there."

They paced back and forth across the sandy soil, poor Noelly needing to count the steps under his breath, *one-two-three, one-two-three* as Izzy lightly hummed the melody. Away from Bill and the others, Noel was at least more cheerful, laughing at his stumbles and not gritting his teeth. Despite this, despite Noel's natural singing voice, despite the rhythms that drove his days—the sweep and toss of shovelling, the sweetness with which he moved in bed—his feet lacked any sense of it, and persisted in going their own way whenever possible. If the step was left, he went right. If he was meant to step backwards, he trod on Izzy's toes. After a good hour he threw up his hands.

"That's me done. I can't do it, Iz. I'm sorry, cobber. Sorry about your toes." He nodded at Izzy's boots, printed with the mud of Noel's.

"Never mind. We'll sort it out." He linked his arm around Noel's and they started for the house, pushed by a rude wind which sent leaves and grit swirling across the ground and smelled of the coming rain.

Rather than eat in the roofless courtyard the household had assembled in the newly plastered dining hall. With the circus cohort in attendance the long room was close to full, knots of people chattering at top volume. Fierce with hunger and feeling more than a little entitled to first servings, Izzy began making for the end of the room nearest the kitchen, Noel close behind.

"Gentlemen!" Alanson glided to intercept them, in full dinner dress, his starched collar fixed with a pink carbuncle that matched his rosy nose.

"Ah shit."

"But Mr Pound," Alanson oozed, "I merely wished to be the first to commend you for being such a ready and capable student of dance. Though I do wish I could say the same about you, Mr Peters."

Noel took a sharp breath, his chest swelling. "I beg your pardon?"

"I mean no offence, of course, but you're admittedly not the fleetest of foot, my dear b—my good friend."

"Perhaps not all of us are cut out for prancing around looking foolish," Noel gritted.

"Come to think of it," Izzy said the idea forming as he spoke, "perhaps he ought not to be dancing at all. His part in the play, that is. The angel's meant to be a bit soft in the head, right?"

"I'm afraid I don't follow," Alanson said through his tacked-on smile.

"I mean, he's a bit rubbish at things, ain't he? He can't tell men from women, he can't hold his drink, so why's he meant to be any good at dancing?"

"Suits me fine," Noel all but spat. "Well?"

For a moment and only a moment, Alanson looked like just what he was: an aging man in middling health with thinning hair and thinner prospects, living off handouts from a wife who despised him. Then he smiled, with a broad and genuine smile that knew nothing of disappointment.

"I see no reason why we cannot make such accommodations. Not to mention it allows me to focus more of my attentions on our star performer." He turned his broad and genuine smile on Izzy, whose guts suddenly filled with ice.

"Ah shit."

They kept the length of the room between themselves and Alanson until dinner was served. Mrs Owen had flat out refused to wash up for so many, and they used the basin of water in the kitchen to clean their own dishes. The rain had set in and made for a wet and nasty trip to the cottage. Without moon or starlight the little room was impossibly dark and Izzy knocked his shins several times feeling his way to the cupboard for a candle. By the time he had it lit, Noel was already out of his clothes and in bed.

He lay facing the wall, his shoulder rising and falling as if he were asleep, but when Izzy got in bed he rolled to face him. "Is it alright?" he murmured.

"Is what alright?"

"That I get let off of dancing in that farce and you don't?"

"It's part of the story, innit?"

"Yeah, but what do *you* think?" Noel's face was hard to read in the wavering half-light and Izzy answered carefully.

"I think it's not up to me what you do or don't do. You're the one who's got to do it."

"That's no kind of answer."

"I dunno. I don't suppose I mind. Like I said, you do what's best for you. If you're happy, so am I."

"But—"

"Hush. Let's leave it at that. It's been a devil of a day. Let's put it behind us."

La tempête

NOEL'S SENTIMENTS towards the play softened now that he needn't dance. One even caught him singing the tunes to himself, usually in the garden, most often *Mine Eyes Art Open*, a sentimental piece with a hymn-like pace perfectly suited to Noel's deep tenor. A love song by the angel on first seeing the actor out of stage drag, and not far off Noel's true feelings for Izzy.

Or so he hoped, though the evidence was there, in Noel's little kindnesses through the day, praising Izzy's growing knowledge of growing things, offering his hat to spare his freckling skin, soothing his aching hands at day's end with salve and tender touches. Even their lovemaking grew sweeter, a languid business of kissing and stroking and delicate teasing, sometimes more of a torment than when Noel took him roughly.

Between the hurly burly of garden work, play rehearsals, his duties to the household at large and Noel in particular, Izzy found his time on the high-wire a blessed respite. The only place where, if he told everyone around him to shut up, they did so without resentment. Best of all was when there was no one around at all, which is why Izzy preferred to do his practicing in the early morning.

There was touch of magic to being up there all alone, with nothing but the wind and the sound of the waves and one thin line keeping him tethered to the earth. Elating, enervating, and that was even when he fell. Which was happening less and less, and not once this morning. A dangerous thought to have in the middle of a transit, but he let it go like smoke on the breeze and kept moving, the upward slant of the hawser telling his feet they were nearing their goal.

As he often did, Miguel arrived to see the end of Izzy's session. Of any possible observer Izzy minded him the least, for he always offered useful comments on how Izzy might improve and more importantly knew when to say nothing at all. As Izzy descended the swaying rope ladder Miguel came to meet him at the base.

"I knew from first seeing you that this was meant for you," he said warmly, throwing his arm around Izzy's shoulders.

"It's not so hard, once you get the knack."

"Yes. The knack. And having got it, I say you are ready for a true challenge."

"Eh?"

"If one wishes to impress the punters, as you call them, it's not enough for you merely to reach the other side."

He shrugged off Miguel's arm. "What about them jumps?"

"Yes, very pretty. I remember when I learned to do that. I must have been oh, six years of age."

Izzy stuck out his tongue. "There's to your six years. Not all of us were born into it."

"Of course not. Now, let's see how heavy you are

on top of me."

His cheeks heating more from the thought of Noel hearing someone speak such words to him than from the words themselves, Izzy followed Miguel to the low pole that served as training for tricks to be done in the air. Here Miguel turned his back to Izzy and stuck out his arse.

"Come, you will mount."

"I will? Oh, I see." Miguel was holding his cupped hand by his hip, offering a place for Izzy's foot so that he could climb onto Miguel's back. "Are you certain I won't be too heavy?"

"We will know soon enough, no?"

Muttering a prayer, questioning both their sanity, Izzy set his hands on Miguel's shoulders and his foot in Miguel's hand.

"On my count," Miguel said, bending his knees. Izzy bent with him, and on the word *tres!* he kicked off with his grounded foot, Miguel hoisting his other.

"Fucking hell! You might have warned me!" For Miguel's shove had levered Izzy so high there was nothing for it but to swing his leg clear over. Likely not the effect intended as he landed hard astride Miguel's shoulder, his cods smack dab against Miguel's ear, his only handhold Miguel's head.

"You are pulling out my hair," Miguel snarled, writhing under Izzy's panicked grip, his legs buckling under them both.

"Let go of my other foot, you berk!" Miguel's legs gave way at last and they collapsed in a shouting, swearing heap, Izzy's leg pinned under Miguel, whose head was pressed unbearably against Izzy's crotch.

"Ow! Gerroff!" With a mighty heave he wrenched

himself out from under Miguel and got to his feet. "Not a chance you'll get me to try that on a wire."

"Not yet."

"Not ever."

"Come, let's try again."

With more sense of what to do, Izzy managed to mount to Miguel's shoulders and cling there for a dozen paces. The dismount was another puzzle, and he slithered off gracelessly then declared the lesson finished.

Noel was alone in the garden, none of their usual helpers in sight. He was digging a trench alongside the celery bed, using the soil to cover the growing stalks and keep them from greening, and for a change he and Izzy stood nose to nose.

"What's your pleasure, Mr Peters?"

"Steady, you," Noel said, glancing about. "We're right out in the open."

"I meant around the garden, you flirt. What d'you need me to do?"

Though it wasn't much past midsummer Noel was already planning for autumn, and set Izzy to seeding spinach in the shade beneath the pea vines, a mindless task that ought to have fallen to one of the youth. All of whom seemed to making a holiday as there was no one about, though it was a poor day for enjoyment, the wind gusting hard, the clouds piling up in the west in a way Izzy had learned meant rain by sundown. Perhaps country life was beginning to stick. His hip ached where he'd fallen on it and he couldn't help but groan as he got to his feet.

"What's wrong now?" Noel called across the beds.

"Nothing. I fell earlier. Only it were on the ground

and not the net."

Noel tsked, shaking his head as he turned back to his task. Long association with a man gave you time to find his faults. Noel's worst was his habit of muttering under his breath. His mother had a dodgy ear from a girlhood bout of fever and missed much of wasn't said to her face, allowing her husband the last word in every argument. Like clockwork, there went Noel, grumbling into his neck as he yanked the spade from the side of the celery trench.

"What's that you said?"

Sucking his lips, Noel jammed the spade back in the soil. "I said, I don't know why you put yourself through all that."

"Cos I like it. Not the falling bit, but being up the air, feeling like I can fly. Up there where I don't have to pay attention to a thing except getting across."

"That'd be why you hurt yourself, because you ain't paying attention."

"That's not what I meant. It's more like I'm paying so much attention to that one thing, I can't be worrying about anything else."

"Like keeping from breaking your neck?"

"Come off it, cobber, what's the matter with you?" Izzy said as Noel carried on digging. "Ever since herself went to Paris you've been in a snit."

"Forgive me for having Ursula's safety in mind."

"Yeah, but you can't do naught about it from here. Besides, she's with Clyde. Best to leave it alone."

"Must be nice, being able to choose not to care for someone."

"That tears it." Izzy marched over to Noel, who surely noticed him but chose to keep on shovelling dirt on his precious celery. "I don't like being cross with you but…well, how dare you!" This fetched Noel up, and he lowered his spade to stare as Izzy barrelled on. "Just because I'm not fretting myself sick about a woman who's more than capable of defending herself doesn't mean I haven't any feeling for her."

"That's not what I said."

"Not in so many words, but what was I meant to take from that? So go on, say your piece. How exactly am I letting you down?"

"What?"

"I must be doing something wrong for you to be so out of sorts."

"You're not."

"Promise?"

And he couldn't, his mouth open but saying nothing. Izzy had used the word 'gutted' of past disappointments but he'd never felt it so acutely, as if Noel's silence was digging a hole in his stomach. Before he started yelling, or possibly crying, he walked away.

"Iz…Izzy, wait," Noel gasped, panic in his voice. "Can't we talk about this later?"

"No. Now, or not at all," he spat over his shoulder, making for the fence.

"It's just I'm right in the middle of something."

"Oh yes, it's absolutely vital the fucking celery get immediately even more planted than it already is. I'll just fuck off somewhere to doubt your faith in me while you shovel some more shit."

Corroded by years of salted air, the old latch on the gate was stuck fast again. Sick to the teeth of second-hand rubbish, of making do with rusty tools and nothing but beans for supper, of putting up with Alanson's jeering and leering, of wondering whether a bit of it was worth it, he levelled a vicious kick at the gate, which rattled but refused to give.

"Damn it! Damn this blasted gate," he cried, kicking it again and harder. "Damn the garden and this whole sodding life!"

Noel's shouted reply was drowned out by a monstrous crack of thunder, the grey wall of oncoming clouds lit stark white as if by a photographer's flash-pan. Another blinding flash and crash tore across the sky, casting the tossing treetops in lurid silhouette.

"My girls!" Noel cried. "I can't leave them out in this."

"You see to the birds. I'll manage around here."

"You sure?" he asked, already climbing over the gate.

"Just get on before it rains, you berk."

As Noel dashed towards the henhouse Izzy began gathering the tools to store them in the hutch. Though the rain had yet to start, the wind was growing fiercer by the minute, bending the trees near in half and sending dust and leaf litter skipping along the ground. He was washing his hands when Miguel came running.

"*Vamos!* All hands!" he cried. "Or we'll lose everything." Without waiting for a reply he took off the way he'd come, gesturing madly for Izzy to follow.

The wind was truly terrific this close to the shore, pulling hard on the wire as the poles swayed, the sandlot a Bedlam of shouting men and women and snorting horses and children running everywhere

190

trying to be useful by getting in everyone's way. Izzy joined Miguel at the end of a gang holding a rope which held the high-wire while on the opposite platform a figure worked frantically to untie it.

As another peal of thunder split the air, a gust came racing across the ground, inflating the staked tarpaulin beneath the wire like a ship's sail. Rather than have it yank out its uprights, they next set to unlashing it, and Izzy was holding one of the loose corners when Noel came pelting out of the woods.

"What in hell are you doing?" he cried over the roar of the wind.

"Being useful," Izzy shouted back

"What about the bloody garden?"

"I was done."

As Noel drew breath to argue further the wind cast a handful of grit in his face and he broke off coughing. Someone shrieked from the direction of the beach, and then the rain was upon them. It was as if the clouds had scooped up the sea and thrown it at them, Izzy drenched to the skin by the time they'd folded the tarpaulin in quarters and brought it under the trees where Noel huddled, rain dribbling down his neck.

"Ours or the house?" Noel shouted in his ear.

"The house is nearer."

Off they ran, splashing through puddles and avoiding the tallest trees, the lighting and thunder unceasing. As they neared the rear of the house, one of the glassed doors to the ballroom opened and someone gestured to them. Annie met them with towels, for the household had gathered to watch the storm from the room's vantage which looked across the terraced gardens to the sea. Not that one could see it past the grey wall of rain.

Though the worst of the storm soon passed, the rain went on until dusk. Wearing dry clothes culled from the play wardrobe, he and Noel crossed the drenched lawn to the garden to assess the damage. A tree limb had fallen, catching on the fence and thus sparing the beds for the most part. They removed this, righted the pea trellises which had canted to one side but stayed upright, then carried on to their cottage. This had fared worse, for the wicked wind had torn away a section of the musty thatch from the roof and a great puddle lay on the floor directly in front of the bed.

"What a shit of a day," Noel groaned, easing himself into the chair furthest from the puddle.

"Never mind," Izzy said as he felt around for damp spots at the bottom of the trunk where they kept their things. "There'll be room for us back at the house."

"That's not the point."

"Then what? So there's a bit of rain."

"This is not a bit of rain," he said, jerking his head towards the hole in the thatch. "What's more, it's going to murder them seeds you put in today."

"So we'll plant more. There was plenty left in the jar."

As Noel sat grumbling, Izzy packed their blankets and a few other bits into the trunk, then between them they carried it to the house. Here they were granted one of the better bedrooms, with a carven monstrosity of a four-poster and a credenza whose drawers were surprisingly free of mildew.

Again Izzy played valet, unpacking their sparse belongings while Noel moped, scuffing his heels and peering behind the curtains as he muttered to himself. As if he hoped for Izzy to call him out, demand he speak up, say his piece and be done with it. But there were ways and there were ways, and Izzy was not going to let one rotten day spoil their happiness.

Noel had sat on the edge of the bed, his elbows on his knees, and didn't look up as Izzy approached. "Noel…Noelly, what's wrong?"

"Nothing."

"It don't seem like nothing. What have I done?" He crouched at Noel's feet to look him in the eye.

With a grunt and a sour look Noel sat upright. "You haven't done a thing, all right?"

"Then what gnawing on you? We been at odds all day, you and me. So if it's not me, what is it?"

He stared at Izzy a moment, the words catching on his tongue, until he threw up his hands in frustration. "I don't know. I don't know why I'm so bloody miserable. I just can't stop thinking about everything that's about to go wrong."

"Like what?"

"Like everything. Alanson's bloody play, and Ursula being gone so long, and us having to keep all these damned people alive. One more bad day could ruin us."

"Noelly…"

"I'm sorry. I'm not making sense."

"You are, but…shit, cobber. You can't be thinking about all that. You'll drive yourself mad. And we'll get by, never fear. Even if we have to chuck the lot of this over and make our own way. If I've still got you, nothing else matters."

"You got me, alright."

"And I ain't letting go."

Noel laughed, a single hoarse gasp, then pulled Izzy up to him, the kiss rather spoiled by their teary sniffling, the kiss not the point.

"So am I forgiven?" Izzy asked once he had settled on Noel's lap.

"You didn't do nothing wrong."

"But if I did, you'd tell me, right? Because maybe I won't know it was wrong until after I done it."

"Of course."

"Promise?"

"I promise."

They kissed again, this one much better, Noel's his lips as soft as his body was hard. "You gotta promise me the same, though," he said as Izzy nuzzled into his musky embrace.

"What d'you mean?"

"Promise to tell me if I ever do something to hurt you without knowing I've done so."

Izzy nodded, his throat tight, his words unequal to his emotions. Noel was satisfied, smiling as he kissed him once more. The best kiss yet.

La jalousie

A DARK ROOM. A broad bed with slippery sheets, Noel faintly snoring beside him. A lingering tenderness below that suggested a lively night. He ought to rise before the maids came knocking. He sat up…and woke properly, the dream that was half memory dissipating as he took in his surroundings: the time-stained panelling, the fading curtains, the grotesque marquetry in the bed's headboard showing a Grecian lady being pounced on by a wizened man with the legs of a goat. Not an overpriced hotel room in Liverpool but a bedroom in Marisol's manor.

Izzy lay back and shut his eyes. If Noel wasn't awake he needn't be either. Yet this early in the day, he could get in a good bit of practice before Miguel or Petra or one of the others got to the wire. Away from their experienced eyes he was free to fail without shame. Or losing his turn, which mattered more when he had only so much time in a day.

His feet were drenched with dew by the time he reached the sand lot, and he dried them on his trouser legs before putting on his slippers, even lighter of sole than the ones he wore for dancing. Two crows were watching from the wire and took off heavily as he began to climb the rope ladder. On the platform he paused to wriggle his toes, loosen his ankles, keeping his eyes on the distant treetops. A trick of the mind as much as the body, as without further ado he took the first step…

And was across. The first crossing of the day was always a blur, a blankness in his memory, as if the knowledge of doing something so patently dangerous was too much to be borne. Yet he'd done it, and with less haste he returned to the other platform. On the third pass he paused in the middle to practice a few hops and switches. Petra did a thing where she lay down, but Izzy hadn't the nerve to try. What he was practicing with Miguel was challenge enough when he was still so new to the sport.

He worked at his steps for a good half hour and had come back to ground when Miguel arrived, slippers in hand. "Good morning, my friend. Have you finished already with your practice?"

"Not if you're up for it."

"I am indeed. I feel strong today, friend."

"Here's hoping. It's a lot farther to fall when I'm that much farther in the air."

Izzy ascended first, the tiny platform creaking ominously as Miguel joined him. "Any chance you're ever going to add another plank to this?"

"*Que?*" Staring at the other platform, Miguel was barely listening, all his mind on the coming crossing.

"Never mind."

Mainly by feel, Izzy turned in place then climbed a little farther up the pole using the pegs driven into either side. Blessing the sweat-soaked cotton tape wound around his hands, he glanced over his shoulder. Miguel stood at the ready, his knees flexed, hand out to catch Izzy's foot.

"*Vamos*," he grunted, not looking back.

"Kiss my arse. I will when I'm ready. Okay, I'm ready."

And now the very most difficult trick of all, as Izzy leaned away from the pole then let go with one hand and foot and stepped onto Miguel's extended hand then with his other hand let go of the only solid object remaining between him and a very long drop. Nothing to worry about, his one leg already over Miguel's shoulder, and now the other.

"Ooh…I hate that bit."

The twenty paces to the far platform was a lot more menacing when was the other fellow doing the pacing. Miguel waited while Izzy found his balance, straightened his spine and firmed up his knees and quit clutching his hair. Setting his gaze on the top of the distant pole, Izzy extended his arms to either side. Miguel sensed the difference in his posture, and with a last deep inhalation set out.

On the ground, Miguel was strong enough almost to run while bearing Izzy this way. In the air, every step was a tiny miracle, Miguel's thighs quivering, his breathing forceful, his grip on Izzy's shins painful but unquestioned. Seconds later, it was done, Miguel was on the far platform, sinking to one knee for Izzy to clamber off his shoulders and grab hold of something solid once again. The pole, and the ladder was right there, and not waiting for Miguel's word he slithered down it and back to solid ground.

Grinning madly, Miguel came down straight after and clasped Izzy to him in a crushing embrace. "I knew you could do it!"

"*We* did it!" Izzy crowed. "Though I can't half believe it!"

"All you needed was time." Showy as ever with his feelings, Miguel kissed Izzy wetly on each cheek. "Did I not say you were meant for this?"

"Do you suppose we'll ever manage it again?"

"Of course. But now is not the time to try. No, first let us celebrate what we have done."

"I gotta tell Noel!"

"Tell me what, exactly?" For Noel was standing at the edge of the clearing, fists on his hips, murder in his eyes.

"We was just trying a new trick," Izzy said as Noel stomped towards them.

"Yeah, well, you best untry it. And as for you," he snarled at Miguel, who was retreating with his hands raised, "touch him again and I swear I'll break you in half." Noel rounded on Izzy again, pulling up short at his furious expression.

"Fucking hell, Peters!" he grated, doing his level best not to bellow. "What in hell's wrong with you?"

"You ought to worry about your own behaviour. You and that…Miguel." He said the name like a curse.

"So he had a hand on me."

"And his mouth."

"That's just his way. He kisses Clyde, for fuck's sake! Come off it, Peters, why are you being such a shit? You can't think…" There it was again, that gut punch, that hollowness, to think that Noel still didn't trust him. "Is that what's got you so bent out of shape? You think I'm plotting to give you up for *him*? Stars above, credit me with a bit of sense, will you?"

Chewing at his lips, his cheeks flaring, Noel looked

away. "You saying he ain't handsome?" he mumbled.

"Handsome is as handsome does, but he ain't got nothing on you."

Noel hissed, shaking his head. "I ain't nothing to look at."

"To my eyes you are." Izzy stepped nearer. "And that's not the point. He could look like a bleeding Adonis but he's still not gonna be you. Whom I love. Him who I don't is just a pretty man."

Noel shook his head again. "I still don't trust him."

"It's not him you've got to trust. It's me, and you ought to know well enough where I stand."

"But what if he tries something on?"

"Then I'll bleeding well break him in half! Noel, cobber…I punched a prince for you. I've put lords on their knees and made them weep."

"So what are you saying?"

"So I ain't afraid to fight a man, is all I'm saying. So who gives a damn whether Miguel fancies me? He can take his fancy and shove it up his arse for all I care. After what I put him through on the daily, looking at me he likely thinks, saints preserve me from this gormless twit."

Noel didn't reply, kicking at grass, looking anywhere but at Izzy, though he didn't balk when Izzy took his hand. "If I'm being honest, I don't half mind you being a touch jealous. It's a bit of a compliment, ain't it?" he went on as Noel looked up sharply. "For you to get this fussed over little no-account me."

"You're no such thing. And I'm sorry for acting the fool. It's stupid of me to think I can't trust you."

"Maybe a bit. But I won't let this come between us. I want—" He wanted more than words could encompass: safety, security, freedom from persecution, wealth enough to sustain them, a future for them both.

"I want us to stay happy," he said gently as he slipped his arms round Noel's waist. "I've seen what happens when someone holds a grudge against a person they're meant to love. It's poison and I'm not doing it."

He rose up to kiss Noel, who for a change didn't stiffen and pull away in fear of being found out, instead kissed him back, held him closer. A mythical kiss, amid towering trees alive with the wind, the sunlight glancing through the leaves, and the world's most perfect man in his arms.

"I don't half deserve you," Noel murmured, his forehead pressed to Izzy's.

"To hell with deserving. No one alive deserves a blessed thing. If it ain't earned, it ain't yours. And I earned you, Mr Peters. Didn't I?" Mute with feeling, Noel nodded. "Good. Now for fuck's sake, and I mean that in the most literal terms, for the sake of a fuck, take me home."

"But the garden—" Noel started.

"It can wait."

"And I'm meant to talk to—"

"It can wait. Everything can wait. Except me. Please?"

PUTTING ONESELF IN peril left a man with a powerful hunger. Add an ugly row and a boisterous mid-morning bedding, and Izzy refused to touch a garden implement until he'd put something in his belly.

Whistling a snatch of *Month of Sundays*, one of Alanson's better songs, he pranced through the front door, along the corridor, and into the kitchen where he skidded to a halt. The girl Esme was sitting on her usual stool by the scullery door, gazing at him with her startling eyes, their vivid blue ringed with lashes so blond they seemed white. Sober, placid, and frighteningly observant, she seemed less a child than a miniature adult, always spurring in Izzy an urge to apologize for his very existence.

A clatter of crockery announced Sal, who emerged from the pantry with a pile of roughly cut jam-and-butter sandwiches on a plate. "Here we are, Ducky," they said to Esme, holding out the plate. "Help yourself."

"My mummy will come home today," the girl said in her tiny voice as she took one of the sandwiches.

"Is that so?" Sal asked, exchanging a look with Izzy.

Esme moved her eyes to and fro as if reading from a page. Then she nodded. "Yes. Will there be enough supper?"

"We'll be sure to tell Mrs Owen to make a little more."

"I expect you wonder how I know who my mummy is," she said, holding the sandwich in both hands though she had yet to take a bite. "Would you like to know how I guessed?"

"If you feel like telling us."

"I saw myself in a looking-glass in Lady Marisol's room. It was last Tuesday. I had guessed already, for I often saw her at the park speaking with Papa. But when I saw the glass I was quite certain." She bit into the sandwich, not the mouse's nibble Izzy expected but with a great chomp, her cheeks puffing.

"Are you sad she didn't tell you?" Sal asked gently.

Esme pondered, chewing hugely. "Yesh," she said around her mouthful. Then she swallowed. "But then I'm quite often sad."

Sal glanced at Izzy again, whose stomach was knotting around Esme's matter-of-factness. "I expect she had a good reason not to tell you," he said.

The girl tipped her head, considering this. "I think that she must have been afraid."

"Of what, ducky?" Sal asked, leaning down to better see the girl's face.

"Of me."

"Of you?"

She nodded solemnly. "Afraid that I would be angry with her. That I might not want her to be my mother after all. That would make any mother at least a little bit afraid."

Sal chucked the girl on her tiny chin. "Anyone ever tell you how smart you are, Ducky?"

"Not in those particular words. Mrs Pennyworth very often said I was too clever for my own good. I think what she meant was that I was too clever for *her* good."

Sal laughed out loud. "I think you're right, Ducky. Maybe we can ask Mrs Owen to cook something special for your mama's homecoming."

"I think she likes honey," Esme said as Sal helped her from her perch. "We might put some in a cake."

"That's a good idea," Sal said, taking the tiny hand, though when they tried leading Esme towards the back door the girl balked.

"We're going this way, Sal."

"As you like, Ducky."

Hand in hand the pair left the kitchen. Izzy went into the pantry and cut himself a thick chunk of bread and a piece of cheese then scrammed before Owen arrived to tell him off for overeating or spilling crumbs or whatever he'd done wrong without even knowing it. With so many people putting expectations on him, it seemed he couldn't take a step these days without earning a scolding.

A quiet afternoon in the garden was just the tonic his jangled nerves required, yet not halfway to the patch he heard a shout go up from the roadway. He wasn't so stupid as to face trouble on his own and unarmed, so kept on towards the garden to collect Noel and something sharp to swing at whoever was attempting to storm their castle. Yet there was Noel, standing on the drive, smiling broadly at the newcomers, waving like a boy at a boat launch. Izzy trotted to meet him, his questions answered as he saw the cart approaching, Ursula riding tall in the seat, Clyde as usual more comfortable walking beside.

By the time they reached the house the whole gang had assembled, circus folk and whores together, and they greeted the pair with a cheer. Smiling more than usual, that is to say at all, Ursula addressed them from the cart.

"You are most kind to welcome us so. I have sorely missed you all. And so that I may answer your questions in advance rather than have to tell again and again: yes, my business has concluded successfully. I met with no difficulty but delay, for which I apologize."

"Never mind that, ma'am," Annie called. "Just so

long as you're well."

"I am, and again, I thank you."

Someone aided her down from the cart, the crowd parting to allow her to pass. Partway to the house, she paused to speak with Sal. Whatever she heard, her face froze. Sal beckoned and wee Esme came scurrying from her hiding place behind the pillar on the porch, clutching her rag-doll.

She stopped five steps away from Ursula, who returned her daughter's glacial stare. Then Ursula reached out her hand. Esme looked from the hand to her mother's face. With careful steps she approached, then took the extended hand. Ursula inhaled sharply, her shoulders lifting as though she was about to take wing and soar into the sky.

"You need me right now, Ducky?" Sal asked. Esme shook her head, making her blond plaits twitch. Then she went into the house with Ursula, though it was not clear which of them was leading.

The stalwart Clyde meanwhile had organized a crew to unload the crates from the cart. The largest were empty, claimed at once by Alanson for constructing the stage sets. The last crate was much smaller, and Clyde pried off the coarse planks to reveal a neater box with the words *Etude H Gallant* stencilled on the side. He pointed to Izzy and Noel then the box, suggesting it was theirs.

"That's a big box of seeds, cobber," Izzy teased as Noel levered off the nailed-on top of the box with his knife. "You going to try growing coconuts?"

"I haven't a clue what's in here."

"She tell you anything?" Izzy asked Clyde, who began to spell with his fingers, a talent he'd been teaching anyone willing to learn but which wholly surpassed Izzy's scant intellect. "What's he saying?" he asked Sal who had joined them at the cart.

"Photographs, I think."

Clyde nodded.

"Photographs for us?" Noel asked as he peered inside.

"No. *Of* us," Izzy said, for now he recalled the photographer's name. "Hang on, don't take 'em out!" he cried as Noel reached into the box. "That lot's for our eyes only."

Noel carried the box directly to their room upstairs. As well as the original plates, Herve had provided prints of each, and they sat side by side on the bed to look through them.

"Well…" Izzy breathed. "There I am."

"You certainly are," Noel replied hoarsely.

"You look marvellous."

"You as well."

He ought to thank Noel for the compliment. He was having a hard time breathing. This was a sight unseen. Unseeable, for no one bent so far as to be able to see their own arse. Freely available however to the camera's cold eye.

Izzy had gone to the odd art gallery in recent years, wandered past the old paintings and wondered what made them so worthy. Now and then he had thought he understood, from the particular way such and such artist had captured the light breaking through a cloud, or the subtlety in the model's face that made her more than just a pretty girl. Somehow despite the unambiguous subject matter, Herve's photographs had a touch of that beauty, exceeding Izzy's expectations, threatening his understanding of how a man ought to appear.

"We ought to put these away," Noel murmured thickly.

His tongue feeling glued to the roof of his mouth, Izzy nodded. Passed him the clutch of cards. Noel went to the credenza and put the cards in the box. By the time he turned around, Izzy was naked. By the time he reached the bedside, so was Noel.

They didn't accomplish every act depicted in the photographs, but it was only mid-afternoon, and what's more the second tumble of the day. After, Izzy dressed slowly, reluctant to emerge from his lovely haze of spent pleasure, for dinner promised to be rowdy with Ursula returned. He was pulling on his stockings when Noel sat beside him.

"Can I ask you something?"

"You just did, but go on."

Laughing, frowning, he knocked Izzy's shoulder with his. "You're such an arse. But will you show me? How you walk the wire?"

"Of course."

Some youngsters were fooling about on the training pole but at this hour no one was on the scaffold. The afternoon sun glaring in his eyes for half the crossings, Izzy put on his best show, hopping and spinning and trying not to notice when Noel gasped in alarm. One day that might be a hundred people, or a thousand, their breath catching in their throats as they feared for his safety. Trembling from the thought, from the effort, from the two hard fucks and his endless want for another, he descended the wobbly ladder with care. Noel caught him up, held him tightly, near lifting his feet from the ground.

"Can't breathe…"

Noel softened his embrace. "Sorry. I'm just glad you're in one piece. That weren't easy to watch."

"It's not easy to do."

"But you're good at it, aren't you?"

"Seems like. And of all the things I've ever been good at, it's surely the most moral."

"Is it?" Noel asked as Izzy sat on the ground to take off his slippers. "You hear a lot of shocking things about the theatre."

"Oh no, it's not full of sodomites, is it? Heavens, I'll stick out like a sore thumb."

"Be serious."

"I am being serious. I've got to make something of myself, don't I? What else have I got? Without you I'm hopeless in the garden, and I haven't any other trade save for the one I gave up. So why shouldn't I try and make a go of what seems to come natural?"

"I just worry…" Noel said as Izzy got to his feet.

"You, worry? Never thought I'd see the day."

"I'm trying to pour my heart out, you twit."

"Sorry. Go on."

He looked away, collecting himself. "It's only, you've got so much ahead of you. New friends, new interests, a life that has nothing to do with me. I can't stand being on that stage, while you took to it like a fish to water. What happens when you get a part in a proper theatre?"

"*When*? Don't you mean *if*?"

"Serious, though. You've got talent. And what have I got?" He gestured at his stained work clothes. "Nothing but dirt. Dirt under my nails and dirt in my future."

"You've got me," Izzy said, pulling him close. "And I promise you, that won't ever change."

"How do you know?"

"Because I damn well say so. There's no one on earth I'd rather love than you, and you can't tell me that's going to change, because I won't let it."

"But—"

"Noel Erasmus Peters, you shut your foolish mouth. I love you to death, and you're just going to have to accept it."

At the house they sneaked upstairs, avoiding the thronging dining room, the others' oblivious good cheer. Izzy hadn't the stomach for a meal, craving only the surety that whatever came to pass, he and Noel would face it together. Wanting nothing in the world so much as this man's love, his kiss, his touch, to prove once again through the union of their bodies the enduring unity of their hearts.

THE APPLE

"**W**HAT'S IT LIKE?" Telford asked.

"I beg your pardon?"

"The wire tricks. The tumbling. I've a deathly fear of h-heights," the young man explained, the word enough to make him shudder. "I can't imagine what it's like to do."

"Right. The tumbling." Izzy took a drink from his empty glass to recover from his fright, for he'd wholly misunderstood Telford's question. And then to think of how to describe something he'd not spoken of in five years, something he'd not done in thirty…

"It were always a damned funny thing to put into words," he began. "It's a feeling, see? You ever been on a helter-skelter, at a fair or such? Well, imagine going on a slide that's a mile long. Just going and going, round and round." He spun his finger in the air in imitation, Telford following with crossed eyes. "You'd be humming, wouldn't you? Head to toe, flying that far, that fast. That's a bit like what it felt like. Like the wire was electrified and so were you."

"Electrified…"

"That's a wicked feeling in itself and not one I recommend. But never mind that, let's shift. He'll want this table eventually." For they'd talked for hours, until Maury had come out and teased him about whether he'd like to see the *carte à diner*. Or he'd talked and Telford had listened, his chin propped on his fist, his eyes starry, now and then alarmed. Why Izzy felt driven to confess so much was something neither of them was questioning, though there was more than one sort of trouble to be caused by a director becoming too fond of an actor.

Fodder for insomnia, though from the heavy feel of his limbs as they walked he might get lucky tonight. Loping beside him, Telford was chewing on his top lip as he did when making up his mind.

"Come on, out with it," Izzy croaked, for his throat was parched. He began to feel his pockets for his little tin of peppermint drops. "What's gnawing on you?"

"Oh. It's not important."

"That's what you always say. Go on, ask it."

"You don't have to tell me, but I can't help being curious how it is you and Noel grew so close. That is, you went from stealing from him, causing him to get beaten by his mother in front of the entire street to being…in love. Why did he even speak to you again?"

"Except to tell me to shove off, that is? God knows. Felt sorry for me, I expect. He was always a bit soft-hearted for little things." He'd found the tin of mints, but his hands were shaking and he returned it to his pocket unopened. The wind must have shifted, for he was suddenly sweating, his stomach clenched as if he stood on that tiny platform with all the world spread out before him, waiting to watch him fall.

"What's happening? Mr Pound, are you ill?"

He shook his head. "Just tired, lad. It's hard not to

feel my years when I think about myself that long ago."

He retrieved the mints, offered one to Telford, then they carried on walking. To nowhere in particular, but going home meant being alone with his mess of thoughts. Plenty of which had to do with this tale, which he might as well get on with telling.

"After that first time, when I pinched that apple, I stayed well away from Noel. I didn't want to get roped in by those brothers of mine again, didn't want to do him wrong, though I didn't exactly know why. But the Peters worked all over the city, so sometimes he ended up where I was."

"How I even got there…I was maybe ten years old when my mum fell pregnant again. I fair wanted to murder him over it. Da, I mean. Cause it was killing her." Fifty years on and his fists still clenched with futile rage. "Poor gel could barely eat, couldn't stir from bed. Da was such a shit he didn't bother buying food for his children. Took up residence at the gin house. My brothers, they found enough jobs to keep themselves out of the workhouse, but no one would give my narrow arse a look, never mind a wage. I tried begging for a bit but it was too hard getting spat on."

"Oh my."

"How deep the well of good old Christian charity, hey? So I couldn't tell you where I was precisely, which part of the city. Some alley I'd dossed down in the night before cause I didn't have it in me to walk home. All of a sudden, there it was."

"What?"

"An apple. He was trying to give me an apple."

"Noel was?"

"Like as not it was bruised, one that had fallen off

the cart, but it was the prettiest thing I'd ever seen."
Even now he could picture it, nestled in Noel's grimy
pink palm, glowing like the sun.

"Bright yellow it was, with a smear of red. And it
smelled like nothing on earth. Like paradise. He sort
of shoved it at me then ran off. I could barely get my
teeth into it. But I ate it down to the seeds. Then I
hear this voice: *you go give him a right clout round the ear
and tell him come here.*"

As Telford goggled at Izzy's mimic of Mrs Peters
he went on. "Next thing I knew, he was back. Said
his mum wanted a word. I said I weren't in the mood
for talking. So he did what she'd said, gave me a
smack—"

"You mean he hit you?"

"Not too hard. A little love tap. Anyway, it put
paid to me arguing. I couldn't have fought him to
save my life, the state I was in. Mrs Peters, though,
was she ever fierce. Talking about all she'd do to my
father if only she laid hands on him. I must have ate
about six apples in a row. She just kept putting 'em in
my hand."

"My goodness. She saved your life."

"Maybe she did. At any rate, after about a week of
this, Mum lost the child, thank the Lord. But she got
her strength back, started taking work again, washing
and mending and such. Things levelled out at home.
I quit hanging round the Peters' stall so much. Still, it
was good to know I had someone in my corner. I owe
that woman so much. I wish…" More than he had
strength to say. "I wish I'd got the chance to tell her
how sorry I was for taking her son from her."

"No," Telford said urgently. "You didn't take him

from her. You *loved* him."

"But I changed him."

"People change regardless. I've changed."

"Since you've met me, which makes it my fault again."

Telford smiled. "Fine. You're a dreadful person who ought to be locked up."

"That's more like it."

THE TERROR

TELFORD TOOK HIS time going home, weighed down by his thoughts: of nature and desire, longing and loss, and the struggle to go on living when your life has been taken from you. Lessons he had learned first-hand, though the teaching had nearly killed him.

He'd been too young, too hurt already by fear and poverty when his mother died to have much strength left for living. It had taken the orphanage nearly a month to find his next-of-kin. Not one day of which he remembered, for he had lain catatonic in bed the whole time, frozen in impenetrable grief. When his aunt at last came to retrieve him, he had needed to be carried to the hired car. His uncle had shown less patience, and when his curt manner had failed to move Telford from his miserable stupor, he had turned first to threats then to violence.

Shut out of the house one night for blubbing, he had heard the neighbour's boy crying. Had asked through the fence if he was hurt. Had been told off most obscenely by young Cian, recently arrived from a Londonderry orphanage, apprenticed to Gilbert the tailor whether that was his wish or not.

Yet Telford had persisted, making up to the boy across the fence with the caution of someone luring a stray cat. An act of pure necessity, for he had had no playmates, been given no time for play. Those stolen moments of conversation, at times confession, those stray touches through the gap: these constituted the whole of their friendship, save for the rare nights he'd taken refuge in the Gilberts' potting shed when Ned's rage had been truly terrifying.

Soon Telford would have no need to hide in a shed. He was going to make his mark on the stage and leave these humble beginnings behind. Get lodgings of his own, somewhere he'd never have to see his uncle. Even if it meant not seeing Cian again.

His steps slowed then halted, as if his feet were unwilling to take him any nearer that future. It didn't have to be so. If anything, his freedom would grant him the chance to know Cian properly. Assuming Cian wished to know *him* better. They'd shared so little time he couldn't say with certainty that there was anything to their friendship beyond the natural sympathy shared between the downtrodden, as if they were prisoners in adjoining cells.

He carried on, no answers to be found by lingering in the darkening streets. As he started down the alley behind the bakery, the Gilberts' gate opened a crack and Cian slipped out.

"What's wrong?" he asked as Telford joined him in the shadow of the wall.

"Nothing's wrong."

"Don't be daft," Cian chided, though he was grinning. "I know when you're not yourself."

"There's no fooling you, is there?" Why would he bother? There was no one he trusted more than Cian. His best, his only friend. The very last person he wanted to harm. "And you're right. I'm not myself. This life, the stage and all that comes with it, well, I know it's going to change me. But I promise you, one thing will never change."

Alone, unseen, wrapped in the shadow of night, he reached for, found Cian's hand. "This. Us. No matter what the future brings, you shall always mean more to me than anyone. You're the reason I've come so far. And I won't ever leave you behind."

"You can't say such things," Cian whispered, his hand trembling in Telford's, his eyes sparkling even in the dark. Starry eyed, star-crossed, and if Telford's life were a play, this would be the last scene, the resolution, when all the audience's dreams came true…

It was only his life, the spell breaking at the clatter of bin lids from the next yard over. Letting go of Cian's hand, he stepped back, away from the impossible. "I best get in before I'm missed."

"God bless you, Telly." A whisper and he was gone.

Telford slipped the latch on own gate and edged through. He tiptoed across the moonlit yard, retrieved the spare key from behind the loose brick, and unlocked the door. A corridor ran from the back of the house to the front, with the rooms opening to the left. From the nearest doorway spilled the fluttering light of a kerosene lamp turned low.

Telford nearly slammed the door and ran. The last time he'd dodged his uncle's judgement, Ned had dipped the strap in carbolic first. Yet that had been years ago. Telford wasn't a boy any longer but a man. A man paralyzed by a fear that went down to his bones.

"Hurry up, lad. And lock the door."

"Yes, Uncle Ned." He pulled the door to, put the key in and turned it halfway, then back. He left it in the keyhole then walked towards the flickering light, which was suddenly occluded by Uncle Ned's bulk.

"I told you to hurry up."

"Sorry, Uncle." He entered the kitchen, casting his eyes about for anything out of place, any particular cause of Ned's rage, but it was as neat as he would have left it himself.

"Get used to the sight, lad. You'll be seeing nothing but, from here on."

"What do you mean?"

"I got rid of that boy. I told you not to get tangled up with that vile little man. But like always, you're too stupid to learn a lesson I don't beat into your thick skull." He advanced on Telford, who stepped back, trying to keep the table between them.

"Don't touch me."

"I'll do what I have to, to make sure you know your place. As of this moment, you're done with that theatre rubbish, permanently. You set foot in that sinful place again, I'll burn it to the ground."

"Why do you hate me so?" A question Telford had always wanted to ask, even at the cost of hearing the answer.

"It's not you I hate," Ned spat. "It's that godforsaken queer who's ruining you. Just like your wretched father ruined my sister."

"You know nothing about him."

"It's you who don't know anything. You didn't see how that man twisted my sweet sister around his finger. Dragging her up and down the country on his seditious business. Not even his death set her free. He'd already poisoned her mind as surely as he poisoned her body with drink."

"You're wrong!"

"And you're a fool. If it wasn't for worrying about you, she'd have given up that nonsense and come home like a sensible girl, instead of hauling you off to the ends of the earth. She deserved everything that happened to—"

"Shut your wretched mouth!" Telford cried. He ducked away in time for Uncle Ned's open-handed slap to only catch him a glancing blow to the side of his head. It still stung like anything, sending him staggering against the benches.

Blocking Telford's way to the door, Ned circled the table with the doubled strap in his other hand, his eyes demonic, his face in a rictus of rage. Here it came, the end Telford had feared every day of the last ten years, the beating that went beyond. The one that ended his life. If he stayed.

The bench tops were clear of any object he might hurl, even to cause a distraction. The table as well, its bulk the only thing between him and his uncle. *It's simple, you twit. You shove the box, the box shoves him.* Mr Pound had shouted those very words at him this morning: the stage directions for the song *Switcheroo*.

With every bit of his strength, Telford hurled himself not at his uncle but at the table between them. It shifted a surprising distance, the legs scraping noisily over the stone floor as Uncle Ned stumbled back. Scant protection, but it halted his advance enough for Telford to bolt from the room, thanking the Father, the Virgin, and Divine Providence just in case, for having granted him the wisdom not to lock the back door.

Uncle Ned was after him before he'd crossed the yard, swinging the belt so it whistled through the air and caught Telford a wicked blow across the back of his legs. Not enough to slow him, and he burst through the yard door and took off down the alley as if all of Hell were at his heels.

HE LINGERED FOR a very long time in the doorway across from Mr Pound's flat. First to be sure no one had followed him, and then because he was ashamed. Ashamed to have been so dismissive of Mr Pound's offer to put him up for a night in this very situation. Ashamed to need help of this measure, and then of having tolerated a bad thing for so long, for having convinced himself he owed the Vandurenburgs everything.

On the landing outside Mr Pound's door he hesitated again. It was now quite late and the old man was certainly in bed, was unlikely to answer, would probably resent the intrusion. Telford pictured rehearsal tomorrow, the scolding Mr Pound would give him when he found out he'd slept in the park. It was an insult to spurn such a generous gift, wasn't it? It was likely too late in the evening to wonder, and so he knocked on the door.

After a half a minute, he heard the clatter of latches, and the door opened a crack. "Who goes there?"

"I'm sorry to bother you so late."

Mr Pound opened the door, his grin fading as he looked him over. "So. That bad, is it? Never mind, just come in."

The flat was less tidy than before, books standing in piles beside the shelves, some of the posters unpinned from the wall and lying on the table. The plant still lived in its coffee tin by the window, the tawny cat who'd assaulted it laying in that awkward cattish way across the back of the settee. Mr Pound waved a cushion at it to shoo it away. It opened one green eye, closed it again and resumed doing nothing.

"I don't mind," Telford said as Mr Pound went to scoop it up. "I like animals."

"If you're looking for a cat, I've one to spare. In the meanwhile, how's about a cuppa?"

"Let me make it."

"Be my guest."

Drinking the tea, they spoke of nothing much: the weather, the sample Mr Pound showed him of the poster for the upcoming show. The cat moved from the back of the settee to Telford's lap where it lapsed into its draped slumber as he absently petted its flank. He wanted to warn Mr Pound of Uncle Ned's shocking threat, but the danger seemed so distant, just noise. His uncle was prone to bursts of rage, not to breaking the law.

Well past midnight, Telford set aside his empty cup. "Thanks for the tea. I really I ought to be going."

"The hell you are," Mr Pound rasped, grabbing for his cane. "Are you out of your bleeding mind?"

"He usually does calm down after a while. Although this wasn't quite usual." Telford had succeeded in moving the cat, but his own legs proved less willing, his arms shaking and his palms sticking to the velour as he tried to push himself to his feet.

"Sit your fool arse down, Cline. Oh, bother…"

A man ought not to cry, but there was no stopping it, the long-lost name unleashing a cataclysm of emotion, the tears dripping through Telford's fingers as he sobbed into his hands.

"Here." Mr Pound held out a red flag the size of a dinner napkin, spotted all over with blue fleurs-de-lis. "It's clean, honest."

Telford took the handkerchief and blotted his face. Then cried some more for kindness' sake. Mr Pound sat beside him, saying nothing, now and then gently patting his back, until his tears ran dry.

"Well. Maybe I'll stay the one night."

"That's more like it."

THE TAIL

AFTER A NUMBER of hours spent lying down, during some of which he slept, Izzy accepted that the day had begun and that he'd soon need to greet it. Rising from bed, he groaned as he did every morning. From the sitting room came the sproing of the settee springs, followed by the cat's angry hiss and the sound of Telford falling all over himself in his haste to rush to the door of the bedroom.

"Are you all right?" he cried. Quite a question given Telford himself looked like he'd leapt backwards through a hedge and got stuck halfway, his clothes askew, his eyes panicked.

"I'm as good as I ever get. Now bugger off, I don't know you well enough to want you to see me like this." In nothing but his night shirt, his hair stratospheric, his old twig just wick enough with morning wood to both do him credit and shame him into the grave. He'd beg forgiveness for being curt when he had wit to do so.

Dusted and dressed, his teeth polished, his hair cruelly subdued by a perhaps overly generous dab of pomade, he emerged from his bedroom to find Telford had already made tea.

"You're certain there isn't anything wrong?" the lad

asked as he poured Izzy a cup.

"Nothing this and change of scenery won't cure," he replied, saluting Telford with the tea.

"That sounded painful, is all."

"I've felt worse of a morning. You think dancing takes the wind out of a man, try doing it on a wire thirty feet in the air."

After toast, which they bravely ate dry as there was nothing at all to put on it, they went together to rehearsal, which was one near-disaster after another. A doorway in the set had been built a hair too short and the door had to be taken off and planed so it would open. The piano's lower registers had slipped again and Larson spent half of rehearsal tuning it. The first lot of posters got printed wrong and would need to be remade, though Izzy was damned if it was going to be at his expense. And all of it with a mere three weeks until opening night.

Several blurry hours later, he sat at his desk, his head in his hands, waiting for Whitley to bring him a tea. Instead Telford brought the tea things, one rattling step at a time, wholly different from Whitley's cat-like creeping. There was a pause as the lad considered how to both hold a tea tray and open the office door. Stowing his grin, Izzy went to give a hand.

Whitley had done the lad a mean trick, loading the tray with the whole service, china cups and a sugar bowl and creamer and all, rather than the standard teapot and pair of chipped tin mugs. Izzy took the tray from him, poured for them both. Telford took up his cup like a holy thing, shutting his eyes to breathe in the steam.

"I see I'm not the only one feeling a bit rough."

Telford looked up, his blissful expression falling. "I'm sorry for last night. I shouldn't have burdened you with—"

"Hush. I offered, didn't I? And anymore it don't take much to keep me tossing and turning through the night."

"I'm amazed at your vigour."

"So am I, son. But never mind that. It's your shout today, innit?"

"I wish," Telford said, with a pained smile. "Money's a bit tight. And likely to stay that way," he added under his breath.

"I don't mind if it's sandwiches. It's been a few days."

Telford ducked his head. "Well, it's actually very tight. As in, I haven't a penny on me."

"Were you not planning to eat today?"

"Of course I'll eat. When I'm home."

"I've nothing much in the old larder, if you recall."

"Oh no, I couldn't impose again. I meant my home. My uncle's."

Izzy stared at the younger man, sick to his back teeth at the notion of Telford putting himself in such danger. Yet the lad had pride enough to chance it. "In that case, I guess it's my shout again."

"I can't possibly ask—"

"You didn't ask. I'm telling. I'm famished so I can't imagine how a great big thing like you must feel. Drink up and let's shift."

They returned the tea things to the tray and Telford carried it down to Whitley, who received it with his butlery blankness, save a certain tightness around the eyes when Izzy winked at him behind Telford's back.

Served Whitley right, to have to wash up what he'd dirtied. Given the man's essentiality to the Palmetto's operations, Izzy let him get away with his sly teasing of the new recruits, in the name of helping them grow thicker skins. There were worse men on the West End than Whitley.

Little wonder Izzy was so damned suspicious. A hard habit to break, and he paused at the mouth of the alley before setting out. Like as not they were both perfectly safe, but Izzy had survived enough danger to never not be on the alert.

"Do you ever have the sense that someone is watching you?" Telford murmured after a few minutes walking.

"Says the stage actor."

"No, I mean right now. I can't help feeling someone's following us."

Izzy hissed, hunching his shoulders at the cold stab of remembered terror. At the newsstand ahead he stopped, looking over the board of headlines posted beside so he could turn sideways and see where they'd been. Either every other man in London had taken to wearing a watch cap, or Izzy had in fact seen that same man on his tail three days in a row.

"Slim cobber, bad shave, knitted cap?" he muttered to Telford, who merely hummed in the affirmative. "Shit. I hoped I'd imagined it."

"What shall we do?" Telford asked quietly as he looked at the news-board.

"We get something to eat so whatever happens next, we've got something to run on."

Bless the lad for snickering and not gasping. Or blubbing, or showing any outward sign of concern. A consummate actor. A man used to looking over his shoulder. "You know you can't run with your crook knee," he said softly.

"Yeah, but he don't know that. Besides, I'm capable of an awful lot when motivated."

FROM THE NEWSSTAND Mr Pound bought a copy of *Punch* which he tucked under his arm as they carried on walking.

"I wonder which of us he's following, you or me," Telford said.

"What does anyone have on you?"

"Not me so much as my father."

"Cline? What could he have to do with this?"

"More than you know."

"Perhaps this is the moment to enlighten me," Pound said with that tone of unnerving politeness he'd employed on Uncle Ned. "Given the circumstances in which we presently find ourselves."

"I suppose it's only fair, I've asked enough questions of you."

"That you have. Me, I can't get past your parents taking you to see that play of mine when you was small."

"I'd seen a lot by then. On stage and in my life. Nowadays one might call my parents bohemians. Free thinkers, in love with life. Not very good at the living of it, however. After my father died, my mother…well, she did her best, but she was grieving, and things were not easy for us. She slipped into bad habits, and…"

His steps had slowed, the foot-path blurring with sudden tears. Years and years, and the pain was as fresh as ever. Mr Pound took him by the elbow and pulled him into an alley.

"You don't need to tell me that bit, lad."

"I'm already moping. You might as well have it all. It could pass for one of your plays."

"How so?"

"They were unionists. Fiercely principled people. He was involved in the miners' strikes. He was a tall man, had a good voice, so he spoke at a lot of marches and rallies and such. One night…"

His throat pinched shut on the words. Who had he ever told? Not even Cian, for the fear had never left him that someday he might count as someone's unfinished business. To burden this blessed man with his awful past was too cruel. This man who feared nothing. Who had promised to protect him. Who had given him a chance.

"I know my father didn't die by accident," he said, speaking slowly to make up for the tremor in his voice. "I know it now. And I know I'll never learn who killed him, whether it was the company or the police."

"Sweet mercy, lad…"

"And then we started getting letters. I have no idea what they said, as my mother burned them, as soon as they arrived. All I know is she was terrified. We left in the night, like fugitives. I suppose we were. We ended in this wretched little village up north. Perhaps if we'd been there in springtime, she would have had time. Time to mourn him, come to her senses. But it was such a bitterly cold winter, so that when she got lost coming home that night…" He covered his mouth, swallowing the bile that rose with the memory of her blue and bruised face, for they'd brought him to the riverside to claim her.

With his hat over his heart, Mr Pound was shaking his head, his lips pressed tight. "What an awful business," he croaked.

"It was. I'd give anything to…well, it's useless to even say, isn't it?"

"It's beyond us, either way. The past is the past. Can't change it. The best you can do is forget."

"Sometimes that's not possible."

Mr Pound huffed a bitter laugh, replacing his hat on his head. "What's best and what's possible are rarely the same thing. Indeed, I take it as given that Man at almost all times fails to do his best. That's what makes us merely human and not divine. If one truly believes in original sin, then what else is there but accepting our flawed nature?"

"But one's meant to strive to do better."

He laughed again but more kindly. "Better on whose terms? I never killed no one, not with my hands nor by act of Parliament. I loved with all my heart. I've done everything I could to leave this world better than it was when I showed up. And they still say I'm going to Hell. So striving be damned. I bloody well am striving. Just because I don't pay heed nor tithe to some pederast in a frock doesn't mean I'm wicked."

"Did you not call yourself a wicked little man?"

"Well. So I did. But you can't say I'm evil. Those lords I used to lord it over? Every man jack of them paid for the privilege of having me smack them about. Damn well told me, in specific, and on occasion excessive detail, precisely how they wanted me to frighten the living daylights out of them."

"I understand. I think."

"All I mean to say is, no matter what wicked things I've done, it was never anything the other fellow didn't ask for. Or that he didn't bleeding well deserve, them who've threatened my person or the safety of someone I love. But I don't count those times. That's not evil. That's surviving."

"Speaking of, what are we meant to do?"

"Well, if he's following us, I ain't leading him nowhere but in circles. Perhaps we can trick him into revealing his intentions." Returning to the street, Izzy caught sight of the owner of the watch cap surveying the contents of a shop window some hundred yards away. Why hadn't they sent a man in a bowler like every other gent on the street?

"I feel like I know him," Telford muttered as they started walking in the opposite direction. "As if I've seen him before."

"Perhaps this ain't his first attempt."

Another few minutes brought them to the sandwich stand. Despite its humble construction, being banged together from mismatched boards all painted a morbid shade of ashy green, the little stand served one of the finest ham sandwiches Izzy had ever met, slathered with grainy mustard, the meat laid on two fingers thick. He bought two for himself and three for Telford and a bottle of ginger beer each.

"I was rather hoping to get inside," Telford said as they resumed walking.

"Inside nothing," Izzy retorted. "There's no good us getting pinned down like that. That's what they want."

"Yes, but who are *they*?"

"I dunno. Our aim right now is to keep moving."

"In that case, why don't we catch that 'bus? It's just about done boarding." Telford nodded across the square to where an omnibus stood, a harried mother attempting to squire a gang of children up its front steps.

"That'll do." Clutching the sandwiches, his cane under his arm, he scuttled across, dodging bicycles and businessmen, Telford quick-marching behind. They crammed on by the rear door seconds before the 'bus rattled into motion.

"I wonder where we're headed," Telford said, leaning into Izzy as the vehicle swayed into motion.

"It's all one to me, as long as it's away from here."

"You don't suppose we imagined it?"

"Could be. I don't know who's even still alive to want me dead."

"You're not serious, are you?"

"I ain't lied to you yet, lad. I ain't about to start now."

Cry an island, leave me on it
All alone to think upon
All the things I might have done
To prove my heart is yours

"Island of Tears"
from "The Last Man on Earth"
Music by T. Whitley
Lyrics by E. Pound

Le désastre

ALANSON WAS FIXED on opening *Exasperating Times* in a little under a month. To no audience, with no advertising, and no real reason for there to be an opening night other than everyone was more than happy for the enterprise to be coming to an end. What had started as a lark had become an obligation, with everyone not appearing on stage press-ganged into being prop assistants, set builders, costume makers, cleaners and the like. Sal's construction crew built benches for the non-existent punters, wings for the actors to stand behind, and much to Izzy's relief a parti-wall projecting from the left side of the stage to serve as the dressing room.

Though Noel no longer needed to dance, he was still required to move about on stage while others danced around him, though as they attempted their so-called pas de deux for the tenth time this morning, Izzy began to wonder if Noel wasn't botching it on purpose.

"Please, Mr Peters, your marks," Alanson gritted through his teeth. "Let's try it again from the top."

"Not a chance," Izzy groaned. He lifted the petticoat and kicked off the heeled slippers Alanson had assigned him for this number. "And I ain't wearing those toe-crushers in the show. Punters ain't gonna be looking at my feet."

"Ain't no one gonna be looking at all," Noel muttered.

"Now, Mr Peters, let's be optimistic," Alanson started.

"To hell with optimistic. I've had it." He hopped off the narrow stage and turned to Izzy. "You coming?"

Izzy kicked the shoes right off the stage then jumped down to retrieve them. Noel joined him backstage to help him out of the petticoat and bustle frame, the only parts of the get-up needed for rehearsals. Noel put the bits back in the trunk designated for Izzy's costumes while Izzy put his trousers on.

"I don't know if I can keep this up, Iz."

"Couple more weeks won't kill you."

"Yeah, but then what? I spend more time than I like to prancing around for bloody Alanson, and the shit still ain't satisfied. I dunno if I'll be able to see it through once he gets an audience in."

"He'll never get an audience."

"So then what's the point of any of this?"

"I dunno," Izzy said, buttoning his braces. "Just something to do, innit?"

Alanson knew better than to speak to them as they left the ballroom. Somewhere a farmer was burning stubble, the tang of smoke clinging to the air. "It's too hot to work," Noel said to Izzy's surprise. "Let's go round the orchard."

Izzy wasn't going to argue, though he expected it would only lead to a different sort of work, looking for grubs or rabbit holes or simply fondling the ripening apples as he'd caught Noel doing on occasion. The wizened trees had set a good crop of fruit, its scent leavening the smoke. Noel however said nothing, nor did he stop to look at any of the trees, wandering morose, his head down, until Izzy made him halt.

"Say what's on your mind, cobber. Ain't no one to hear you but me."

His hands deep in his pockets, Noel sighed, kicking his heels. "D'you really suppose you're gonna be able to go through with it?" he said at length. "I mean, if by some miracle Alanson does pull an audience?"

"You're going to do just fine, Noelly. No one's going to mind if you stuff up your steps now and then."

Noel stared at him then looked away, shaking his head. "Forget it."

"Tell me. Noel, love, didn't you and me promise to tell each other things like this?"

"It's nothing you've done."

"That don't matter. You're hurting. Maybe I can stop whatever's hurting you."

"I don't want to be in the play, Iz," he blurted, his words running into one another in his urgency. "Not at all. But it's gone so far now, and it's meant to be ready in a few weeks and I don't want to let you down, but I just know I'm going ruin everything."

"You won't let me down, love."

"But what if I forget what I'm meant to do? It happens. I been hearing all sorts of stories, from everyone. I just know I'm going to set one foot on that stage and forget every damned word, every step, everything I'm meant to remember."

"A couple more weeks' rehearsal, you'll be right as

rain."

"It won't make a damned bit of difference. Iz, I just can't do it." He swallowed hard, as if on the brink of being sick to his stomach. "Every time I step out on that stage, I can't keep from feeling like I'm back in Ursula's parlour, as if the whole point of the show is to put us on display."

"Ursula said we're free and clear. That we ain't on the menu."

"Like that's going to make a difference."

"She won't let anything happen to us."

"She don't run the world. Look what happened already. He might have killed you."

Izzy swallowed past the visceral memory of his near miss, when that wretched toff had tried to throttle him into obedience. "This is different."

"How?" Noel hissed. "You were right, there's nothing whatsoever protecting us. We're in the middle of bloody nowhere, with no one to help us."

"You're talking nonsense."

"I'm right and you damn well know it." He stormed away through the sunlit trees, grasshoppers whizzing out of his path. Izzy caught up at the edge of the orchard and went with him to Ursula's study. The door stood a little open, which meant one might knock, which Noel did with an agitated rat-a-tat.

"Vous en prie," came the high, sibilant answer. Esme, whom Ursula was educating in the entrepreneurial arts, the two of them bent over a ledger book, Esme with accountant's cuffs over her thin wrists to keep her dress clean of ink.

Vibrating with pent-up feeling, Noel strode into the room. Much improved from its mildewed state in the spring, the library still had no shelves, but Ursula had a fair collection of books atop the desk, held upright by a pair of bookends Sal had crafted from blocks of hardwood, their surfaces inlaid with marquetry. Sal was loafing in an armchair nearby with their feet on the windowsill, near but not looming over their two charges.

"Mr Peters, Mr Pound," said Ursula. The reunion with her daughter had brought her back to life, her eyes clear, lips gentled with what she allowed as a smile. "What can I do for you?"

"Is it possible to have a word in confidence, ma'am?"

"Of course, Mr Peters."

"Mummy, may I show Sal where I saw the crab?" Esme said.

"Yes, Esme. You must tell me if it found a new shell."

The girl nodded, solemn as ever as she tugged off the cuffs. Ursula helped her from the heavy chair. The child put her arms around her mother's waist, resting her fair head against her hip. Then she dashed from the room, Sal chasing after, both of them giggling. Izzy shut the door then joined Noel, who was standing at attention, his hands clasped behind him, his chin proudly lifted and trembling.

"Please do tell me what's on your mind, Mr Peters," Ursula said as she sat in the vacated chair.

"It's this stage-play, ma'am. I'm simply not able to carry on with it."

"I see. And what has Mr Alanson said to this?"

"Oh. I ain't told him yet."

"Then I am obliged to ask why you have chosen to

tell me first."

"You mean you don't care if I quit the show?"

"I am concerned only with your responsibilities to my own enterprise, Mr Peters."

"So you're not fussed at all?"

"I assure you," she said with that heaviness of tone she employed with argumentative lords right before calling for Clyde, "my business and Mr Alanson's are wholly unrelated. And shall remain so."

"Oh. All right. Good to know."

"Have you any other matters you wish to discuss, Mr Peters?"

"Nah, I'm right."

"And you, Mr Pound?" she said to Izzy.

"You know me, I'm just here for atmosphere."

They left her with her books, closing the door like she asked. "Are you going to tell me what just happened?" Izzy said as they crossed the hall. "Have you quit or not?"

"I have."

"Alanson's going to go clear out of his mind."

"To hell with him," Noel spat. "In fact, you can tell him yourself. I see that mug, I'm like to kick him through a window."

"Not a chance, cobber. This is your decision."

"Please, Iz," he said, taking his hand. "I just want it over and done. I don't need him crawling all over me, calling me his *dear friend* and pretending he don't hate my guts."

"He doesn't hate you."

"Well, he will now. Please, will you do this for me? I swear I'll make it up to you."

"Shit. All right, but if he murders me promise

237

you'll avenge my death."

"Of course." He pulled Izzy nearer and kissed him thoroughly, until he was clinging to Noel's neck. "Now get on. Meet me at the cottage, yeah?"

THOUGH IZZY WAS braced for one of Alanson's little fits, the director merely sighed on hearing the news, shaking his head and setting the ringlets across the back shimmying. "I had a sense this day would come. Which is why I acquired us an understudy, for when your dear friend inevitably broke under the strain."

"He didn't break—"

"Yoo-hoo, Laurent," Bill called, waving coyly at someone in a group nearby. "Laurent, my boy, come meet your counterpart."

A tall fellow with Noel's complexion and delicate features and the torso of a carven statue detached from the group and came dancing towards them. Or perhaps he just happened to walk like that, which anyone might who was in possession of such elegantly powerful thighs. The sort of thighs that were going to give Noel jealous nightmares.

"I didn't agree to this."

"Don't worry, my, er, good Mr Pound," Alanson said with his shiny smile, patting Izzy gingerly on the shoulder. "Laurent is a consummate performer. Aren't you, Larry? In fact, we've devised a little choreography just to suit him."

"Exactly how long have you been secretly planning

238

to replace Noel?"

Bill's shiny smile spread unpleasantly. "As long as he's been secretly planning to quit. Now, let's try that pas de deux with a proper dancer."

"Later," Izzy said, shying away from Alanson's steering hand. "I've got things that need doing."

"More important than this?"

"Infinitely so." As Izzy left the ballroom, Laurent began to sing in a magnificent, heart-melting tenor. He was singing *Mine Eyes Art Open*.

Noel was pulling weeds from around their stoop and followed Izzy inside the cottage. "So? How'd old Bill take the news he'd have to rewrite the blasted play all over again?"

"He ain't rewriting it."

"You don't mean he's giving it up at last?"

"Nah. He had someone lined up for the role."

"Miguel?"

"Why would it be him? He can't carry a tune in a bucket."

"So who is it?"

"Some chap named Laurent."

"Fantastic," Noel said bitterly. "Something else to worry about." He dragged a chair out noisily and sat, arms crossed, face stony.

Despite a strong urge to kick the chair out from underneath him, Izzy pulled out the other chair and sat facing him. "You don't have to worry about no one, you berk."

"You mean you're not bothered by this?"

"Why should I be? You got what you wanted."

"You aren't bothered by having to pash some...actor?"

"We'll see if we can't get rid of the kissing bits."

"And the dances?"

"They're part of the show."

"And when he sings that song to you while you're on the balcony?"

"If you're trying to get me to quit as well, just come out and say it."

"That's not it."

"Then tell me why you're so stuck on this idea I'm about to throw you over for every boy who dips his lashes at me."

Unable to answer, Noel dropped his head. Izzy scooted forward, bending down and craning his neck to force him to meet his eye, and Noel sat upright again with an exasperated grunt. "Fine. I just dunno how anyone could act so…in love and not end up wanting to take the next step."

"Acting in a way you don't feel is the whole point of, well, acting! Me making doe eyes at that Laurent ain't no different from me topping some squirming lord. Fucking hell, Peters, I used to fuck men for money, and you never said boo. I gave that up, largely out of consideration of you if you'll be so good as to recall, and now you don't trust me because…because I don't even know why!"

He was yelling. He didn't need to be yelling. He ought not to have to say any of this but they'd promised honesty and Noel was getting an earful. "By the saints, Noel, why are we doing this to ourselves? It never used to be like this. How can it be we're better off in the trade than out of it?"

"What do you mean?"

I mean you and me got on better when we were

whores than we do now. So if accepting their money is what convinces you that I don't care about other men, then perhaps I ought to go back to doing so."

"You can't mean that."

"What if I did?" All the air seemed to leave the cottage, the only sound Izzy's thumping heart as Noel stared at him.

"Is that what you really want?" he breathed.

"Want's got naught to do with it."

"Then why?"

"Gotta earn a crust somehow, don't I?"

Izzy got up, Noel's proximity sorely testing his resolve, for it would be so, so easy to say *I'm sorry, I'm the fool, forget all I said.* To lie and pretend he wasn't burning from the inside out, full to the brim with a wicked stew of anger and sorrow and longing and fear and honest-to-God embarrassment that Noel didn't have the guts to say *please don't do this.*

In their hovel the door was always in reach, and before he started sobbing like a child he opened it and stepped outside. The sky had closed, the sun a silvery blot behind featureless grey clouds. Behind him Noel was muttering, the old grump, just loud enough Izzy heard him say the worst words he had ever uttered in Izzy's direction.

He turned on the doorstep. "Worst mistake of your life? Is that so?"

Confronted, Noel fell silent again. Izzy was sick to the back teeth of those silences, that stubborn fear. "In that case, sorry to have ever bothered you." He stumbled down the steps and started running towards the house, dashing tears from his eyes, Noel at his heels.

"Izzy, wait…" He grabbed for Izzy's sleeve but Izzy shook him off and kept walking. "I didn't mean what you think."

He spun about, gratified to see Noel in tears, wishing there were more of them. "If that's so, why did you damn well say it?"

"I didn't mean *you*."

"But it's still my fault, ain't it? All of this." He gestured around, at the garden, the whorehouse, their meagre cottage, the blackening sky. "I could have left you alone. Then you would have been happy, hey? Back in Bromley, at your parents' beck and call. All the dirt you could ever want."

Noel's sorrowful expression hardened as he stuck out his chin. "And then you could make eyes at whomever you liked."

"For the love of all that's holy!" Izzy cried. "You still think this is about some other man? Like this is all some clever way for me to cast you out and start over?"

"Without me holding you back from this marvellous new career you're set on having."

"Without you finding fault with the mere notion of me trying to better myself, you mean? I don't know what you think I do all day, but I ain't never worked so hard at anything in my life. And damn it, I'm good at it. Not just the tumbling but the dancing, acting, all of it."

"Good at pretending to be something you're not?"

"Cobber, if I couldn't pretend to be something I'm not, I'd have never become anything at all. After all, Mr Peters, I've learned more than a few tricks about dazzling the eye and ear," he said, putting on what Noel called his Headmaster's voice: crisply accented, not an 'aitch' dropped, a velvet purr that spoke of absolute control. And he could turn it on and off like water from a faucet. "Speaking of putting on a show," he went on as himself, "what I can't get my head round is how me singing and dancing can bother you more than how I used to earn a wage."

"That's not what this is about."

"Then what? What is it you want from me? Just tell me what to do and I'll do it. We can leave here, go to Spain, Italy, go north, to bleeding Australia. I'd go to the moon if you only asked it of me. But I can't keep going if we aren't going on together. Saints above, Peters, it's all for you anyway. That's the only reason I do anything, to make you happy. I'd do anything to make it so. So if you can't stand me being in the play, I won't be in it."

"What?" Noel gasped in horror.

"Forget the blasted show. They can find a new sap. I quit."

"You can't!"

"Like fun I can't. You did."

"Izzy, you don't have to do this."

"It's quit or have this same godawful argument every time you get the wind up you. I'm sorry it makes you nervy, but I won't let anything come between us. To hell with fame and fortune, to Alanson, to the whole bleeding lot of it. It's not worth it, not one bit. Without you, it'll all be ashes."

Le divorce

"NOEL…DAMN IT, Noel, say something, will you?"
Panting like he'd run a mile, his heart hammering in
his ears, his guts hollow with despair, Izzy shut his
mouth and waited. He was damned if he was going to
let Noel off so easily, without a word. They'd only
end here again, shouting things they didn't mean,
breaking all their promises.

His eyes wide open and brimming with tears, Noel
took a deep breath…

It was the most alarming sound he'd ever heard a
man make, and it came not from Noel but from Clyde.
Clyde, who had only half a tongue, who'd never made
a sound beyond a wheeze, was pelting towards them
from the direction of the beach, bellowing like a bull.
Izzy whistled for Sal and the rest, then they dashed to
meet him.

Clyde at once began to spell with his hands, then
made his signs for Esme and for Sal. He fingered the
letters again, Noel speaking them aloud: "A-b-d-u-c-t-
e-d…Abducted?" Nodding, Clyde made a yanking
motion, then pointed towards the beach. "Fucking
hell, someone's grabbed Sal and Esme?"

Clyde nodded more frantically. He shouldered past
them and ran to Ursula as she emerged from the

house. As the two began to converse in signs, a snatch of shouting rose above the ceaseless murmur of the sea.

"Maybe we can catch up with 'em," Izzy said. "Come on!"

They spent precious seconds running to the garden for weapons, for they didn't stand a chance against a force of any strength with just their fists. Though the sand was churned by half a dozen pairs of boots, only two people remained on the strand, locked in vicious combat, the taller clutching the other's head to his chest as if to suffocate him.

"Is that Sal?" Noel gasped.

"Then the other must be that brute, Stanley! He's going to twist Sal's head clean—hang on."

For as they approached they saw that of the two, the smaller had the better of it, Sal hammering their fists into Stanley's unprotected stomach as Stanley hung on Sal's shoulders, his knees wavering, his lip split, his face sickly green where it wasn't red or purple from Sal's earlier blows. Sal had taken their own share of knocks, their nose bloodied and more blood trickling down their forehead from where Stan appeared to have yanked out a handful of Sal's hair.

"Say you'll divorce me!" Sal snarled, grabbing Stan under the chin to make him lift his head. Stan merely gurgled, his eyes glassy. "Say it or I swear to God I'll cut your balls—"

"Stop!" the man shrieked, jerking his head from Sal's grip. "Please, Sal, have a heart."

In answer Sal kneed him in the groin. The big man toppled to the sand, clutching his middle and moaning piteously. Sal stood over him, one foot to either side of his head. "Now say it, Stanley. Say *I, Stanley Emerson Terwilliger-Dupree do hereby renounce marriage to Hazel Imogen Parker*—"

"You know this isn't binding," Stanley gurgled.

"It's a start." With that Sal snorted, then spat magnificently onto Stanley's bashed face.

"Sal," Izzy cried over the waves. "Are you hurt?"

"Forget about me," Sal hollered, pointing towards Calais. "They've got Esme!"

"We can't just go running after," Noel said as Izzy turned to do just that. "What would you do if we caught up to them?"

"I dunno, save her…ah shit, you're right."

Clyde was returning from the house and Noel went to meet him. They spoke in signs then Clyde nodded and started jogging towards Calais while Noel came to explain. "He says the ferry ain't due to depart for hours. Either they've hired a lighter or they're going by road or they're sitting tight. Whatever they're up to, we'll go see if we can't find out."

"Oh, please be careful."

"I will." He kissed Izzy's cheek then ran to catch Clyde.

"I love you," Izzy shouted after him, wishing he'd said it sooner, wishing he said it hourly, his heart taking flight as Noel dashed back to embrace him tightly, kiss him properly.

"I love you too. I'll be careful, I promise. You as well, yeah?"

"I will. Now get on and save that poor girl."

Izzy and Sal returned to Stan, who had managed to rise to his feet and stood swaying, punch-drunk and bloodied, his fawn linen suit smeared with sand.

"Hands offa me," he slurred. "Y'got no jurisdiction—"

"To hell with jurisdiction," Sal snarled. "You're coming with us."

"'m an 'merican citizen—"

"You're a colluding son of a bitch engaged in an international kidnapping case. Either start walking or I'll have to whup your American ass a second time."

"I'll be only too happy to lend a hand," Izzy said, who was beginning to wish Sal had knocked the git out cold.

"You? 'd like to see you try, ya limey bastard. I'll take y' both on. I'll beat y' into next year. I'll—"

"Mind if I shut him up?" Izzy asked Sal.

"Be my guest."

Stan had his hands up in an unsteady boxer's pose. Rather than pretend he knew a thing about boxing, Izzy hooked Stan's leg out from under him. He fell to the wet sand like, well, a sack of wet sand, though Sal's repeat of their offer to castrate him got him to his feet again in a hurry. He went with them meekly to the stable, where they gaoled him in a stall under the eye of Laurent, Annie, and whoever felt like pelting him with rotting fruit, as per Sal's generous offer.

"I ought to tell you this before you find out on your own," Sal said to Izzy as they started for the house, "but one of your brothers is here."

"Shit! Where?" Izzy spun about, his fists at the ready.

"No, I mean he was one of the mugs who took Esme."

"How do you know? You've never met my brothers."

"Nope, but he's a pock-faced East Ender who

looks like a taller you if you were ugly, and answers to the name Pound. I figured he had to be one of 'em."

"Big gap between his front teeth?"

"Yep."

"Pete. By the saints, I'll murder him myself."

They carried on towards the rear of the house from which came the sound of many voices. Ursula sat on the paved terrace in her wheel-chair gazing fixedly ahead as Marisol gave orders to a gang of men and women from the circus, each bearing a cudgel or club, one of them clutching a fearsome spear with feathers dangling from the base of the blade.

Others gathered in clusters, the circus wives muttering about their own children's safety, their obligations to the household, Ursula's staff in hot debate about who despised Muldoon the most and therefore deserved to be the one to slit his throat.

Izzy summoned two of the garden apprentices and sent them to coop the chickens. Not that the girls were at risk, but it would want doing soon enough and Noel wasn't here to… Noel was safe. Noel was with Clyde. Repeating this silently, Izzy rejoined Sal who was describing the assault to Ursula.

"After poking around the rock pools for that crab, we sat on the sand and she did her thing, you know, dug holes and so on. We were watching this rowboat about a quarter mile offshore. The oarsman didn't have a clue so they were just going in circles."

"A distraction," Ursula murmured.

"Could have been. Next thing I knew, they'd sneaked up on us from behind the rocks."

"How many?"

"Half a dozen, give or take. Stan and another fella

tried to haul me away but I wasn't having none of it. I booted Muldoon's boy a good one and he took off with the rest. You should have seen the look on Stan's face when he figured out they'd left him in the lurch. Well, I just about wiped his face clean off, didn't I, Iz?" Sal started laughing, a high, panicked giggle that ended with a sob. "Oh hell, what have I done?"

As if they'd taken a blow to the stomach they crumpled at Ursula's feet. "It's all my fault, ma'am," Sal bawled. "I should have been more careful. Oh Ducky, I'm so sorry."

"I don't blame you," Ursula said in the same low tone, stroking Sal's hair as they clung to her legs. "But why was Stanley with them?"

"Jailbait," came the muffled reply.

"What do you mean?"

Sal sat up, shoving their tears away with the flat of their hand. "Muldoon might not be a genius but he's a hell of a lot smarter than Stan. I guess he heard some Yankee swell was spreading cash around London, looking for dames dressed like they weren't. He sweet-talked old Stan into footing the bill to bring a crew over here and nab me."

"Do you mean Esme was a lucky grab?" Izzy asked.

"Esme was the prize. I'm the lucky grab. Muldoon's using Stan as cover for his own crime."

"But what does Muldoon want? It can't just be revenge."

"No," Ursula said, once more gazing out to sea. "It's not revenge. It's..." She gasped, her eyes flying open. Scarcely breathing, she held out a trembling hand towards Clyde who was approaching from the beach with another man in custody. "Harry?"

She began trying to rise from her chair. Sal sprung up and offered their arm as Clyde mounted the half-dozen steps at the side of the terrace, propelling before him a fair-haired, muscular gent in a costly suit that looked to have been slept in. He offered no resistance, nearly stumbling when Clyde thrust him towards Ursula, who held out her hands and beckoned.

"My darling!" the man cried. He rushed to her and pulled her into a desperate embrace. Clyde, Sal, Izzy, everyone surged forward to defend her, but she had flung her arms around the stranger's neck and was peppering his face with urgent kisses, without a care for being seen. Ursula, who touched no one if she could avoid it, who barely smiled except at her long-lost daughter.

The man stepped back, speaking urgently though he still held Ursula's hands. Seeing his face properly, Izzy's memory snapped to attention. That square chin and broad brow belonged to a face he'd once taken great pains to know, so that if he ever saw it he could run the other way.

"Saints above, Sal, do you know who that is?" he muttered from the corner of his mouth.

"Yeah," Sal grunted, dabbing at their torn scalp with a bloody handkerchief. "It's Esme's dad."

"He's *what?*" Izzy cried, so struck he had to take a step back. "That's the last blessed thing I thought you'd say."

"Why, how do you know him?"

"That's Lord Harry fucking Bolton! Prince Bobbie himself, deputy head of the whole metropolitan force!"

"Oh yeah. So he is."

"**I**'M NOT ASKING too much of you, am I?" said Ursula as they returned to the dining room.

"First off, it weren't you who asked," Izzy replied. "And second, you know there's nothing I won't do for you."

"It will be dangerous."

"That's not a worry. I feel dangerous." Felt downright lethal if truth be told, for on top of all else Noel had still not returned from Calais. If Pete, if anyone dared harm Noel… Izzy shook himself, covertly crossed himself, and joined the others at the dining table. Bolton had sketched a map of the area on the back of a discarded wall panel, variously shaped pebbles standing in for the principle players of the piece.

"Unless they've moved on, this is where they're keeping her," he said, pointing to a rough box indicating the port-side tavern where Muldoon's crew had been spotted. "I've got men watching but I haven't the authority to do anything."

"You've no authority?" Izzy said innocently. "Prince of the bobbies?"

Bolton shot him a dirty look but said nothing, having been properly chastened by Ursula five minutes after his arrival for lording it over the rag-tag gang of whores and actors on whose goodwill his future now depended. "A title to which I no longer have claim," he said with a bitter smile. "In fact that's what this is all about."

"Does Muldoon want you gone?"

"I've already resigned. He wants me back, but under his thumb."

"Christ, imagine? He'd be nigh unstoppable."

"Indeed. At first he thought to leverage Ursula herself. Once she'd put paid to that by leaving the country, it was only a matter of time before he came for Esme."

"And us going to the gendarmes ain't in the cards?"

"Do you trust the local police?"

"Must I answer that?"

"Whether we want the police or not may make no difference, as our enemies have arranged more than one diversion. They set a fire at an abandoned house on the east side of town. Once that had drawn the gendarmerie away, they started an enormous fight on the beach. All of Calais is in an uproar."

"How do you know all this? If you don't mind saying."

He looked to Ursula, who raised one pale eyebrow. "I suppose there's no harm in my telling you at this stage," he said with a guilty flush. "I had heard a gang of Muldoon's underlings had assembled at Dover, preparing for a ferry crossing. We'd been waiting for such a thing and we were able to get passage on the next. As for now I've men watching the tavern where they took lodging and the two main roads from Calais. I've a few informers along the lesser routes, but I'm spread thin, and this is by no means official police business."

"And who are these men of yours?"

Bolton coughed, glancing again at Ursula. "Let us say, times have behoved me to assemble a small crew of operatives I can call on in a pinch."

"Vigilantes, you mean?"

He coughed again. "If you must think of them as such. But not men for hire. They do as I ask out of friendship."

"That's a big ask, crossing the channel to help you start a war."

"No. We're here to end it."

A SLIM, PALE woman with a cane and dark, mannish clothing limped through the raucous crowd at Calais port, her wide bonnet swivelling this way and that as she searched for someone. She paused, leaning heavily on the silver-headed cane as she felt about for her reticule, oblivious to the opening door of the mud-spattered post-chaise beside her. A coarsely dressed man jumped down from the driver's seat, grabbed the woman round the waist and shoved her bodily into the carriage, shutting the door behind her.

Had they been using the coach as a latrine? So the odour suggested, the sludge on the floor staining Ursula's gloves and soaking through her dress at the knees. *Get up off the floor. Sit on the other bench. Move before he touches you.*

"Yes, do make yourself at home, my dear," a man sniggered in a crawling nasal voice. Peter Pound, without a doubt. His boots were filthy, little else visible past the cowl of Ursula's bonnet as the coach jerked into motion.

And now to wait until the last possible moment. If Bolton's spycraft held true, the raiding party were aiming to flee Calais on the eastward road to make a crossing at Dunkirk. They would first need to retrieve Esme from the cut-throat tavern where she was being held. Ursula's cane felt heavy, the pewter head gleaming dully in the scant light through the closed drapes, asking mutely to be wielded against the monster seated on the opposite bench. *Wait…*

"I gotta ask, love, what you thought you was doing, running away from him," Pete sneered, kicking at Ursula's boots. "Don't you know the world turns on the word of men like us? Silly little women like you got no right to be messing in men's business. I just hope I'm in the room when he gets his hands on you and puts you in your place. Flat on your back, under him."

Wait. Hold onto the anger and use it, only wait…

Not for much longer as the coach clattered under an echoing archway then drew to a halt. The vehicle creaked and rocked with the driver's dismount, then his steps faded into the distance. Time passed, but not the silent urge to do manifest harm to the man on the other bench.

"What in blazes is taking so long?" Pete Pound muttered, his watch-fobs tinkling as he jiggled his knee. From the courtyard came the sound of running footsteps, then the angry grunting of fighting men, their boots scraping over the wet paving stones as they struggled. Pete slid across the bench to peek out the window. He gasped then jerked the door open for someone to shove a long and unwieldy bundle into his arms. He wrangled the heavy object onto the bench beside him then shut the door again.

"Oh. Hello, Mr Pound," said Esme, whose face

was just visible protruding from the end of the tightly wrapped blanket. Her cheek was red like she'd been slapped and her hair was spidering out of her plaits but she seemed otherwise unharmed.

"Eh?" Pete wrenched around to face her. "How d'you know my name?"

"Because I'm very clever," she said to him, blinking slowly. "I heard them say it."

"You best unhear it, missy."

"How can I possibly unhear something?" Esme lisped.

"In that case allow me to smack it out of your stupid little head," he spat, raising his hand to strike her.

"You touch that child again, I'll slit you neck to arsehole and hang you by your miserable guts," Izzy snarled from beneath Ursula's bonnet.

Pete stared back, his arm frozen in mid-air, his mouth hanging open so wide Izzy might have shoved his fist down his throat. He settled for ramming the head of Ursula's cane into Pete's unguarded stomach.

"Sorry, love," he said to Esme as Pete doubled over, gurgling.

"I don't care one bit, Mr Pound," she replied, squirming violently against her confines. "He said simply awful things about Mummy."

"I've known him all my life and trust me, he's a filthy liar."

"So then he isn't your brother?"

"No, that bit's true, sorry to say."

"'s anyway to treat your own flesh and blood?" Pete rasped, trying to shove himself upright.

"It is when he fucks with me and mine." Izzy

struck again, a vindictive open-handed slap to Pete's ear, like Pete used to do to him on the daily, creeping up behind any time he let his guard down, right up to the day Izzy quit his parents' house. Pete shrieked, clutching the side of his head, his flailing feet kicking the cane from Izzy's grip.

Something powerful was driving his brother, for the next second he had hurled himself across the carriage, slamming carelessly into Izzy to pin him against the seat. Encumbered by the dress and shawl and bonnet, he struggled under Pete's heavier weight, kicking at skirts and air, unable to get a grip on the other man, keeping his chin pressed to his chest to prevent Pete from choking him as they grappled. When Pete's scrabbling hand met Izzy's mouth, he bit down as hard as he could on the meat between Pete's thumb and palm. Held on as Pete screamed and tried to wrench his hand away. Let go when he tasted blood.

Eyes white, face contorted with pain and fury, Pete pulled back his bloodied fist to slam it into Izzy's face. Instead he shrieked and fell writhing to the side. The blanket still wound about her legs, Esme knelt on the carriage bench gripping her mother's cane in both tiny hands. She raised it overhead like an axe, about to smash it down on Pete's spine.

"Christ, no!" Izzy cried. "You'll kill him!"

She lowered her weapon and blinked at him. "And we don't want that?"

"No! He is still my brother. And I'd rather him hang and not you, sweetheart."

"Oh. I didn't realize they hanged children." The door jerked opened, and by it was a matter of inches that Izzy missed kicking Harry Bolton in the face.

"Hello, Daddy," Esme said to him as Izzy fell back on the bench, his heart in his mouth. "Next time, it would be better if you knocked."

Le reunion

ESME HAD JUST about broken Pete's arm with her mother's cane. Clutching his arm to his chest, Pete wriggled out of the carriage under Bolton's pistol to stand with the other conspirators. Each showed signs of their struggle, their clothes dirtied and torn, faces bruised, one tall bearded fellow with a blood-spotted bandage round his shoulder. Izzy's side were themselves the worse for wear, Bolton's lip cut and swollen, his fine suit five kinds of filthy as he swept Esme into his arms and bore her away from the carriage, leaving three of his irregulars to mind the prisoners.

Haggard but seeming uninjured, Miguel was sitting on a barrel by the archway to the road, Clyde standing with him. Peeling off Ursula's filthy gloves, Izzy joined them, hating that the question needed asking. "Have you seen Noel anywhere?"

His arms resting on his upraised knees, a flat bottle of brownish liquor dangling from one hand, Miguel only shrugged. Clyde began to explain in his way, but as usual his mix of hand-spelling and pantomime surpassed Izzy's understanding. Before he could oblige Miguel into giving clarity, Bolton tapped his arm. "Esme wishes to speak with you."

She beckoned for Izzy to bend down, which he did, holding up his skirt as best he could to spare it getting any dirtier.

"That was very brave, Mr Pound," she said in her soft murmur, "and I'm sorry that I nearly ruined the surprise."

"No, lovey, it was no fault of yours," he said, taking her tiny hand. "I wasn't going to be able to keep fooling him much longer. I'm sorry you had to see that. And for those rude things I said to him."

"That was nothing as rude as what those men said about Mummy," she whispered, though her grip was fierce.

"I'm so sorry, lovey." Maybe this was it, a father's instinct, for Izzy very badly wished he'd let her break his brother's back in recompense. Too great a burden for such a tiny thing to bear for the rest of her life. "Some men are properly dreadful."

"Not you though. You're always very kind. Mr Peters says so all the time. I do hope he's not in any danger."

He'd not wanted to say it aloud. Nor even to think it, in case he brought it to pass, in case he used up all their luck. She was only a child, and he managed to put a smile back on his face. "So do I, lovey."

Serious, she laid her other hand over his, indelibly her mother's child. "It's quite all right if you feel sad, Mr Pound. Mr Peters is a very nice man. I think he must love you very much."

That cut too close, and he stood up to spare her the sight of his pain as he crushed his eyes shut, feeling like he might fly apart, well and truly explode.

"We're just about finished here," Bolton said,

setting his firm hand on Izzy's shoulder. "We'll return to the house. I'm certain he'll be there."

Izzy nodded, biting his lips. Surely he'd know if Noel had met with harm, would have felt it like a blow to his own heart. He shook off Bolton's hand and began searching through the countless pockets stitched all over Ursula's dress for one with a handkerchief.

Inattentive, he had strayed near the prisoners, who posed little threat with their hands bound in front of them and three guns levelled at them. Pete stood muttering at the end of the line, and in a fit of daring Izzy plucked the red silk from his brother's breast pocket. He blew his nose with enthusiasm, then shoved the soggy handkerchief back in Pete's pocket.

"Mum's died," Pete said bluntly. "And no, it weren't by my hand," he went on with a poisonous sneer. "Or his. Just time."

Izzy ought to be weeping. Instead it felt as though a stinging pain had been soothed, to know her life of misery had been brought to a merciful end. "Then she's finally beyond hurt."

"You ain't gonna ask about Da?"

"I couldn't give a rat's arse. Unless he's dead too."

"Some brother you are. Turning your back on your own flesh and blood."

Izzy laughed joylessly. "Of all the pleas you might have made to move me to compassion. I've been starved, beaten, abandoned, exploited, and vilified by that self-same flesh and blood. All my life, that flesh and blood of mine has nearly been the death of me. I don't owe any one of you a damned thing."

"Fine, walk away," Pete spat as Izzy turned. "Go

back to bending, you tuppenny whore!"

A meaningless slur. Idle words from a fool. Yet Izzy turned back, for he'd never have another chance to learn the truth. "Tell me something, brother. How is it such a clever man as you got suckered into Muldoon's game?"

His lips pulling into a snarl, Pete didn't answer. "Lemme guess: you tried to pull one over on him. What was it, oh brother of mine? Cheat at a card game in some dockside hell? Skive off a debt you ought to never have taken on? Some little thing you thought he'd not even notice, I expect. And he caught you, and he made you his slave. Am I coming close?"

"You wouldn't understand," Pete grated. "It's a matter of honour."

"And you're so weak you believed him."

"Like you ain't tied to the Life," he spat at Izzy's retreating back. "You're in just as deep as I am."

"We'll see if that holds water, hey? Have a nice ferry ride. Sorry we spoiled your holiday abroad."

Bolton ordered Muldoon's men into their carriage. The fellow with the bleeding shoulder and a round-faced chap with a gash on his forehead complied willingly. The other three less so, dragging their heels despite the odds against them. Their resolve crumbled once Bolton called Clyde to help.

"You might just as well shoot us," Pete blurted as Clyde bundled him up the step. "You know he'll do worse to us if we don't come through. He'll make it take hours." The others began shouting agreement, pleading for mercy of one kind or another. They made a miserable party packed in the stinking coach with their hands still bound, their shoulders round their ears and their knees crushed together. Bolton hammered on the side of the coach to silence them.

"I'm giving you all two choices," he said. "And you must all agree on which you'll take. You may either accompany me to England where we will permit the relevant authorities to decide how to apportion the charges of espionage, kidnapping, extortion and all other relevant crimes of which you may be guilty. Or I'll give you each twenty pounds right now to go very far away and stay there."

The conspirators muttered furiously amongst themselves. Then one of them hissed the rest to silence. "We want twenty-five."

"Done." Bolton shut the door. "Take them at least ten miles out of town," he said to his man who had mounted to the driver's seat. "Further if the horses are up to it." He gestured to the irregulars who had been guarding them and the men took up places on the front and back benches.

"Now what?" Izzy asked as the coach creaked into motion.

"Now we bring Esme to her mother."

THE CARAVAN THEY'D borrowed from a family of acrobats was parked conspicuously in front of one of Calais' better hotels, under the assumption none of their enemies were bold enough to approach it in plain sight. It appeared untouched, and Ursula opened the door at once to Bolton's particular knock. He handed Esme up and Ursula shut the door again. After some minutes of standing about in the street, Bolton accepted that the women weren't likely to exit the vehicle any time soon. He helped Izzy climb up beside the driver and they started for home through the deepening twilight.

Conscious of disturbing the occupants, the caravan's driver allowed the mismatched team of horses to keep a leisurely pace. Izzy thought more than once about leaping down from the seat and running the rest of the way home, but the dress was heavy and hot, as heavy as the fear of discovering the very worst had come to pass. Surely Noel was at the house, or comforting his chickens, or waiting in their little cottage praying that Izzy had come to no harm. Or sulking, indignant that Izzy had put himself in peril without thinking of the consequences.

His mind turned these last two possibilities over and over as they swayed along the road. At last they started down Marisol's long driveway. As they neared the cottage Izzy asked the driver to stop and let him off. If nothing else he could undress in privacy, but he had scarce set his foot on the ground when Noel came pelting from the house.

"Oh hell," Izzy groaned, "what n——"

This. Noel in his arms, Noel's lips against his, their hearts beating in time. Noel crying so hard he was gasping for breath, crushing Izzy to him: "praise the Lord. I've been losing my mind."

"Unghhh…"

"Sorry…" Noel released him though kept his hands on Izzy's shoulders. "When I heard what you done, I thought…"

"That I was soft in the head?"

"No! Well, a little, but just…" He looked down, cheeks darkening. "I dunno if I could have been that brave. But you didn't even think twice. You went ahead and did what had to be done."

"You'd have found a way."

"I'm so glad you're not harmed."

Another kiss, calmer, more joyful and less panicked. Though the corset had absorbed the worst of it, Izzy had taken more than one blow from Pete's fists and perhaps his knees, and he groaned as Noel squeezed him.

"You ain't lying about being hurt, are you?" he asked with a frown.

"Nah. A bit roughed up, but not so bad seeing as all I had to do was wear a dress and knock the stuffing out of someone who deserved it."

Noel grimaced. "I heard Pete was mixed up in this."

"The rat had the audacity to say I was betraying my family. He don't know what family means. *You're* my family. To hell with the Pounds. Ezekiel Peters, how does that sound?"

Noel blushed again, taking Izzy's hand as they started for the cottage. "Does that mean I'm forgiven?"

"Forgiven? For what?"

"For being such a shit before. For being scared of trusting you. Not just around other men but entirely." He stopped, tugging on Izzy's hand to make him pay attention. "Iz, I don't want you to quit doing what you do. Not being in the show nor what you do on the wire. Who am I to keep you from something that makes you happy?"

"You make me happy."

"But not my trade," he said with a wry smile. "And

that's not something I can change by badgering you about it. Or by preventing you from doing what brings you joy. So if that's acting or tumbling or whatever, don't quit just because you think it'll please me. It won't, because I'll have taken something from you."

"Then figure out how to be okay with it. Believe me, there's no difference between this and what we did for Ursula. If anything this is better. Everyone keeps their trousers on. Well, more or less," Izzy said with a laugh, glancing down at his costumed self.

Noel laughed along, though his brow was pinched. "It's hard to watch, though."

"Then don't watch. It makes you mental, it makes me forget my lines, and it's all faked anyway. You don't gotta keep tabs on me. All you gotta do is holler, I'll come running, if ever you need me."

"Come inside with me now," he murmured.

"Mr Peters, please! What a thing to ask of me after such a day."

"We don't have to get up to anything. I just want to be near you."

So simple a want, yet it struck Izzy harder than any flattery or randy wind-up. Lost for words, he nodded, then followed Noel inside the cottage, where for a very long time they stood and kissed and nothing else, both of them too full of feeling to need any more of each other.

"What's wrong?" Noel asked when he felt Izzy's tears on his face.

"Nothing at all. Only, it doesn't seem real to have someone so worth loving."

"Izzy, heart…"

"What a sap I am, spotting your shirt like that," he said, brushing at the damp patches on Noel's front.

"Forget it," he chuckled.

"Oh, but it's such a nice shirt, Mr Peters."

"Just like that?"

"Eh?"

"From weeping to flirting?"

"I never said I was sad," Izzy replied. "How could I be? I'm with you. I don't care about nothing else. Only this," he said, touching Noel's hot cheek. "Only you." They kissed once more, a passionate kiss to defeat all doubt, to prove that love triumphed over all.

THE NIGHT

They had ridden to the end of the omnibus line and all the way back into town. Back to the theatre, for Telford had nowhere else to go. Back to Izzy's office, where they were standing side by side before an enlargement of the photo of the group on the beach, all those faces now with names and stories behind them.

"So there it is. Your happily ever after," Telford said wistfully.

Izzy just about choked, his chest seeming to cave as if under a heavy blow, the pain of remembering as strong as the feel of living it. He covered his mouth, his eyes pressed shut against tears too old to shed, too fresh to hold at bay.

"But…" Telford stammered, "but you'd gone through so much together."

"Rescued the wee princess and saved the day, hey? Sorry to say that don't earn you a prize."

"But you said…but *The Alabaster Angel*…did you not say that play was based on a true story? Your life, but made fantastic?"

"Who said life always has a happy ending?" A truth he was tired of telling. Tired like never before. "Find us a chair, will you?" Telford eased him into the nearest, where he sat breathing slowly, willing the heaviness to lift.

"What can I do?" Telford asked, fluttering nearby.

"Bring us a cuppa, there's a lad."

"Not a doctor?"

"I'm sad, not dying."

"Sorry, sorry." He dashed off, leaving Izzy to run down his mental list of ways a man of his age might die, to see if this felt like any of them. His doctor was likely tired of his questions. To be fair, Izzy was tired of asking, but his stubborn heart persisted, his weariness subsided, and he was just settling behind his desk when Telford returned with the tea tray and a paper sack.

"Where'd these come from?" Izzy asked as Telford tipped out the sandwiches.

"The pub across the way."

"You were quick getting over there."

"I was hungry. And I know it's what we had for lunch but I saw Whitley and—"

"Never mind," Izzy said, unwrapping the first to hand. "Sandwiches is fine. D'you get cheese and pickle? Here, give us half of it for half this ham…"

They ate the sandwiches and drank the tea, Telford wise enough not to ask how he was feeling. Much better with something in his belly, even if it was only another sandwich. "Well, I'm for home," he said as he crumpled the paper bag and lobbed it towards the kindling bucket. "You coming with or staying here?"

"Here?" Telford replied, folding his own bag into neat little square. "Is that allowed?"

"It is by me. I don't much care otherwise."

"You won't mind me being in your office?"

"If you don't mind sleeping in it. Though you might do better in the set department. That's a real bed, remember."

He left before Telford refused. Whitley was in his office beneath the stairs, burning the literal midnight oil, though hearing Izzy's step he put away his papers. Most of Whitley's songs were written thus, in solitude and silence, the only instrument the one in his mind.

"Spare us a bit of silver, will you? I want a cab."

"Not walking home?" Whitley asked, opening the drawer where he kept the petty cash.

"Eh, I been walking all over."

"There's something else, isn't there?" he asked Izzy's reflection in the mirror on his desk.

"Can't hide a thing from you, hey? Maybe it's nothing but I've come all over suspicious. On account of some cove in a funny hat I keep seeing about town. Same with Fords, he reckons he saw him too."

Whitley swivelled his chair about. "What have you gone and done, you old fool?"

"Beg your pardon?"

"The last cove in a funny hat following you about town was named Ioan Sales."

Izzy hissed, the con-man's name stirring a vile stew of emotion. "Nothing doing. It was a different hat entirely."

"Don't be obtuse."

"Don't be an old woman." Whitley only glared, that one muscle by his left ear twitching with his held-back emotion. "So you going to lend me the money or not?" Izzy nodded to the silver in Whitley's tense grip.

"*I'm* not lending you anything. You're lending it to

yourself out of your future receipts." He dropped the coins in Izzy's waiting hand.

"Seeing as I pay your wages, amounts to the same thing, don't it? And just so you know, the lad's bunking here tonight."

"Why?"

How much did Whitley need to know? "His home life's gone for a shit, let's just say. I can't have my second tenor getting bashed up a fortnight before we open, can I?"

"Gone for a shit, indeed."

There were still plenty of hansoms plying The Strand and Izzy was home in no time. Climbing the stairs just about undid him, his knees twin orbs of fire, every creak and knock behind him suggesting an imminent ambush. Foolishness, just memories, but he still made sure each corner of his flat was empty before getting into bed.

He had nearly drifted off when a bang from the sitting room had him bolt upright and reaching for his stick. He relaxed as the green agate chips of the cat's eyes gleamed from the bedroom doorway. The thing crossed the room and hopped onto the bed, where it paraded up and down before curling up just south of Noel's pillow.

"Scratch me and you're going straight out the window," Izzy grumbled as he settled again, tugging vainly at the blanket pinned under the creature. Nothing new, for Noel had been a notorious blanket thief. Lulled by the snoring drone of the cat's purr, by its warmth in a bed that had gone cold for too long, Izzy let go of his worries and fears, like so much smoke on the wind.

TELFORD SAT ON Mr Pound's itchy sofa waiting for Mr Pound to return. The offer was too grand, too special. Too kind, when he'd not so much as asked. At a noise on the landing he sprung to his feet and ran to open the door. Mr Whitley stood there with his hand raised to knock.

"You're a quiet one," he said, one black eyebrow bent, possibly with humour. "Himself usually can't keep his mouth shut, even without an audience."

"He said I might stay here tonight. Is it all right?"

"Don't leave if you can help it. Fire laws mean the back door isn't locked from the inside, but you won't be able to get back in should you leave."

"I understand."

"Unger will be here by seven. Try not to make a mess."

"Yes, Mr Whitley."

"Do you need money?"

"Mr Whitley?"

"For lodgings after tonight."

"I can't ask that of you."

"You didn't ask. And this isn't Pound's offer but mine. An advance on your pay."

"But why?"

"Call me mercenary, but you're integral to the show, Mr Fords. We can't have you getting damaged." Whitley didn't press, only brought him downstairs to remind him of the operation of the gas ring in the canteen, in case he wanted tea. He then left, and

Telford was alone.

His watch was lagging but showed half twelve. The city slept, and Telford was alone in the unlit and echoing theatre. And safe. No one could get in without a key. No one had a key but Unger, Whitley, and Mr Pound.

As his eyes accustomed to the dark, he found there was just light enough from the amber-shaded electric lamps at the exits to feel his way about the auditorium. He grew bolder, passing through the pitch black lobby and creeping up the stairs to the mezzanine.

There lay the stage, cloaked in shadows, the site of his future reckoning. Being made up wholly of students' family members, the audiences at St Barnabas hadn't had a choice whether or not to attend. Further, it had made no difference at all if they enjoyed the show, for he had never heard fiercer applause than from the parents of a boy who had flubbed every line and knocked over half the cardboard forest while playing Puck the year they'd done *A Midsummer Night's Dream*.

Mr Pound intended to charge people money to see Telford. Money they might well demand returned to them if his performance was unsatisfactory. Pound was no fool, though. He'd have never given Telford a thought if he didn't believe him able to rise to the challenge.

Feeling both hot and cold, he returned to the auditorium and mounted to the stage, his footsteps ringing in the stillness. The row of chairs representing the train stood in a line on the wheeled platform centre stage. This spun about to show the train's interior for certain scenes, but without all the pieces of the set it was merely a row of plain wooden chairs.

Like everything else that happened on stage: a sham, a pretence, a way of making the profane fact of a row of chairs and some painted planks into the beautiful lie of two people finding sanctuary in each other's love. A lie Mr Pound told with such heart-breaking precision because he'd lived it himself.

> *And though we are divided*
> *Our hearts beat in parallel*
> *No more could I desire*
> *Than to ride the longest rail*
> *And share the journey*
> *With you to the end…*

Unaccompanied, Telford's voice wavered in the still air. He'd have to put in a better showing on the night. Set aside his own sorrow, become as dear old Father Gilchrist had so often said *a conduit of glory*, his humble form a mere vessel for Creation. He sang it again, his head held high, his voice ringing clear across the auditorium, his eyes closed so that it did not matter that he was alone.

HE SPENT THE rest of the night attempting various postures on the wretched sofa in Mr Pound's office. Once he tried the bed in the set department, but he kept startling at the sound of the mice skittering about backstage. He seemed to have only just nodded off when he heard the hollow thunk of the stage door swinging closed. Rubbing his bleary eyes, patting vainly at his upright hair, he left the office and went downstairs to find Mr Pound filling the kettle.

"What time is it?" Telford asked.

"Dunno. Sixish," Pound grunted, shuffling to the gas ring. "You remember how to light this thing?"

Tea made, they went up to the office to drink it. Telford felt hollowed, like bread with its soft middle plucked out to leave the brittle crust. Mr Pound hardly looked better, holding his mug in both hands with his elbows on the desk as he breathed in the steam. He took a sip of the scalding tea and set it down.

"The worst thing was, it was all going so well," he said without preamble, though the ache in his voice made it clear what he meant. "Running like clockwork, until I gummed up the gears. And all on account of my pride. Pride that weren't nearly merited. If you learn nothing else from me, lad, let it be that kisses might end an argument, but they won't solve none of your problems."

L'étoile

WHETHER MULDOON WAS plotting further mischief or had simply cut his losses, they heard nothing more from him, nor from Pete Pound, though Izzy did receive a letter from his eldest living brother Matthew confirming that their mother had indeed passed over.

Sal and Clyde meanwhile took Stan to London to see Ursula's solicitor and have the Duprees' marriage dissolved. Ursula remained to set up Bolton and Esme in a house in Calais where the child would not be bothered by the particulars of her mother's business. What Bolton thought of these particulars was not a topic for general discussion, though Izzy and Noel swapped many a theory privately.

The fright of losing Izzy had awoken a new compassion in Noel, who ceased complaining of the wire tricks, the play, even Laurent. It helped that Laurent was so wholly professional, having no shame in performance yet no inclination to carry the staged romance into real life. It was he who suggested dropping the lights on every kiss between their characters, as it was very evidently putting Izzy off his stride to have to put his mouth on a man who wasn't Noel.

Thus it was that against all odds and expectations Ursula opened her club for business on the same night Bill debuted his masterwork. Only Ursula could have achieved it, and it must have cost a pretty penny given the army of cleaners, cooks, and urgently summoned workmen she engaged that last week. Where she'd got the custom from was another undiscussed subject, but they'd been arriving all afternoon, until the ballroom rang with masculine laughter, cigar smoke blueing the ceiling as Annie cinched Izzy into his costume.

"This is ridiculous," he said for the thousandth time as she shoved the stuffed 'improver' down the front of his corset to make up for his lack of breasts.

"No good thinking that, Iz," she said around the pins in her mouth. "You can't quit now."

"Don't damn well tempt me."

She spat the pins into her hand then gripped the shoulder of his under-shift. "You quit this bleeding play and I swear I'll hunt you down and drag you back here by your balls and nail you to the stage."

"Eh?"

"We've all put up with too much for you to get cold feet, Pound," she said with the steel-eyed sincerity of a gangland daughter. "You're the bleeding lead. Now go put on your make-up. Curtain's in twenty minutes."

"Since when did we have a curtain?" he squeaked as she marched off. She made a rude gesture and kept going, nearly colliding with Noel who was on his way in. He smiled on seeing Izzy, which went a long way towards making him feel less ridiculous. The others could rot if Noel was content.

"You're going to do great," he said, smiling hugely, his hands sizzling hot on Izzy's bare shoulders. "I just know it.”

“I’ll settle for not making a complete arse of myself.”

“Nah, you’re golden.” Noel kissed his forehead, then both cheeks, and was just starting on a lovely, long kiss of Izzy’s lips when Annie rang her little bell to signify the quarter hour mark.

“Fuck.”

“Later,” Noel grinned. “When you’re a star of the stage.”

“You twit…”

“I love you, okay? I’m glad you saw it through.”

“Let’s wait till I’ve done so before we say that, yeah? And I love you too. Thank you. Don’t ask for what. For all of it.”

One last kiss, cut short as Noreen and Antonia came into the dressing room. Noel left, and then all was haste and stumbling over each other’s feet and shoes, fighting for space at the mirror, straightening wigs, and all of it in panicky whispers as the muttering of the audience grew louder and louder. And then it was too late for anything except lining up at the bottom of the steps to wait for one’s cue.

“*…fancies herself quite the eyeful.*”

Up the steps, past the wooden wings, hand on his silky hip. Blinded by the shaded lanterns across the front of the stage, the audience a mass of whispering black, unseen and unimportant.

“*Eyeful, mouthful, either way I’m a morsel…*”

Thirty seconds and a thousand years later Annie was grabbing one of his hands and Laurent the other and they were bowing to the unseen mass of black who were no longer whispering but clapping and whistling, a gang near the back shouting the mangled chorus to the song *Short End of the Stick*. Laurent lead him offstage where Noel was waiting, beaming with joy, his arms open wide.

"That was wonderful. You were wonderful," he said as Izzy clung to his neck.

"I didn't bitch anything up, did I?" he asked the front of Noel's shirt.

"You don't remember?"

"Barely." In the way he'd sometimes lost sight of himself when serving Ursula's more needy clients, those men who'd wanted more than to simply surrender, who had wanted his very worst and then some. Nights which had passed like a hazy dream "Not so as I can gauge whether I did anything wrong."

"Seemed good to me," Noel said, still grinning. "And I watched the lot."

"Well, if you ask me, you did fantastic," Annie said as she crowded near, pinching his bum through the swathe of shiny white fabric of his final costume.

"Fantastic to say the very least!" cried Alanson, appearing on his other side. "One might add magnetic, incandescent, heart-stopping—"

"That'll do," Noel said with a sly wink for Izzy. He stepped back as Annie began unpinning the brooches that held the costume, allowing Alanson to grasp Izzy's hand and pump it vigorously.

"A born showman you are, my good Mr Pound! They simply couldn't get enough of you."

"Well, that's all they're getting of me for the night." He yanked his hand away from Alanson's greasy grip. "Now if you don't mind, us ladies is getting undressed."

"Oh come, my dear, we're all one big company, are we not?

"That's beside the point of me not wanting to strip off in front of you."

"Yeah, fuck off, Bill," Annie said, shoving his shoulder and none too kindly. "You're getting in everyone's way."

"A better stage manager I couldn't hope for, Miss Billings," he beamed, bowing his sweaty head.

"Save it, Chuckles."

The last number of the show ended with most of the cast in their underclothes, and the room cleared quickly as Ursula's women joined the clients in the dining room, from which drifted giddy laughter and the occasional popping of a cork. Izzy took his time, cleaning the rouge and eye paint off with cold cream while Noel puttered about with a bit of knotted string, measuring the walls he'd built, doubtless plotting improvements.

Trusting the security detail of Clyde, Sal, and Bolton to manage any miscreant clients, they sneaked away to their cottage. Not to fuck, or at least without that as the intent. It was as on the night of the rescue, when what they both needed more than anything was simply the other's presence. His warmth. His strength.

"I really did think you did good," Noel said, his breath tickling Izzy's hair, his voice purring in Izzy's ear as they embraced.

"I don't want to talk about it. Nor even think."

"Then kiss me."

THE NEXT NIGHT they did it again. Then the

night after that and so on, with each show Izzy feeling more present in himself, more aware of his own actions, which might have made him self-conscious if the audience weren't lapping it up like dogs.

They laughed at his jokes. They cheered when he sang. They gasped as one, as if he were truly in peril, when he jumped across "the River Lethe," a wide streamer of blue fabric Annie and Petra waved in time to simulate waves.

They sent him flowers. Cards filled with dreadful poetry and obscene entreaties, as if he and his onstage role were inseparable. Gifts now and then, in little velvet boxes brought to him by Alanson on the sly and always refused, though some of the cuff-links and tie pins had tempted him, even if only to pawn. Unthinkable, for to accept any of their gifts was to suggest possibilities that did not exist. They made do with his company, which he began to dole out in small quantities and always under Noel's chaperone, passing arm-in-arm through the crowd at the inevitable party that prevailed in the dining room at the end of every performance.

Ursula hired the owner of one of the circus carts to offer transport to and from the Dover ferry, and by the third week *Exasperating Times* was showing every night save Sunday, and Alanson was stumping for a Saturday matinee. Patrons began to complain of a scarcity of lodgings in Calais, most of the fellows unwilling or unable to cover the price of a room at the house. Those who could took every advantage, so that one might find people fucking nearly anywhere about the property at nearly any hour of the day, until Noel painted a sign for the cottage which read *WARNING:*

DYNAMITE to keep eager sorts from trying the door.

In other words it was a riot, sunup to sundown and right the way round again. Unfettered madness yet a raging success. Of course it couldn't last. Not because of Muldoon. Or an embittered aristocrat, or his wife, or pressure from the local police, or any of the other risks they ran, but because Marisol hadn't thought to pay her taxes.

Izzy and Noel were minding some of their helpers in harvesting apples on a balmy day in late September when they heard women shouting. Leaving the kids to carry on, they jogged towards the house, rounding the treed corner of the drive in time to see Marisol bolt from the front door, holding up her skirt and howling, Ursula in shockingly close pursuit.

It was she who was shouting. Ursula, who barely raised an eyebrow at the boldest indiscretion, whose usual show of anger was the flaring of her fine nostrils, was hobbling after Marisol with fire in her eyes, shaking a sheaf of paper and shouting hoarsely, suggesting she'd been yelling for some time: "Goddammt! You lie and you lie and still I believed you! I put everything I had into this, and now it's to be taken because you lied again!"

"I'm sorry," Marisol sobbed, turning to Ursula though she continued to retreat.

"To hell with you and your apologies! You've ruined me!" Flinging the papers which scattered across the gravel, Ursula fell, or perhaps only gave up, subsiding on the drive and hiding her face in her hands.

Inky tears running down her painted cheeks, Marisol tiptoed near. "Sala, please—"

"Go away," Ursula spat.

"But Sala—"

"Never speak that name again!" she shrieked, her porcelain face contorted with fury. Cursing in Norwegian, she swung her fists vainly at Marisol who skipped out of reach. Then Ursula covered her face and began sobbing in earnest.

The papers had blown onto the lawn and Noel picked up the nearest. "You suppose *tax* is the same word in French and English?" he asked, squinting at the letterhead.

"Let's pick up the rest of em. No matter what it is, it looks important."

Rose joined them in gathering up the pages. About to deliver one to Noel, she glanced at it and froze, her mouth hanging open.

"What is it, Rosie?" Noel asked.

"I dunno much about local money but sweet merciful Christ…"

Shaking, she passed him the page. He reacted as she had, his eyes popping, the blood draining from his cheeks. "Fucking hell…no wonder she went spare."

"Three noughts…" Izzy murmured, looking over Noel's arm at the numbers on the paper. "Hang on, does that say forty-seven *thousand* francs?"

"Fucking hell…" Noel repeated weakly. "We're fucked, ain't we?"

"And not in any way I like."

"Be serious," Noel hissed. "This is a real problem."

"What was your first clue?"

"Look, you—"

"Shut it, the both of you," Rosie said sternly. "This is no time for your little tiff."

Anne had helped Ursula to her feet and was aiding

her back to the house, the other onlookers gathering to discuss the events in quiet murmurs. Marisol was nowhere to be seen. More pressing was the matter of what to do about the evening's performance, the audience for which was due to start arriving in slightly more than an hour.

It seemed callous to carry on, but foolhardy to give up any chance to earn money. The argument went back and forth between the boys, Rose, Annie, Bill, and Giles the bandleader, until Miguel arrived to reveal that Laurent had quit the premises in the company of Marisol, bound for Paris. Fucked indeed.

Le fin

AGAINST ALANSON'S HYSTERICAL entreaties, and his even less sensible assertion that he made a suitable replacement for the romantic lead, they cancelled that night's performance. Sal's prop painters got to work on some hasty signage to hang at the front gate and place along the road to Calais, and a sandwich board for one of the circus kids to wear around the ferry port for the rest of the evening to dissuade any further interest.

A full caravan of musicians deserted that night under cover of darkness. By the end of the following day, the troupe was well on its way to disintegrating. The tax department took possession in a little less than a week, that in itself reason for Ursula's aggression, for the trouble had been in the works for months, the hearth in Marisol's room yielding fragmentary evidence of many prior letters.

Meanwhile, Ursula staged a fire sale. Every piece of property not nailed down, and much that was, she set about flogging to everyone in the locality. Even the terracotta tiles, claimed by a sunburnt housebuilder and his wordless apprentice who spent two days and countless cart-loads stripping the roof to the rafters.

Thankfully Leveque was happy to take Noel's

chickens, even paying a fair sum, for they were busy layers and in good health. Izzy and Noel stood at the fence of Leveque's chicken run watching the hens edge their way around the local flock, as nervous as birds had sense to get, the pecking order yet to be established.

"Wish we were half so easy to get housed," Izzy sighed.

Leaning on the high fence, his chin resting on his folded arm, Noel grunted. "Give us a minute, will you?"

"You sure?"

Noel merely grunted again, ducking his head. Izzy left him to it, half feeling though that he ought to stay, offer the comfort Noel claimed he didn't want but most evidently needed. Love was blind indeed, for who was truly able to see what the other hid from themselves?

In his soggy mood he barely heeded where his feet were leading him, and he fetched up at the front of the house where Alanson was bidding farewell to another cartful of itinerants. The driver tipped his wide straw hat to Izzy as he passed, the contents of the caravan clinking as it swayed along the drive.

"Ah, Mr Pound," Alanson said before he could slip away. "You're just the man I wanted."

"Make it good, Alanson, I've about half a nerve to spare."

"Yes, we're all a bit at sea with this recent turn of events. Which is why you should be so glad I've arranged for you to accompany me to Paris."

"Like fun I will."

"But Mr Pound," Alanson oozed, "I have nothing

but the purest of intentions." He looped his arm around Izzy's and began leading him towards the house. "Not that you'd know given our being stranded in this cultural backwater, but I've so many people to whom I might introduce you. Directors and casting agents, people of merit, all of them eager to elevate a brilliant new talent."

"Brilliant? You can't mean me."

"Oh, but I do. Believe me, my good Mr Pound, I've seen plenty up-and-comers who merely up and went. Away, that is." He chortled at his own joke, giving Izzy a stagey wink. "But you've got more than just talent, young man. You're a fighter, you are. And one who's not afraid of fighting dirty if it comes to it."

He winked again, patting Izzy's arm, and Izzy shook him off. "I ain't made up my mind what I'm doing."

"Regardless, I do hope you'll think it over. I'll be leaving on the morrow. You and your Mr Peters are more than welcome to attach yourselves to our little company." He went inside, whistling *Short End of the Stick* with nary a hint of irony.

Someone else whistled: Noel, trudging along the drive, hands in his pockets, face glum. "What'd bloody Alanson want?" he asked when Izzy reached him.

"Reckons we ought to go to Paris."

He frowned harder. "Why would we want to go to Paris?"

"He knows people. Might be able to get me in with a proper company."

Noel snorted. "So what happened to all this theatre nonsense being a lark?"

"Whatever happened to you not minding if I kept at it?"

"I didn't think you'd—" He broke off, hissing through his teeth.

"Didn't think I'd what? Be any good at it? Go on, tell me what you were going to say."

He looked up and away, lips working, and Izzy was about to goad him again when he huffed, setting his hands on his hips, his father incarnate. "Is this theatre guff honestly what you plan on doing for the rest of your life?"

"Fucking hell, Peters…how am I meant to answer that?"

"How can you not know what it is you want?"

"Then tell me what is it *you* want, Mr Clever-clever-got-his-life-all-planned."

"Don't be cheeky."

"Then don't be an arse!"

"I just thought…" He grimaced, started over. "I thought we'd go home."

"Do you mean back to London? Are you out of your blessed mind?"

"Why wouldn't we?"

"Maybe cause we just upended Muldoon's plans in a most public and conclusive fashion and going to London seems a bit like suicide. We won't get five steps from the ferry before he nabs us."

"But what about my folks?"

"What about 'em? They can't protect us."

"What if it's them who needs protecting? Did you ever think about that? Or were you too busy thinking about yourself? Fucking hell, Pound, you didn't even cry when your own mother died."

The words hit like falling in cold water, rendering Izzy breathless. Noel had shocked even himself, his eyes popping as he covered his mouth.

"How dare you…" It came out as a whisper. He wanted to shout it. Fling the words like daggers. Make Noel bleed, just a little, for his lack of faith. Instead, Izzy ran away, before he made things any worse, before his anger overcame his true feelings.

Away to the shore, the rocks at low tide offering just enough cover for a man to crouch behind to cry unheard. What he wanted, he couldn't have. What mattered to him didn't matter to anyone else. Everything was going wrong, completely and utterly wrong, just like Noel had feared, and he was powerless to stop it.

Sick with feeling, he wandered on, coming to the sand lot. The wire was already gone, and all the rest of it save for two dirty holes where the uprights had stood. Miguel was on the far side of the clearing, steadying someone's carthorse while its owner cinched its harness.

"You have heard bad news?" he said as Izzy joined them.

"Nothing you don't already know."

"A very bad thing, this. Very unprofessional."

"That's not the word I'd use, but yeah."

The horse hitched, the cart-man drove from the clearing, Miguel and Izzy walking behind. "What will you do now?" Izzy asked him.

"Find another job."

"How?"

"However. Maybe it will not be the best, but there will be another job after that. Come with me."

"Where?"

"Wherever."

"I thought you meant right now."

"I do. I am going with them." He nodded towards the cart ahead. "Well?"

"I ain't going anywhere without Noel." Even if he was letting the bad times sour his mood. They'd weather this storm together and come out smiling, like they had before. "Which might pose a bit of a problem as he seems to hate your guts."

"A waste of time, for him to be jealous. I don't take men to bed."

"Shit. I wish you'd made that clearer a couple months ago."

"But you are married," Miguel said as if it were both true and obvious. "In your way. And I am no Casanova. My mother, God bless her, would beat me senseless if she discovered I was party to breaking such a sacred vow."

"Yeah, but Noel don't know that, does he?"

Miguel laughed kindly, gripping Izzy's shoulder. "I am sorry to have caused you such trouble."

"Nah, the old goat caused it himself. And if it wasn't you it'd have been someone else. Fucking hell, Mick, what do I do?"

"You can't be any more faithful than you are. He must learn to trust you."

As if it were that easy. As if they had time to spare. Miguel gave Izzy his mother's name and the Catalonian village where she lived, in case he wanted or needed to reach him. "You must have faith," Miguel said as they embraced for the last time at the gate-head. "In him and in yourself. With love are all things possible."

"I pray you're right."

"I know it to be so." Then the driver whistled, the cart already a hundred yards down the road. Miguel ran to catch it, turning once to wave goodbye.

"Dropping like flies, they are." Noel was leaned on the gatepost, glaring at the departing cart. "And what about you, have you made up your mind?"

"About what?"

"You know what."

"We can't go back to London, cobber. It just ain't safe."

"Nothing's gonna happen to us."

"Don't make me laugh. Plenty could happen, at any minute. I ain't putting my neck out for Muldoon or any other man to step on."

"Yet you're prepared to trust bloody Alanson?"

"I don't trust him."

"Then why would you even think about going with him to Paris?"

"Because I've got bugger all else!" Izzy was shouting again. He was making things worse, and he forced his fists to unclench. "What happens if we go back to England?" he went on more gently. "We go hide out at your parents until Muldoon comes knocking? Scarper back to Liverpool or somewhere even more miserable and hope he don't send someone after? Noel, cobber…there's nothing for us there."

"So I'm on my own, then."

Izzy's heart dropped like a stone, straight to the pit of his stomach. "You can't mean you're going," he rasped, his tongue bone dry, his head throbbing with a sickly feel of falling.

Noel cast another filthy look down the road at the departing cart. "Sometimes a man has to choose, don't he?"

"Between Bill and suicide?"

"Between what's right and what's convenient." He turned as if to leave and Izzy grabbed his arm.

"Don't you dodge me, Peters. Not at a time like this."

Noel shook off his hand. "You don't understand."

"You're right. I bloody well don't. So how's about you explain it. Explain how keeping company with a malignant old fool is worse than getting out-and-out murdered."

"It's not Alanson that's the problem. It's this whole flash life you're so intent on having, with or without me."

"Is that what you believe? By the saints, I don't know what I ever did to make you doubt me."

Scuffing his heels, Noel said nothing, for what could he say when of all his fears this was the only lie? "Then why?" Izzy pleaded. "Why can't you believe that I love you?"

Noel stiffened, a bitter pinch to his lips. "If you really did, this wouldn't be so hard."

"You're right. It shouldn't be so hard for you to give up being a jealous shit."

"That's a fine thing to say to someone you claim to love."

"That tears it! You want to be a sour old man, you can do it alone. Come see me when you're done being miserable." His arms locked over his heaving stomach, Izzy started for the house, wanting to run, hating the world.

"**A**ND THEN…"

"Yes?"

Gazing past Telford at the photo on the wall, Mr Pound took a deep breath, exhaled slowly then turned to him with an ocean of hurt in his pale eyes. "And then he was gone."

"What?"

"Noreen and Brigid were leaving on the next steamer. He went with."

Winded, Telford fell back, raising another puff of dust from the musty cushion. "I don't believe you."

"I hardly believed it myself," Mr Pound croaked. "I was running about like a maniac, shouting for him. No one wanted to tell me that it was already too late."

"Why did he leave you?"

"Damn fool took me at my word. Of all the times…"

This. This was how Mr Pound had learned of heartbreak. Why his plays spoke of it so eloquently. Even Telford's own character, the forlorn valet Jeeves, torn again and again from his lover's arms every time the train left the station. This was why someone was always getting left behind.

You're asking too much of the average man
To pay attention to causes
Better to get your point across
In a way that earns applauses
In which case I'd advise
It's most certainly wise
To learn how to run a riot

"How to Run a Riot"
from "Jules, Seize Her!"
Music by T. Whitley
Lyrics by E. Pound

THE TENOR

ON WENT THE show, or at least that day's rehearsal, testing every ounce of Izzy's strength. Telford's as well, though his rendition of *The Longest Rail* reached new heights of dramatic power. An extraordinary performance driven by a desperate passion, Telford's rosy cheeks and tremulous voice putting Izzy in mind of an actress he'd known who had given a world's best performance then died that night of the cancer which had been eating her alive for the prior three years. Morbid thoughts from a morbid little man, but by the end of rehearsal they were both knock-kneed, Telford climbing the stairs with an old man's slowness and raising a cloud of dust as he dropped onto the sofa in Izzy's office.

"I hope you save some of that for opening night, lad."

"Hmm?"

"Never mind."

They drank their tea and spoke of nothing. At least the boy had the sense not to prattle on when the mood was low, both of them steeped in sorrows past and present. Quiet contemplation turned to outright unconsciousness, and Izzy woke in his chair sore and stiff with Whitley shaking his shoulder.

"Shit, it happened again."

"Why are you even still here?" Whitley asked as he began putting the tea things on the tray.

"Because I'm too much of a fool to go home and sleep in a bed."

"As I suspected."

"What time is it, anyway?" Izzy asked, for Whitley always knew.

"Just coming up on half eight," he replied, glancing at the bookcase where the stopped clock had stood at ten past three for the past year and a half because Noel was the only one who had known how to set it.

As Whitley started down the stairs with nary a clatter from the china, Izzy shoved himself to his feet. "Come along, back to mine," he said to Telford. "I expect we'll both sleep better that way."

"Why couldn't you sleep?" the lad asked through a yawn as he stretched his arms overhead.

"Sick from worry."

"You really mustn't worry about me."

"I will if I please. And who says it was about you? There's plenty gnawing at me as it is."

Downstairs, they crossed to the stage door by the comparative shortcut of the stage rather than the maze of back rooms. Whitley and Unger were by the stage door, in conversation with the costume mistress who had stayed late working on a dress to replace one that was too worn. All paused at the loud knocking.

"Christ, good thing there ain't a show on," Izzy groaned. "Whitley, tell whoever that is to fuck off, will you?"

"Yes, dear." Whitley opened the door and his spine stiffened. "Fine, you can see him," he said with unusual venom to whoever was waiting. "But make it quick."

He stepped back to admit Bowen. A glossier, prettier Telford, a Telford who'd been well fed and well treated all his life, Artie Bowen had a slender nose and a waspy waist and a great big soaring tenor voice that Izzy didn't give a rat's arse for if the git couldn't mind his responsibilities.

"Oi, did I say you could let him in?" Izzy spat.

"He's been coming round all day," Whitley said dryly, "but I told him you were occupied."

"I still am. Occupied in going the fuck home."

"I'll only take a minute of your time, Mr Pound," Bowen said, stepping forward with his press-card smile. He'd lost weight, as one did in the poke, but had at least taken time to shave and dress politely. It wasn't going to help his case.

Izzy fished out his watch and flipped it open. "Clock's running."

Bowen's shiny smile slipped a little. "Er, yes, it's only that when I was here before and asked Mr Whitley for my copy of the libretto, he said to ask you."

"Your copy? You don't have a copy."

"Then how am I meant to learn my part?"

"You don't have a part."

"Since when?"

"Since you got your randy arse sent up the poke."

"You mean you cast someone else?" Distraught, Bowen stared around, seeing but not registering Telford hovering at the edge of the stage.

"What was I meant to do, let the role go unfilled while I campaigned for your compassionate early release?"

"But I'm out now," Bowen whined, gesturing needlessly at himself.

"It's too late now. I thought you understood. Or did you think I was joking when I came to see you?"

"I thought you meant you'd find an understudy."

"What kind of a shop you think I'm running? Everyone's already going hell for leather, my budget's topped out and then some, and the bleeding show opens in two weeks. I can't do nothing for you. And your time's up." He snapped the case closed and pocketed the watch as Bowen stared, tension gripping his jaw.

"It was a moment of weakness," he hissed.

"Of stupidity, more like. As if you don't have two working hands of your own. You can do what you want on your own time but when you're on my payroll, I damn well own you. That's how it's always been and it's never going to change."

"That's not fair!"

"Fuck fair! When have I ever treated you or anyone else fairly? You had a responsibility to me and to the cast, and you threw it over for thirty seconds of thrill."

"That's rich coming from the likes of you."

"How dare you!" Despite his pain and weariness, despite Bowen hardly meriting the expenditure of effort, Izzy's restless anger ignited within him. "That's it, you're banned from my productions, from here on."

Bowen flushed, setting his hands on his hips. "You can't do that!"

"Can, have, and I'd do it again."

"But I have a contract!" he squealed.

"Which you violated." He stepped back, wishing

he had his cane, as waving a big stick at a fight usually ended it quick. "I owe you nothing. Now take your glad hands and get the hell out of my theatre."

"But—"

"On the double or you'll be going out the door head first! Then I'll have Unger drag you back in so I can throw you out again!"

This last he delivered as Bowen tumbled out the open door. Whitley swung it closed behind him and was about to speak when Bowen began hammering again.

"Oh help!" he shrieked. "Whitley, for the love of God, let me in!" He resumed pounding.

"Don't you dare open that, Whitley!"

"He sounds to be in some distress," Whitley said, reaching for the handle.

"I'll give him bloody distress," Izzy gritted. Whitley was going to catch it as well, for defying him, for allowing any of this to happen, for opening the blasted door again.

Bowen hurled himself back inside, his eyes wild. "There's a great big mob out there!" he cried, shoving the door closed and leaning against it.

Not a lie, as the door now admitted the muffled sounds of angry shouting and heavy boots. Someone much bigger and angrier than Bowen began thumping on the door, his shouted words lost in the general clamour. At a scuffle on stage Izzy looked around. Telford had retreated to the other wings, a trembling shadow within shadows.

"Do you expect they're looking for our Mr Fords?" Whitley said, sidling up to Izzy.

"That's not something I'm leaving to chance." He

mounted the steps and hurried to Telford, who was clutching at his chest, his breathing panicked.

"It's all my fault," he whispered, looking past Izzy to the door where the violent thumping continued.

"It's not."

"It is," he replied urgently. "That night I came to you? My uncle swore to—" Gasping, Telford hunched his shoulders, curling in on himself.

"Come on, out with it," Izzy urged. He put his arm round Telford's waist, for the lad was beside himself, quivering like a penned rabbit at the sight of a fox. "You know you can tell me anything."

"He s-said he'd burn the t-theatre. If I ever came back here."

"It's best he don't find you here in that case."

"But I can't leave you to—"

"Don't you dare question me," Izzy hissed. "Not at a time like this. You want to do something brave, save your own neck. You're who heard him say it. If there's a trial, it'll be your word that will undo him."

At this Telford stood up straight, his agonized expression giving way to a pale resolve. "You're right. But please, Mr Pound—Izzy. Please be careful."

"You don't worry about me, lad. He ain't gonna know what hit him."

FROM THE COSTUME department Whitley supplied Telford with an overcoat and a cloth cap which covered his prominent ears. He then led him through the auditorium to the gloomy lobby, their footsteps echoing off the tiles. In the ticket booth Whitley opened a lock-box and took out a handful of banknotes.

"You can't possibly—"

"I am perfectly capable of remembering your debt, Mr Fords," Whitley replied, unlocking a narrow door in the back of the booth. "Go to the bistro. Maury will mind you till this is over."

"That man who followed us," Telford said as he stepped through the door. "He's one of my uncle's chums from the boxing club. I'm sure of it."

"I'll be sure to tell him."

"Mr Whitley…don't let him get hurt."

The man nodded curtly, as if to a stern command. "As much as is in my power, Mr Fords. He means a great deal to us all." He closed the door which all but disappeared, painted as it was to resemble a stuccoed archway like the wall beside it.

There were still many people in the streets, making it much less likely he'd be seen. He hated having to think thus, having done it too often in the past, scuttling down alleys with his mother when she'd drunk through her funds and then some and needed to evade the publican. Or the night they'd left Coventry and fled northward, to that miserable hillside village whose name he'd made himself forget.

He could hear the shouting from the alleyway. He'd serve nothing by staying. Still he lingered in the darkness, torn between self-preservation and a searing sense of duty towards his benefactor. His duty was to do what he'd been told.

Pushing aside the useless images of Mr Pound bruised and battered, bleeding out on the alley's greasy stones, he straightened his shoulders, pulled the hat more firmly over his ears and stepped out of the dark alcove by the hidden door and into the spotlight of the street lamp.

"Cian?"

For there he was, leaned on the lamp-post, his hands buried in the pockets of his much-patched coat, his cap down around his eyebrows. Seeing Telford he sprang to attention then hurried to him.

"Thank the lord you're not harmed."

"Why are you here?" Telford asked, drawing him into the shadowed corner.

"I couldn't stay away, Tel. It's one thing to know what he does to you in his own home but to come after you like this…I couldn't let it stand."

"But what good is it for you to be here?"

"I don't know," he said rubbing at his eyes with the back of his hand. "But I had to see you. After all you said last night, I had to know you were safe."

"You're a blessing, you know?"

"Am not."

"You are." Concealed by the night, the dark, their own bodies, Telford took Cian's hand, held on when the other man would pull away. The strange feeling was coming over him once more, that this was not his life but a play: the street and the shadows, the oblivious passers-by, and two desperate men in the dark, speaking impossible words to each other. A tale of make-believe worthy of a production by Whitley & Pound.

If this were such a play, he knew what should happen next. If this were a play then he was merely a player. They all were, and it was for him to claim the lead role of his own life. Act like the man he wished to be, and pray that he was believed.

For the years of their friendship, it was rare to be face to face with Cian. More often they spoke through the fence, and he very nearly laughed to think of it. Just like old Alabaster, if one swapped the fence with a statue in a goddess' grotto, standing in mute witness to Porteo and Melenus' words of love, all they were forbidden to say to one another. Yet this wasn't Fairyland or Albion but the hard and dirty world where nothing stood between them, and daring everything he raised Cian's hand to his lips and kissed it.

Cian gasped, then grabbed Telford round the waist and threw himself into his arms. Shaking all over, he butted his head into Telford's chest as they clung to each other.

"I'd just about given up," Cian murmured hoarsely, his breath penetrating Telford's shirt.

"Given up what?"

"Hoping." Blinking back tears, he raised his head and kissed Telford's burning cheek. A sweet kiss, a boy's kiss, and suddenly Telford understood. The reason for kisses, the thirst, and he cupped Cian's darling face in both hands and kissed him the way he had always wanted to: softly, completely, square on his beautiful, sweet-spoken lips. His best friend, his saviour, his life.

THE DELEGATION

IF IZZY HAD only known that day in the park that giving the lad a chance would lead to violence…he might still have done it all the same, done everything could to spare Telford from a fate no one deserved.

"Don't this take you back," Unger said with too much glee, swinging his broom handle menacingly."

"Steady on, Tim," Izzy said, emptying his pockets into his hat, upturned on the edge of the stage. "We ain't trying to make things worse."

"You've done enough of that already, have you?"

"Shut it. And where's Bowen?"

"Shitting himself in the dressing room."

"At least he's out of the way."

Whitley had returned from locking his office and was taking off his tight jacket. He sighed as Unger passed him a second broom handle. "I had thought such days behind us."

"No rest for the wicked, eh?" Izzy said, hoisting his cane. "Mrs Wietz, you be careful."

"You also, Herr Pound," the diminutive costume mistress said in her whispery voice as she knotted her bonnet beneath her chin. She hurried away, to leave by the same door Telford had used. Thinking of the boy's persistent habit of touching his hidden cross in times of spiritual need, Izzy touched his breast pocket where the two photo cards lay. United once more…

"Right. Let's have at em."

The shits had at least quit hammering on the door. Izzy stretched to peek through the slot, then waved to Unger to flip the switch for the electric fixture they'd had mounted over the stage door just last week. Not that this had been its intended use, but one used the tools to hand, their assailants crying out like awe-struck peasants at the sudden burst of artificial light.

He yanked open the door and stood back for Unger to toss out a lit string of firecrackers, the little whizz-bangs they used on stage all the time that barely made a spark but let off a hell of a noise. Ned's crew scattered, or tried to, careening into each other and the alley walls in a muddle of shouting, squinting men. Unger whistled, in that paint-peeling way he had, gaining everyone's attention in an instant.

"What in blazes is going on?" Izzy hollered. "This is a place of business, not a wrestling ring."

Ned pushed his way past his fellows to stand blinking in the ring of hot light. As a whole they made a sorry lot, a dull assemblage of ten or so middle-aged working men, the seedy chap with the watch cap among them, all in dull black and brown save for one swell in an ugly red and brown tweed easily spotted should he come round again.

"Where's my boy?" Ned panted, cutting a less than intimidating figure with his hat twisted sideways and his coat collar bent.

"I don't know who you mean," Izzy said clearly, eliciting a snort from Unger and a little hiss from Whitley, standing to either side of him. "Wait, now I recall," he went on, stepping carelessly towards Ned, lightly swinging his cane. "You're that soft cunt I caught causing trouble for my star tenor."

"You didn't tell us he got top of the bill," muttered a mustard-faced man to Ned's right.

"That don't account," Ned snarled. "And you, stop waving that pick about!"

"My walking stick?" Izzy said, holding up his— Ursula's—cane to look the raven in its pewter eyes. "D'you mean you're come over all nervous that a little old man is going to do you down in an alley with his walking stick in front of all your friends?"

"Little old man, indeed. You can't fool me."

"Who said anything about fooling?" He lowered the cane, leaning on it as he gestured to his own time-worn face. "I'm sixty-three years old! And here you come charging like the bleeding Light Brigade, and for what?"

"Never mind that, where's Telford?" Ned gritted, his hands on his hips.

"Gone home."

"I don't believe you." He made to step around Izzy. Stopped at the feel of Izzy's cane pressing into his gut.

"If you got any designs about trespassing on my property, Vandurenburg, you ought to cut em out at once." Unger chose this moment to toss another string of crackers. Ned flung himself backwards like he'd taken cannon fire, colliding with his shouting fellows.

"Easy, Tim," Izzy hissed as the mob collected itself. "If they charge at us, we're cooked." They had only to hold them at bay a few minutes more. Already a few of the set-riggers from the Olympic Theatre two doors down had gathered at their own stage door. Across the alley, Miskiewicz the printer was watching from the upper storey, the ink-blotted faces of his two apprentices pressed against the ground floor window. Bringing Izzy's forces about even with Ned's, should it come to pitched battle. The chances of that were already in decline, Ned's friends beginning to mutter amongst themselves as they took stock of their weakened position.

"To the devil with you and your tricks, you sinner," Ned spat. "Now where's my boy?"

"Telford ain't your boy. Your own nephew and you couldn't be arsed to adopt him. Is that because you didn't want him inheriting your grotty shop?" Ned grimaced and Izzy knew he'd hit the mark. "Cor, what a monstrous thing to do. How does your wife feel about that?"

"It's none of her concern."

"Suppose you wrote her out of the will too, hey? That'll be a nasty shock when she's grieving. How deep is thy fucking well?"

"You got no right to judge me, you piece of Cockney filth!" Ned snarled, surging closer. "Now you're going to bring my boy here or I'll be bringing the sort of trouble that did for his cursed father."

"Bet you didn't intend to say that so loudly," Izzy said as the men nearest drew up short to gape at Ned, himself purple to the gills and visibly sweating.

"I don't know what you mean," he grated, his eyes darting, fists shaking.

"Don't bother to lie. You ruined his life."

"Cline deserved—"

"Cline's *son* deserved none of this. You took all

that boy had, and then you beat him till he gave you more. And now this," and Izzy flung his arms wide to the gang of would-be arsonists, to himself and his two colleagues, fending them off with a handful of sticks. "We're grown men, Vandurenburg. Acting like children. Did any of your friends know you were planning to set my theatre on fire?"

Izzy couldn't sing for anything, but he knew how to make his voice carry. All eyes turned to Ned, who stood wilting under the hot light, sweat beading across his rubbery brow. Into the crackling silence fell the sound of footsteps. Grumbling followed, Ned's mates standing aside as Telford passed through their ranks, followed by his friend Cian.

"It's over, Ned," said one of his chums, plucking at his elbow. "Let's clear out."

Others were crowding around Telford, not to chastise but to shake his hand: "He never said you'd got top of the bill."

"Suppose you can get us a break on ticket prices?"

"Me mum, she loves a show. Ought I to bring her?"

"Whitely, be a dear and see if you can't keep that boy from scarpering," Izzy murmured, nodding towards Cian lurking at the back of the scrum. Ned's mates had begun to slip away in ones and twos. Already the boys from the Olympia had gone inside. In a matter of minutes only Telford and his uncle remained. And Izzy and Unger, to bear witness.

ACT THREE: THE denouement. The final

revelation, the end, as he faced his enemy. The man meant to be his refuge, who had instead been his tormenter. It was like facing a dragon.

Dragons could be slain.

"I suppose you think you're clever," Ned grunted, jerking his head towards Mr Pound and Mr Unger, watching from the stage door.

"No," Telford said plainly. "Just done with you." There was so much he might say, so many hurts to avenge, and nothing at all to be gained by the saying. He already had what mattered most. "Don't wait up for me. I expect to be out late."

"We've still rules in our house," Ned muttered with another vicious glance towards the theatre.

"Then feel free to obey them yourself. I'll be seeking my own lodgings."

"You? Where are you going to go?"

"Wherever I wish. You can manage without me from now on."

"We had an arrangement—"

This old lie, that he owed his family for his own keep. "No. We had one terrified boy and a bully."

"That's no way to speak of the man who raised you."

"Excuse my language, but you can go to hell." He was trembling. He could do nothing about it, but he did not look away as Ned stared at him with a reptilian hunger, a want for violence. Nothing Telford had ever done had satisfied, not because he was a failure but because his uncle wanted it that way.

And so he turned his back. A ruinous mistake at any other time, the heights of disrespect, to not submit to the full force of Ned's rage. Never again, and with slow but sure steps he walked away from his uncle.

"Oh, and one more thing, Vandurenburg," Mr Pound called to Ned as Telford passed through the theatre door. "I swear, as God is my witness, if you so much as lay another finger on this boy, I will make you pay. You won't ever be rid of me, I promise."

Inside, Pound and Unger began to argue quietly while Telford sat on the steps to the stage and tried not to be sick to his stomach. Heaven alone knew what he had wrought. With only a few words he had changed his life forever. At a touch on his shoulder he made himself sit up.

"You're looking a bit green round the gills, lad," Mr Pound said, frowning kindly.

"I can't believe I did that."

"Well, it's done. Not much you can do about it now."

"I don't regret it. Please don't think that. I just never thought I'd be free of him."

Free to cease looking over his shoulder at the slightest sound. To never again to deny his emotions in case he revealed his fear. To live on his own terms, the struggles, the failures, the victories for himself alone to judge. Freedom, and he hadn't the slightest idea what to do with it.

Whitley had reappeared, he and Unger debating some point of order over the head of…of Cian, who was watching the flow of words between the two men with an expression of baffled admiration. Intending to rescue him, Telford tried to stand but his legs weren't quite ready to sustain his weight and he sank down again.

"That boy dares break your heart," Mr Pound grunted, "I swear, I'll stomp him to bits."

"What do you mean, break my heart?" He looked at Cian who glanced his way and smiled before turning back to whatever Whitley was saying.

"See. He loves you to bits."

"All he did was smile."

"So you say," Mr Pound retorted. "I've been around long enough to know what love looks like. And to know how foolish it is to deny it." Grappling with the weight of this, Telford said nothing as Mr Pound lowered himself onto the step beside him with a sigh.

"The world is a horrible place, lad," he said with that old sideways smile. "No one alive has any more right to happiness than you or me. No one deserves a damned thing at all. Everything you ever want, you have to take, or it'll be taken from you. So when you find the good, you don't let it get away. Don't you ever refuse it. But you do as you see fit," he went on, settling back with his elbows on the stair behind him. "You're the only one who knows what you truly want. Lord knows it took me long enough to figure it out."

Le cite

PARIS WITH MARISOL had meant the best of everything: luxe hotel rooms, five-course meals, theatres and spectacles and hand-tailoring. Paris with Marisol's husband was anything but, as they tramped from one flea-bitten rooming house to the next, eating stand up meals at the zinc bars because it cost more to sit, Alanson attempting with ever growing desperation to find a backer for his masterpiece.

He'd persuaded an old acquaintance into a proper dinner this evening, to which Izzy had agreed for nothing more than the chance to eat anything other than café sandwiches. Admittedly the French did sandwiches well, but his mouth was watering from the scent of meat as they waited for their meals in this swish restaurant full of crystal and the soft murmur of the well-to-do while Alanson and his contact Béliveau faffed on about who knew what.

Him: they were talking about him, for Izzy kept hearing his name. As everything else was said in rapid Parisian he could only guess at the context, but he was well past caring. Noel's leaving had done that, though at first it had caused him to care far too much. Inconsolable wasn't just a word, it was a physical condition, a state of being in which he had dwelled for what had to have been days but which he now remembered as a grey fog, a vale of tears. In that time, Ursula, Esme, and Bolton had departed for Australia of all places, under the unwavering protection of Sal and Clyde. The women had dispersed to friends they'd made in the locality or back to London to take their chances. Rose was staying, her and her mother having found work at a hotel in Calais.

All of this Rose explained to Izzy after the fact, as he sat numbly on the bed in that same hotel. Ursula had left a lot of money for him, and so he surely wouldn't starve, but he had run out of reasons to go on living. None the less he'd taken the money, as well as whatever personal goods he could fit in one case. The crate of photographs remained, too heavy and fragile to carry about, too precious to discard, even if he was too sore to ever look on them again. In a last desperate act, he had shipped the lot to England under the name of the only person he knew who might both appreciate the pictures and have the titled clout to dodge a jail sentence for their possession.

The food came and he ate it, and though it was certainly better than sandwiches he found he had little appetite. Only the knowledge of how long it might be until he ate so well again enabled him to clean his plates. He polished off the wine as well, for then he'd not mind so much the grotty room they'd taken. At least Bill wasn't so stupid as to try him. Only to rob him, for more than once Izzy had come into his room to find the greasy git poking through his things under the false pretence of wanting some inconsequential thing, tooth powder or a pin.

"But William, we are being so rude to your friend

Monsieur Pound," the theatre man Béliveau said as the waiters removed the cheese plates. Tall and lean, Béliveau had a narrow face and heavy eyes and very nice clothes. The owner of several playhouses in Paris and its surrounds, he was said to be the very sort of man to have the broadness of view, which Izzy had taken to mean financial liberty, to appreciate Alanson's self-declared genius. Which made him a fool, if it were true.

Cesar Béliveau did not seem a fool. Of course who knew with rich men, of whom Izzy had met plenty without being very often impressed by their cleverness. Most came by their wealth by chance, but Béliveau had earned his, entering the theatre at the age of twelve as a costume-maker's apprentice and slogging his way to the top. He was waiting for Izzy to speak, Bill urging him silently with pleading eyes to do same, after having roundly ignored him for the past hour.

He cleared his throat. "I ought to put more effort into learning the language. Can't expect to be coddled, can I?"

"And yet I feel ashamed of myself," Béliveau hummed. "Allow me to offer redress. I have some excellent cognac, to outshine any barkeeper's offering. Shall we enjoy some? We are very close."

"Bien!" Bill cried with a clap of his hands. "Allons-y chez Béliveau!"

A few minutes' walk brought the trio to a gleaming new Haussmann. Béliveau's *appartement* covered the entire third storey and was decorated with restrained elegance, the furnishings slim-legged and all upholstered in the same gold-striped damask. Romantic paintings hung here and there, depicting cavorting muses and sleeping youths in Grecian dress. The cognac was indeed a pleasant drop, and though he was already well-watered Izzy drank all he was given as the others resumed ignoring him.

He set down the heavy bottomed glass and strolled about the sitting room once more. Béliveau had said the next room gave a good view of the square and when he passed the open door again he went in, if only to spare himself from Alanson's raucous laugh. Though the lamps weren't lit the curtains were open, the amber glow of the gaslights casting the vining shadow of the wrought iron window grille onto the parquet. A thin drizzle was falling, and the lights in the place below glowed like a row of hazy yellow moons. Atmosphere by the bucketful, and he was watching the progress along the pavement of a bent-backed old gent under an immense red umbrella when he heard the door shut.

The unlit room was very dark, Izzy's eyes spoiled by the glow outside, and Béliveau seemed to emerge from thin air. "So, this is where you have hidden yourself."

Izzy had no reply, the room suddenly hot, Béliveau's steps echoing off the high ceiling as he approached. "From what William said I expected a little firebrand. And yet you have been most reserved this evening, Mr Pound. Have you no passions?"

"None I'm advertising."

"Not even for your craft?" Béliveau paused at the edge of the slab of amber light. "I should think anyone with your potential would be champing at the bit, as you English so grotesquely say."

"Having potential ain't a guarantee of success, is it?"

"No, it never is. And yet I perceive a greatness about you."

"That's quite a thing to perceive from watching me eat a meal."

Béliveau smiled, his eyes traveling covetously over Izzy's form. "Yes. I believe I could obtain satisfaction from watching you do just about anything."

"What d'you mean by that?"

"Only that I like to look at handsome men."

"Handsome? You're having me on."

"Have you never been told so?"

"Yeah, but the person sort of owed me."

"Now *you* must explain."

Like fun, but he had to say something or Béliveau would make a case of it. "I mean that's the sort of thing you say to someone you love. Even if it isn't quite true."

"For you, it is entirely true." His gold rings gleaming in the light, he stepped nearer. So near Izzy could taste the man's shaving water on the air, Béliveau's unrelenting gaze pinning him in place so that he gasped in honest surprise when Béliveau stroked his curled finger along Izzy's jaw. "I only want to help you. I've great influence. You'd never even have to audition. It could be so very convenient. For both of us."

His other hand was now on the back of Izzy's neck, but as he bent to take his liberty Izzy jerked his head to the side so that Béliveau's lips found his cheek. Even if he never saw Noel again, no such man as this deserved to kiss him. This man deserved nothing at all, was merely another wealthy man with too much power over Izzy's future, a future to be bought at the cost of his obedience.

"As you like," Béliveau murmured, his breath tickling Izzy's ear. "A kiss is so sentimental, isn't it? So unnecessary." He began to feel down Izzy's front, his other hand gripping the back of his head.

"Please…" Izzy rasped, his throat bone dry, his heart booming.

"Yes?"

"Please stop."

"Why?"

Of all the questions, the man's sheer arrogance stirring what remained of Izzy's dignity. "Because I'm damn well asking you to."

"You don't mean it."

If flesh were all there was to a man, Béliveau spoke true, for Izzy's idiot cock was already stiffening, responding to a masterful touch that ought to have thrilled him. He grabbed Béliveau's wrist and wrested the hand away. "I very much mean it. Now quit or you're going to get hurt."

Béliveau chuckled cruelly, digging his nails into Izzy's scalp. "Why, are you going to break my heart?"

"No, I'm going to break your teeth."

Saying it was enough as Béliveau let go. "There's no need for violence," he sniffed.

"There is if you don't lay off."

With a little huff of irritation, Béliveau stepped further back. "I ought to have known not to trust *cet idiot.*"

"That makes two of us. Don't worry, I'll be happy to make him regret it. Convenient for both of us, hey?"

Béliveau laughed dryly past the cigarette he had just lit. "He told me you were a whore."

"Was, once. Not any longer."

"Merde, you didn't go and fall in love did you?"

"Not with the custom. Someone far worthier."

"And yet you're here and your worthy man is not." He exhaled, the smoke glowing orange in the lamplight. "What a pity. Love is so rare. True love, that is. The kind men like us can't afford."

Izzy gained nothing by sticking around to dispute Béliveau's dire philosophy. Not when his dearest wish was to be well away from all of this. Leaving the man to his cigarette, he returned to the sitting room. Alanson was at Béliveau's writing table poking through one of the drawers. He slapped it shut, his crawling smile falling as he saw who had caught him.

"My. That was brief."

"Did you think it'd take him all night to fuck me against my will?"

Alanson grimaced, patting his lank curls. "No. Not against, as such."

"But drunk to the gills, half sick on fancy food, lonesome and afraid, that was perfectly acceptable to you, hey? As long as I put in a good word for you whenever I didn't have his cock in my mouth?"

He grimaced again, as if the truth tasted bad. "No one said this was going to be easy."

"You shit, you damn well said it yourself! You had so many people to introduce me to, didn't you? Directors and casting agents, people of merit, dying to get their hands on my brilliant talent. Get their hands on my arse, you meant. I should have known it for a lie. Like everything else you've ever said." There was nothing more to say, not to Alanson nor to Béliveau. Ashes, all of it ashes, every promise, every hope, and here is how it ended, with him to bear it alone.

"Where do you think you're going?" Alanson said as he started for the door.

"As far away from you as possible."

Alanson moved surprisingly quickly for his size, which was wide enough to almost fill the narrow doorway from the sitting room to the entry. "I think you ought to reconsider, Mr Pound," he said through bared teeth, his moustache bristling like an indignant hedgehog.

"Like fun I will. Get out of my way."

"I don't think you understand what's at stake."

"If it's your career, then to hell with you."

"Look, you coxcomb scum," Alanson snarled, all jollity gone, replaced by a manic tension as he grabbed Izzy's left arm in a fearsome grip. "I've used a lot of favours to get us here, and I'll not have you ruin this for me!"

Manic, panicked, he was therefore unaware of Izzy's incoming right hook, which connected with his chin with a satisfying rattle of teeth and sent him staggering backwards. "To hell with you, I said! You can fuck him yourself. Except he'd not have a bar of it, would he, you oily parasite?"

"You miserable peasant!" Alanson shrieked, clutching his jaw. "I'll ruin you!"

"Get off your high horse, Alanson. You're from bleeding Croyden!"

"Do you think I don't know that? Do you think I haven't spent my whole life trying to make more of myself than that?"

"Well, you're not doing it on my back. You want to know how I've spent my life? Getting pushed around by people who were bigger and stronger than me, people who made me suffer if I didn't do what I was told. And I ain't having that anymore. You come near me ever again, for as long as God allows you to haul your wretched carcass around this mortal coil, and I swear I will tear you apart."

"You don't have the balls," he spat.

"It's you who'll be short a pair." No one knew. No one knew he'd spent a good lot of time and attention learning how to manage the weapon with which he'd equipped himself while in London in the spring. Not even Noel, who thought of knives as the devil's own, the swiftest path to a criminal's death, in the gutter or on the gallows.

At the mere sight Alanson shrieked, leaping backwards through the doorway. He threw himself at the front door, grappling with the handle like it was greased, casting terrified glances over his shoulder at Izzy, who had done no more than pull the wicked little knife from his pocket and bare its blade.

At last Alanson wrenched open the door and went thumping down the stairs. Izzy stowed the knife in the slim pocket Annie had added to his trousers for this self-same purpose, she the one who had taught him to wield the slippery weapon, having spent the first two decades of her life as the daughter of a very successful and now thoroughly deceased stand-over man from a gang who'd once rivalled Muldoon's. All gone, as were Izzy's prospects here.

"A pity you don't speak French," Béliveau said. He lingered in the door from his bedroom, a new cigarette between his curving lips. "You really are quite the little showman." In reply Izzy bowed.

Laughing, Béliveau turned away. "Pull the door shut when you leave," he said over his shoulder. "It will lock on its own."

Izzy lingered in the vestibule of Béliveau's building for some time, contemplating the steady rain and his own sorry prospects. Once again he was down to the clothes on his back and what money he had in his pocket, which was thankfully all of it since he hadn't left his purse behind once since Bill started snooping. It might have been nice to retrieve his overcoat, but with the photo-card safe in his breast pocket, there was truly nothing else on earth he needed. If it was too late to catch a train to the coast, there were hotels all around the station, and plenty of trains tomorrow. No matter what, he was leaving France at his nearest possible opportunity. At least his grave could be on home soil.

L'emploi

ONE HOPE REMAINED: that he'd said to Noel *come see me when you're done being miserable.* Pretty much impossible when he wasn't about to be seen. Dover port authorities took as true his tale of a dowager aunt he'd been escorting about Europe for the last year once he dropped a good hint about the fictional dame's pending bequest of her enormous fortune.

And then he was home. So to speak, for England felt like a foreign country. It was him who had become foreign, not merely to the nation but to London life, having lost that sense of comfortable solitude amidst the maddening hordes.

He took a room in a new hotel near Charring Cross and didn't stir for two days. Much of that time he spent in the bathtub, which was deep and broad and served with unending hot water through the copper spigots. Sunk to his chin, only his knees and head clear, he treated himself to indulgent visions of finding Noel on his doorstep, bearing flowers and a healthy dose of contrition. Noel on his knees, apologetic, adorable. Noel on his knees…

Izzy slipped down further until his head was under the water. When he couldn't hold his breath another instant he sat up. What was he doing loafing about like a lord? Noel couldn't show up on his doorstep if he didn't know Izzy had doorstep on which he might do so.

It was with no little agitation on a blustery day a week short of All Saints that he travelled by omnibus then foot to Noel's parents' place in Bromley. Walking from the bridge, he passed the Peters' allotment, which was still thickly planted despite the frosty nights, the silvery hummocks of German cole surrounded by a palisade of browned onion stalks. A man was bent over working at the far end and Izzy hurried along, not quite ready to engage. Similarly he passed Auntie's laundry rather than stop, for the dear old thing would keep him hours.

The Peters' whitewashed cottage seemed larger than it once had, but then again he'd been living in a dwelling little bigger than a potting shed for the last year. His guts in a knot, he passed through the low gate, waited until his heart quieted, then knocked on the door.

"Who's been feeding you?" Mrs Peters said in lieu of a greeting. "Never you mind, come in, come in. Not there, boy," the robust woman said as he stepped towards the sitting room. "Can't be messing my settee, we just paid it off." Somewhat kindly, she shoved him down the corridor into the kitchen then into a chair at the heavy table.

"It's good to see you again, ma'am," Izzy said as she placed a bowl of mutton stew before him.

"Hush and start eating."

"Yes, ma'am."

Noel's mother asked no questions, simply kept placing food in front of him, which he ate eagerly, then diligently, then out of sheer embarrassment that she thought him so bereft. She had no questions but neither had she answers, saying nothing about Noel's whereabouts or wellness. As Izzy picked at the edges of a third and rather unwanted curry pie, the front door opened. Unable to raise his head, scarcely breathing, Izzy listened as a pair of heavy boots thumped towards the kitchen. A dirt-creased hand landed on his shoulder.

"Where himself?" His eyebrows sprigged with grey, Noel's father frowned down at him.

Izzy's tongue uncleaved from the roof of his mouth. "I was hoping you knew, sir."

Dropping into the other chair, Mr Peters hissed. "He were here a day and a night, no more. Went down to the city and no one heard naught since."

"Rass, don't lie," Mrs Peters said, turning from the workbench to slap her husband's shoulder.

"If you're talking about that picture postcard, that don't amount." He nodded to a card on the windowsill, a photograph of the glasshouse at Kew Gardens.

"May I?" Izzy asked. Mr Peters shrugged, which wasn't refusal, so Izzy got the card and sat again. With his former reading tutor Mrs Peters looming near, he mouthed his way silently through the few words. Noel had found work. It paid very well. He would visit when he might but was too busy to say when. He mentioned no one by name, which was just as well, but the card bore no postage stamp, which meant it had been brought direct by someone who knew where to go. It was all he had of Noel, and he read it again and then again while the Peters talked over him. At length Mr Peters left, off to the public bathhouse by the laundry to rid himself of the day's muck. Mrs Peters fussed about the kitchen for a minute, then sat across from Izzy and set her hand on the table between them.

"Ezekiel, boy…what happened?"

He wanted to explain. Take all the blame. Say *I drove him away, do you think he'll forgive me?* "I don't know. I don't know…" And then it was too much to think about, all the ways he might have saved their love, the words he hadn't said, the choices he hadn't made, and he put his head down on the table and surrendered to his tears.

It was growing late and he accepted the offer of both another meal and a bed for the night. Noel's unmarried sister had taken live-in work as a domestic in a Hertfordshire manor and Izzy had the girls' old bed to himself. Noel had made do with the settee so that his sisters might have privacy.

After so many months in the countryside Izzy had grown accustomed to quiet nights, and he barely stirred despite the lumpy mattress and Mr Peters' resonant snore which shook the very rafters. Even more calming than the absence of city sounds was the absence of Alanson, his creeping, his scheming, his covetous leer and his lack of morals. A worse danger than a man who confronted you face to face. And Izzy had put himself deliberately in the path of that danger. No wonder Noel had cut him, not trusting him to know trouble when he saw it. And yet… *Come see me when you've stopped being miserable.*

THOUGH MRS PETERS fussed about his health and Mr Peters fussed about not having a hand in the garden, Izzy returned to his hotel in the city the next day. Christmas pantomimes were still casting and he was determined to show himself the equal of any man qualified to play the role of the back end of a horse.

A determination wholly mismatched to the likelihood of its satisfaction. That is to say, he got barely a look, the greater population of would-be stage performers being mainly taller, fitter, and handsomer than him, and all of them having been at it for what seemed years. More than that, they all knew each other, and all the directors and the people backstage, at every theatre. He knew nothing and no one. The people to whom he mentioned Alanson's name turned up their noses as if to a bad smell, so that Izzy mentioned him but the once.

What cut the hardest, what he'd never expected, was how badly he'd been deceived by his own abilities. Those drunken toffs in Marisol's ballroom had cheered him so robustly because they were drunken toffs on holiday at a seaside bawdy and they would have cheered curdling milk if you'd put it in a pretty dress. Compared to these fleet-footed choir boys Izzy was a squawking crow. Yet he gamely turned up at the theatre doors, filled in his docket by memory, waited his turn to sing ten notes then be thanked and asked to leave the stage.

Here he was again, standing in a rough queue of shuffling, muttering men in a crowded wing of a shabby vaudeville theatre nearly a mile off the Strand.

As the queue progressed he noticed his bootlace was untied. He knelt to re-knot it, silently cursing as the frayed cord came apart in his hand. Running out of bootlace: it had been so long since he'd confronted poverty, but between lodgings and meals he was spending money like water. Once, a hundred pounds would have seemed a lifetime's earnings. He'd spent five pounds this week alone. Ashes, ashes, his life made ludicrous, all his strengths revealed as weaknesses, his sinful history a stain on his present, his future increasingly limited.

"Let's have the next one," the director called from the seats. A high-toned cultured voice that sounded bang out of place in a vaudeville. The next man stepped out on stage and the queue shuffled forward once more. Still crouching, Izzy scooted aside, his legs watery, his heart too loud. The lights on the stage were blinding, the auditorium a black chasm where anyone might be lurking. And he was meant to go and stand in that blinding light and shame himself again when he couldn't even manage to stand up...

"Pound? Is there a Pound here?" drawled the stage manager.

He couldn't reply, his chest caving in, his skin prickling where it wasn't sweating or icy. Thankfully no one knew him. Thankfully it was dark backstage so that he went unnoticed, shivering behind a bit of plank painted to resemble a rowboat.

He emerged once the singing had stopped. Most of the auditioners had already gone, the last few being herded towards the back door by the paunchy stage manager.

"It's not up to me, now is it?" he was saying. "And

no, Pentland, you ponce, I don't care what you offer, and he'd better not hear you say such to me again. It'll be posted tomorrow, same as always." With that he shut the door on their moaning. Turning, he spied Izzy sidling through the shadows. "You there, what are you doing?"

You're guilty of nothing. "You mean me, chief?"

"Yes. Aren't you the rigger's new boy?"

"Sure am, chief."

"Well then?" He folded his arms, waiting for Izzy to comply with some unspoken command.

"Sorry, chief," he ventured, "it's only I'm still getting used to where everything is."

"He's going to be waiting for you. You'd better get on." The man nodded at a narrow ladder bolted to the wall. It ran up into the gloomy heights, from whence came the noise of hammering, then a clatter of falling metal and a man's cursing in Broad Yorkshire.

"Sounds like I'm needed on the double," Izzy said with a grin. The ladder was an easy climb, being firmly fixed to the wall and made of wood rather than being a pair of ropes and a handful of sticks hanging in mid-air. It lead to the unseen realm above the stage, a nautical world of rafters and planks and lashed-together poles and the great sails of backdrops, all of lit from below so that every shadow was reversed.

Sensing the vastness of space beneath him, Izzy carefully kept his eyes level as he stepped onto the main catwalk. The head rigger was at the far end of the walk, flat on his front and peering over the edge. Izzy gave a low whistle as he approached. The man glanced his way, then rose on his elbow and looked at him more carefully.

"Who're you?"

"Your apprentice."

"I thought you were taller."

"Must be the odd angle. I don't believe you were lying on the floor when you hired me."

The fellow's surly brow smoothed as he laughed. "That I was not. Though I thought you was blonder."

"I'll come clean," Izzy said, crouching beside him. "I ain't the man you hired."

"So where's he?"

"Buggered if I know."

"Then who are you?"

"I'm the man who wants the job more than does the man you hired, evidently."

The Yorkshireman laughed again and sat up. He had a round, childlike face that showed his age when he laughed, wrinkles spidering from both eyes. "So where'd you work before?"

"Nowhere, but listen," he said as the man frowned. "I'm quick and light on my feet and I take direction and I ain't afraid of heights. Show me what to do, I'll do it. No task too large or small. I've put up with some nonsense in my day and you'll be saving me from a heap more of it if you give me a chance."

He rose and stepped back at a gesture from the rigger who got to his feet as well. Head tipped to one side, he looked Izzy up and down. "Given you've spoken more in that wee speech than that turnip said in the last week, I'm game."

"You won't regret this," Izzy said as they shook hands. "What do you need me to do?"

"Figure out how we're going to reach that bleeding hammer what I dropped."

They fished it up with a loop of stiff wire from where it lay across the tops of two backdrops. Then the man, whose name was Miller, set Izzy to coiling rope. "You'll think this a thankless task, but it matters muchly, so mind you do it careful. A kinked rope is a missed cue is the pair of us out of a job."

"Aye aye, cap'n."

Miller chuckled, as he had every time Izzy replied thus, which was precisely why he kept doing it. "Just mind yourself or you'll be walking the plank," he said with a wink. He then retreated to the crow's nest of an office-cum-storehouse where they kept ropes, pulleys, lamps and such goods as needed at the top of the theatre. When scene changes took seconds, no one had time to be going up and down a ladder.

Seated on the broad catwalk, Izzy wound hanks of rope for a good hour, until his hands burned from the coarse hemp fibres and he began to wonder if Miller had forgotten him. He was preparing to make his way to the office when he heard someone ascending the ladder beside him. A head appeared, that of a man about Izzy's age, with badly cropped hair and a red mark on the side of his neck and the decided scent of woman clinging to his face.

"Who're you?" the head demanded.

"Rigger's boy."

"You ain't any such," the man said, coming up another step. "I am."

"You mean you *were*."

"I am still."

"Then where've you been?"

"I was having a little kip."

"That's odd, because you smell like minge."

"You rotter!"

Izzy sprung to his feet as the fellow climbed the last rungs in a hurry. As he was stepping onto the catwalk the yelling commenced. They both looked over the rail to see a plump woman with a measuring tape around her neck come storming from a back room, dragging with her a young woman in a wrinkled yellow dress. The ex-rigger's boy caught his breath and stepped back.

"That'd be the owner of the minge, would it?"

"Look, you bleeding cuckoo's egg," he hissed, rounding on Izzy. "I'm giving you one chance to clear out."

"Shiffley!" hollered the stage manager from below. The ex-boy caught his breath again, his finger stilled in mid-air. "Shiffley, get down here at once."

"You heard him," Izzy murmured when the fellow didn't move. "Go on, Shiffley, and shift."

"This ain't over," he replied through his teeth as he began to descend the ladder.

"Sure thing, Shiffley."

As the stage manager laid into the stammering Shiffley, Izzy sank to his knees. Stand-offs were one thing, but at this height he was left shaking, and he sat with his back against the wall until Miller emerged from the office. He came and sat beside Izzy, took a little snuff from a box from his time-creased waistcoat.

"I heard Mr Herkheim tearing someone a new arsehole," Miller said when he'd done sniffling.

"Shiffley got sacked. And Marjorie from costuming."

"Ach, I knew she were too pretty."

"Is that possible?"

"For backstage, you ken. Shame she ain't got a voice."

"Why you think I'm up here and not down there?" Izzy said, nodding towards the stage beyond the shadowy curtains.

At least he had work. At least it was in a theatre. It was nothing near what he'd been promised, what he'd so foolishly dreamed of, but it was brass in his pocket. It was a start.

I thought I'd never know a man who's lonelier than I
But there you stand in solitude beseeching
Some higher love I long to find and keep it by my side
So here I wait before you, ever reaching

"Heart of Stone"
from "The Alabaster Angel"
Music by T. Whitley,
Lyrics by E. Pound & R. Clarence

Le triomphe

IF IT ONLY mattered. If there were only someone with whom to share his little triumph. He kept on, if only to have a way to occupy his solitary hours. Rigging was a demanding craft, requiring strength and attention to work the ropes, and moral fibre to put up with the stage manager Mr Herkheim, who never spoke when he could yell, never praised when he could point out one's singular failure. Izzy rarely saw the director Mr Kingswood, and only from a height, knowing him by the gleam of his bald scalp.

On Miller's recommendation he took a room in a nearby lodging house largely populated by other theatre types. The room was hardly bigger than the closet he'd had in Liverpool, but it was clean and very affordable. When he at last visited Auntie Owen in the laundry, she scolded him roundly for his shabby suit, then allowed him his pick of items left behind by long-gone clients, which she then insisted on altering to better fit him.

Neatly dressed, gainfully employed, free thus far of any harassment from Muldoon or anyone, Izzy was nearly completely miserable. Until its collapse, Ursula's bawdy had been his whole life. In that time his childhood friends had dispersed, some to the grave, some merely to prison, the others to more or less respectable lives. He neither wished nor expected to befriend his former clients, none of whom he'd much liked at the time. Noel's parents were kind, but Mrs Peters' doting bordered on oppressive, her loving too much like Noel's, with his lanolin and scolding talk.

Now and then he stopped for a meal at the public house where he'd brought Noel that foggy night three years ago to tell him of his scandalously lucrative new career. Dropping in on his old friend out of the blue, stinking of new money and offering same, luring him whether by intent or not into vice and thence into disaster. And yet…

For those three years they'd been in lock-step, distance no obstacle to their love, for Noel had tracked him down in Liverpool like a dog after a reeking fox. Noel was still alive. He simply had to be, for Izzy would have felt his passing. Yet short of scouring the streets or putting up a missing person notice, he couldn't think of how to find him.

At Mrs Peters' stern insistence, he generally stopped with them for Sunday dinners, often accepting the offer to stay the night rather than trudge back to his lonesome room in the city. Monday morning he was at the breakfast table munching sweet-bread when a letter came for him, brought by a coyly pretty youth from the telegraph office. The cream-coloured envelope was addressed in a beautiful looping hand that sorely challenged his reading talent. Mrs Peters standing at his shoulder, he peeled back the wax seal and extracted a folded card of similar creamy stock. He opened it and found Noel.

His photograph, rather, but it was enough to make

Izzy cry out, his eyes pricking with sudden tears. The one of Noel alone, dressed to the nines, gazing at the camera with perfect confidence. With a similar cry, Mrs Peters snatched up the photo-card and carried it to the window to see it in better light. This revealed the note penned in the card, in the same fancy lettering which Izzy muddled through mainly by context: *Something of yours has come into my household. May I assume you wish to have it back?*

It concluded with an address in Marylebone and a scrawled monogram that matched the letters on the seal. No further instructions, no time proposed as convenient, nothing incriminating, and Mrs Peters sobbing into her kerchief as she clutched the photo of her absent son to her bosom.

VISCOUNT WEXFORD'S TOWNHOUSE was a grand old sandstone facing a treed square in Marylebone. Izzy had been here only once before, at the end of his and Noel's strange adventure to Liverpool and back. Between his sympathy to Noel and Izzy's circumstances and his invulnerable social status, Lord Leslie had been the only one Izzy had thought to trust with his and Noel's photographs. The Peters would have died on the spot if such a thing had arrived on their doorstep unannounced. Or murdered Izzy on sight, or at the very least thrown the pictures away. If he couldn't have Noel, he'd make do with memories, and now that he had more permanent lodgings he could at last safely retrieve them.

The tawny façade of Leslie's house was separated from the foot path by a chest-high hedge of juniper, a narrow strip of turf, and a much wider garden bed. This late in the year the plants were trimmed well back, the turf littered with the husks of chestnuts plucked by birds. Two gardeners were engaged in wrapping a rosebush in sacking. The one was a wizened Indian, his round cap and long white shirt reminding Izzy of their very first helper from the circus gang. The other was Noel.

He glanced up, then looked again at Izzy staring at him over the juniper. He rose slowly, eyes wide, lips trembling, perfectly and wholly and magnificently Noel and only an arm's length away. Not across the sea or across the country but right there in front of him.

"You know this man?" the elderly chap said, still squatting on the lawn.

"Yeah," Noel breathed, not turning away. By God, was he gorgeous, even in distress, his cheeks bloodless, his jaw taut with the unspeakable. "Yeah, I know him. It's, uh, good to see you, Iz."

"Yeah. Same. Same to you." Of all the stupid things to say, when what he wanted to say was *what will it take to make you love me again?* He was standing in a public street speaking to the love of his life across a juniper hedge and he couldn't say a word.

"Speak to your friend if you will," the old fellow said as he shuffled sideways to start on the next rosebush. "Go to the conservatory if you wish to speak in private."

"You mean it?" Noel asked with surprise.

"Don't be heard, is all."

Blushing furiously, Noel met Izzy at the gate. They did not touch or even speak, all the words too raw, all touches too dangerous as together they went around the corner of the house and along a stone path to the back where a substantial glasshouse was built against the sunny south-facing wall.

Inside was an Eden of green and blooming things, the air rich with the wet funk of earth and old leaves and softly damp against Izzy's cheek as they walked the length of the room, Izzy carrying his hat and trying not to crush the brim in his shaking grip. In a brick-edged bed in the centre of the long glass hall a small, many branched tree grew, its yellow-tongued pink blossoms as big as his hand. Noel still did not speak or touch him, pacing slowly beside him with his eyes lowered, blooming brighter, smelling sweeter than any flower.

At the far end a statue of pale stone stood in a sort of alcove formed by the thickly planted beds. Noel stepped around the statue, revealing a low stone bench beneath a vine-covered lattice arch. A secret place in a private home, and Izzy had a sudden inkling of the sorts of conversations Lord Leslie carried on here. Hence Noel's hot cheeks, hence the naked marble arse of the beautiful youth and the sweet scent of flowers all around them.

"So what—"

"How did you—"

They both fell silent again. "You first," Izzy said. Because if he started talking, he'd break into bits. Throw himself at Noel's feet and start blubbing. Beg forgiveness, take every bit of blame, warranted or not, and nothing else would get said.

Noel's face had gone grey, but he nodded and cleared his throat. "Are you well?" he asked solemnly.

"Well enough. Sort of fell into a job. Nothing dodgy," he added as Noel tensed. "I'm on the stage crew at this little theatre."

He grinned, Izzy's heart flip-flopping in response. "So you've made it," he said.

Izzy had to laugh. "Not by a mile, cobber. I'm back at the bottom. I'm the one whose fault it is when things go wrong."

"How so?"

He explained the whole sorry tale, the salvageable ending, the cheery Northerner whose apprentice he'd accidentally become. "I'll never land a part," he concluded. "Not with my reedy little voice. Short of a blooming miracle. Turns out bloody Alanson was full of shit after all."

"Ah hell…I'm sorry, Iz."

"I ought to have known. But for truth, I might have had all the success in the world and it'd still be ashes." He stepped towards Noel who stepped back an equal measure.

"At any rate you look well," he murmured.

"What, this lot?" Izzy glanced down at the fusty grey suit. "Straight out of Auntie's rag bin."

"Well, you needn't pretend I look near as nice." Noel gestured to his garden togs, his linen shirt dusted with dirt and bits of leaves, sacking tied about his knees to cushion them.

"You look good as ever. You look like you. I mean, this is you all over, innit?" Izzy went on as Noel frowned. "Elbow-deep in the garden, dirt on your knees and under your nails?"

"Some things never change," he said wryly.

"Eh?"

"I mean we're right back where we started, ain't we? That night you came down the garden I hadn't seen hide nor hair of you for months. Then you sailed in, wearing that posh chequered suit, kid gloves, smelling like a lord, and there I was, covered in muck."

"And I said to myself, saints above, that Peters chap grew into his looks something marvellous. Even with the muck." Izzy took another step towards him but Noel shifted aside.

"Whyever did you come to me that night?"

"I dunno exactly." It seemed so long ago, thought it had only been three years. Three years more full of happiness than any man deserved. Long enough that he had lost touch with how empty life could feel. "I said to myself, he's the only man I know who's never judged me. Never turned me aside. I didn't mean for all the rest to happen. I only ever wanted your friendship."

And out of habit and daring and longing he reached out and brushed a speck of dried mud from Noel's cheek. Noel gasped, tears springing to his eyes. As if the darling man hadn't thought it possible that Izzy might still care for him.

"Fucking hell, Iz," he stammered, "I'm so sorry."

"For what?"

"Excuse me?" He gaped, incredulous.

"Right, right. But go on."

"I should never have done that to you, left you like that, without even a word. As soon as I set foot on that ferry, I knew I'd done wrong."

"You could have come back."

"I tried. Annie had to keep me from jumping over the side."

"You can't swim, you berk."

"You think I don't know that?" he said with a bitter laugh. "But I wasn't thinking right, not at all. Then when we landed England-side I tried to sneak back aboard. Christ, what a row. Spent a night in the poke."

"You did not."

"Honour bright. Don't expect I'm welcome round Dover port any time soon."

"You duffer!"

They were both laughing, yet again when Izzy reached for him Noel stepped aside. Rubbing at his earlobe, he wandered a few paces, snipped a browned leaf off a vine with his fingernails. Somewhere a fountain plashed, a tiny murmuring like a swift-running gutter after a hard rain, as every want and wondering, every word he might say, all came bubbling up Izzy's throat at once. All the words he should have said before to keep their love alive. All he wished to say today in hope it hadn't fully died. Too many words, and they all came back to these.

Now or not at all…

"Noel…why did you leave?" A simple enough question, and it left him trembling, biting his lips, both craving and fearing the answer.

Noel didn't reply at first, gazing into the thicket of green. Shaking his head, he blew out a shaky breath. "God's honest, I don't know. I was just so angry."

"At me?"

"At everything. Marisol for lying, Ursula for trusting her. You for trusting Alanson."

"I never trusted him."

"Yet there you were swanning off to Paris with the greasy brute. Bound for fame and fortune."

"For all the good it did me."

"So then why did you go? Why did *you* leave? Since we're asking and all."

Trembling, he clamped his lips shut and waited, all over him the look of a man on the edge of running away, so near yet so closed to him, a stone.

"In truth, I didn't know what else to do," Izzy said, his voice muffled by the thump of blood through his head, the untouchable nearness of Noel. "You were gone. The house was gone. All I had to my name was a bag full of fancy clothes and a box of photographs I couldn't bear to look at."

Not stone but ice, and the ice was melting as Noel's stern expression softened to that look of heart-stopping tenderness. "Oh Iz…I didn't mean to set you off."

"You asked," Izzy snuffled from behind his handkerchief. "I was so frightened of what might happen if I went back to London, I couldn't find the nerve. And even without Muldoon, what was there for me to go back to? Whoring? Starving? Sponging off your parents? Though I guess you made out well enough."

"More than I deserve."

The air thick with feeling, they fell silent once more. Izzy was steeling himself to beg forgiveness for his desertion when Noel grunted and stepped back, shaking his hands like they hurt.

"Ugh, I'm hopeless at this…having feelings business. Half the time I used to want to punch myself, some of the things I said to you. And then there's all the things I never said, that I ought to have but never had the nerve."

"You can say 'em now, can't you?"

"It don't matter now," he said with a helpless gesture. "I've stuffed this up well and proper, haven't I?"

"What are you on about? What have you stuffed up?" Izzy stepped nearer and at last Noel did not retreat, though his face was stricken.

"This. Us. Everything."

"We've been dinged about a bit, I'll give you, but nothing that can't be mended."

"But I left you."

"Cos I bleeding well told you to, if you recall. Right when you needed me the most. And you were right about Bill. I should have never given him a chance. I'm sorry if I made you think you didn't matter to me." Daring all, daring his last, he took Noel's hand, and when the darling fool made to pull away he held on tighter.

"Iz…"

"Hush. I did not survive all of what we've been through, Muldoon and bloody Alanson and everyone else's disasters, just to lose you to nothing at all."

"But—"

"Shut up and take it like a man, Peters."

"But—"

"I've more to say. I love you, Noel Erasmus Peters. Like no one's ever loved a man before. I die without you."

"Don't be a fool," he grumbled, purely by rote for the light in his eyes spoke the truth of his feelings.

"For you I can't be anything else. You're in my

heart, Noelly. My soul, if I've got one. So stop feeling sorry for yourself, accept that I've forgiven you for your momentary lapse of good judgement like I hope you've forgiven me for mine, and damn well kiss me. Please."

He stepped nearer, closing the gap between them as Noel gazed down at him in wonderment. "I don't half deserve you," he murmured.

"To hell with deserving. You've got me whether you want me or not."

"Eh?"

"Go on, try getting rid of me. It didn't work this time and it won't work the next."

"I'd never want to be rid of you."

"Then kiss me like you mean to keep me."

And like a dream, like Izzy's every dream, in daytime or the pitiless night, he did, tipping Izzy's chin up as he brought their lips together. A dream made real in this green and leafy grove, this tiny paradise, this place of perfect solitude amid the madness and despair. A world away from all their woes where they were purely and simply together, at last and for all time, for nothing would tear them apart ever again, this Izzy's secret yet most solemn pledge, sealed with this magical kiss.

Magical didn't mean mannerly, and like they'd never been apart, like they'd been apart a century, they clung to each other, staggering about as the kiss grew fiercer, their avid breathing echoing harshly off the glass roof, until they fetched up against the unyielding form of the statue.

"I suppose there's a limit to what that marble chap can keep hidden," Izzy quipped, the carven youth's cold buttocks hard against the small of his back.

"Alabaster."

"Beg your pardon?"

"The statue," Noel said. "The rock's called alabaster."

"I don't care if it's solid gold, it's no substitute for a bedroom door."

"Then come downstairs with me."

"No one's going to mind?"

"Not if they don't find out." He was grinning hugely, his hands firm on Izzy's backside.

"Why Mr Peters, what's come over you?"

He hummed, a low rumble in his chest as he squeezed Izzy's arse. "You. I missed you so much, you milky little bugger."

"And I missed you, my prince."

With a soul-deep groan Noel bent to claim his mouth with twice the kiss as before, a kiss of legend: enduring, possessive, paradise. Paradise lost, as a door opened somewhere beyond the green. Izzy stiffened, trying to pull away from Noel, who let him go with reluctance. As if he wasn't afraid to be caught in another man's arms. A man who ought not to be here at all.

"I better shift," Izzy whispered.

"Old Les won't mind you being here."

"Says you."

They left the alcove, Izzy following Noel's lead, for he hadn't a clue where the exit lay. In the centre beneath the tree with the pink blooms, a fair-haired man in a fine grey suit was engrossed in reading a letter. He looked up sharply on hearing them, then smiled, returning the letter to its envelope as they neared.

"Afternoon, your lordship," Noel said with a bob of his head.

"Hallo, Noel. And to you as well, Izzy," Lord Leslie said warmly. "I thought I might be able to lure you here."

As Noel frowned in confusion, Izzy brought out the photo-card the viscount had sent from his inside pocket, for it went with him everywhere, a talisman of hope, a hope now realized. "I shipped the lot here from France for safe keeping."

"I must apologize," his lordship said to Noel, who was staring at the card in something like horror. "I wasn't certain how it would appear to you that those were in my possession. Have I overstepped?"

"No, you did the right thing," Noel replied, though he couldn't take his eyes off the card. "I'm likely too much the coward to have done much about it."

"You're no coward," Izzy chided. "Don't ever say so."

Noel snorted. "I'm afraid of my mother, Iz."

"Cobber, anyone with half a bit of sense is afraid of your mother."

"They ought to be, if she can cow the two of you," Leslie offered merrily.

"Well, at any rate, your lordship," Noel said, his voice hitching with embarrassment as he began shunting Izzy towards the door leading to the house. "We was just going to take advantage—I mean make the most of no one being downstairs at the moment. If it's not a problem for anyone. I mean, I know I'm meant to be working, but it's been so long since we've seen each other, and—"

"Noel, please," the viscount said, putting up a hand. "It's perfectly understandable that you'd like some time together. I know how much you mean to one another. Which is why I'm letting you use the Opaline room."

"But sir—"

"Don't bother to argue, Peters," his lordship said firmly, though he was still smirking. "It's unbecoming to reject a kindness."

"Yes, sir."

"I suspect I shan't see you after, Mr Pound," he said to Izzy. "My friend Mr Clarence's play opens tonight so I shall be out quite late. But ask my man Henry and he'll fetch the rest of your photographs."

"Yes, sir. And thank you. For everything."

His lordship bid them good evening and they left him in the conservatory. They came out into a longish room with the same black and white tile flooring and an open archway at one end which let onto a staircase. "Who's Mr Clarence?" Izzy asked as they climbed, for Lord Leslie's expression had softened on saying the man's name.

"His lordship's, uh, you," Noel mumbled. "That is to say, they're like us. I mean—"

"Point made, but what about her ladyship?"

"Permanently moved to her mother's. From what I've heard from the household it's been to everyone's benefit."

The Opaline suite was the same where they'd stayed last year, the night his lordship had offered them sanctuary. Wanting light, to see and be seen, to enjoy Noel in every aspect, Izzy felt his way across the room and opened the blue velveteen curtains a sliver so that a blade of sun fell across the pearly grey carpeting.

"Now, Iz," Noel said, approaching with cautious steps, his hands up. "I know it's been a bit since we been together so I don't expect you to—oh."

"*Oh* is right," Izzy replied with a wicked grin as he tossed aside his jacket to start on his shirt studs. "Now get cracking, Mr Peters. You've got to make up for lost time."

Le directeur

WORDS COULDN'T CAPTURE, nothing could capture the wealth of feeling granted him with Noel's return to his life. Noel was his life, and not one worldly ambition could match the magic of the simple fact that this man was his to love.

He would leave the stage to the show-offs, the glory hounds, those whom Nature had blessed with either beauty or talent. Izzy was happy to have work. Though it was hardly what he'd expected or aimed for, it paid well enough and he seemed to have a knack for it. Rather than pretending to the stage, he would become the fleetest rigger in the whole West End. Employ a swarm of lads to do the climbing. Get him and Noel a nice little house on the edge of town where they could make all the noise they liked. He would be happy for now with what he had, because he had love.

It seemed best for Izzy to keep his cheap little room and Noel to stay on at Leslie's. Save their wages until they could secure good lodgings. They still managed to see each other almost daily through the winter, while Noel learned from Leslie the finer arts of managing the tender tropical plants in the conservatory and Izzy learned how to stage a show.

The chief man Miller was a patient man of good

humour. The middle son of a rope-maker from Hawes, he was continually amazed by Izzy's physical daring., though perhaps it was merely his ignorance of the dangers of the job that made him able to walk the rafters like they were city streets and not narrow spans of wood with nothing below them but air. There was talk of safety ropes, and he'd given it a try, but he found it too great a hindrance to be dragging it behind him as he travelled the maze of catwalks.

After Christmas the theatre closed for a few weeks, but Izzy had money enough to sustain him. More than enough, for he was able to make an extravagant gift to Noel of a pair of fancy pruning shears with vines stamped into the blades and leather wrapped around the handles to spare his fingers. In return Noel gave him a new suit of daring unmentionables to replace what Izzy had left in France, of which they made vigorous and frequent use.

Lord Leslie was a brick, granting Izzy free run of wherever on the property Noel was permitted, which apparently included permanent rights to the Opaline. Of his lordship one saw very little, his 'friendship' with Mr Clarence at an emotional climactic so that one most often found him strolling the chequered tiles of the conservatory, sighing over one of the playwright's letters or simply lost in blissful thought.

By February, Izzy was working flat out again with a new show in production, a translated French farce laden with double entendre and absurd twists of its racy plot. None of that bore on his job, which was to raise and lower the backdrops and curtains on time. Miller saw to the lighting equipment, mainly a task of watching to be sure the gaslights stayed lit and the phosphor didn't catch the rest of the theatre on fire. As seemed to be the way with every one of Izzy's jobs, the work was a mix of frantic action and standing about doing not much at all. Scenes only changed so often, and most of the time his task was to stay out of everyone's way.

Midway through the second act of a Wednesday night run, he was leaned against the wall by the pulleys wondering yet again whether the chaos before him was typical of the professional stage or merely a quirk of this theatre in particular. The actors for the next scene were assembling in the narrow wings, hissing and jostling, the pasteboard helmets of Roman soldiers mingling with the braided up-dos of the "sylphs" they were meant to be pursuing. Mr Herkheim the stage manager stalked among them with his ever present notebook, whispering last minute reprimands.

There was a sudden shuffling of many feet and a woman's indignant squeak. One of the Romans stepped back sharply, his spear hooking on the edge of the canvas. The whole backdrop rippled, a pleat forming as a few of the thin cords binding it to the pole high above gave way.

Izzy sprang to attention. "Oi, Herkheim!" he hissed, for the actors only minded the stage manager and never the crew.

"Did you just say *oi*?" Herkheim's eyes bulged as he bore down upon him.

"My mistake. Begging your pardon, guvnor, sorry to bother, but can you keep them eejits away from here?" He gestured at the squabbling actors, the sagging backdrop. "Now I've got to go up and fix that, don't I?"

"You've a cue in four minutes!"

"You're right," Izzy said, crossing his arms as he leaned against the wall again. "I'll just wait for it to all come undone and collapse on top of—"

"Fine," Herkheim spat. "Just get on with it."

Izzy vaulted up the ladder, his soft shoes making no sound. For no apparent reason but to cause trouble, the uncountable mice inhabiting the theatre made frequent meals of the ropes securing the backdrop to the rail. Lying on his belly on the catwalk just above, Izzy pulled a short length of the same stuff from the hank draped around his neck. He looped it about his wrist then began to unknot the first of the snapped cords from the eyelet on the backdrop. Four had come apart along the first foot of the edge, and he was making useful progress when another rustling ruckus broke out below. Both hands on the pole of the backdrop, his knee braced against the nearest strut of the catwalk, he leaned out greedily to watch the little human drama unfold.

"Touch me again, Banner, and I'll massacre you!" a woman hissed, so loud they might have heard it in the audience. She shoved the miscreant, who went staggering into his mates, who went careening into the backdrop in force, sending it swinging. There went Izzy's hand-hold, and he was quite suddenly held up by only his leg, his torso dangling in free space. As the backdrop swung towards him he grabbed at the pole, this his undoing, for the huge canvas outweighed him by orders of magnitude. He was yanked violently forward as it swung away once more. And then he was falling…

Except he wasn't. He still had a hand on the pole,

his other flailing for something else to grip as he collided with the canvas at speed. His dead weight set the whole thing swinging again but aslant, the shrieking of the actors and clamour of the audience barely reaching his ears past the rattle of his heart. He made a mad grab for the pole, caught the top of the backdrop only, three more of the old ropes giving way in a shower of oakum.

Miller was above him, shouting something about his hand. "Just lower the bleeding backdrop!" Izzy hollered. His flailing foot found purchase which immediately gave way, for all he'd done was kick a hole through a worn part of the fabric.

Leery of the soldiers' tin spears he dared to look down. Herkheim's control had broken completely, the backstage a melee of shouting actors and crew, two of the soldiers wading towards him with a wooden ladder though there was nothing near to lean it against, and all of it visible to the audience who hooted and stamped with equal frenzy. Someone on the ground had nonetheless heard him yell as the pole began to suddenly drop.

"Fucking hell, not so fast!" His arms blazed with pain, his hands cramping from his desperate grip as the pole dropped again, the backdrop swamping the stage and wrapping around his kicking legs. Another few cords snapped along the pole. His upper hand was suddenly bearing all his weight, and then it wasn't, and he fell a few yards in a hurry, scrabbling for a handhold as the huge canvas subsided around him and on top of everyone foolish enough to be under it, along with the pole which landed heavily across Izzy's lap. With something akin to solid ground beneath him, he clawed his way free and slithered off the writhing canvas-covered mound of angry actors.

"You little hellion!" Another angry actor, the fellow whose scene had been interrupted, was clambering over bits of fallen set to reach him, murder most evident in his twitching eyes. Driven by equally savage intent, Herkheim was battling towards him through the scrum from the other direction. Behind him, the remaining cast were on the brink of a full blown riot, all their bottled-up enmities and spoiled feelings bursting loose, chorus girls hurling insults back and forth as, waving a hatpin like a sword and shouting about split seams, the costume mistress pursued the chief centurion.

The only way out was straight ahead, and without much thought Izzy somersaulted forward, freeing his legs of the snarl of canvas and ending up neatly on his feet, at the very same moment that Herkheim and the red-faced actor converged on the place where he'd been. Collided was more the word, the pair bouncing off one another and falling on their backsides amid the rabble.

Izzy found himself alone at the front of the stage with the actress. Her pretty face contorted by a snarl, she swung her fist at him. He ducked just in time, then again as she swung at him from the other side. He came up under her flailing arms and grabbed her around the middle. For a handful of staggering steps he bore the struggling woman on his shoulders. Conveniently enough, Herkheim and the actor were there to catch her, and the trio collapsed in a hollering heap.

The left wing of the stage was barred by a fistfight

between two Romans, the right by a costume girl and the prop manager as they warred over a piece of tapestry. Izzy dithered centre stage, the audience's shout of warning coming too late for him to dodge Herkheim, who grabbed him fiercely by the arm, earning a chorus of boos as he dragged him away. Izzy waved to the crowd and the whistling and cheers reached new heights. If this was the end of his theatre career, he'd at least go out with applause ringing in his ears.

He expected to find himself deposited outside the stage door. Instead, Herkheim hurried him along the carpeted corridor leading past the boxes on the lower level and out to the foyer, where Mr Kingswood the owner was descending the stairs from the upper boxes in full evening dress, accompanied by two other men.

"Thank you, Jim," he said as Herkheim thrust Izzy at him. "That will be all for now."

"But sir—" Herkheim started. Kingswood cast him a look over Izzy's head and he choked back his words. "Yes, Mr Kingswood," he gritted. Then he stalked away, leaving Izzy alone with the director and his two companions.

"This here is my associate, Mr Nyland," Kingswood said of a tall, grey-haired man of similar patrician appearance, also in costly evening wear. "And Mr Clarence, the playwright." He indicated the shorter fellow with the well-worn jacket and deep eyes.

"I say, what an impressive performance you put on just now," said Clarence warmly. "Given it was wholly improvised. Aren't you in need of acrobats, Elliot?" He looked to Kingswood, who smiled indulgently.

"I am indeed," he replied. "Why don't you show

me what else you can do?"

"You mean right here?" Izzy glanced about the empty foyer, the hard floor of gold-edged marble, the twinkling chandeliers.

"Don't be nervous," Kingswood said in the soothing tones of a man who assumed the obedience of everyone around him. "I promise to remain wholly indifferent to your charms. Of course I can't speak for these two ne'er do wells." He glanced at his friends and Clarence laughed, Nyland groaning as if at a joke he'd heard countless times before. From the auditorium came a burst of applause.

"Sir, I'll be needed soon," Izzy murmured.

"He'll manage without you a little longer," Kingswood replied. "Carry on."

"Thing is, I dunno that I've much to show you. I was really more of a high-wire man."

"So you *are* trained," Clarence said with a bright smile.

"A bit. Plus I used to be able to climb just about anything as a boy."

"He's scarcely more than a boy now," Nyland muttered, his heavy features unmoved.

"I'm twenty-three, if you please."

"Can you learn a routine?" Kingswood asked.

"I don't see why not."

"If you can, you'll be doing me no end of good."

"Hmm." Avenues of opportunity laid themselves out before his imagination, along with the likely impediments. "Can I get the rigging job back if it don't stick?"

"I'll be sure to find a use for you," Kingswood said with a gilded smile. "Tell me, have you ever tried trapeze?”

“Don’t tell me I’m funding a circus next,” Nyland said tiredly. The others laughed, Clarence’s eyes alight.

Any other man would use every advantage to hand. “I beg your pardon, Mr Clarence,” Izzy said, “but are you by any chance acquainted with his lordship Viscount Wexford?”

“I am,” he replied easily. “Why do you ask?”

“Only that he’s spoken to me of a Mr Clarence who was a playwright, and I wondered if he meant you.”

“Are you friendly with the viscount?” Kingswood asked with only a hint of disbelief.

“We’re on excellent terms, yes. Please do give my regards when you see him next, Mr Clarence.”

“I shall, Mr…”

“Pound. Ezekiel Pound,” he said, shaking Clarence’s offered hand. “Though his lordship will know me as Izzy.”

THE REST OF the show ran smoothly. There was no good rehanging the backdrop, which was torn along the upper edge and had several holes straight through it from the tin spears and Izzy’s feet. The audience were well worked up and cheered the slightest bit of comedy. The night before earning a laugh had been like pulling teeth. At last the curtain came down, but Izzy had scarce let go of the rope when the soprano, the woman who’d wanted to punch him, grabbed his arm and dragged him to centre stage.

The applause doubled, the audience a hot loud

mass beyond the footlights which blazed in his face like a string of bonfires. He waved and the mob roared back. Removing his cap with a flourish, he bowed deeply. Was suddenly choking as Herkheim grabbed him by the back of his collar to frogmarch him offstage to a chorus of jeers.

Miller let him leave at once with a promise to come early tomorrow to mend if not wholly replace the backdrop. He fair ran to Leslie's, slipping quietly through the gate and along the side to enter by the conservatory as a concession to propriety. Noel was in the kitchen, for he'd been to see his parents who had sent him home with food, including a special curry pie for Izzy made with Mrs Peters' minimum of spice. It was still enough to make his head sweat and the insides of his nose tingle as he told the story of his fall and subsequent elevation.

An elevation no less impressive than Noel's own, for thanks to Lord Leslie's training and relentless boosterism he had secured a position in the tropical plant house at Kew Gardens. A prestigious role of the sort that entailed even earlier mornings, even harder work, for he had kept his placement at Leslie's to keep himself in lodgings. It was however a joy to see Noel's eyes light up when speaking of some rare new species, a quieter yet more robust comfort to know he was being valued for his talents at long last.

"I knew you had it in you," Noel said at the end of Izzy's tale. "It was only a matter of time before you got noticed by someone important."

"Time, and luck, and me just about dying."

"I sure ain't going to miss you being a rigger. That's proper dangerous."

"Too right, cobber." Izzy dusted the pastry crumbs off his front. "But don't fret, I ain't ever going up again without being tied to something."

"I'll like it more when you never have to go up at all," Noel said, chasing a few crumbs around the table-top with his fingertip. "I'm scared every time you work that you'll not come back in one piece. But I didn't want to fuss. You seemed so happy."

"You're what makes me happy. That was only ever a job."

The household was quiet, upstairs and down, but when Noel started for the stairs, Izzy led him the other way, to Noel's little room below, craving the very opposite of the opulent bedroom above. Longing for the safety of quiet unseen places. Space enough for the two of them, no more. A bed so small they need never be apart. A love so grand it filled the universe.

THE KISS

"COURSE, MR KINGSWOOD treated me about as well as I treat you," Mr Pound said with that slanted grin of his. "I quit him and went on to another shop quick. Not that it made much difference, the mix up they was in, cor. But by then there were a good twenty theatres or more in the End. I'd gotten a name as an easy-going sort who did what I was told. And with legs as pretty as mine, or as they used to be..." Mr Pound shrugged.

"A regular Henry Dixey," Telford quipped.

Mr Pound snorted, rolling his eyes. "I should have been so lucky. At least he can sing. Me, I did all right for myself, no more."

As seemed their habit, they had left the theatre together and begun walking without purpose or destination. Telford ought to have been exhausted, but the velvet twilight and the admirable company had filled him with a radiant optimism, a warmth of the heart that affected his mind so that these familiar old streets seemed wreathed in a brand-new beauty. A night for one's prayers to be answered.

"So tell me, what started you on directing?" he asked, simply for the pleasure of conversation.

"The same thing what got you your speaking part,"

Mr Pound replied, swinging his cane as he walked. "After a few years taking my tumbling act round the vaudeville circuit, I got sick of the travel, sick of getting hurt, so I went all in with this little rep up the top of St Martin's. I was the comic relief, I guess you could say, playing four or five bit parts every show, mainly as they hadn't the money to hire more actors. Then the director went and did a bloody Bowen and ended up in the poke. We all showed up for rehearsal, and when there weren't a director…well, we had a show upcoming, hey? And what with me having all those parts, I knew near everyone's cues. It was either give it a go or fold the show, and we'd started selling tickets at that point."

"Don't tell me you stumbled into that as well?"

"That's me all over, at my best when I roll with the punches. I don't like telling people what to do."

Telford laughed openly, picturing the old man standing in the theatre aisle only that morning, waving his stick at them as he shouted commands. "That's literally all you ever do."

"That don't mean I enjoy it. My main talent is paying attention to what's going on around me, so as I've got half a clue how to salvage what's important when the wheels start falling off the cart. Ugh, speaking of wheels, I could do with a set. Save me having to walk myself home."

Telford's steps slowed as he realized where they'd come. He hadn't meant to return to the bakery. Mr Pound seemed oblivious to his mounting fear, waving to the two figures who had stepped away from the shadow of the wall.

"Evening, Mrs Vandurenburg," Mr Pound said,

sweeping off his hat in a regal bow to Telford's aunt. "It's a pleasure to finally meet you."

"Mr Pound, I presume," she murmured with an odd glance at Telford. "I hear I have you to thank for Telford's success."

"He did it wholly on his own merits, ma'am, but you're very much welcome."

"How do you know Cian?" Telford asked her.

"We've only just met," Cian replied. "I came out to see if you weren't back yet and she was at the gate."

"We've been enjoying a very nice chat," Telford's aunt said with one of her rare smiles.

"About what?"

"You, mainly," said Cian, with a wink for Aunt Beryl, who was suddenly gripped by a need to brush the creases from her long apron.

"See, lad?" Mr Pound said, slapping Telford on the back with unnecessary vigour. "With the lot of us in your corner, you can't lose."

"Don't be long with your friend, Telford," Aunt Beryl said as he stood gawping at them. "I'd like to lock the gate"

"Oh. Yes, auntie."

"A good evening to you, Mr Pound. And thank you." She had been backing towards the gate and now slipped through, swinging it nearly closed behind her.

"Gilbert, is it?" Mr Pound said to Cian, who snapped to attention.

"No, sir. It's Doherty, sir."

"Very well then, Mr Doherty. You take care of our Mr Cline. He's got a big part to play, I don't want him getting damaged."

"Yes, sir, Mr Pound."

"You and your *sir*..." He shook his head, though he was grinning. "Same goes for you, Cline. Take care of this one." He pointed to Cian with his cane.

"But he doesn't need my help."

Pound snorted again, rolling his eyes at Cian. "Thick as, this one, ain't he?"

"What are you talking about?" Telford said as started down the alley. "Mr Pound... Izzy, wait!"

A shadow in the shadows, he paused. "Leave it be, lad," he called back, his voice like the rasp of dry leaves over stone, like the turn of a page. "Me, I'm for home. I'm getting too old for mucking about the streets late at night, don't you know? You'll see me tomorrow. Or tonight if you need somewhere to doss down."

"But—" And then Telford forgot what it was he so desperately needed to know from the old rascal. Forgot everything but the fact that Cian was holding his hand.

"Come in the yard, Tel," he whispered. "I don't want to say good-night just yet."

His feet seeming not to touch the ground, Telford followed Cian through the battered green gate into the dusky shadow of the shed. This was how things ought to be, how a night like this should end: the villain defeated, the heroes triumphant and finally free. Free to claim what happiness they could, snatch it from the jaws of cold reality and never let it go.

Now or not at all...

Now and forever, as Cian went into his arms, clinging to him fiercely. "I was so scared for you, Tel. If that devil had touched you I'd have murdered him, right there in front of everyone."

"Hush. It's over. And thank you. For coming to find me. For all you've ever done. I can't imagine what might have become of me if you hadn't been there on the other side of the fence."

"Ah, when I came to the Gilberts' I was as poorly as you. Snivelling over my little hurts."

"Those weren't little hurts."

"Nor were yours. But we pulled ourselves together and got on with things, didn't we?" Cian said with a crooked smile. His only kind of smile, the taut skin on the left side of his face unable to bend so far. Remnants of the burn he'd sustained at his mother's hands when he was yet too young to remember how it had been done. Cian's foster family expected much, but they had shown none of the viciousness of the demons who had birthed him. No one so young should have so many scars. But that was in the wretched past. The future was free.

"We did. Cian, you're my very best friend. I've tried to be the best friend to you I could. But I've so little to offer you. I may never get another part. I may end up back at the bakery. And I want to give you more than that. I want you to have everything good in the world. But it's just like you said. I can't bear to say good-night to you. I can't keep saying goodbye."

"What are you saying?"

"That I love you. Completely, maybe helplessly. But so very much. I love you so much, Cian."

"Oh, Telford, I love you too. I never thought…never thought you'd want me, the way I am."

"But it's you. It's part of you. Your strength, the beauty in your heart. I can't bear that you suffered, but I'd not change a thing." As he had before, as he would again and again, as often as Cian would allow it, Telford cradled his beloved's face in his trembling hands and kissed him. On his lips, his cheeks, his eyelids, salted by his tears. On his freckled nose and softly, so very softly on the ruined skin beside his mouth, because nothing about him was ruined. He was perfect.

"What's changed?" Cian asked, wiping his eyes on his sleeve as they stood in each other's arms. "Why say it now?"

"Because I've learned to make my own happiness. Life offers us nothing. All that we desire, God makes us seek. Sometimes for a lifetime. But whenever we seek with patient honesty, we are doing His work. Looking for the good in every man and woman. Celebrating it when we discover it. Cian, you are so good to me. I don't know how I could not love you."

Fresh tears in his darling eyes, Cian dropped his head, nuzzling into Telford's chest. "Faith, you'll turn my head with that sort of talk," he murmured, though it sounded like he was smiling.

"Turn it towards me, though."

"Always."

Another kiss; he'd never say no, never refuse his beloved anything within his power to give. A house, a life together. Love in abundance, which would have to suffice until he'd the means to provide more.

They stepped apart as a bang and clatter rang out from the far end of the alley. Smirking, Cian brought him into the potting shed, where eyes of the world could not reach them as they kissed for a very long time. A kiss for every kiss they had wished for in the past, and a kiss for all the kisses yet to come.

THE END

"**T**HANK FUN THIS eejit can sing."

"I thought Fords did quite well," said Whitley as he rose to join the ovation. "For a beginner."

"He'll do," Unger grunted from his other side, though the old dog was grinning as he too got to his feet.

A standing ovation was a bit of a stretch for the calibre of the performance, but opening night crowds tended to the demonstrative, leaving Izzy the only one sitting amid a forest of tailcoats and sequined gowns and grinning faces. Unger was on the aisle and leaned out to speak to someone. Izzy was suddenly being hauled to his feet, dragged out of the row by Unger, who handed him off to Leonard, who took his arm to persuade him up the aisle and onto the damned stage, followed closely by Whitley, whose fool idea this must have been.

"Oh, take it like a man," Whitley murmured to him, preparing to bow. "At least it's not a flop."

"Yet." But Izzy bowed and waved to the audience; refused a bouquet of roses, giving them instead to Marguerite, who gave them to a bewildered Telford.

Izzy endured a full half a minute of unnecessary celebrity before escaping to the rumpus backstage.

These were the people whose opinions mattered most to him, the actors and actresses and prop boys and costumers, everyone whose efforts made the show into a performance and not just a gang of people standing about. A poor opening could sink a show before it left the harbour, but tonight the mood was electrified, on every face a smile. He accepted a lukewarm glass of fizzy wine, shook every hand offered him, turned away all praise. When he saw Unger he waved him up to the office, then went to find Telford.

He was alone in the men's dressing room, still half in his butler's costume. Izzy shut the door and the clamour dropped. "How you feeling, lad?"

"Good," Telford answered, smearing cold-cream on his painted eyebrows. "Tired. Happy. You?"

"More or less the same. Gotta say, I'm proud of you. You came through when I needed you."

"You realize I'd have done whatever you asked," Telford said to him in the mirror. "Really, I can't ever thank you enough."

"Now, now, enough of that soft stuff."

"You started it, you old grump," Telford said with an easy laugh as he reached for a clean cloth.

"Suppose I did." He strolled about the room while Telford finished. Like everywhere else in the mangy old theatre, the walls were papered with leaflets and bills for shows long past. Shows from even before Izzy's era, the paper yellow with age, the names worn to dust. As was the way with everything, all fame and acclaim in the world not enough to stay the hand of time.

Time would catch even him soon enough. He took

out the old card, the two photographs reunited. How grand his dreams, that cheeky boy, posing with his lover, daring the world to object. How lucky they'd both been, to have had a love worth keeping.

Now he'd done it, set himself off, and he put the card away before he wet it with his useless tears. He was still patting himself down for his handkerchief when one appeared in front of him, offered by Telford.

"Whitley told me," he said gently, his own eyes bright with tears. "Last night. I'm so sorry."

That arsehole... "Ah...thanks, lad. And thank you for bringing him back."

"What do you mean?"

"All them tales I been telling you. Gosh, it was good to feel it all over again. Even the bits where I nearly ruined his life. And mine. But we stuck it out. Forty-three years, we had, which is more than most. Guess he saw something in me worth hanging about for."

"I'd say he made the right decision."

"Eh, let's leave off this soggy business, shall we? It's your big night. You ought to be celebrating."

"I couldn't have done it without you."

"That's for certain. Mine's the only shop you auditioned at, you twit."

Laughing, they left the dressing room, and though Telford frowned when Izzy lead him towards the office he went upstairs without a question. As he waited on the landing for Izzy to join him, Unger came out of the office.

"All yours," he said to Telford, who frowned even harder.

"Go on, then," Izzy said nodding to the open door.

"This is all rather mysterious...oh." Telford stopped in the doorway, blinking. "Why is he here?"

"To see the play, you twit."

"Did you arrange this?" he said over his shoulder as Izzy steered him into the office.

"Eh, might have been me who made sure he had a ticket. It'd be Unger's fault if he managed to sneak backstage."

"Hello again, Mr Pound," Cian said, rising to meet them.

"Evening, lad. Hope it wasn't too uncouth."

"Not at all." He cut a fine figure, for Izzy had got Mrs Wietz to cut down an old suit of Whitley's for the occasion. What one noticed first of all was his eyes, glowing like the dawn, for Telford alone.

"I'll let you two have a moment to yourselves, how about?" Izzy said.

"Wait, where are you going?" Telford asked with a note of panic, as if he were being left in the company of a crocodile.

"Down them blessed stairs while my knees will still allow it. Don't worry, that pack of mongrels of mine will be baying for hours. Join us when you like. Or don't. You'll be missed but no one will mind."

He left them to it. The pair were such lambs they'd likely do no more than hold hands, bill and coo, say to each other the sweet little words on which love sustained itself throughout the years.

Grand gestures were for the stage. Love, real love, was a daily affair, built on trust, and sacrifice, and agonizing honesty. All things you couldn't see. The only things that mattered, beside which earthly wealth and fame were ashes.

The world offered nothing. Love was what one made out of that nothing. A truth told for centuries, for all of time, the truth behind every fairy-tale, every dream of the human heart, every lover's secret wish: that love would always be enough. Now and then, it was. Sometimes there was still a touch of magic in ending a story with a kiss.

THE PARTY

"**B**Y THE SAINTS, is this ever going to be over?"

Whitley shot him another filthy look. Izzy judiciously did not stick his tongue out in reply. He was uncomfortable enough with the attention being paid him without making things worse, though the Kew Gardens people had all been perfectly lovely. They seemed to know everything about him, and to take for granted the closeness of his 'friendship' with Mr Peters. Not a one had been rude about it. Indeed, they had spoken of Noel with reverence. Story after story about his cleverness, his generosity, his innate sense for growing things, and the fact that he never shut up about Izzy.

The sun was glaring off the glasshouses and cooking Izzy's back as the photographer's assistants mucked about on the fringes of the group. Izzy was smack in the middle, pinned between Whitley, cool and unsweaty as usual, and the late Viscount Wexford's daughter, Lady Geraldine Taymore.

He'd never met her ladyship, though he'd seen portraits of her in her youth in Leslie's house. Their introduction today had been fleeting, for the garden was awash in the cream of society, lords and ladies and sirs flitting about the lawn like twittering, overdressed birds. And all here for Noel, or at least for the dedication of the Noel E. Peters Memorial Pavilion.

A weighty title for a band-stand, though the choice of structure was clearly meant as a tribute to Izzy, which was both a very nice gesture and wretchedly embarrassing. He'd just about died when Whitley had read him the invitation. A gift, he'd said, from the cast and crew, who'd barracked for months around Izzy's old contacts until they'd raised the bequest.

He'd come close to dying again at the ribbon cutting ceremony when the band had started in on a medley of some of his more sentimental tunes. Yet again Whitley's fault, for which Izzy would be devising a savage revenge. Later, when he wasn't being shunted about by a pair of boys in plus-fours, being told to smile, reach out and shake her ladyship's hand.

The photographer's boys retreated from the scene, leaving Izzy and Lady Geraldine hand-in-lace-gloved hand, a pose which required both of them to lean a little forward.

"I do wish he'd hurry," her ladyship murmured in her papery voice, for she was not much younger than Izzy.

"So do I, your ladyship. I'm too old to be bending in half like this."

Taymore exhaled a laugh, her placid smile unmoving. A consummate actor, and not to be outdone he maintained his expression of benign approval until the photographer emerged from behind his apparatus and signalled the group to stand down.

"Do you know, Mr Pound," Taymore said to him as chatter broke out around them. "I had always thought you'd be taller."

"Eh?"

"The way your dear friend Mr Peters spoke of you. You seemed this tower of strength." She lifted her lacy hand to the sky, smiling more naturally now than in the photo, and he took the compliment for what it was worth.

"I may have had my moments, back in the day."

"Well, I must say it was a pleasure to finally put a face to the legend."

"Excuse me, but did you say *legend*?" But her ladyship's chaperone, a sharp-eyed woman of middle age and indifferent dress, was already at her elbow to steer her on to the next guest.

Hot all over, Izzy sidled through the chattering throng, catching up with Whitley near the entrance to the marquee. "Get me a lemonade or a bloody gin or something," he muttered as they passed under the awning's blessed shade. "And if you ever spring anything like this on me ever again, I'll slice you open in front of everyone, so help me God."

"Steady on, old boy."

"Don't you *old boy* me, you—oh, forget it. Just find us a drink, will you?"

Whitley deposited him in a corner then disappeared. Though the shade was a relief, the closed marquee blocked the breeze, and Izzy shivered when a breath of cool air slipped in through a gap between the canvas walls and touched his sweaty neck. No one was paying him the least attention, not even Whitley, who was talking with one of the Kew people on the far side of the marquee. It would serve the bugger right, to be left holding the bag. Eyes peeled for eager well-wishers, Izzy edged towards the gap in the canvas.

And then he was outside. He'd not been to Kew Gardens in an age, and only a few times since Noel's retirement five years ago. It was still beautiful, even under the weight of the summer's brash heat, and he wandered aimlessly across the emerald lawn, the party a persistent buzzing in the distance.

Ahead, two men were sitting on a bench framed by a pair of late-flowering trees, and he was about to change course to avoid them when he recognized Telford's ears. As he started towards the lads, Telford stretched one long arm along the back of the bench behind Cian. Briefly, but so tenderly, Cian laid his head on Telford's shoulder. Then he sat upright and the two went back to gazing out across the verdant green.

Izzy let them be. Telford gave him time enough. Let the lovers have their stolen moment, their quiet paradise, that fleeting touch that said so much…

Damn if a song wasn't brewing in his soggy old head. *The emerald grass, the sapphire sky, a paradise for you and I,* and of all the times for Whitley not to be looming over him with one of his little notebooks. Ah well, if it was worth remembering, he would. If not, it hardly mattered.

He'd told that story before, on stage and off it. Of wanting what you shouldn't have, then not knowing what to do when you got it. Of loving and being loved, claiming your right to happiness, in the face of all opposition.

If he'd ever had a purpose, dare he say a calling, perhaps this was it: to give hope to the hopeless, to show the world how grand love could be, how deep and wide and all-embracing. He'd felt that love. He'd

lived it. A gift too great to keep secret, that someone
as unworthy as him was still worth loving. A story
he'd never tire of telling, for as long as he rode that old
rail. He'd tell it for the rest of his life.

Thanks for reading

I'd love it if you took a moment to leave a review!

ACKNOWLEDGMENTS

Massive thanks to editing superstar Britt Hanowell of Boundless Words. You were a beacon in the dark, and this book (and the series) wouldn't be the same without your insight.

Thanks as well to my cover artist Joan Belda, for bringing my rambling vision beautifully to life.

As always, my endless love to my wonderful husband and to our frighteningly grown up offspring, who have had to put up with years of this nonsense.

Special thanks to Terri, my muse, my ride-or-die, whose presence in my life defines the word 'blessing.'

Lastly, a tip of the hat to my high school drama teacher the late Art Fiddler, a mainstay on the London (Ontario) theatre scene and a man who wasn't afraid to think big.

LONDON HUSTLE: THE COLLECTION

"But surely they do more than kiss…"
'The Old Razzle Dazzle' is a story told to a sweet young man who doesn't need to know what his mentor used to get up to in bed. But in case *you* wondered…

BACKSTAGE PASS

Made to Measure – For His Eyes Only – A Proper Homecoming – Sleeping Beauty
Four gratuitous episodes of unabashed eroticism. Dressed up, dressed down, in costume or stripped bare, Izzy never fails to satisfy Noel's every dark desire. For two unrepentant sinners, theirs is a match made in heaven.
FREE DOWNLOAD
https://books.willforrest.com/BackstagePassCollection

JUST LOVE ENOUGH

The passionate first book of the London Hustle collection

He wasn't looking for love. He only wanted a job…

Izzy wants more than the miserable life he's been granted. Sick of living by his wits, he'll take any escape, committing to a life of sin and luxury at a notorious London pleasure house where the rich and powerful come to be humbled by the very lowest.
But when an aristocratic client demands more than a little bought time, Izzy does what he must to protect his lover Noel from the truth of the devious lives they lead. Even if it means breaking his heart.
https://books.willforrest.com/JustLoveEnough

About the Author

Author, blogger, and general nuisance Will Forrest
writes unusual (and usually queer) Historical and
Paranormal Romances with a dash of mischief and
mayhem, and grew up on a steady diet of Douglas
Adams and 'Sweet Valley High.'
Will has a diploma of fashion design, a degree in social
theory, and a bad habit of changing careers, life goals,
and continents. Currently Will lives in a very warm
part of Canada with three lovely humans and a
succession of martyred houseplants.

find more books at willforrest.com

Will overshares on Instagram more sedately on
Facebook as WillForrestTheWriter

Join the 'Mischief & Mayhem' readers' club for free
books, great deals, and exclusive content at:
willforrest.com/newsletter

Will writes Victorian-era erotica under the pen name
Tori Fehr
torifehr.com

hardcastlebooks.com